NOREEN AYRES

"A MAJOR NEW TALENT
ON THE MYSTERY SCENE"
Donald A. Stanwood, author of *The Memory of Eva Ryker*

"A TRULY TALENTED NEW WRITER . . .
She's sometimes funny, sometimes spooky,
and always perfectly fluent
in the language of dread."
T. Jefferson Parker, author of *Laguna Heat*

"BOTH AYRES AND HER HEROINE
CAN TALK THE TALK AND WALK THE WALK."
J.A. Jance, author of *Tombstone Courage*

CARCASS TRADE

"Hard-hitting crime fiction . . .
Chilling and well-told, combining dark humor,
gritty realism, and plenty of gut-wrenching,
eye-popping action."
Booklist

"With **CARCASS TRADE**, Noreen Ayres
takes her place as a formidable player
in the emerging world of female mystery writers."
Southbridge News

"Smokey Brandon is a fascinating new addition
to the genre, one we hope to see again."
Kalamazoo Gazette

Other Smokey Brandon Mysteries by
Noreen Ayres
from Avon Books

A WORLD THE COLOR OF SALT

CARCASS TRADE

A SMOKEY BRANDON MYSTERY

NOREEN AYRES

AVON BOOKS  NEW YORK

AVON BOOKS
A division of
The Hearst Corporation
1350 Avenue of the Americas
New York, New York 10019

Copyright © 1994 by Noreen Ayres
Published by arrangement with the author
Library of Congress Catalog Card Number: 94-7040
ISBN: 0-380-71572-4

Published in hardcover by William Morrow and Company, Inc.; for information address Permissions Department, William Morrow and Company, Inc., 1350 Avenue of the Americas, New York, New York 10019.

First Avon Books Printing: July 1995

AVON TRADEMARK REG. U.S. PAT. OFF. AND IN OTHER COUNTRIES, MARCA REGISTRADA, HECHO EN U.S.A.

Printed in the U.S.A.

RA 10 9 8 7 6 5 4 3 2 1

For Tom
alongside in the dream

ACKNOWLEDGMENTS

Grateful thanks is offered to the following for their help during the long haul:

Members of **the Fictionaires,** with special thanks to **Barbara DeMarco**

Orange County Sheriff-Coroner's Department
    Cherry Van Stee, Deputy Coroner
    Maureen Albrecht, Deputy Coroner
    Larry Ragle, Director of Forensic Services, Retired
    Larry Harris, Lieutenant, Search and Rescue Reserve Unit
    Michael Lynn, Sergeant, Coroner Support Reserve Unit
    Richard Olson, Lieutenant, Public Information Officer
    Gary Bale, Investigator

Long Beach Police Department
    Larry Chowen, Police Officer, Patrol
    Bob Mahakian, Police Officer, Administration

Los Angeles County Sheriff's Department
    Larry Mitchell, Crime Scene Investigation, Scientific Services Bureau
    Barry Fisher, Director, Scientific Services Bureau

Newport Beach Police Department
    Patrick O'Sullivan, Detective Sergeant

California Highway Patrol
   Bruce Lian and **Greg Moorehead,** State Traffic
   Officers

Federal Bureau of Investigation
   Randy Aden, Special Agent

U.S. Customs Service
   Michael Fleming, Public Affairs Officer

Other experts of talent and grace
   **Shirlie Banta, Greg Block, Cecelia Fannon, Dr.
   Kathleen Ryan, Al Tank, Sandy Tourigny, Harold
   Trask, David Vincent,** and **Ryan Watje**

Wise and Sharp-Eyed Editors
   Bob Shuman and **Liza Dawson,** and copyeditor **Kathy
   Antrim**

*Wise and Charming Agents of the William Morris Agency,
East and West*

Michael Carlisle and **Amy Schiffman**

My families, both of them

And again, in memory of Gary Brazelton

There must be wisdom with great Death;
The dead shall look me thro' and thro'.

—Alfred Lord Tennyson, "In Memoriam"

CARCASS TRADE

1 \ Up on the hill CC Rider ambled along with his red tail curled over his back and his nose down, sniffing. He stopped just over the burned car wreck that lay on a ledge in the canyon below him and gazed toward us on the roadside just getting out of our cars.

We were in a cut of Chino Hills called Carbon Canyon, a part of northeastern Orange County where, at the start of the century, an oil probe hit a gusher along the Whittier fault line and released centuries of compressed single-cell diatoms that flooded the area with oil boomtowns. Now these same canyons shelter restive yuppies and biker barons taking the narrow curves that snake from the coastal valley to the desert plain by way of Cleveland National Forest.

CC Rider moved downhill on the roadside nearer to where there might be some evidence of a car going over the side, but not so close that anyone could throw a net over him and haul him off to some county dog motel.

"Keep that dog away," I called to the deputy standing near his cruiser. A red county fire truck was parked ahead on the shoulder, with only one fire fighter in the cab that I could see.

"We been trying," he said. He removed his pistol from the holster and mock-shot him, and CC on the hill watched and then rose and walked over a little way, tucked his rear under, and defecated near a clump of creosote bush. Then he gave two finishing kicks, sending a weak plume of rain-softened leaf bits into the air. I first came across CC Rider a year or so ago, when I'd been called out on a cocaine-related homicide near a patch of defunct oil rigs crouched and ready for calisthenics in the weeds. While we worked, the dog ran around the steel structures and watched to see if we were doing it right, the investigation, and the park ranger told us then that the dog belonged to no one, but the bikers at Los Lobos named him CC for Carbon Canyon and fed him scraps and got him drunk every once in a while.

The morning sun had broken through the mist and the air carried an unsettling smell of char as I stood by the trunk of my car waiting for my passenger, Doug Forster, to hear the last of "Devil with the Blue Dress" on the oldie station and bring me my keys so I could get my evidence kit out. Doug and I are civilian employees of the sheriff-coroner's department, in the forensic services section, commonly called the crime lab. He shoots most of our photos since the man who used to be on this shift got canned for using crime-scene shots in an art exhibit in Laguna Beach.

While I waited for Doug, I tried to figure how a two-ton missile landed sideways on a table ledge with its wheels to the canyon wall, assuming it flew off the road going up an incline on a right-bending curve.

I heard Doug's voice behind me say, "I know a recipe for roadkill." He nodded toward a ribbon of brown ants I'd disrupted coursing toward a flattened snake the color of straw near my rear tire, but at first I thought he meant what lay in the burned wreck, humor being one of the ways cops and their cousins cope. Wearing a white turtleneck and jeans, Doug looked like a college student. His dark hair shone and his skin was baby smooth with no beard shadow. Once I heard our front-office clerk say she thought Doug was real buff, meaning cool and hunky. My own taste runs to the old and ragged, Joe Sanders style. I expected Joe to be pulling up in a moment. I'd put a call in for him.

Doug nudged the snake tail with his foot and said, "We could whip up a peanut sauce, thread him on a stick and roast him: snake satay." He put his finger and thumb together like a delicate waiter, then looked across the road into the canyon at the charred car.

"Are you trying out for the Laff Stop, or what?"

"Think I'm good enough?"

"Hell no."

"Damn," he said, and brushed his hands across his jeans as if grass were sticking to them.

We crossed the road some distance from where the cruiser and the fire truck were parked and went partway down the slope and stood, getting the feel of the scene. Except for the black mar against the cliff, the surrounding area was not touched by flame or fury. We had been warned that this one was ugly: The car, with whoever was in it, was entirely burned. Though the paint on the license plate had boiled away, the numbers, which were raised, could be read, and when the deputy ran the plate he learned the 1974 Cadillac was owned by a woman from Beverly Hills, and stolen. That qualified it as a crime scene on a slow morning, even if it did look like a simple accident. The call had come in around six in the morning to the San Bernardino sheriff's from a motorist who'd seen a smoking car over the side on Highway 142. The civilian, doing his Good Samaritan best, had shagged down the hill with his heavy-duty flashlight and tried to get a look inside, but the ledge and the slippery debris prevented more than a verification that it was indeed a beached vehicle, so he plowed back up the hill and phoned from the market in Sleepy Hollow just over the county line where he'd had his morning cup of coffee not ten minutes before.

I said to Doug, "How much damage do you think the fire crew and the civilian did?"

Before he could answer, a deputy shouted and waved his tablet at us. We trudged back up to the shoulder.

While Doug was signing in, I suggested we do the area sketches and wide shots before going down to examine the wreck, and he said, "I hate a woman boss."

"Not as much as she despises you. Now boogie on up the road and get me some tire impressions, Private."

The deputy smiled and stepped away so he could motion to a couple of slow cars to keep on moving. I'm not really Doug's boss. I just happened to be the lead on this investigation. I've got five years' seniority on Doug, both at the lab and in life, and at twenty-eight his urges to compete are in full flower. Or maybe he was just trying to impress the deputy.

I signed in, Brandon, initial: S.

Samantha's my given name, but most people know me as Smokey, so the letter works either way. In my younger, stupider, and in some ways happier days, I was Smokey Montiel, a dancer, an entertainer, you might say, in Vegas. A stripper. When I first sought a job in law enforcement, they ran a routine background check because, among other things, they don't want embarrassment to come to an agency from a person's previous employment. But if my former foolish job interested anyone particularly,

I never heard about it, though I admit I downgraded the job to "dancer," and right after that got to list a few years' stint behind a grocery store cash register while I went to college. Way back then I stopped wearing makeup, cut my hair and wore it straight and stayed out of the sun so it wouldn't be so blonde, and took to wearing clothes that if not hid then didn't announce my figure, and in no time I was a cop working jail duty up north. And then one day I wasn't, but dealing with the aftermath of minds much weirder than mine, and feeling my chip was at least on the stack for justice.

"Let's go have a look," Doug said, following me down the slope.

I put my kit down, took out my pad, and set an N on top of the grid paper for the north marker. At the bottom, I wrote my name, the date, and the words "Tape-measured—not to scale."

"Come on, let's see what's up," he persisted.

"Doug, do you know you sound like a whiny little kid?"

"I *am* a whiny little kid. That makes me smarter than you, see, 'cause I get what I want."

"Go take your pictures."

"Okay, I'm going down."

"No." I made a swift motion to the roadside.

He said, "See? That's what I hate about women. Changing their minds all the time."

"I meant the road shots." The reason I wasn't in a hurry to approach the wreck was that a man who'd been around the lab a long time before me told me from the start: Go slow and you might get lucky. Go fast and the expressions on the faces of the victim's family when the court case fails because of something you botched will stay with you for years.

Enunciating slowly and in a near whisper, I said to Doug, "Find us some skid marks, will you, before every looky-loo in the county messes them up." He followed my gaze to the road shoulder where a car and a bicyclist were stopped as if the deputies' orders shouldn't pertain to them. Only when one of the officers began walking toward them did they ease away.

Doug pointed a finger at me and said, "You lack a serious level of prurient interest, you know that?" then hunched away, turning back for a quick grin. It's not that he has no respect for the dead. It's just that each of us handles this kind of work in a different way. I require a long lead-in.

I noted an approximate distance from roadside to rubble at about sixty feet. My rendition of a jumbo sedan with its wheels to the cliff face looked like a Crackerjack box with loop handles, but a sketch doesn't have to be a piece of art. Above me, while I sketched, I heard the whir of Doug's autowinder. I glanced up and saw CC Rider observing this new occurrence from a higher perch on the incline. Let's put our thoughts together, CC. What do you think? I pondered how the driver missed the curve and tunneled into a bowl of darkness to connect with the unforgiving clay-and-sandstone backstop. Maybe he was fleeing, in his stolen car, from someone. Maybe he'd been blinded by opposing headlights, or his tires had skied on a skin of water from the night's hard dose of rain. Perhaps he was a night-shift worker who took a final snooze in the car he borrowed from a friend, waking for a last few precious seconds as his body shifted in the capsizing car.

Whatever the cause, I wanted Joe Sanders to get there soon. After twenty-three years of service, he's an expert in arson, explosives, drugs, blood, trace evidence, toolmarks, or whatever, and the rest of us dummies call on him when we get in a bind. He used to be the supervisor of CSI, Crime Scene Investigation, but that was three years and a heart attack ago, and now he assists the lab director and is available for teaching classes at the academy. On the way to the scene I learned he was finishing up a seven o'clock class at the training academy, so I left a message for him to drop by if he could.

I was getting out my steel tape measure when Doug came back and stood braced above me on the slope. He said all the fire crew had done was check for embers; otherwise, they had not disturbed the scene.

"Did you get some skids?"

"Nope. A diet Pepsi can. Good shot of that."

"Wonderful."

"I bagged it. Want it for evidence?" He withdrew a brown paper sack from his camera bag, a pleased look on his face. "My lunch sack."

"Why not?" I took it and put it next to my kit.

"If nothing's on it, give it back. I'll recycle for the five cents."

"Things are tough all over, Doug."

"Do you know how long it's been since I had a raise?"

"Yeah, I know. You're so poor you're eating jam sandwiches: two pieces of bread jammed together."

"I *am* poor," he said. "My roof leaks so bad my whole bed's a wet spot."

Joe's gray sedan pulled up and parked ahead of my car and behind the deputies' cruiser and the fire pumper. He got out, crossed the road, and stood with his legs apart and his hands in his suit pockets, then came down the hill toward Doug and me sideways, experienced with fallen eucalyptus spears that act like a million minisleds on slopes. With the steady look that sufficed for hello, he said, "Did you call for aerial?"

"No."

"Why not?"

"It's just a stolen car."

"With a body. There could be another one some-where, or an injured person. You goofed."

My hackles were up, him talking to me like that. He may be an expert, but he's forgotten that these aren't the good old days when Orange County was rolling in citrus money and aw-shucksing itself in the presence of certain gol-durned Republican ac-tors, one of whom went and got a whole airport named after him. John Wayne is still one of Joe's favorites. Over the holidays, he watched seven of his movies.

But I didn't say anything because I figured he was giving me a small dig for a reason. We'd been a pas-sionate pair for a while until I asked for a reprieve, not because dating someone you work with is a bad idea to my mind, despite the popular notion. What better petri dish than a work environment to learn someone's values, temperament, and reputation? But I admit to a restlessness I sometimes have to defend, and a memory of a husband lost to sudden death. His memory slips through me like a shadow in a stream, there, not there, solid, broken, like life itself, and a certain wariness takes over. You're ei-ther ready for commitment or you're not, and I'll take the blame.

"Who all's been down?" Joe asked. He glanced back up to the road where the one fire fighter, a small man with little hair, sat on the backstep of the truck, pulling on a stick of red licorice with his teeth. Now I noticed a female fire fighter at the side writ-ing in a report book.

"We haven't yet," Doug said. "Everyone else has."

"I haven't seen Homicide yet," I said. "If it's just

a stolen, maybe nobody's coming out. Maybe Dispatch didn't—"

Joe looked at the car a moment, then said, "Somebody arsoned it. These canyons are used all the time for body dumps."

Doug asked, "What if the car just flew off the road and burst into flames?"

Joe shook his head. "Cars hardly ever explode. Except Corvettes. All that glue and resin. No, somebody wanted to hide something. I've got the sniffer in the trunk. I was using it in class." He was referring to a device called a catalytic combustion detector, a CCD, used to see if anyone dumped gasoline, kerosene, or lighter fluid before the blaze erupted. "Get all the shots you can up the road, okay?" he said to Doug.

Doug started uphill immediately, and Joe waited a moment, then asked, his face softened, "How are you, kid?"

"Semi-lonesome," I answered, and buffeted him with a shoulder as I passed by.

"I'm free tonight," he said, catching up.

"Let me think about it."

He nodded once, and after a time we both stopped and just stood there, looking ahead at the wreck behind the twisted yellow cordon tape swinging in the breeze.

Up on the road, Doug was talking to a detective named Les. The less I see of him the better I like it.

Joe said, "Your buddy's here."

"I see that."

Les was in a brown suit and an orange tie, a favorite combination he claimed went with his faded red hair. He and Doug moved off to the deputies' car.

Joe looked me over, and I couldn't tell if he was remembering something else he should have brought or he was about to give me another lesson. "You look pretty today," he said.

"Thanks."

"You do."

"I don't want to hear it."

"Why are you always so touchy on that?"

"On the job I'm neuter."

"Sweetheart, you will never be neuter."

"I know someone who will if he doesn't be quiet. Looks are an accident of nature. They're not earned, and I don't take credit."

"Well, I wouldn't want to spoil your fantasy," he said. He smiled and left me, taking slow, careful steps, the steps of a man who'd learned all things have their natural rhythms, whose favorite expression was "It takes the time it takes," said about almost anything, from paperwork to investigations to the winding and unwinding of love.

I needed to measure actual distances, so I headed over to a boulder where I would tuck the end of the tape and walk up the slope, then come back down and measure from the boulder to the table ledge, then measure the ledge's height and width. All the while, I was thinking of what I would see in the car, how badly burned the person was, how terrible the act of burning alive must be. And I hoped dearly that we would learn that the fire was merely an attempt to hide an already completed crime, or better yet, that it was an accident after all; for someone had surely once loved the someone in the car. Someone had heard him or her laugh, and watched whoever it was ride trikes and discover things, and someone had sacrificed to keep whoever it was in clothes and in schools and to give the child what we've come to expect is the right to reasonable living. When a life is deliberately taken away, it's a theft from dozens of people. And theft, to my mind, each time it happens and no matter to what degree, is a little killing, a murder of time and thought and caring.

I finished the measures and stood for a moment looking at the narrow passageway between the car's tires and the backstop. My height at five five plus the height of the door with the car on its side would not allow me a perspective if I approached that way. I passed to the left where an aluminum ladder still lay, probably from off the fire truck, along the thirty-inch-high ledge. Lifting the ladder, I propped it against the car frame, setting the legs firmly in the mix of soil and leaves. I wasn't too worried about getting ash on me because I had on an old green twill jacket and pants; they'd survive.

Les Fedders came toward me. He saw me at the ladder and turned his palm up. "Ladies first."

"Oh, you go right ahead."

"Nuh-uh. I like to see women climb ladders."

"Les, does your wife make you sleep on the porch?"

He laughed, and with his hands in his pockets, looked down and made sure leaves weren't lapping over his gleaming brown shoes. He said, "You go on and do your thing, Smokey."

Joe told me a long time ago, "They pay you to think." They pay you to think, not feel. And so a certain practiced dispassion overtook me while I climbed. The abundant smell of carbon, purged fuel, melted rubber, and incinerated flesh overtook my nostrils. I stilled myself at the thought of what lay inside the blackened salvage. What mute thing would send its plea for recognition: I *was*, therefore I am?

I would look inside the ruin that yet released its heat to the morning air, and I would listen for what the blackened being within would tell me of its life and death. And afterward, at the morgue, I would explore the heart of the Greek word *autoptos* meaning "I see for myself." I would see for myself. I would listen and learn. And if there had been a helper in the victim's hard release from this world, I would be alert to it, and come to know that too.

2

When I peered into the chute, the shock of what I saw almost threw me off the ladder.

At first I thought it was a dog, CC Rider's size. Against the driver's side lay a thing that looked like a burned duffel bag. The legs were gone to the knees and the arms so consumed they were not in the usual pugilistic posture of severely burned persons when ligaments and tendons shrivel, pulling the fists up as though the victim in final frenzy could box the flames away. Where the head should have been, a stump of leaden vertebrae remained.

I lifted my eyes while steadying myself with a keener grip on the window frame. Above me, two ragged ravens swept through the sky and came to rest in the branches of a Monterey pine a few dozen yards away.

Believing the shape of the head would form itself once my eyes got used to the shades of blackness, I looked inside again, but nothing there resembled a skull. On the chest wall were two burned lumps that said the victim was a woman.

Joe and a coroner's investigator with an explosion of coppery hair backlit by the sun were approaching as I got down. Les moved aside for them.

I said, "The head's gone. Maybe it rolled under. I can't see that well. We're going to need lamps."

"It's not gone," Joe said. "It's just not in one piece." He put his hands to his head like ear mufflers

13

and said, "You've got a prison of bone here. High enough temperatures, it explodes." Expanding gases, he explained, would send bony shrapnel jetting into the leaves and lumpy eucalyptus buttons we'd have to search through on the canyon floor. "Our job just got a little harder, is all."

Les moved to the ladder, went up, looked a long while, then climbed down. "Get it out. We'll see what's what."

Doug came along with the CCD and set it down by Joe. He handed over the car keys, and Joe took them, bounced them twice, and gave them back. "You'll need the sifter, too," he said. "You're a good man, Charlie Brown," Joe said, as Doug gamely headed back up the hill to Joe's car.

Joe told Les, "I need to get to the underside of the car, but I'll wait till the body is cleared. I guess you know it's registered to a woman in Beverly Hills."

Les nodded. "We'll give her a call. If she's callable." His gaze went to the wreck.

The polished silver pin in Joe's lapel with the numbers 4–190 on it glinted in the sun. A lot of cops have pins and belt buckles designed with 187 on them, the penal code section for homicide, but Joe's meant he was *for* 190, the section that allows a judge to impose the death sentence for murder in the first degree.

Joe went back up the hill as I stood waiting for Doug to bring back the screened flat we use for sifting. The coroner's investigator, dressed in street clothes and wearing flat shoes, climbed up the ladder and looked in. She came back down wordlessly, then glanced at us and said, "Whew. Get your pictures. I'll call Transport." I didn't know her name and she didn't offer it. As she turned to go up the slope, she folded her arms tightly around her waist. Sometimes it's too early in the morning.

When Doug came back to give me the sifter, he got up on the car and began taking shots as I laid line in a grid for our search of the surrounding area. In a while the transport team arrived in a plain-wrap station wagon, two young men in blue jumpsuits with "Coroner" in gold letters on the back. They came down the hill with a collapsible gurney and a body bag. I told them to walk a single line along the ledge and when they were in the car itself to keep an eye out for anything foreign and try not to disturb its position. Then I went back up to my car, removed my jacket, took out a pair of coveralls and stepped into them, also bringing along the Polaroid I keep as a standby. I couldn't see that Les Fedders was doing anything but bullshitting with the woman fire fighter.

Doug's autowinder was still going as I began brushing aside debris in a corner grid with just my gloved fingers. In the next fifteen minutes I found and dropped into a paper bag what I thought were fragments of temporal, occipital, nasal, and maxillary bone, this after snapping shots of the surface of the gridded area. I also found a tooth.

Pretty soon I heard Doug's camera buzzing again off my left shoulder and saw him photographing something by the trunk of an oak. Next thing I know, he was standing near me, saying, "Guess what I found." His camera was capped and sitting on his bag near his sneakered foot, and he held both hands behind him. When I looked up, his white shirt hurt my eyes. Holding out a piece of gray bone in the shape of a croquet hoop, he said the jaw had been resting on a pot-sized rock against a tree.

"The mandible," I said.

"The magic mandible," he said.

"Minus teeth."

"It's got a few."

"Find the upper, then we'll celebrate."

"I can do that."

"Hotshot. Here," I said, and gave him a bag. "Mark it right."

I heard him drop the bone in the bag. I wasn't looking when he said, "Guess again."

"What?"

I looked up and found him standing in the same stupid way, with the same stupid, satisfied smile. He brought around to the front the maxilla, the upper jaw, had it hiding somewhere. "God, Doug."

"I'm great, ain't I?"

"You are."

"Hear that?" he said, looking around for witnesses. "She said it."

Doug pointed to a canyon sycamore. "Found it in that wedge of roots." He turned it admiringly. The front teeth were intact, but only two others remained on each side. Finally, he admitted a raven found it. He saw the bird poking its thick black crunchers into the leaves and snatching its head around like a shoplifter on the lookout.

I was jealous. But now ID would be that much easier, especially if I found more teeth. From dentition—the kind, number, and arrangement of teeth—an odontologist can read the patient's history like a kindergarten book, and the morgue people delight in keeping the rate of their unidentifieds way down.

The transport team brought the body out. They had used a sheet to extract the corpse, threading it under the remains in the tight interior. Then they tied the ends to make the bundle easier to lift up through the car door. The whole thing, sheet and all, would be put into the body bag, to make sure no evidence was lost.

The corner's investigator wore latex gloves as she stepped around, bent, and untied the flaps, throwing the sheet open. When she rose from bending over the body and blocking our view, we all stood silently looking at the thing that seemed no more than a charred humanoid wick, the limbs seared away and the head gone, the two charcoal knobs glued to the chest.

"It was a woman," one of the men said.

The investigator flipped the sheet back over the corpse and said, "There's not much to examine here," and began pulling off the gloves. "We'll get it to a safe environment."

I needed shots of the car interior after the body was removed. Since I had coveralls and Doug didn't, I'd have to go into the car myself. I asked Doug to stand by in case I needed anything, took some shots from above, then lowered myself in. It was like standing in a dead fireplace. I cast a light around the whole interior, then reached over the frame of the front seat for something that lay like an ashy helmet in the curl of the backseat springs, and pincered it, bringing it forward. It looked like one half of the parietal. Lightly, I ran a finger over the piece of skull. The borders were smooth, flames having eaten away the serrations by which it would fit like a jig-saw piece with the other half.

"Find any money under the seat, it's mine," Doug called.

"Very funny."

I did retrieve a few coins, and dug off the door a melted blob of blue plastic with one comb-tooth protruding, and spied a metal barrel I thought at first was the front seat track until it moved with a touch of my glove. Lifting the object, I unstuck a small handgun buried like a corn dog in a crust of sheep-skin-padded leather. The two halves of the cover came away, the side with the sinuous zipper falling down my thigh.

There was more scorch on the bottom side than the top, and I imagined liquid accelerant running underneath before the fire erupted. The plastic on the grip had melted the magazine shut, but I needed to check to see if there was a cartridge in the chamber because the whole thing would be in a volatile state. I could read the letters *BOA* between the head and tail outline of a snake on the slide. With the muzzle pointed down, and holding firm on the corrugated metal finger grips, I cracked open the slide, then let it go home when I saw no cartridge.

"Doug, toss me a firearm box," I called. "This victim didn't know that if you're going to pack a gun under a seat, you don't tuck it into bed like a baby. She never had a chance."

"Women and guns," Doug said. "It's the in thing. I'm afraid to go out on a date anymore."

"*You* should be," I said. "Where's my box?"

I sat on the southern rise of the canyon and watched the transport wagon pull away with its pitiful cargo. In the splayed eucalyptus branches above me, a burly raven clucked. Joe was down by his car, putting away his equipment. Les was back talking to the woman fire fighter, whose truck, I'd learned, was out of Station No. 4, on the corner of Olinda Drive and Olinda Place in the tiny village of Olinda not a mile south, where the house numbers still run to three digits, so I guess that's why the pumper crew had time to sit around during our whole investigation. Doug had already gone.

A second raven flew above me and sat by the first in the leafy veil. The common raven, called common for a reason. The heavy boldness of their size pleases me, their iron shape taking big bites out of the sky. Once I saw a pair of ravens fighting their own reflections in a bank window, making guttural noises in their hackle-covered throats. The lower window was shaded black, drawing their own images sharply in the reflected sidewalk light. The two flapped and hopped and spit at themselves the whole time I was at the ATM, miniature gangsters in each other's faces.

To the bird on the lower branch, I said, "Hello, big guy," because if you put your face up and talk to a raven, he will talk back, maybe not the first time you come across him, but by the second. Big Guy gave a metallic *tok-tok-tok*, then a prolonged *grauk*, as he tipped his head my way.

Creosote resins released by rain the night before scented the air. I concentrated, trying to imagine who the person in the car could be. A woman, coming down the hill in the early A.M. But coming down to what? Three kids waiting at home, the father ready for his day shift? And she, the mother, returning from nine hours of tending bedpans, the only job she could get in these hard times? Or maybe a woman who'd run away from her husband, receiving a call, tears on both sides; then the grateful agreement, yes, I'll come home.

Or something darker? The pistol would say so. It looked to me like a .25, not a power gun, a gun an amateur might select for defense. And how did it add up that we had a stolen car from Beverly Hills, a city populated by movie stars, Arab sheikhs, and rich plastic surgeons, yet the car was old, its carapace lying sixty miles south, in northern Orange County?

Orange County is in its adolescence, its face and figure changing. Eight hundred square miles and forty-odd cities surround a shrinking island of peaceful bean and strawberry fields. Stark white finance centers and design-free hotels loom next to freeways. In the last decade, builders bolstered by a flood of Pacific Islanders, Filipinos, Guamanians, Koreans, Vietnamese, and Hispanics hiked housing prices to sucker levels, then fled to Colorado when the market dropped. Yet while red-tile cloned homes invade forsaken farmland, cul-de-sac drug dealers and arts center supporters eat at the same pizza bars. Most of us go to work, to fairs and games and stores and movies without event. The golden weather, the knowledge that the endless, rhythmic ocean lies mere miles away, makes us complacent. Cows still graze on hillsides. The air is mostly clear, and there are places where horses lope on fragrant bark trails, and protected pockets where wildlife can be seen. Yet beneath this docile surface, the bottom currents churn.

When Joe's shadow came shooting over the white morning glory vine, the sun an hour past its apex, I was talking to my ravens again.

He said, "Keep that up and somebody'll pin you down and pull a tox on you," meaning I must be on some behavior-altering drug and should have a toxicology test for drug use. He sat on his heels, handing me a can of soda.

"You want to be the one to do it?"

"Can I? What's this lonesome business you tell me? You're the one wanted some time off."

I said, "It doesn't mean I don't miss you." I stood up and walked to the edge of the hill, avoiding the morning glories. He followed. I looked at the soft skin by his eyes with a yearning. Both of us had said the L word, then qualified it in special ways, casually, over salad or while philosophizing about life, using those sidelong glances to see how the other person took it. Twice he'd mentioned the difference in our ages. I told him it was not a problem.

He said, "Do you care what people in the office think? Office affairs are never a secret, not really."

"People think what they think. If we weren't see-ing each other, they'd think we were. Who knows what they think? Who cares? Besides, you can't call it an affair if it's two single people, can you? A friendship. A very friendly friendship. What are we talking about this for? That's not the issue, and you know it."

"What is the issue?"

"If I knew that, I guess I wouldn't be asking for a time-out," I said. "What'd you find with your sniffer?"

"It dinged when it should. They used an acceler-ant. We'll find out which one when I can get to my rate sheets." The CCD pumps vapors over a coil, measuring heat resistance. Joe would match the re-sulting numbers with retention rates to identify the particular fuel.

"This is the way I figure it," he said, pointing across the canyon. "The car didn't go off the road in this direction, where we're sitting. I walked up there on the bank. There's chunks out of the edge there. I think the car was pushed over. Not rolled. It goes down, wheels in, wheels out, wheels in, bang." He broke a dried grass stem into bits and chewed on the last length while he looked into the far landscape. "The door panel's caved in on the up side."

"So?"

"Like it was rammed over."

"You read a lot into a scene."

"It makes up for a dull life."

We headed down the hill toward the road, the ravens uttering rude sounds as they took a couple of hops and flew to another tree along our path. Their pebble eyes stayed on us in case they got lucky and we both keeled over from poison oak rash or something. Out of the scrub a gray mockingbird swooped near us, spreading its black-and-white tail fan and squawking about our infringement of territory. "Mockers have more guts than sense," I said.

"Like some people I know," Joe said.

Overhead, the bigger birds just gave an empty stare and flew to the ground for something, hopping like prisoners in foot chains with too short a lead.

When we reached the far side of the canyon where Joe felt the car had gone over, the ravens had flown away to the north, and I thought they were gone to better hunting, but they came flapping back and settled in another tree. Glancing up at them, I said, "You know what they call a collection of ravens? An unkindness."

Looking over the side at the gray hulk below, noting the flattened weed on the road edge and the open wound of dirt where the car had bit off the edge, Joe said, "An unkindness? That's an unkindness."

"No argument from me."

He pointed: "We have lemon and white splash on the metal inside the car. That means a fire of around two thousand degrees Fahrenheit, even in the rain."

I looked around my own feet where we stood, wondering if Doug had got pictures here, wondering if we were trampling on tire and shoe impressions, and saw nothing and mentioned it to Joe.

"It's pretty sandy here, and I think it rained after the event. It'd blur easy."

"Could it have been a pipe bomb?" I asked.

"Pipe bombs don't usually do the kind of damage their malicious little engineers hope. Juveniles and amateurs settling a grudge. No, we'd see wide searing on the undercarriage, and we don't. The salvage guys'll look for toolmarks on fuel lines, melted motor mounts, that sort of thing, just to be sure I'm reading this right. If some guy was just pissed at a car company, he'd probably set fire to the engine compartment. The radiator lead would liquefy, the fan belt would be burned. But I think the fire started from accelerant poured in through the window. One thing's for certain: Somebody was sure pissed at somebody."

He hiked his pants as he sat on his heels, one finger on the ground for balance as he looked down at the scene once more. A cop's eyes. A scientist's eyes. Not so different one from another.

The harsh racket of motorcycles preceded two monster bikes around the bend. The riders were without helmets. Two more bikers came roaring by, one a woman, her long brown hair whipping in the wind. As she passed, the sun struck her just right and I could see on her bare thigh below her torn stone-washed jeans a blue skull with a rose in its teeth.

My pal from the California Highway Patrol, Ray Vega, told me about a rider he personally cited over twenty times for no headgear. The guy said he'd pay as many fines as it took till the legislature came to its senses. The *very* next day Ray found him with brain seepage out his ears and nostrils, his head a hockey puck that had connected with a bent fence pole near a newly razed gas station.

But now as I caught the black leathery gleam off the backs of the last riders, the smallish one with his arms cocked out on the handlebars and a full head of snowy hair free in the wind, I had no ill thoughts about them. God help them, if they want to dare death, let them. Death, like life, has its own illogic.

I looked at Joe squatting there, another weed in his mouth, and felt a sudden sadness. He must have felt me looking, and turned with a question in his eyes.

I said, "How about taking me to the Cowboy Boogie Company tonight? Honey."

He said, "You're absolutely on. Baby."

3 Every butt was synchronized. The band was on break, but the canned music didn't stop anyone. A couple of grannies in cowboy boots were dancing with the rest of them while Clint Black's voice dipped to a passionate growl and you just knew he was singin' straight to you.

Joe and I sat on barstools at a long table and watched Ray Vega and his new girlfriend Francine doing the Push Tush, the line dance that made even country music sexy. When the song finished, Ray and Francine came back grinning and reached quickly for their abandoned beers. She collected the condensation from her bottle and slipped her hand under her hair to pat the back of her neck.

Doug Forster came alone but lost no time asking women to dance. In his Western-cut shirt and his roommate's black hat matching his hair, Doug could be old Glintin' Clinton himself. When he squeezed by Francine to get to his stool, his hand dragged across her waist all the way, but Ray didn't see it, or if he did, didn't care.

"I say *day-am*. I do believe I'm gettin' the goshdarn hang of this," Doug said, smacking his thigh like a ranch hand learning poker. On the level below us, a sea of cowboy hats flowed by, the hardwood floor a rose color under the lights.

"Well, you've danced with every woman out there, you should," Ray said.

"And here you were the one who didn't want to come because you didn't have a date," I said.

Joe was offering a credit card to the waitress and giving the go-round circle with two fingers and not paying particular attention to Doug, who maybe'd had one too many already.

Doug said, "I have a date," and looked at me with an expression I had not seen on his college-kid face.

Ray caught it and said, "A date with your hand under the sheets."

"*Ray!*" Francine's eyes went wide and her mouth hung open, the lips glossed in deep pink. Her black hair shone and she looked really pretty in the warm light and her purple silk blouse. She had that full kind of figure that looks comfortably waterlogged, if a guy didn't groove on the anorectic look. A flush began at Francine's neck. She looked at me as if I should do something, because Raymond's a friend of mine and an officer with the highway patrol, and sometimes he thinks he's my brother. Ray's face went taut with warning, and I couldn't believe it myself, what Raymond had said to Doug, and wondered if all the Dos Equis had yet to be danced off out there on the floor.

"Well hell, it was a try," Doug said. He shot a quick look at Joe, who was back with us now and none the wiser, his cheeks apple-rosy with the help of Absolut and tonic.

Another song started, and then I saw Doug's glance catch on some point over my head in the direction of the snack bar. In a moment he said, "There is a God." A bleached-white blonde in white jeans strode toward us, wearing red cowboy boots and a red hat, and under her denim jacket and low-cut white knit shirt were two of the biggest, bubbliest bazooms that ever bounced the earth. She swung by, towing a good-looking guy, her frontal burden trav-

eling freely. Joe Sanders choked back a swallow even
before I kicked him hard on one of his new boots,
and Francine's dark eyes stayed wide with wonder.
In one of the few moments of the evening that found
Ray agreeing with Doug, he groaned, "Touch me,
turn me on, and burn me down," and laughed, shaking his head.

Doug was out and around the table before I knew
it. "Watch this," he said, preparing to follow the
couple down the step to the dance floor.

I said, "Doug, don't. You're going to make a fool
of yourself." But since it's permissible to dance with
two partners or none in country dancing, I guessed
Doug was going to try for a ménage à country before
these two knew what hit them.

Tipping his Stetson down and putting a backhand
to his mouth the way you do when sharing a secret,
he said, "Make a fool of myself? Who was it found
the maxilla, Smokey? Hm? What was that?"

He left me fuming, then tried to catch up to the
girl in the red boots, but a happy lady in a long blue
skirt hooked him and they slipped into the Two-Step
as if they were old friends.

"Found a what?" Francine asked. Ray's nose was
pinched between her fingers as she kept his head
rigid so he couldn't follow the blonde woman's passage around the floor.

I said to Joe, "So I couldn't find all fourteen bones
of the face and eight of the goddamn cranium. Order
me a Sex-on-the-Beach. Tell her I want the L.A. version, no pineapple juice. I'm goin' to the john."

Removing my straw hat, I scrunched it onto Joe,
holding his whole adorable sandpapery mug in my
hand to snug the hat down. The beaded feather dan-
gled in back.

"Got you where you live, didn't he?" Joe's hand
landed on my thigh and rubbed up and down, and

all the muscles in my groin tightened in a needy way.

"Forget him, Smokey," Ray said. "Snot-nosed kid."

I said, the booze assisting self-pity, "Why are all you men such competitive assholes?"

Raymond came around behind Joe and massaged my shoulders. "Why, that's just part of our charm."

His smell was rich and sweet and maybe I leaned on my stool and into him too far. The music started again, Tanya Tucker suggesting that if your heart ain't busy tonight, neither was she.

I patted Ray's hand on my shoulder, then left and went to the rest room. While there I was thinking of Doug finding the maxilla only because a raven found it first. How petty of me. How *competitive* of me. An unkindness. In Germany, bad mothers are called *Rabenmutters*, because ravens often abandon their offspring. Doug was a baby. What did he know?

In front of the mirror, I fluffed my hair, thinking I'd let it grow again, maybe even lighten it, what the hell. I tore off a paper towel and dampened it to dab at the shine on my face, saw the flush of my skin drowning my lips, my Bardot lips, one man once told me, so I added two swoops of a brownish lipstick, and went out the door.

When I got back to the table, the band had started up again, and I heard Joe saying to Ray, ". . . from Beverly Hills."

"Are you talking about the canyon?" I asked.

He nodded, midswallow of his vodka, then said, "Miranda Robertson, on the registration. Six, twenty-three, sixty-three."

"That her measurements?" Ray asked, appalled. Then winked at me after looking at Francine.

Francine gave him a quick, disgusted look, then

surveyed the dance floor, her gaze stopping on a man who looked like a TV star, a James Dean type with dark eyebrows and hollow cheekbones, who stood at the perimeter with his left thumb in his pocket, just watching for the right bird to fly by.

"My much-married brother," I said, "had a wife one wife back named Miranda." I had to kind of shout it, the music was so loud. The band stopped abruptly, the lead laughing into the mike, saying, "Sorry, folks," and adjusting something on the amplifier, then launching in again, this time not so loud.

From Joe: "Might you say he Mirandized her?"

"Miranda, Mirandized? Why do I know you?"

"Destiny, my dear," Joe answered. He narrowed his eyes in thought and said, "Trenton. I got lost on that street once, trying to buy a car cover."

I asked, "In Beverly Hills?"

"That city ain't what your average Hubert from Ohio thinks. Real people live in real houses and go to work at crummy businesses just like anywhere else."

"How disappointing," Ray said.

"One dream after another shattered," Joe said. He looked at me with swimmy blue eyes, grinning through the fog. I asked him if he wanted to dance. He shook his head and said, "Bad knees. Old football injury."

Ray laughed and said to me, "I'll scoot boots with you, Smokey."

He took my wrist and we started away, and Francine's black eyes, when I thought to look at her, held on me, and then she looked at Joe and said, "So, you have a neat car, or what?" and tucked her purple blouse in her waistband, raising her breasts into the soft glow and smiling slyly at an old man whose glance fell upon her as he was passing by.

* * *

"It's not even Friday night," I said, in my bathroom.

"Does it have to be?"

"We have to get up in the morning."

"We will. We will get up in the morning, and we will get it up in the evening, and—"

"Hey, what are you doing?"

"I'm lifting you up on the sink, my dear. Have some imagination."

"God."

"What'd you call me?"

"Your bad knees," I whispered.

"What knees?"

"Oh, hon."

"Say it again."

"Oh—"

"I've missed you, baby," he said. "Where you been?"

The light above the mirror gilded every single shiny thing in the room so that I thought I was back staring at polished brass rails and hearing the Kentucky hunk singing sexy about his achy-breaky heart.

"This can't be done, can it?"

"Hush up. Kiss me."

"Joe."

"Just kiss me. Jesus. Slide forward."

Deep in my throat, those sounds.

"Doll, is this what you want? Hm? Just tell me."

"Oh."

"Hm?"

"Oh hon . . ."

4 On the way over to the morgue two blocks away from the lab, I told Doug, "You don't have to do this, you know. We don't both have to be there."

"And let you be the only lucky stiff? Ha-ha. Get it? Lucky stiff?"

"Please."

"You make it home all right last night?"

"Of course."

"You seemed a little wasted."

"Did I?"

"You're different than in the daytime."

"Yeah?"

"Not so serious. Kinda . . . you know."

"No, I don't know."

The morning was bright as clear glass. A deputy driving by waved at us, and I waved back though I didn't recognize him.

Doug said, his gaze straight ahead as we crossed the street, "Joe drive you home?"

"Well now, you're the nosy one."

When we reached the other side, a Santa Ana police car passed and popped its horn at another cruiser with a female officer at the wheel. Doug put on his shades and looked as hip as could be, smoothing down both sides of his hair. He was wearing clean jeans, a white shirt, and a navy blue sports jacket with gold buttons, no tie.

"You two doin' the wild thang?"

I tossed him a look without answering.

"Didn't think so. Too old for you."

"What's the matter with you, you ask me a none-of-your-business question like that?"

"So you *are* doin' the wild thang."

Shaking my head, I said, "I'm glad to see *you* aren't sporting two black eyes, chasing after Miss Buxom last night."

"Nah," he said. "People love me. Once they get to know me." As he walked he bounced as if his tennis shoes had tacks through the heels.

"Must be nice to be Mr. Personality," I said.

"Hey, I am *stud du jour.*"

"I'm surprised you didn't go after Ray's date."

"Francine? Two years, she'll be packing burritos around her middle like one of them life jackets."

We went by the big white building that served as the jail and walked through a treeless parking lot. Opposite the inmate Intake-Release Center, we turned down a walkway lined with yellow pansies minus faces shuddering in the wind. Approaching the morgue, a building of gray blocks with orange tiles breaching the middle, Doug asked, "How many autopsies you seen?"

"I don't know."

"A hundred?"

"No."

"Fifty?"

"I doubt it."

"I want to notch a hundred. Say, Happy Hour, some chick goes, 'What do *you* do, stud?' "

He brushed away a giant John Belushi bee that zipped out from a hibiscus bush near the entrance.

I held the door and said, "I've got a feeling you're a much nicer person than you make yourself out to be, Doug. Who you trying to impress?"

"Does it walk? Does it talk? Does it wear size thirty-six D?"

Two million people will die in the U.S. this year, fifteen thousand in my county. Of that number, one out of four will undergo the medicolegal procedure known as autopsy.

No one I know enjoys observing that procedure. But nearly everyone I know bears a profound urge to disperse mystery. Mystery, from the Greek word *myein*, meaning to be closed (of eyes). In a disciplined hour, the coroners and technicians at the morgue, the observers like me and my dippy cohort, Doug Forster, would open our eyes to see, in the knowledge that someone has to, and in the knowledge that we could.

Doug's sneakers gave off a loud *sneeek* in the entry room, piercing through the piped-in Muzak. While I wrote my name on the register, three women clerks behind in the office were talking about a Kevin Costner movie, one saying she didn't understand what all the fuss was about, he looked like a geek to her. Another clerk moved papers while she had a phone handset clamped on her shoulder, a Mexican girl in a pink suit who just got her A.A. degree in business. "Yo, Smokey," she said, and looked at Doug with a half smile. "I'm on hold."

"Is the canyon Jane up yet? The burn from yesterday?"

"We had an officer-involved case, so it got delayed."

"Good. So are we. Delayed." I looked back at Doug. "You two know each other?"

"Hi, Doug," Janetta said, all cheeriness. "How you doing?"

I left them smiling at each other and went in the other door and down the hallway, passing by the office of a deputy coroner, his high forehead gleaming as he hunched over the phone.

Thirty-eight people, including clerical help, cover the twenty-four hours here. Even so, only about eight autopsies are performed a day compared to L.A.'s daily twenty-four, and the techs don't have to forklift bodies three to a shelf the way they do there.

The odor of formalin and alcohol filled the air, and I patted my pocket to see if I still had my Mentholatum stick. Most corpses we see do not have that much of an odor because the amine-type chemicals responsible for decomposition—cadaverine and putrescine—haven't yet begun their work.

It's the smell of the formalin that slugs me. In its usual state as a preservative, it's a solution of formaldehyde and water but it's also used in powder form, sprinkled in the cavities of bodies so violently disrupted by autopsy. Early household deodorizers contained formalin, not so much to hide the odor as to numb the ability to smell. Unfortunately, it doesn't work all that well. Not so much in the autopsy room, but in the refrigeration room where the treated corpses wait until removal to a funeral home, I have to use something for my nostrils, sissy or not.

Dr. Schaffer-White was working on a male in the first station. Schaffer-White's a strong sister and very feminine. Always she has pearls or diamonds around her neck. Tall, slender, and blonde, she works fewer hours than the rest of the staff because she has a two- and a four-year-old at home. The only chink in her armor is that she doesn't work on child cases.

Dr. Watanabe was at the second station, with his two favorite assistants, both women. The air vent beneath the basin by his legs had filter papers with blood smears on them drying against the louvers. Later, the filters would be plucked off and stored in the freezer. On Watanabe's table was a young man with distinct ligature marks around his neck and what I could recognize as electrical burns on his ankles even from where I stood. A torture victim. The doctor was showing the techs how the electrical cord that still bound the victim's left ankle had been shaved back on the ends, the better to apply power.

A doctor who looked to be East Indian and who I didn't know, was sitting in a chair at the next station, watching a young man who looked like a college halfback use rose cutters to sever the ribs of a heavy woman.

On the table next to her, a tech was preparing to remove the tongue of a suspected cocaine courier. I shifted positions so I wouldn't see. Removing the tongue is the one step in the autopsy procedure I avoid. It's done to check for injury to the larynx. But when they sever the piece and lift it dangling to the scale, it's as long and limp as a salmon, and the loss seems so cruelly nullifying. Without a tongue, is a being human, even in death?

In by two, out by seven. That's the unofficial motto at the Orange County morgue. Our coroners work on a contract basis. When you come right down to it, that's piecework, and in this impartial inventory of parts, something is lost to the idea of reverent handling.

Once I watched a performance here in a case of severe decomp that gave me new respect for the morgue people. Severed hands had been brought in after they had spent a few days in a moisture-filled trash bag. A morgue tech named Barney, for Rubble, we tell him, slipped the skin off and soaked it in saline to bring up the ridges. When it was ready, he pulled it on like gloves to ink for prints. Even if a corpse is mummified by heat, the fingers can be hydrated by injecting saline, inflating into slender balloons ripe for rolling.

At the last station lay a thing that looked like burned and sea-soaked timber off a ship that had broken apart after an explosion and floated ashore. The legs, or stumps, were as shiny black as japanned wood. This poor piece of human flesh and sometime bone that the coroner's caddies extracted from the husk of ravaged steel in Carbon Canyon would be examined systematically and thoroughly; and if we were lucky, the thing would emerge a person with an identity.

Doug, behind me, looked solemn and very pale, but when I gazed at him, he whispered, "I'm okay." He looked away from the bodies and into the empty viewing room where people come to ID their relatives.

The photographer leaning against the wall between Watanabe's and the East-Indian doctor's stations stepped forward to shoot, fulfilling the requirement for all autopsies to be photo-doc'ed. In high-profile cases, such as those involving serial killers, a couple thousand shots may be filed; and in jail deaths, the autopsy is videotaped; cover your fanny, the first rule of the road. I did not know this photographer very well, and sort of missed the man he replaced, a cheeky guy named Billy Katchaturian, the one who was fired for using blood spatter shots in a photo exhibit. You grow older, your tolerance level deepens, I guess, and so even I, after a while, along with the rest of my tasteless colleagues, came to think his flagrant lack of judgment was funny.

At our Jane's table was Dr. Margolis, without a mask, as were all the doctors except Schaffer-White in her clear plastic guard, though all but one wore gloves. There are eyewash areas and first aid kits nearby, but I think we all get a sort of fatalistic attitude about what might happen to any of us who hang around the dead. A story went around for a while about a killer virus that escaped from a corpse into the air-conditioning system of a morgue, knocking off members of the medical examiner's office somewhere in the East. I was never sure the story was legit and the doctors here didn't seem worried, even about squirts and splashes that might be carrying the AIDS virus.

Doug took a position so he could observe only our corpse, not the others.

Dr. Margolis's shoulders bumped the scale, sending it swinging on its hook. He looked up, switched off his mike, and said, "Pretty picture, huh?"

"Not too," I said. There was no sign of Les, and I was surprised they started without him. "Is Detective Fedders here, Doctor?"

"Who?"

"The homicide investigator for this case."

The doctor and a male technician moved out of each other's way as the tech finished suctioning out the pool of blood filling the peritoneal cavity, using a device much like the one in a dentist's office, with a screen in it to capture any possible bullet fragments. Dr. Margolis picked up a scalpel, stared blankly at me a second, and I'm sure forgot the question.

The tech was busy at the sink, and so the doctor asked if I would get him the turkey baster from the cart. He always recognizes me but never remembers my name. Once he called me Stormy. I thought, hey, not half bad.

"Could I get you to aspirate here?" He pointed to a pool of bright blood in the lower cavity. "Give me some of that in the vial there, will you? Flush the rest."

I didn't really want to do it, but I did, and would have even if Doug weren't watching. I put the baster down on the counter and stepped back as though that was enough of that while the doctor dictated, lifting out a 60-gram ovary distended with chocolatey fluid. Then he removed the 7- by 6- by 5-centimeter, 132-gram uterus, laying it in the scale. A woman named Mai Lu who stood at the erasable board at the end of the room wrote this information on it as the doctor recited.

"Presence of papillations suggests neoplasm," the doctor said. Then to Doug, whom he didn't know, "Likely cancer."

Maybe the woman knew she had a malignancy and decided not to go through with the rigors of treatment, driving her car off a cliff. It crosses one's mind: Not long ago I worried about the same thing. My mother took a drug called DES. It kept me in the womb when I was in my first restless mood to move on. In my case there was no cervical dysplasia, no precursor of cancer, but because of other chronic problems, my doctor rid me of the pear-shaped organ similar to the one now in the scale. If today I have regrets, they pass soon. On whom should I inflict these renegade cells? I used to wonder what a child of my union with my dead husband would have been like, but that's a don't-think zone.

I asked, "What would you say is the age of this victim, Doctor?"

His glasses were on the tip of his nose. The fluorescent light gave his olive skin an unhealthy green glow.

"By the look of the hipbone," Dr. Margolis said, "and the involvement of suspicious uterine tissue, I'd say this victim was thirty-five or forty." He put the tip of his knife on the bone. "In the public symphysis we see residual ridging. Older than middle-aged, these ridges would be gone. Also, the edges would be worn and the bone material fairly porous under microscopic examination. Now, over here," he said, shimming more tissue away from the hipbone, "we see a slight concavity. In a youngster, this area is furrowed. Later it becomes flat, and later still concave. There's no remarkable arthritic degradation, though I see here by this grainy area at the major muscle attachment that she may have had some occasional inflammation."

I stopped making notes because there was no way I could keep up with him, and we'd get the transcribed report later.

Doug said, "How tall, would you say?"

"Femur measurement indicates she was five six to five ten. On X ray, no sign of trauma to the ribs or shoulder blades. Has not borne children, either." He pointed out a barely visible groove in a bone near the lower spine. "This groove would be wider and deeper. In some women after childbirth, what we call dorsal pits form on the front of the pelvis."

I asked, "Did X ray show any wound damage, gun—"

He shook his head no. "Lungs are clear."

My gaze went automatically to the chest, which lay open, with the ribs folded back and the two bean-shaped organs already removed.

"She was dead before the car burned, then."

"No smoke inhalation," Dr. Margolis said. Then he added, moving forward to the chest area and folding back a chest flap, "We have implants in both breasts." With his scalpel, he probed the base of the charcoal weld, exposing a rubbery flap that resembled a brown mushroom petticoating a tree.

Doug gave me a look, and I lifted my shoulders to say don't ask *me*.

"X rays show no fractures of the hyoid bone," the

doctor said, "which means she was not strangled. Of course, a full osteobiography is only done on skeletonized subjects." He looked at me over his glasses, raising his wiry white eyebrows. "You have Meyer Singer coming in for the teeth?"

"Yes. Thank you, Doctor. We appreciate your help," I said.

Mai Lu came around behind us from Dr. Schaffer-White's table and laid a liver in the scale.

Doug and I could leave now, return to the day's sun and the tall stalks of purple lilies of the Nile taking deep encores in the breeze as the lunch crowds exited around Civic Center Square.

In the hall by the rear door, Dr. Watanabe's assistant was squawking her wide pen on a whiteboard propped against a wall on an empty gurney. She drew a red box around a note in green letters. It read "ATTN TECHS: Please do not put B.G.'s brains away—she's coming in tonight."

I looked around as I heard the back doors slide open and the grumble of wheels from a new gurney being wheeled in. The nude form of a young Hispanic male was aboard. Three hot, raw holes pegged his chest.

The beat goes on.

5 ╱ The next morning I stood on my balcony
⟋ overlooking the Upper Newport Bay, called
╲ Back Bay by locals, and searched for a hint
of heron among the soaked bulrush tassels. Sometime during the night, a cloister of cloud had drawn
down. I looked for a clearing in the fog and hoped
to see, at the bottom of the reeds, the bowling-pin
shape of a brown bittern, or the flashy pink legs of
a black-necked stilt, these names, these birds, all new
to me in the last three years since I'd come to live in
my aunt's condo.

The telephone rang. It was my brother. Even though
my feet were cold, I brought the portable phone back
out to the balcony and continued to look through my
field glasses. On the near bank, a cat darted out of sight
as if falling from earth.

I'm eleven years younger and an entire personality apart from my brother. Nathan calls from his
home in the East maybe once a year. Despite our
emotionally distant family, he carries a peculiar sen-
timentality about the twenty-fifth of December. Usually he'll slip in a minilecture about my not keeping
in touch with our parents, but I doubt he does a
much better job at it. Once he said keeping in touch
is what women do. Not this one, I said. The truth is,
I do, but at my own choosing, not out of protocol. I
figure our parents in Florida are doing fine and so

is he and so am I, so what more needs doing? They never call me.

"Don't tell me I owe you money, Nathan. I haven't borrowed money since college."

"A simple hello would do."

"It's a joke, Nathan."

I pictured my brother. Even with infrequent sightings, when I did see him I could recognize him as a good-looking man: trim, five eleven, even features, with a vertical crease in the tip of his nose that made him look much less serious than he was. The last time I saw him, a flattering gray had crept in among the dark brown hair at his temples.

"You sound like you just got up."

"I did."

"It's late."

"Is it?" I knew what time it was. Already I was beating myself up, counting the number of errands I could have accomplished by now. "Fancy that."

Northeast, a cattail bent nearly horizontal in the foggy layer, bobbing from the weight of a yellow-headed blackbird.

Nathan said, "Pretend the phone just rang."

He could be a smug SOB. But I went along. "Oh hi, Nathan. Good to hear from you." I walked back in, closed the slider, and took the phone into the kitchen, thought I'd try out new tea.

"I'm fine. How are you? See, that's how it's done," he said, but his voice sounded funny.

"Something wrong? Are Mom and Dad all right?"

"You could phone them once in a while." I let silence reign, as the saying goes, while I filled a cup and put it in the microwave. He said, "I'd like to stop by if you're going to be home."

"Sure," I said, an edgy feeling overtaking me. "What brings you out here?"

"I live here."

"No shit."

"In Sierra Madre. You know where that is?"

"Above Pasadena. Nate, I just talked to you Christmas. What is this, summer home/winter home?"

The microwave quit beeping, and I took out the cup and waved a raspberry tea bag over it until it landed and began to bleed into the water. Unraveling the terry dish towel from the oven handle and tossing it on one shoulder, I took my tea and sat down with my feet propped on a chair and wrapped the towel around them. Popsicle toes. There used to be a song. . . .

I contemplated Nathan living fifty miles away, up against the San Gabriel Mountains near the City of Roses, the parade city we blame for drawing defectors from snow country every sunny January. When would Nathan have moved there, packed up all his cares and woe and come clear across the country to a little enclave of exiled hippies, conservative Catholics, and people with maybe a fifth his yearly income? To make his fortune, Nathan sold second trust deeds, then stocks, then handled home refinancing, all the stuff that bores me silly. I guess he could do that by fax or modem and live anywhere he chose.

He said, "I asked you a question."

"Of course you can come by. I'll give you directions."

"I've been to Aunt Markie's before."

"You have? When?"

"Long time ago. What's it matter?"

"You're happy today."

His turn for a pause. "I need to talk to you about something. I think you could help me."

It came to me as I listened to him: Miranda, the name on the car registration. As I told my friends at the cowboy club last night, Nathan had a Miranda. But it could not possibly be.... "I'm sitting here, Nathan, drinking tea and warming my toes, with nothing else to do in the whole world but listen to my wise, old—very old—big brother."

He didn't laugh. "You're going to be home, then?"

"I'll be here."

"Noon all right?"

"We'll do lunch. You have to get used to saying that out here—*do* lunch."

"We say it in the East too," he said, sounding that far away.

"Nothing's sacred," I said. "They probably say it in Nebraska. What's the world coming to?"

"What's the world coming to?" he repeated softly. He must be hunched over the receiver, not standing up, I thought. Nathan stands up for phone calls. It frees the diaphragm. You sound more in control.

"Do I get a hint of what this is about? I mean, you're not going to ask me to invest money in some scheme I'll never be able to figure out, are you?"

"I'm not going to ask you to do that."

"What, then?"

"You remember—?" He stopped himself. I thought I could hear him smoking. "I need to find somebody. Maybe you could help."

Swinging my feet down, I asked with great dread, "Who's the person?"

"I'll tell you later."

"Jesus, Nathan."

"I'd just rather wait till I see you."

"I'm not a cop. I'm a civilian, working *with* cops. I don't just go around looking for people."

"I should just get a private investigator then, is that it?"

"That might be a better idea," I said with more irritation than I meant. I walked into the living room, peeling away my bathrobe down to my cutesy magenta underwear, and threw the robe over the back of the couch. The collar hit a vase of drying flowers I'd meant to empty, and the green water spread over my pine table and onto the cream-colored carpet. "Shit," I said. "Oh, not you. I spilled something."

"You want to get it?"

In the kitchen I tugged paper towels off in a long white train that wouldn't stop rolling till I put my foot on it. "It's okay." While I mopped, I said, "Talk." Then: "You're still smoking. I can hear you. Your lungs are black sponge."

"You're going to tell me you've seen cases."

"Yeah, exactly. Ugly black sponges. Californians don't smoke anymore. Don't smoke in my apartment when you come, okay?" I sat on the couch arm, holding the bunched towels like a torch.

"You always this cranky when you get up?"

"I'm sorry. I have things on my mind."

I expected him to say something equally carping. What he said was, "I miss you, Sammi." Sammi, my little sister name.

"You're a businessman," I said. "You don't miss anybody."

But I listened intently when he said, "Do you remember when I let you fly that red radio airplane off Humpback Hill?"

"Boy. That's going back some."

"Remember?"

"You notice I didn't enroll in flight school for a career," I said.

"I'm sorry I yelled at you then."

"Are you drunk, Nathan?"

"I'm not drunk. You've never seen drunk until you've seen your big brother blotto. You didn't know that about me, did you?"

"That's a picture that takes some imagination, yes." I got up to go back in the kitchen. "I'm glad to hear it."

"Guess what? Tightasses are people too. Are you going to help me, or am I going to have to stop filling your bank account anonymously?"

I laughed and threw the wet wad of paper towels into the sink and glanced at the clock. "Sure."

"You're a great girl, you really are. Only remember, I'm drunk and I don't really mean that."

"Get off the phone so I can get some things done."

"See you around noon."

"Make it one."

"So long, Smokey." He used my other name. And took advantage of my pause.

"See," he said, "I know more about you than you thought. And your old, your very old, brother never rubbed it in, now did he?"

6 He said he needed to walk. "Let's go down to the bay," I said, since the fog had lifted by the time Nate got to my place. The sweet fragrance of white sage, encouraged by the sun, drifted through my open slider as he paced and I sat.

"I think I want to eat," he said.

"Fine. There are great places on the island."

"Maybe we should just stay here."

"Out," I said, pointing to the front door while I unfolded from the couch.

We drove down Jamboree, a boulevard wide enough to be a freeway. It was named for a vast Boy Scout gathering that took place decades ago, when there was nothing around for miles and bulldozers could scrape out a campsite without people yelling about endangered gnatcatchers. At its end a mile down, we crept across the tiny bridge that leads to Balboa Island, which lies between the inland mass and the nearly four-mile-long Balboa peninsula, leaving a channel of water on both sides. A small strip of what's called town runs down the middle of the island, and the rest is a packed architectural mix of houses that range from funky to grand. We could stroll the sidewalk that runs right next to the sand, and watch the ducks waddle up from the beach to nip at flower salads in people's plate-sized yards.

I parked next to a bakery that offered sandwiches

for lunch, and sprang for drinks and bean sprout–walnut–avocado–cream cheese fodder on wheat bread for us both. Halfway down the walk, he told me to hold his sandwich so he could peel off his green cable-stitch sweater, revealing a burgundy knit shirt underneath. His skin seemed flushed, and his eyes watered from the sun-bright droplets in the air.

"Well?" I said, waiting.

"Just a minute."

"Okay." We walked some more.

Ahead, a young woman in shorts and a carpenter's apron rose up from looping a length of orange power cord in her hand as she worked on a house whose owners were adding a second story. Her hair was blonde and wavy to the waist, and I was happy for her, that she got to work outside. Her gaze lingered on Nathan.

I talked about ducks. I told him I'd joined Audubon. I knew a little something about birds now. He looked at me without comment other than "good." "I mean, I don't know how much I can ever know. There are over eight hundred species in North America, after all. I don't want to be a nut about it, you know?"

He nodded and finished his food. We talked about the unusual houses we were passing, some like Cape Cod cottages, others a Spanish motif. When we were nearing the curve of the island, he said quietly, "It's Miranda." We stopped. He looked at me briefly, and said, "You remember her."

"Yes, I remember her." A picture of Nathan's Miranda flashed into my mind, this woman the third of his four wives. She was a beauty, I remembered that. Her best feature was the hair that fell in one long hefty auburn braid all the way to her hips. She would tie off the rope with an orange or aqua ribbon, or whatever color heightened her golden skin and accented her penny-brown eyes. Fifteen years his junior, she'd been both his pride and his slight embarrassment, for Nathan was not the type to call attention to himself. I never knew her well: met her once, talked to her a few times on the phone. His multiple marriages were always a puzzle to me, not fitting a man who wouldn't jaywalk on an empty street after a nuclear holocaust. Early on, I figured this wife for a quick bite of sandwich between his real estate lady and the heiress who talked like Lily Tomlin's telephone operator and no doubt counted the ringy-dingys.

Off my right shoulder, in someone's garden, a tin sea captain stuck on a pole was running in place with the wind, over the heads of lavender holly-hocks.

Nathan said, "Something might have happened to her." In my heart I didn't want him to go on.

"I was supposed to see her. She didn't show up."

"That doesn't sound too serious to me."

"Don't be flip, okay?"

Flip? I thought. We walked on.

"We were to meet Tuesday. We meet every Tuesday." He stepped over a low concrete wall and sat on it, his shoes in the sand.

"You've been out here awhile, then," I said.

Glancing at me, then looking away at three mallards walking flatfooted under a boat tie-up, he said, "I was busy. I tried calling once—"

"How long have you lived here?"

"Since February."

"Three months."

"Convicted," he said, and held out his wrists for cuffs.

I smiled. "Forgiven. And you've been seeing her all this time."

He nodded. "Now you know about your big brother."

This was a new thing, not a Nathan thing, I was hearing. Then I thought, What do I know about how he conducts his life? Maybe that's how he developed and lost his other wives.

"How does wife number four feel about this?"

"She has a name," he said.

"Okay, how does Bridget feel about this?"

"Of course she doesn't know. I don't know how it happened. I didn't plan it."

"Is that why you're out here, to be near her?"

"It didn't feel like cheating, since Miranda *had* been my wife. We were like old friends. It's not that uncommon after a divorce. Really."

"Mm-hm."

Nathan stood up and stepped over the wall to the sidewalk and began walking, his hands in his pockets.

He said, "Don't judge me."

"Of course I won't judge you."

But I did. In my heart I did. But more, I feared for him. Don't let it be the corpse in the canyon, I thought.

Nathan gestured and said, "The old spark was there, what can I say? You'll learn someday things are not all so simple."

"I never thought they were."

"You should see her. She's positively glowing."

"Glowing. So, let me see: She's either pregnant, or she just swung a movie deal."

I moved ahead of him and jumped up on the wall and tried to see how far I could walk there, little kid style, since I had on my rubber-soled shoes. I didn't want to be talking to Nathan about his personal life. I didn't want to be paying attention to two Mirandas in one week. Yet in my gut I knew. There's a lot more coincidence in police work than people want to hear. Still, I hoped for two Mirandas: the one in the canyon and his. As the campy comedian Judy Tenuta would say, it could happen.

"She didn't sign a movie deal."

Stepping off the wall, I asked, "The baby then. It's yours?" What had Dr. Margolis, the pathologist, said about the Jane? He said she had not borne children. Were we safe then? We were safe.

Nathan's voice sounded like number 2–grain sandpaper on tin. "It's not mine," he said. "They're working things out . . . she and that, that Bob."

"I can tell you like him fine."

"He's a doctor. He's a jerk."

"When did Miranda tell you this, she's preggers?"

"In the motel, the last time. They had a knock-down drag-out." He waved his hand. "I don't know about what. Something. He filled the bedspread with all her stuffed animals, took it out on the lawn, and burned it. She started beating on him and he threw her in the pool."

"What a cute couple."

"After they made up, they decided to have a baby."

"That's sick, Nathan."

"No, it's not sick. It's human. You never got to know her. She's a great girl. You never saw that."

"I guess I didn't."

Trying to picture what it would be like to be so happy about such an event you'd celebrate with an ex-husband while whispering on pillows, I couldn't, but maybe that was a shortcoming of my own.

"Before this, was she having fun?"

"She was unhappy. I told you that."

"Was she fooling *around*?"

Maybe he didn't like the baldness of the question; or maybe he didn't want to contemplate it himself.

There was a long pause. "She might have a friend."

I looked away, hiding my expression.

"Her husband's into Harleys. Her too. This guy paints their tanks or something."

"Nathan . . ."

"If she and Dr. Jerkoff had a fight, she wouldn't come to me, if that's what you're thinking. Pride. She wouldn't come to me. She might go to this guy."

"Oh, Nathan."

The old impatience showed in his face. "You have to realize people are people," he said.

"I know what people do," I said.

"If I could just be sure she was all right . . ."

"I'm not a cop anymore, Nathan. I haven't been for a lot of years."

"But you know things."

"And you can get me on the cheap."

"That's not it," he said tautly. "But I'll pay you, if that's what you want."

"I'm just being snotty. That's my job as a kid sister."

We were approaching the ferry dock that would cross to the peninsula where there were shops and restaurants and an amusement center complete with a ferris wheel. Twin red VW Jettas were on the ferry's deck, the drivers out and leaning over the rails.

I said, "Maybe Miranda decided to call it off."

"Not possible," he said, shaking his head.

"What happened between you and her—to your marriage?" Out in the channel a sailboat drifted by. Behind the sailboat came a slow-moving yacht trailed by a canoe with eight paddlers in white jerseys, pulling flashing yellow oars.

"She came home one day and told me she was in love with somebody else. I thought it would be someone younger, closer to her age. Shit, I didn't know who it would be. But not a doctor. He's al-

most as old as me. I said, 'Is this guy your gyne-
cologist?' "

"That made her cooperative, I'll bet."

"She threw a pineapple at me."

"Fond memories."

"Maybe that was part of the attraction. The un-
predictability. Me, well . . ." He shrugged. "They
met on the golf course, Ladies' Day. A neurologist.
A doctor who rides Harleys. Feature that."

"I have friends who say bikes are no worse than
cars if you know what you're doing. It depends on
the person, the training, and the charity of luck."

"Bridget volunteers at a convalescent hospital—
yes, Bridget."

"I liked Mary Lee."

"You were too young. You liked her because she
made you brownies."

"Yeah man, why didn't you keep *her*?"

"Convalescent hospitals, they're not what people
think. They have a lot of young people in there, too.
Accident victims. Bikers. Pardon me, let me revise
that. Squashes. That's what they call them, squashes.
Nobody home. They're all kinked up"—Nathan
made claws of his hands, opened his eyes wide, and
lolled his tongue—"and people have to come in and
put casts on their limbs so their bones don't break
from spasms. This prick doctor must know that." He
arced his soda can into a trash barrel ahead of us. A
woman's laughter pierced the air above the periodic
explosions of nail guns, gull calls, and the talk of
people passing by. We stepped off the walk and onto
the sand.

In Nathan's brow and eyes was my father, and in
the cheekbones and full lips, our mother. Creases at
the eyes said he smiled more than I knew. He took
a cigarette from the pack in his pocket and lit it,
saying, "You're thinking I should leave well enough

alone. But that's not going to happen. I can't do anything about Bridget right now. I'll handle that when the time comes."

By the side of a beached boat two male mallards were butting chests. Mating season should be over and territories already established, but these two, I guessed, bore old grudges. We crossed the sand again to the sidewalk and mounted steps made of cut-down telephone poles to reach the sidewalk. As we did, a teenager with headphones handed us a flier advertising Rollerblades and surfboards and a free drawing for tickets to see Dire Straits at Irvine Meadows.

Nathan said, "She wouldn't say so, but I think she's staying in her marriage because she's afraid. Afraid of the world. See, I never gave her anything when we divorced. We weren't married that long. I should have. God, she's only a kid, really."

"She's just a few years younger than I."

"But you're different."

"Yeah. I have a job."

"She never trained for anything."

"You just have to be out there. You get a measly job, you quit it, go on to the next one until you find something that will work."

"See? You're so judgmental."

"She could go to school. I did."

Nathan blinked his eyes and shook his head as if telling himself, yeah, but it's different for her.

"Now there's the baby to think about," he said. "I should have given her something at the divorce, but I was mad. Out screwing around while I'm busting my ass. I sound mad now, but I'm not. I'm not a saint either. I just hold with the double standard."

It was the second time he showed a sense of humor about himself, and in that one moment I gained an insight into him I hadn't had, and forgave him half a dozen things in our past.

"I hate to say this, but maybe she had a sudden attack of conscience. After all, this is the second time she's fooled around in a marriage."

"I'm telling you she wouldn't. Not the way it's been with us. I had someone call her house, one of the girls in my office. That shows you how loose my screws are. A maid answered the phone. She said, 'Mrs. Robertson's on vacation in Europe.'"

"What?"

"What?" he echoed.

"Her last name."

"Robertson."

The name rang through. Miranda Robertson: the name on the canyon car registration.

Nathan was still talking. "Miranda isn't out of the country. She just returned from Italy last month. Why would she go back right away? I know she would've told me if she was going back."

"That was her new name? Robertson?"

He nodded, and crossed the sidewalk to a snack stand to get another Coke.

The birth date on the registration, what was it? Something, something fifty-three? Ray Vega had made a joke of it. Or was it sixty-three? Didn't the doctor say the body was in her forties? Thirty-five or forty. That's what he said. Miranda was, as I remembered, not yet thirty. The corpse had breast implants. Miranda wouldn't have had breast implants. She already had a good figure. Miranda was pregnant. The woman from the canyon burn wasn't pregnant. I saw the uterus put in the scale. Would I know a mildly pregnant uterus if I saw it? No. But the doctor didn't say. . . .

I realized I hadn't asked my brother where Miranda lived. Maybe because I knew what he'd say. Maybe because in my heart I knew the pretty girl with the auburn braid and the golden skin was gone.

When he came back, I said, "Nathan, I've got to ask you a question you may not like or may not know the answer to, but try to keep it in perspective, okay?"

We stared out over the gently rippled water to the pitch of Balboa Pavilion, the grand 1905 building that when lit with stringers of lights at night takes on an aura of nostalgic innocence.

"Let's have it," he said.

"Do you know if Miranda ever had breast surgery?"

"Why would you ask such a thing?"

"Nathan, did Miranda . . . does Miranda live in Beverly Hills?"

His eyes searched my face, fear and anger at war with each other.

"Does she?"

"Yes." His breath was coming hard. The embroidered alligator on his shirt rose and fell.

"What is it?" he asked. "What do you know?"

"There was a car found Thursday. A woman was in it. The name on the registration . . . but I didn't connect—"

"You knew! You knew all along something happened and you didn't tell me." He let go of the can, which rolled against the wall, and a moan came out from somewhere in the deep bend of his body. I went to him and tried to hold him, but he wouldn't let me.

"Nathan, no positive ID has been made. How would I put it together? I didn't know Miranda's last name. The address on the registration said L.A.

We're down here. It's almost like two different worlds. Who would put it together?"

He walked between an opening in the seawall onto the sand, his face fiery, his body a board.

I looked around for help, but what kind of help I didn't know.

7

I put Nathan back on the road an hour after the walk around the island. He had clammed up. No matter how I talked to him, or about what, he was a million miles away. In my apartment, he washed his face and called a friend he was going to play tennis with, to cancel. When I asked him if he was all right, he said he was just going home to sleep. I told him I was sure there was some mistake about Miranda, that I'd phone her husband myself if that's what he wanted. He said, "No, wait, I'll think of something," and left me feeling irrelevant, superfluous, as he often did.

My mind needed a rest. I went to see a movie with John Goodman in it, because John Goodman was in it, and spoke to no one except the woman in the ticket booth. Afterward I wandered in a department store in Triangle Square without knowing what I was looking for. I ignored the sales associates, as they like to call themselves, and hoped they thought I was a mean and shifty shoplifter.

Later, I walked a couple blocks down the street, headed for a coffeehouse with pretensions of hippie-beatdom. Alongside me, slick-looking cars swept along the boulevard, their cloth tops down, the music up, the drivers busy with gum and lush with new spring tans and expensive sunglasses.

The walls in the coffeehouse were painted black

and jazz was playing. I ordered a blend of something African with a dollop of whipped cream and went to sit at one of the round blue tables. Across the room a single, skinny, morose man with a gold ear cuff and a pointy beard turned pages in a worn *New Yorker*. He humped the pages over with a long finger, whish-pause, whish-pause, regular in the rhythm, as though he were a speed reader with the knack down pat.

On the chair next to me was a thin book with ornate letters on front: *SCPJ*. I opened it and saw it was the literary journal from Cal State Fullerton, and it was all poems. I read a few. I don't know much about poetry, but it seemed good, and I read about deer and candles and things I hadn't thought about in a long time. The caffeine and silence eventually brought me around.

"I tried phoning you earlier," I said to Joe, reaching him about ten that night.

"I was out with Jennifer."

"Oh."

"She needed to talk about David. His college, like that. We hadn't made plans, you and me."

"Where'd you go?" I asked.

"Are you jealous?"

"Of course not."

"You are."

"I understand you have to talk to her about stuff. Where'd you go to eat? New place?"

"I tried *you* at four," he said.

"Nobody's ever home."

"It seems that way, doesn't it?"

"I didn't see a message," I said.

"There's a strain in your voice."

"I just wanted to tell you something. My brother came to see me. Nathan. He's living here now."

"You didn't know that?"

"Our family's a little different."

"Are you all right? You sound depressed."

"I think the victim in Carbon Canyon could be my ex–sister-in-law."

"No way."

"Bullshit, no way. Listen to this," I said, and then I told him about Nathan seeing Miranda while he was still married, while *she* was still married, and when I did, it felt like a betrayal to them both. But I pressed on. I told him about the discrepancies in what the pathologist said and with what I knew about Miranda: the pregnancy, the presumed age. For some reason, I held back about the breast implants. Nathan hadn't directly answered yes, that she had had them, but I thought I read it in his eyes. I held back because I didn't like to talk to men about women having surgery on themselves. It's too easy to joke. And who knows, I may have a lift and tuck someday myself, even though I currently disapproved. I wondered if it was Nathan who encouraged her to do it.

"You just said it doesn't add up."

"But what's her car doing out there, then? Joe, I'm sure that body in the canyon is Miranda Robertson. It's got to be."

"You want me to come over?"

"No. What good would that do?"

"I just thought . . . I don't know. We could get coffee, something."

"I don't need taking care of. I need answers."

"You're sure I can't come over?"

"Go to bed, Joe."

"'American Gladiators' is on. We could watch together. They've got new games."

I said, crankily, "They keep changing the male

gladiators. I liked that older black man, what was his name?"

"I know who you mean, but I don't remember."

"All those women have implants, you know."

Implants. I said it.

"Whatever they've got, it's all right by me."

"You *like* all those muscles? You like that look?"

"Whatever they've got, it's all right with me. What about tomorrow?"

"I have to do stuff."

"So do I. But you're coming here for dinner."

"I am?"

"That's better. Glad you agree."

Early Sunday I phoned the morgue. I learned that a deputy coroner had reached Miranda Robertson's physician husband to ask if he was missing a wife.

Miranda was on vacation in Italy, Dr. Robertson said, and, no, he didn't know who would have been driving her car. His wife was in the habit of loaning her car to people, even the help.

Afterward, I left a message on Nathan's answering machine repeating all this and saying I'd let him know the minute I knew anything else. The rest of the day I did bills and laundry, read the paper, and at dusk took my neighbor's dog, Farmer, for a run. Someone told me there's a fictional P.I. from Chicago who takes her landlord's dog for runs. Mystery loves company.

Later, showering, I genuinely looked forward to the evening with Joe. While dressing, I heard on the radio an old song called "Me and Mrs. Jones." It was a pain-racked tune about infidelity. My brother's pained face came to mind, and then his calmer face, the way he looked when the girl carpenter on the island gave him the long once-over.

I put on a green silk shirt, green jeans, gold bracelet and earrings, and a touch of one of those expensive perfumes you get as a free sample while fleeing through the makeup section of a department store. A song by Nat King Cole came on, one of romance with fewer complications than the one with Mrs. Jones.

When I got to Joe's, he had wine waiting. He fed me grilled shrimp in lemon sauce, nutty rice, tangerine salad, and a chocolate truffle, the last an after-dinner aphrodisiac, he said. My kind of man.

8 Joe told me about a nasty one off Ortega Highway in South County. It was Monday morning and I was in my car and Joe in his, but he was sitting in the Cleveland National Forest and I was on the freeway headed back to the lab from a scene in Laguna Hills, a meth death easy to conclude. "I phoned your boss and requested you," Joe said, "because I know you were down this way."

"You keep pretty good tabs on me."

"Absolutely."

I thought about the scene I'd just left. Deputies had staged an early-morning raid on a modest stucco house off Moulton Parkway and Alicia that fronted for a speed lab. They seized firearms, cash, cars, and enough methamphetamine oil to make forty pounds of crank, the addict's answer to fast food, worth half a million dollars.

Worse news was that one of the amateur chemists took a breakfast snort of crystal intended to last all day. Instead of the usual euphoria and excitation of the brain, the magic diet pill shorted out her cardiac circuits and she keeled over onto the flagstone patio while still in her robe and nightie. It was not clear how long she'd lain there while her brother and husband were cooking up in the lab, but the dog was looking depressed and soulful under a canopy of trumpet vine as though he'd already surmised there'd be no ball today.

In a bedroom upstairs, decorated with stenciled Dutch girls and boys holding hands around a ceiling border, her fifteen-month-old son stood in his crib smiling and babbling to us when we walked in. I'd taken off my gloves, and when I went to shake a small blue rattle at him, his fat legs danced, and when I brought his diapered bottom to my body lifting him out, the sog drenched and warmed me, and I felt the quick vibrations of his heart.

When Joe called from his car, I was coming up on Alton Parkway, so I took the off ramp and curled around to head south.

"Who's out from the coroner's?" I asked.

"A guy named Oskar."

"Don't know him."

"You know how to get here?"

"Blue Jay? Isn't that past San Juan Hot Springs?"

"Eight miles," he said.

"Want to noodle around naked out there after?"

"It's closed. They went under, so to speak."

"Damn."

"I don't think I'd want to get naked out here under any circumstances, anyway," he said.

"Why not?"

"Well, right now there's a vulture looking at me from the top branch of a digger pine."

"Are you dead?"

"Not the last time I looked."

"Then don't sweat it."

"They're sure ugly sonsabitches."

"Ugly's in the eye of the beholder."

"You'll see a sign for Riverside, but it turns to Orange County again. Once you make the turnoff to Blue Jay, the road goes to washboard. There's fallen rock everywhere. Be careful."

"I just don't know how I made it in this life before you, hon, I really don't."

He grumbled, then said, "Well, be careful anyway."

Famed for its spectacular vehicle flights off cliffsides, the thirty-two-mile narrow stretch of treachery through the Santa Ana Mountains inspires bumper stickers that boast of surviving it. Like Carbon Canyon, it's also a favorite place for body dumps. Our crew would be mulling around the mountains scaring off carrion eaters for the second time in five days.

The phone began to crackle and Joe's words break up as I entered a phone cell that didn't want to cooperate. "You there?" I heard him say. "Smoke?"

"I'm here. Wait."

I turned off the freeway onto the highway named for Sergeant Jose Francisco Ortega, a scout for the Portola Expedition in 1769. His adventure started a chain of land grab beginning with the king of Spain and ending with the Bank of America and finally the county of Orange. Passing through an intersection, I waved at a highway patrol car waiting in the other direction, whose driver wasn't my pal Ray but easily could have been, his substation being not far away. "I'm on Ortega," I said. "I'm going to lose you."

"Okay. Be—"

"Right."

When I hung up, my free hand brushed the diaper dampness still on my clothes. I deliberately brought my hand to my face to sniff, remembering the blue-eyed baby I'd kissed on his fragrant temple twice and handed over to the female deputy to take to the county shelter. I thought of his mother, how her hands, arms, and face were covered with numerous small scabs and "picks" from fighting off imaginary bugs. She was bony, her pallor extreme, and the froth at the nose and mouth indicated overdose.

Now I wished her *up*, free of monkeys, preparing her baby for a walk in the sun.

Signs along the road announced the way to the county dump, these days called "landfill." Farther on was a long crest of hill with a row of transplanted palm trees, their tops still neatly tied into upswept hairdos to protect the heart of the palm for six months until the twine rots and they come tumbling down. I quickly counted groups of five. The fifty trees made the dune look like a spined fish heading for sea. I knew the palms marked the property of a builder wanting to put up a castle for himself, newsworthy because various interest groups were saying no way.

I lowered my windows and felt the warm air rush in, and enjoyed a moment of spring. Over the acres of dried grasses, blackbirds twitted and flitted. The sky was knit with faint curtains of contrails left by jets out of El Toro Marine Base. A peaceful day. A tranquil day. I thought how when a baby reaches for you, he grabs you with all four limbs.

Joe walked with me to where the corpse lay on hardpack twenty feet away from a campground trash barrel. A coroner's assistant standing by a stretcher kept bringing the V of his elbow to his face to breathe through the fabric of his shirt. For every ten degrees of ambient temperature, the chemical reaction causing decomposition doubles. It had been hot the last two days. The heavy, repulsive smell reached me.

Joe pulled a Hav-A-Tampa out of his pocket and gave it to me. I peeled off the wrapper, and he leaned near with a colored lighter and lit me. I took a couple of puffs off the small cigar, then bit into a shred of leaf, and went forward with my camera. "Where's Homicide?" I asked.

"No soft shoes but you guys," the deputy standing near Joe said. His voice sounded hoarse, as if he'd been yelling in a bar all night.

"He'll be here, but late," Joe said. "Frank Rubio. His girl's been in an accident on the freeway."

"Bummer. Is she hurt?"

"Just mad because she can't get to her job, is what he said."

Camera in hand, I focused on the body and snapped off two shots. I moved in close and knelt over Mr. Doe as he lay on his side, the left arm a fat plank of faded tattoos extending from his sleeveless shirt. Near the shoulder was a fierce eagle carrying a submachine gun in his talons; below that, a dripping heart wrapped in blue barbed wire. The dead man's eyes were blackened and puffed like a toad's. His nose, lips, teeth, and chin were covered with a dark issue that carried down to the dirt. "He was killed here," I said, pointing downward. "Blood was still flowing."

Joe said, "Look in his eyes."

He motioned in the direction of his evidence kit where I could get some gloves, and I left my camera with Joe and returned to the corpse. With my thumb I pried open one spongy eyelid. My breath was held, and the silence as I peered into that brown, dead orb was like none other. There was a ringing in my head and a whiteness at the edges of my vision as though the void between the man and me was seen and heard in a high pitch through thick Plexiglas.

I stood up immediately, and Joe said, "Are you all right? You look a little green."

"It's hot. I was rushing. Maybe it's the cigar."

"What'd you see?"

"Nothing."

"Look again."

Joe knelt with me. As the other eyelid went up

under my thumb, I noted the dark pink spots on the cornea. "Petechial hemorrhaging," I said, referring to a condition caused by the increase in blood pressure because of compression of the airway. "He suffocated. Maybe strangled."

I didn't see a ligature, and no fingernail wounds appeared on the neck, the victim's attempt to be rid of a rope or whatever instrument of death he would have had to fight. But there couldn't be, for his arms had been bound behind him with silver duct tape. The tape had loosened and gone wavy in the heat, so that the swollen-eyed man looked as though he was about to break free from a nap anytime. One leg was at the wrong angle. I said, "Looks like they broke a kneecap."

"He must have been a very bad boy," the deputy said in his loosely strung voice. His rusty, freckly arms at my eye level were a farm of golden hair. He squatted then, too, and told me he thought the creeps had kicked the body around some by the look of the scuffs and shiny digs in the hardpack. As he added notes to his field report sheet, I saw him write in block letters: KACKY PANTS, GRAY MUSCLE SHIRT, KACKY SOX, BLACK SHOSE, and I wondered what his sergeant had to say about his spelling. The deputy's nose twitched frequently.

I kept looking at the victim's neck, the way the flesh piled out and the color waned at a fold, while the rest of the flesh had progressed to the colors of decomp, beginning with the measleslike Tardieu spots from ruptured capillaries, and progressing to the deeper lividity at the downward position where the draining blood had collected.

"I think under that fat, we've got a ligature," I said. I pressed the flesh at the neck. It blanched. My finger touched something hard embedded in the folds, but I reflexively drew back when what looked

like a living mole moved at the crease, a whitish
wart that wiggled. I flicked the maggot aside and
spread the folds again. One of the flies that feed on
corpses is aptly named *Calliphora vomitoria*.

"Wire," I said.

The deputy coroner, who stood off Joe's right and
who looked more like a girl's soccer coach than a
body snatcher, nodded. His name, Oskar, showed
over the right pocket of his jumpsuit. He was checking air temperature and recording the barometric
reading.

Through the victim's sparse hair, I saw a crusty
stain, and I figured he'd been hit on the head as well.
A rove beetle ran across his cheek. Beetles favor the
outside, flies the orifices.

I said, "Cripes."

"Yeah, I know what you mean. We should carry
Raid," Oskar said, and barely were the words out
when a larva emerged from the victim's downside
earlobe. At the lab there's a man who insists on calling the ear canal the external auditory meatus, but
instead of pronouncing meatus in three syllables, he
says "meet us," and every time I hear the innocent
phrase of people joining one another, I see instead a
landscape of convoluted gristle.

With fat-ended tweezers, I gathered the insect
specimens, put them in a small paper envelope,
folded the top, and stapled it.

"Killer," Joe whispered in my ear. "No air."

"Shut up," I said.

Other insect casings would be collected at the
morgue from the water used to wash the corpse.
They'd be air-dried and placed on cotton. The length
of the insects' life cycles can determine time of death.

Our guess now was that the victim had been dead
about thirty hours. Rigor mortis, a phenomenon
caused by the release of lactic acid, had come and

gone. Rigidity begins in the shortest muscles of the face and progresses throughout the rest of the muscles within eight to twelve hours; then the muscles begin to relax in the same order they contracted, and the body becomes limp again.

I stood and walked over to a pipe bench near a wooden sign that said BLUEJAY CAMPGROUND. There, I tamped out my cigar and put the stub in the Velcro loop of my camera case.

Joe was walking around carefully, keeping eyes out. He spotted three small-caliber shell casings, but they seemed old. Nonetheless, we put them in one of my empty film roll canisters and labeled them. At every crime scene, something is taken, something is left—it's called the theory of transfer.

Turning away, I walked to where I could see out over a plateau on which yellow flowers big as biscuits were growing in the shadow of an oak. Joe came up to stand beside me, his jacket still on in the eighty-plus heat. "It's pretty here, huh?" I said.

"In some directions."

I asked, "Where you headed now?"

"Probably to hell."

"Can I come too?"

"Probably you will," he said. We walked past the trash barrel. Joe looked in. "It's empty," he said. We crossed to the edge of the campground and looked beyond into a valley. "Hear any more from Nathan?"

"I've been working all morning."

"And I kept you busy last night."

"You did indeed. But thanks for asking. The whole thing feels like a duck in the desert. Last night I was sure she was gone. Now I'm sure she's not. Sometimes, you know, you just have a notion."

Joe nodded toward the victim lying on the

ground. "Have a notion about this poor schmuck, will you?"

The quiet was broken by a motorcycle engine. A deputy put up a hand to stop the riders. As the bike started to turn, he called for them to stop. On the apehangers was a man in a black T-shirt with a skull and red rose on the front. Thin puffs of brown hair curved out of his black-leather, silver-studded cycle cap. He was clean-shaven, porky, and he grimaced into the sun, showing a mouthful of what looked like long and ill-spaced wooden pegs. The woman behind him was a frizzy redhead with a bony chest visible under a black bikini top.

In the stillness, we could hear the deputy ask the two what they were doing there.

"Enjoying the springtime," said the girl.

"You been up here before?"

The man said, "No, sir. That's why we wanted to check it out."

"How about shutting that thing off a minute?"

The canyon got quiet again. The sun seemed to increase its vigor.

"What's your name?"

"I'm Harlan, she's Helen."

"What's your last name?"

"Smith."

"You ever been arrested before, Harlan?"

"No, sir."

"How about you, dear?"

"Two years ago, up in Kern County."

"What was that for?"

"Doing nitrous."

"They got nitrous up there in the valley?"

"Major."

"I thought that was mostly kids."

She lifted her shoulders, sucked in her cheeks, and looked like a bored thirteen-year-old.

"Are you clean now?"

Harlan said, "Oh man we don't fool with that, none of it." The woman's eyes fixed on Oskar and his assistant as they were laying out a body bag for the dead man. Harlan saw it then, too, and said, "Shit, what's that?"

"A homicide. You two wouldn't happen to know anything about it?"

"Man, no."

"Are you sure this is your first time up here?"

Helen said, "First time. Last time, too, by the looks of it. Man, that's heavy."

"If I ran your plates, would I learn anything about you you'd be sorry you didn't tell me? Would there be any warrants out for you?"

Harlan said, "I got some, but I paid last week. CHP sat on me."

"I'll bet they got you for no helmet." The deputy dragged out his ticket pad.

"I hate them brain buckets."

"Well, I'm going to cite you both for not having them, you understand? Helmets save lives. You may not want to believe that, but they do."

"There's evidence to the contrary, Officer. I don't want to argue with you, but—"

"No, you don't want to do that. Now, we're going to run your plates, Harlan. And, if I find you're lying to me about having any warrants out, that won't make me happy, you got me?"

"I understand, Officer. You won't find nothing. Look, I'm just up here with my girl, trying to make a little time, you know?" Harlan twisted back to wink at the woman, her neck arching away from him in a deadpan look of boredom. I saw then that she had a tattoo running over the top of one breast in rainbow colors. It said EASY LOVIN'.

The deputy said, "What's your last name, Helen?"

"Baker."

"What's the name on your driver's license?"

"Helen Baker."

"What's the name on your birth certificate?"

Glancing at Joe, I saw his expression change, and a faint smile come to his lips as he looked at me. The woman did not answer right away. She dropped her hands to her sides as though the muscles had lost grip on the bones, and rolled her eyes and looked away.

He asked her again, "What's the name on your birth certificate?"

"Henry Babson."

I opened my eyes wide to Joe, and he was turning now, stifling what promised to be a wide smile, and stepped away and around to me then, coming close and saying softly in my ear, "See the Adam's apple?"

"Do you think it's news to Harlan?"

"Not at all."

Harlan was in fact looking impatient to move on.

The second deputy came back with results from the plate run off the mobile data terminal in the car, and said, "No warrants on Harlan."

Harlan looked pleased, and said, "She'll come up clean, too, Officers. I'll vouch for that."

9

We were at the only lunch place around for miles, above the hazy flats near the city of Lake Elsinore.

I asked Joe, "The bikers, do you think they were up to anything?"

"You heard them interviewed."

"I think they were just out riding," I answered myself.

"Where I would be, if I was twenty years younger."

He was gazing through a filmy window at the boiling patch of gritty desert country below that drew blue-collar workers, retirees, hot-air balloonists, speedboat enthusiasts, and until recently, a serial killer nabbed only after he'd made a sizable dent in the female prostitute and drug abuser population.

"Didn't you see that one biker the other day with white hair? You're never too old," I said.

I thought back to the burn scene in Carbon Canyon five days ago, the bikers flying down the highway as we were getting ready to leave, with their hair free in the wind. We were fifty miles from there, as the raven flies.

"My son goes dirt biking somewhere out here," Joe said. "Lot of decomposed granite. Ruts don't form. The rain just soaks on through."

"Now you won't want him to go."

He shook his head. "You get killed quicker in Santa Ana than out here in the mountains."

Three men, all with beards, came in and pulled out chairs around one of the dark wooden tables. The big man wore a pale yellow knit shirt that form-fit a keg belly so smoothly the navel contours showed. Printed on the shirt was a lobster with an oversized pincer. Crawdaddy's Lobster Shack in Sacramento, the place for tail and ale. As he caught the eye of the woman behind the sandwich bar, he ordered a pitcher of draft, then levered pressure off his flesh with both thumbs under his belt, and sat down.

He said, "Go for that upper gate, man. The eyes are soft as putty."

"Oh, I don't know," the man with a tan shirt with his back to me said. "You ever butcher a cow?" On his right arm he had a short flesh-colored cast.

"Not lately," the big man said, and laughed. He leaned back and humped his shoulders a few times to work out the kinks.

"That cornea is one tough motherfucker."

I looked at Joe, who flicked the men a glance.

"Greg says to watch the middle gate," the second man said. "But I'm tellin' ya, man, you got a guy one step, one thrust away, with a knife big as your bone, you're going to be watching the arm. I don't care how much discipline you have. Natural instinct."

Leaning toward Joe across our table, I said, "Self-defense tactics. Think they're cops?"

"Jerks." I smiled and watched him sip his coffee I knew was lukewarm, the way he liked it.

Yellow belly stood up in response to the pitcher being placed on the bar. He hooked three mugs and brought it all to the table. "The guy goes for it, whack the ulna," he said. "That's pain. I guarantee, he's going to drop the weapon."

"Sure sounds like day-off cops to me," I said. "Who else says 'weapon'?"

The short man facing me had a blowsy white beard and hair that curled thickly over his collar. He fixed his bright blue eyes on me until I looked away.

I heard a softer, marbled voice I hadn't heard before and figured it was the white-haired guy. "Let me tell you something," he said. "You're faced off. Attack first. Don't wait for him to come to you. You need that element of surprise. Render a devastating, neutralizing, lethalizing attack, if that's what you have to do."

Joe offered me a fry. "They're showboating for you, honey."

"Think so?"

The waitress brought the check and I asked for a Pepsi to go. The men were quiet for a while, and then, when the woman came back and as we were trying to read the writing on the check, one of the men said something about exotic loads. He was referring to soft-jacketed ammunition also known as manstoppers. I raised my eyebrows to Joe and said, "They like guns too."

We laid out money for the waitress and walked outside to the hot white brilliance at four thousand feet, my Pepsi in my hand.

In the gravel parking lot was a Jeep with a lift kit and roll bar, and next to it a pickup truck with three dirt bikes in the bed, and I realized what our bearded buddies were up to when they weren't playing Baddest Dude in the Whole Damn Town.

"Dirt bikers," Joe said. "A little old for that."

* * *

Joe squinted into the sun as we walked to the cars.

I said, "Joe, do you think I ought to call Miranda Robertson's husband myself?"

"No." A quick frown arrived then fled across his face. "Homicide will handle that. She's either in Italy or she isn't. In any case, we'll know pretty soon." He maneuvered me over to my car.

"You're mad. You think I'll meddle."

"You had enough trouble six months ago."

"This Pepsi is watery."

"Are you listening to me?"

"Yes."

"I know you're worried because your brother's involved. But it'll be nothing, you'll see." By my car door he moved into me, the dank sweet smell of his body comforting.

"I reek of cigar," I said.

"So do I." He lifted my chin and kissed me lightly. When we broke, I said, "I'm going to throw this away," and looked around for a trash barrel.

"Let's just take the afternoon off," Joe said.

"Oh yeah, sure." I knew he didn't mean it. Well, he meant it as far as the urge went, but neither of us would indulge on county time, though we both knew people who did. What's unethical for one is not for another, but stealing paid-for time is stealing just the same, to my mind.

I saw a trash can and went toward it. Joe got out his keys and went around to his car.

Wasps looped over the barrel. A cone of stench emanated from it. I decided to avoid that one, and went a distance away to a can with a paddle-shaped homemade wooden cover on top. When I raised it, I said, "Joe, wait." He came over.

Two empty cardboard rolls of tape lay in the middle of the trash. One had a fragment of silver duct

tape still attached and the other's center held a
walnut-sized wad of tape. Coiled over all was a
prickly length of shiny single-strand aluminum wire
with small triangular nubs on it.

"That looks wicked," Joe said.

Gingerly, I plucked it out, the tail releasing from
the confines of the barrel and whipping into the button panel of Joe's shirt.

"Down, girl," he said.

"Look at this stuff. What is it?"

"I don't know."

"Should we take it along, for grins?" I asked.

"We're nine or ten miles from the scene, if that's
what you're thinking."

"That's what I'm thinking. Pretty unlikely, huh?"

I leaned the coiled wire against the trash barrel,
remembering a call I went on with my husband in
Oakland. We were searching for a weapon all the
bystanders said they saw in the hand of the suspect
a moment before we arrived. I was sure the suspect
passed it off to someone, but Bill said evidence hides
in strange places. He went up on the roof of the
house next door. The kid had tossed the pistol there.

I said, "Our victim had wire around his neck. It
was so embedded. It could have been this. I never
pricked myself, though, when I touched it."

"Take it. It's your call."

Picking the scary Slinky up again, I said, "You
couldn't grab this for a garrote," I said. "You're
right. I'll leave it."

Joe said, "Take the tape rolls. What the hell, we
might get lucky. I'll get a bag." Prints can be obtained off tape these days, even the sticky side. They
can be obtained off the inside of surgical gloves as
well, surprise, surprise to the bad guys.

I looked for a twig to move stuff around in the
barrel and found a dark stick of manzanita.

"There's a couple other pieces in here." Using my stick, I lifted out a double-stranded copper wire, spearing through a diamond-shaped separation between the two strands. The diamonds were regular, a part of the design, as though they'd been pried apart by a tiny little Samson standing on the bottom strand. The piece was about a foot long.

Joe shrugged, took the copper piece from me, and dropped it in a bag. He plucked out the cardboard tape rolls and the wads of tape and put them in too.

"Let's tip the barrel," I said. We shook out a trail of garbage. We were poking around in the papers and chili cups when we heard a window slide open in the café and the waitress say, "Can I help you?"

Joe said to me under his breath, "We need a warrant to do this?"

"No way."

"My wife thinks she lost her ring in here. That okay?" he said to the woman, now lost in the brown shadow of screen.

"That's why I don't wear mine no more," she sang back. "Good luck."

I used my shoe to brush aside a bagful of soiled baby diapers, revealing another strip of wire about fifteen inches long, this one so jagged it looked as if tinsnips had been taken to it to slice its length into even, backward-leaning shark's teeth.

"Woho," Joe said. "Don't it make your skin tingle?"

"Let's take it." I pincered it between thumb and forefinger and dropped it into the sack. Hearing the door to the café open, I looked up expecting to see the waitress, but the small man with the white hair who had been with the lobster man stepped off the concrete platform that served as a porch. The wind lifted his beard and blew open his light green shirt, revealing his undershirt and, up by the armpit, a tan holster curved with weight.

"Joe," I said. "That guy's packing. He's got a shoulder holster."

Watching him out of the corner of my eye, I saw him go across the lot to the pickup truck with the dirt bikes in it. He opened the door and slid out a pack of cigarettes from the seat. Looking at us, he shook out a cigarette and lit it. Then he came forward.

I stood up and faced him. The small paper sacks we had were lying on their sides, so I didn't suppose he'd think they were anything but trash.

"How y'all doin'?" he said.

I said, "Okay. How you all doin'?"

Joe rose from his crouch. He said, "My wife lost her ring. I swear I can't take her anywhere."

"I wondered what y'all were digging around in the trash for. I seen hungry and I seen poor, but I hope it don't come down that rough on me," he said, the cigarette dangling from his mouth. He slipped the lighter into his chest pocket alongside the pack of cigarettes. "You never can tell. I seen guys in suits Dumpster-diving before. Well, take care, now," he said, and turned and walked toward the Jeep this time.

My eyes still on him, I saw him jump back, then noticed a brown flutter on the ground and heard a *dee-deeah* cry.

We moved forward, and the man looked at us and said, "Looks like it's got a broken wing."

"She's faking," I said. "She's got eggs nearby. That's a killdeer." The black double bands on the bird's neck looked as coquettish as velvet chokers.

"Eggs? Where?"

The bird gyrated in her fake injury, the white of her neck and breast flashing.

"They lay their eggs in gravel. It's one of their favorite places," I said. With the three of us so close, the bird limped and flapped all the harder. *Kill-deeee*, it shrilled, making Joe wince. "Part of its scientific name is *vociferus* meaning 'noisy.' "

"Well, we'll just leave you alone, little feller," the man told the bird. He gave us a nod, then headed for the Jeep.

Joe said, "What do you make of him?"

"The gun? I told you I wondered if they were cops in there."

"Catch the plate?"

"Sure. I'll get somebody to run it. The other one, too." The Jeep license plate had a B, and a 1, and then BOMBER. "B-one-Bomber. Probably an aerospace guy. Not a cop. But a concealed weapon, man, somebody should rap him. It gives me the creeps, that's for sure. Like Doug. He said when we found the gun in Carbon Canyon he worries the whole country is armed and dangerous. He's afraid to go on a date."

"He should be," Joe said; exactly what I told Doug.

"I didn't think you noticed," I said.

"I notice everything."

"He's a flirt. And a baby. I like my studs seasoned."

"That's what you call me?"

"What—seasoned, or stud?"

"Studly. I think it fits, eh?" Joe pulled back his shoulders and lifted his chin.

"Stud muffin," I said.

I forgot to have someone run the plates on the vehicles we saw on Ortega until an hour after I got back to the lab. By that time, I even thought gathering the wire was foolish, but that was in Joe's camp now, or rather his trunk. In a dead period after I had returned calls left for me on message slips, I phoned and asked Ray Vega to run me the plates. "Clean," he said, when he called back. "No wants, no warrants."

"Thanks, hon. Anything happening today?"

"The usual. We had a slow chase by San Clemente. Some dude stole his dad's car. How's with you?"

"The usual."

"Don't you guys always have a lot of work Mondays?"

"The gangbangers were relatively quiet this weekend. We had a body off Ortega. Guy beaten to death."

"You were down here, you didn't call me?"

"Afterward, Joe and I ate at a place top of the ridgeline, you know where I mean?"

"Yeah, that's a biker hangout."

"All we saw were dirt bikers. I thought maybe they were dirt *bags* for a while there, though. One had a concealed weapon. That's why I had you run the plates."

"Those weren't bike plates."

"I know, silly. The bikes were in the truck. Listen, I better go. I got a call up in Fullerton. That's going to put me in the worst traffic coming home."

"Hell, grab the overtime. I always do."

"Yeah, but you're a greedy bastard."

"Sayonara, Sweetcheeks."

"You too. Talk to you later."

When I did get to Fullerton, the case was a carbon monoxide suicide in a garage that also took the lives of a dog and cat in the house. The man was a tenant of the woman who lived in the house. His furniture consisted of ten-gallon paint cans for stools, two small scratched tables, and a twin mattress on old carpet squares in the corner. The woman said she felt sorry for him, he was a distant cousin or something, but that she couldn't have him stay in the house, he was just too dirty.

"Now look what he done," she said, weeping as if flesh had been torn from her bones. "He come in here and killed my babies." Next to her on the couch lay a puff of white cat and a small black-and-beige dog. "No-good Jessups. That whole family has to look up to see the rim of the toilet. He comes back from the grave, I'll kill him again."

My neighbor's voice was on my machine when I got home. Mrs. Langston said her arthritis was bad today. Would I mind letting Farmer take me for a walk? He was driving her nuts.

Mrs. Langston doesn't have the kind of arthritis that shows. It's in her muscles and connective tissue. To look at her, you'd think nothing was wrong with the pleasant retired schoolteacher, but I learned to recognize when the pain darkened the slight shadows under her eyes.

"It feels like tiny crabs are in there," she told me one time. "Pinching. I don't mean to complain. It just aches."

All over her house are gadgets of wonderful design to alleviate her pain: hard rubber balls on flexible rods that she slings over her shoulders to pound her back; sawed-off broom handles she uses to roll down her legs as if flattening dough; thick plastic coat hangers she burns apart with a cigarette lighter to make a dull end so she can poke and prod the pain away; flat massagers the size of baseball mitts; purring footrests knobbed in rubber bumps; air guns meant to render a blast against the ligaments or in the hollows where muscles attach to bone. For all

Mrs. Langston's suffering, she tries not to mention it, but says some days, "Oh, I hurt," in that way you know she's said it over and over again to herself when no one was around to listen and has forgotten now there's someone near who can.

"A rough one today?" I said.

Farmer gazed at me with smiling eyes, his auburn tail waving like a duster over the end table.

"Somebody jumped me in an alley last night," she said. "If you catch him, give him unholy hell."

"I'll do that," I said.

I'd seen the flapper pictures of her in her twenties, one long pale leg on the running board of a Model T, and in the hand cocked on her hip a racy cigarette. It was hard to put that picture with this, no matter that she looked fifteen years younger than her sixty-two years.

A glance at the other end table told me she'd already put three long-stemmed, raspberry-colored daisies in a vase for me that I knew she'd give me when I brought Farmer back.

"Get your leash, Farmer," I said, and the springs in his legs went off. He wheeled into the kitchen to grab the leash off the high counter, his toenails clicking on the tile as he clutched to hold on.

Farmer scared up a snowy egret. The slender white heron moved through the air in a lazy flap, flicking its head ever so slightly toward its right rudder with what I could imagine was a gesture of mild annoyance.

At the sight of the egret, Farmer went to point, his body rigid as stone. I praised him and he relaxed, joyful, his rubbery grin so basic and elemental I smiled too.

We covered much of our usual trek around Upper Newport Bay before dark, almost three miles. The bay is about half a mile wide. A salt company once dredged there, and another enterprise mined for shell deposits. I don't make the trek every day, but maybe twice a week, and often with Mrs. Langston's setter.

Soon I was lost in the sage smells and the scent of brackish water, and I tried to see how many plants and bushes I could name in the gathering dusk. Always, my eye was out for the rare Laguna liveforever that clings precariously to the steep cliffsides, and the salt-marsh bird's beak that looks like tiny birds and is washed under by high tides. But my mind was on other things, and in the rosy grayness, all the colors merged.

Sometime during our walk, I knew I would be driving back to work, overtime or no overtime.

Back at Mrs. Langston's, I collected my three daisies and told her to quit staying out at the nightclubs so late, she'd feel better, then went to my place and microwaved a frozen dinner of lemon chicken and inedible peas. I watched the news and, without a moment of arguing myself out of it, headed to the morgue to see if I could read the chart for the Carbon Canyon victim and convince myself, as Nathan tried to do so desperately, it wasn't Miranda Robertson lifted from the cinders at all.

10

Freeway construction shunted me off to an unfamiliar route on my way to the morgue. On a dark Santa Ana street, I drove toward the highest building I could see, a dull brown block against the charcoal sky. I was passing through a neighborhood of modest homes where third-shift police patrols get several disturbance calls a night and the parks each evening fill up with dope dealers like leaves blown across a lawn. Maybe it was too early, but I didn't hear boom box music issuing from street corners or see many people about. All the same, I cracked the windows on both sides to listen for tire noise or footsteps. At stop signs I only slowed, taking the mild dips designed for water runoff with reasonable speed, watching my low beams bounce over startled cats' eyes, root-lifted sidewalks, and twenty-year-old car bumpers with red cellophane taped over broken taillights.

Downtown, I drove on virtually empty streets and didn't wait for the full red-light cycles to complete. Here Spanish-named taverns shouldered shops that close before dark. Gutters glinted with broken glass. In the doorway of a storefront with iron accordion grates, a lumpy bag lady stood fussing with her grocery cart.

At Third and Main, I caught the familiar yellow letters on the windowpane of a shop closed as long

as I can remember: EVERYTHING IN THE STORE $6.90
OR LESS. I wondered what had become of the owner,
and if his sons now wore Raiders jackets and flashed
AK-47s from pickup beds. Raiders: *Right After I Die,
Everybody Runs Scared.* That's what one juvie told
us it means.

Monday night blues, or just a mood that had been
creeping up for awhile, overtook me, and I wondered why any of us ever thought we could stop or
even slow down the mudslide of dark forces.

On a back street behind the morgue a few
months ago someone fired a round at a police car
as it was leaving the parking lot. Nonetheless, as I
neared Shelton, I decided to come around the back
way, daring something, I guess. That part of my
personality someone will have to clue me in on
someday.

Now there was no life at all, only the low-wattage
porch lights over butterscotch-colored homes, and
the long expanse of the county parking lot scatter-
shot with maybe two dozen dew-covered cars.
When I opened the door to the building, a Muzak
version of "Proud Mary" was playing. The disk was
stuck on *rollin,' rollin' on the river* and didn't unstick
for a full minute.

A tech with a long ponytail and a jaw still round
with baby fat came from the back. I told him I was
from the lab and showed him my ID. "Could I look
at the file for Jane Doe Five?" He was new, didn't
know where anything was. I said that was okay, I
did. After buzzing me in, he walked silently back to
where he'd come from.

All offices feel foreign when no one is there. I
toyed with the light switch but couldn't get more
than a bluish middle fixture to come on. It was
enough light to find the Doe log book, which gives
the details of a case, and then to find the right folder.

Janetta's desk had boxes on it, so I took the file to one of the other four desks and sat down, noting the miniature pink roses in a paper-wrapped pot near the telephone, and the tiny framed photo of a man with a little boy on his knee. The woman at whose desk I sat I didn't know well, and I felt a bit intrusive.

I turned the pages of the pathologist's report. This bone and that bone, the organ weights and measures, and, because I'm sensitive to it, the phrase, "gross cervical dysplasia," meaning a precancerous condition, the same as I had had. I read again my Jane's estimated age, revised it to early forties. No kids. No evidence of stabbing or shooting. Nor had she burned to death, because her lungs were clear. A head wound, perhaps, but we had hardly any pieces to assemble to complete that puzzle.

I flipped through the autopsy photos. Wedged against the corpse was the triangular stainless-steel block used to prop the body so it could be photographed from all sides. The block gleamed like a new railroad tie. The photos didn't tell me anything new. The first X ray I came to was a side view. Dr. Margolis had noted the plastic implants that did in fact show as white disks on the film. I felt a wave of pity for the woman. It comes to this. A proud or vain woman, attempting to enhance her life; two white, hardened disks like new moons grinning through the black night.

My reverie was broken by hearing Dr. Schaffer-White's voice in the hallway as she gave instructions to the baby-fat lab tech. I replaced the file and went out to see her. Leaned against the wall, she was turning pages in a folder. She was in her lab coat and old-lady shoes, but the pearls were there and the diamond earrings. She noted me, smiled wanly, and lifted the folder higher. "A senior who may be an abuse victim," she said, brushing wayward blonde hairs away from her face. She looked tired.

"From a home?" I asked, meaning convalescent.

"His daughter's," she said, then added without looking up, "I hope there's a short stairway to hell for those kind of people."

I said, "How 'bout we start a vigilante committee. I'd have no trouble getting charter members."

"He was scalded. He was starved. Who would you get to do the same to the daughter?"

"I know a few cops."

"That's not funny these days," she said.

"It never was."

She sighed heavily, closed the folder, and started moving toward the autopsy room. I trailed along. "What brings you out tonight, Smokey?"

"Oh, just reviewing a case from last week. Burn victim, crash victim, we don't know yet."

"That awful one?" she asked, and turned her blue eyes to me as we stopped in the doorway. She had a small cold sore on her bottom lip. Behind her, the vacant autopsy room was quiet and sterile as anyone could make it. With the intercom music off, I could hear the cooling unit for the refrigeration room hum.

I told her about the male Doe we brought in from the campground. "Do you know anything about it?"

"I did that one," she said. "As I remember, he had a fractured skull, four ribs, femur, and tibia, and a dislocated patella."

"Worked him over good," I said.

She tested her sore lip with the top one, then said, "They used his chest for an ashtray."

"God. I didn't see that."

"You wouldn't, with the shirt on. There was wire around the neck, but that was not the manner of death. I sent it to Property."

"What did the wire look like?"

"It was flat but had these little nubs on it, triangles, that dug into the flesh. It wasn't even long enough to strangle him with. I think it was tied to something else that broke."

"Joe Sanders and I found some strange wire about ten miles from the campsite in a trash can."

She smiled and said, "I can't believe you guys."

"Well, it's a long shot."

In the autopsy room, she opened a lower cabinet door and looked inside, then two more. At the far end of the room a life-sized plastic skeleton held a placard painted with a skull and crossbones. The sign is used for morgue tours for drunk-driving arrestees: YOU BOOZE, YOU LOSE.

Dr. Schaffer-White found what she was looking for. She brought out a book. "I'm studying law. I don't want to do this forever. We had some downtime today, then it got busy."

"Law?"

"Keep it to yourself, okay?"

"You got it."

"I think I like what you do better than what I do, Smokey. But then some people are never satisfied."

"Well, neither of us exactly hold the glamour jobs," I said. "But hey. What do they say around here? 'Five hundred a week and all you can eat?' "

"*I* don't say it."

"Pardon me," I said, smiling. "Our victim. He died of the beating, then?"

"He died of a blow to the suprasternal notch, that hollow right here?" she said, and fingered the swale where the two collarbones meet. "Shatter that and all sorts of things collapse. Bones puncture vital blood lines. I saw one of these in med school, I'll never forget it."

"They have to use a special weapon?"

"The hand. The victim's scalp had abrasions

where someone grabbed him by the hair and pulled his head back. Someone else chops downward with the side of the hand," she said, demonstrating. "I told your friend, 'Your suspect will know martial arts.'" She sighed, patted her lab coat as if it had keys in it somewhere, and said, "You take care now, Smokey. I've got to run. One of my girls is sick and my husband's having a tantrum. He's a good father, but he can't handle diapers and he can't handle sick."

Before even reaching the end of the lot I phoned Ray Vega from my car and told him to get his fanny off the freeway and come see me.

He said, "Are you crazy, girl? This is my night for stopping all blondes. Francine and me had a major fight. I need a new date."

"You are really disgusting."

"Ain't I?"

"Be a friend tonight, okay, Raymond?"

"All yours, babe. Where you taking me?"

"How about—?"

"You up for fish?"

We met in a seafood eatery next to a topless joint named Captain Cream's in a dark corner of a lot just off the freeway.

Every time I see Ray Vega in his CHP uniform, I think he's just so darned handsome, like a TV cop.

I gave him a rundown of my day. "I still have baby pee on me, Raymond, from a little boy who won't have a mother to diaper him in the morning."

He squeezed my arm that lay on the table. He was quiet for a while. The waitress brought us water without asking, a surprise after seven years of drought, and took our orders. When she left, I said, "That's not all."

"What's up? Tell your old buddy, or what's a

buddy for? Shakespeare say that or something?"

"Yeah, Shakespeare."

"So, what's eating you?" He watched a young woman come in, her tight beige skirt like an Ace bandage over her perfect thighs. The shade of her stockings matched. "Jesus," Ray breathed.

When I got his attention again, I told him about my brother phoning me Saturday; about our walk around the island and my deep fears. I said I sensed Nathan's ex-wife/present lover was a murder victim, despite none of the numbers adding up, really. And then I said, "I want to go and violate procedure."

"You've got to give me more than that," Ray said, sipping off three inches of his ice water.

"What I want to do, I want to go talk to her husband myself. See if he's lying."

"Why are you telling me this? You want my permission? Listen. You go messing around, you better start makin' blueprints for your home under a freeway. 'Cause you're going to be fresh out of a job."

I thought back to how close I'd come last year to being, as Ray said, fresh out of a job, for involving myself in what should have been strictly a police matter. That time I gave *myself* permission because a friend was threatened. Miranda wasn't a friend, but she wasn't exactly a stranger either.

"What could it hurt, Raymond? That's what I've been tossing around in my mind."

"You're going Fifty-One-Fifty on me," he said, using cop code for a crazy. "How about I just get you blitzed and we go over to my place? I just did the sheets. You'd be proud."

Vinegar and a plastic basket of calamari strips were set in front of us at last, and Raymond dug in without so much as a glance upward. In time, he mumbled, "You know that bumper sticker says

'Friends don't let friends drive drunk?' "

"Yeah."

"I saw one today says 'Friends don't let friends drive Subarus.' "

"That's funny, Raymond. What does it mean?"

"It means a *friend* don't let another friend go lookin' down her own barrel. Do you want a job in a nice clean laboratory, or do you want to, like, start your own business as a bikini-wearing street vendor?"

"I could open a detective agency. Maybe I'd meet Bruce Willis."

"He died hard, didn't he? Man. He fell in the toilet. Who cares? He'll be singing doo-widdy with you under the freeway."

Ray poked a calamari my way and I shook my head no. He said, "I don't want to talk about this. It upsets me."

"Upsets you?" I was amused, insulted, and annoyed. "What do you want to talk about?"

"Francine wants to get married."

"You keep running into that problem," I said.

"How come that is? I don't understand."

"Neither do I. Who'd want to marry you?"

"Right," he said, and didn't blush, but let his guard down. "Smoke, do you suppose all the old people in the world have this thing figured out?"

"I doubt it," I said.

"All those old people, having anniversaries all the time. Golden, diamond, whatever. You think it was better back then? People were smarter?"

"I'd like to think so, Ray. But maybe they just give up. They know that's about as good as it's going to get, so they pretend they're happy."

"That's what I was afraid of," Ray said. He looked at me as if trying to figure how serious I was. "I shouldn't have brought it up."

"I warned you."

He said, "If your husband woulda lived, do you think . . . ? What do you think—?"

"Ray? My turn to change subjects."

He lowered his eyes. His black hair gleamed under the light. When he looked back up, he was smiling. "Hey," he said. "You know what happened to me today? A lady dressed in a suit, she flew by me while I was writing a guy up. Gives me the finger. How you like that?"

11 I met Nathan in Huntington Beach at the mouth of the long pier "rehabbed" in recent years to something yuppies could love. Despite it being a Tuesday, plenty of fishermen stood at the railings with their poles weighted downward from the tug of the sea. Like a spill of bright coins, the sun glinted brokenly off the water. I turned and pointed across the highway, suggesting a couple of great lunch places. He said, "Let's walk first."

Midway down the pier, a small boy ran into Nathan's leg, pasting my brother's slacks with the wet rim of a half-eaten chocolate bar. With a where'd-you-come-from question in the boy's unlit eyes, he stumbled and spun off. "Oh man, he got your leg," I said.

Nathan looked down at the chocolate transfer on his leg and then out at the horizon, as if he'd already forgotten why he looked.

We stood at the rail, watching men in rubber wet suits ride the waves. He said, "Before I met her she never let anyone watch her sleep." He said "her," not needing to say her name. "She trusted me. Maybe she shouldn't have. Who the hell knows anybody?" His knuckles showed through his pocket.

"Why wouldn't she trust you, Nathan?" I said it outright. No waver, no apology, but no accusation either. Sometimes you need to say things for your own confirmation, and sometimes if you do, you get reactions you didn't expect.

But Nathan's thoughts were far away and he gave me no grim surprises. He said, "I called the son of a bitch myself."

"Her husband?"

"You know what he says? He says, 'She's not your charge anymore, Montiel.' What the hell kind of word is 'charge'? Is that what he thinks of her, his *charge*?"

"What difference does it make what words he uses?" I asked. "He's not worried about her, that's clear. That must mean she's fine, she's off doing her thing. Buying pasta makers in Italy."

"He wouldn't tell me a damn thing, that's what gets me. What would it hurt? I ask him, 'Do you think I could talk to her, have her number over there?' No."

"What's she supposed to be doing over there?"

"She's got an aunt, cousins. I never met them."

"You think he knows about you two?"

"Impossible."

"Nothing's impossible."

"He doesn't, that's all. I ask him, 'Have you heard from her or not?' He tells me to get lost. I'll go to goddamn Italy myself, I have to."

We turned to walk back. Ahead of us, a man rode a bicycle, though none were allowed on the pier. A little farther down, a bright wriggling thing whipped frantically on the concrete surface. Nathan stepped ahead and scooped up the fish. "Let's give him back to his maker," he said, and strode to the side to heave the tiny missile over.

When he resumed walking it was as though he'd never lost focus. "I'm sick, Sammi, sick. I don't know whether to scream or jump in the ocean. She's gone. She's just gone."

"I've never heard you talk like this before," I said softly, trying to see his face, but he turned away and stepped again to the side to look over the long expanse of washed sand. A gull glided widely between us and a scattering of sanderlings line-dancing on the shore. "Nathan, I'll see if I can talk to him. Just give me a day or two."

He pulled me to him sideways. That surprised me, since we are not a touchy family. He said, "I can't wait that long."

"You *can* wait that long. Be patient."

"That was never my strong suit."

Nor mine, I thought.

We ate Italian, though that might not have been a good idea, and left each other for separate parking lots after awkward talk about the national scene, our parents, and one cousin who killed himself in prison.

When I got back to the office, on my desk was a copy of Dr. Schaffer-White's report from the Blue Jay homicide. I turned pages and saw that Les Fedders was the dick on the case. So. Now we had two cases together. I'd had the misfortune of working with Les before, though on as lean a basis as I could. He's given to gloating about how he can cover the "poppers" with no wad up his nose, poppers being corpses in that state of advanced putrefaction wherein the buildup of internal gases splits the skin like seismic violence. Teflon nostrils this detective says he has.

But once, on a case in 104-degree summer heat, I watched a gag wrestle in Les's throat when a coroner's tech pulled on the arm of a corpse left too long in a car behind a building and the arm came away at the seam. Dick of the Year saw me catch the reaction, and ever after he gets a dig in when he can.

I no sooner had him on the phone than he said to

someone in the background, "What was the score on that fingerprint, Jesse? 'B' quality? That's good enough for me. I'll sign off on it."

He returned to me. "We got a hit on a serial bank robber. Dumb shit's going to federal quicker'n hell can scorch a feather. He left his prints on a check-book cover."

"Les, you wouldn't happen to have the camp-ground case on your desk?"

"That one down off Ortega? Yeah, I do." I heard the smack of folders. "I got there right after you frenzies left." Frenzies—his word for forensics peo-ple. "That was a pretty one, wasn't it? Le's see . . . Rollie Wilson Pierson, age fifty-five, housepainter. Arrested for public intoxication four times. Two un-paid traffic cites. That's it. Trudy Kunitz says she doesn't think we can get anything off the duct tape. Just a big smudge. But I'll tell you something. Who-ever messed him up was a skilled practitioner of martial arts."

"How do you know that, Les?"

"Experience."

I should have leveled him myself, stealing the doc-tor's evaluation. But I wanted to ask him a favor, and I was working up my courage. "Have you talked to the family yet?"

"By phone."

"Anything there?"

"I talked to a sister. The wife'll be giving me a call."

My pencil kept rolling off the desk. I checked the nicks and scratches on my desk to be sure I wasn't the victim of a midnight swap.

"How about our canyon Jane, Les? What have we got on her?"

"You asking me to go through all my cases with you, Smokey, or what?"

"I was on the scene, Les."

"But you're not responsible for the investigation. What is it you want to know?"

"I just wondered if anyone had talked—"

"No ID's been made on the canyon case."

"I know that, Les. But there was a name on—"

"Stolden. Guy says the car's stolen."

"Yes, we knew that. The 'guy' . . . You talked to someone, then?"

"A Dr. Robertson. That same day. Friday."

I took a deep breath and said, "Okay, Les, I want to tell you something." And then I went into the story of how the Caddy in the canyon belonged to a woman named Miranda Robertson, and how my brother was married to a woman by that name a few years back. How my brother was supposed to meet with her, some business-type stuff, I lied, only she never showed up and he didn't want to call her husband. Then I asked Les if he minded my coming along if he makes a visit.

"I'm not going to make a visit. There's nothing to make a visit about. A report was already taken in L.A. for the stolen car. The wife made it herself."

"And you talked to a sister? *Her* sister?"

"Uh . . . the doctor's sister."

"What if, Les, what if that was Miranda Robertson in the car?"

"Then we will have our interview. You work with the coroner's people and get us an ID. When that happens, and if it turns out to be your relative, I'll put him under a bulb and drive bamboo up his fingernails if you want. But right now I don't have time to go on field interviews for an if and a maybe when all we have is a stolden vehicle. You know the guy, check?"

"Well no, not exactly."

"No matter. Your brother doesn't want to call him, call him yourself."

"Hey, Les."

"What?"

"Is that permission?"

"Yeah. Yeah, it is."

I'd never tell him, but I owed him one.

"What if I sort of dropped in on him? Would that be all right? I'll take along Joe Sanders."

"Take whoever you want. Just don't do it on my budget. I don't want to hear from Fiscal you did it on my nickel."

"No prob, Les. I won't even bill the department overtime."

"*Ciao*," he said.

Ciao. Italy on the brain.

Doing the dishes that evening, I had the classical music station on when I heard the announcer say he was going to play Rossini's overture to the Italian Girl in Algiers. I let my hands drip into the sink while I listened to the music rise and fall and watched an Ana's hummingbird at the feeder outside my window. As I listened, I pictured Miranda Robertson in Italy, her long chestnut hair loose, her skirt of many colors breaking in her strides. Maybe she was this very minute dancing well with a John Travolta type.

Joe was to pick me up in a little over an hour, and we'd drive to Beverly Hills to see Dr. Robertson at eight that evening. Deciding to use the time to burn some calories, I went over to Mrs. Langston's to see if I could talk Farmer into a walk. Yeah, like talking water into running downhill.

Mrs. Langston was limping ahead of me, coming back from getting her newspaper. "How are you to-day, Mrs. Langston?"

"Oh hi, Smokey. Well, today some people would say I was an old lady. You know, we Americans think we can fix everything. But everything's not fixable. It just isn't." She burrowed a thumb into her thigh.

"Your doctors . . . ?"

"Sometimes you just have to make peace with yourself and realize there's a whole lot of stuff doctors don't know. That doesn't make them bad people. They just don't know it all."

"I suppose that's true."

"You want some onions when you come back? I cooked up a whole bunch of them because they were growing beards."

"No, thanks, Mrs. Langston."

"I wish you'd call me Mary."

"I'll try."

Farmer's toenails were already scrambling on the door when we opened it. His owner reached for his leash and said, "You guard Smokey now, you good for nothin', adorable, nasty nuisance, you." Then she took his head in both hands and kissed him between the eyes.

Halfway into our walk, the dog found something in the bush. Instead of pointing, he whined and wagged his tail. A tiny, furry, blond thing with a rounded nose and floppy ears that looked like rose petals was hunkered in the grass. Slowly, I reached down and picked it up, amazed that it let me. No tail, its rump looked like a 1980 Seville, no trunk space.

"What are you?"

It peeped, then began to shudder. No, purr. It purred in my hand, and dropped a pellet.

"Let's see what your new mommy's going to think you are," I said, referring to Mrs. Langston.

* * *

"Joe, it is so cute. You have to come see it."

"I know what they look like. David had a guinea pig. Where are you going to keep it?"

"It's in the bathtub now."

"With water?"

"No, silly. I'll get a cage tomorrow."

"They're work," he warned.

"How much work can they be?"

A guy flashed his lights behind us, and Joe moved out of the fast lane. Joe tends to drive like an old lady, no offense intended. When we arrived at Dr. Robertson's, a corner clump of pink begonias succumbed to his right rear tire, but he didn't know it and I didn't mention it.

"What if he's an asshole, Joe?"

"You said you talked to him."

"I did. He sounded okay this morning. But what if he changed his mind?"

"What if Mexico cedes to the United States? Forget this could have anything to do with your brother's ex-wife. It's just another case, with a peculiarity."

The doctor was wearing a green polo shirt and white shorts, and his legs were tan all the way to his toenails. Over his left brow his blond hair dipped in a foppish wave.

"Come on in. We'll watch our polluted sunset out on the patio." We walked out onto a wooden deck that curved around the house out of sight. It looked down on a wooded canyon. He served us strawberry daiquiris already in a pitcher as the sun became a penny in the horizon's gray slot. "Miranda is not the most responsible person in the world," he said with an apologist's grin. "I mean, she said she'd call . . . Detective Fedders is it . . . ? but I doubt she did. She was going to Vienna. Always in a hurry."

"Is there anyone else who might have talked to her in the last few days?" Joe asked.

"Mm-m. My sister."

"Does she have parents in town?"

"You aren't taking my word for it? What is this, anyway?"

"Detective Fedders told you, didn't he, that a corpse was found in your wife's car?" Joe said this quietly, respectfully.

"Yes. That's unfortunate. Who was he?"

"We don't have that information yet. We don't mean to upset you," Joe said, raising a hand the same way Peter Falk does when Columbo is acting like a doofus. "We're just trying to be thorough."

"I can understand that." He seemed to settle. "Let's go back inside. Once the sun goes down, the air cools right off."

We made ourselves comfortable on plush green leather couches with nowhere to put our glasses. When two people go on an interview, one tries to keep eye contact with the interviewee, the other takes notes. I set my glass down on the floor and withdrew a notebook.

Joe asked, "Do you think you could provide us with your wife's dental records, Doctor? Just to—"

The doctor said, "Excuse me," and stood up. I thought he was leaving us. He went instead to a side table across the room and picked up the gas tank, seat, saddle, and control panel handset of a replica Harley-Davidson telephone. While he punched buttons, he said, "My wife would not like her privacy invaded in that manner. Would you?"

And then: "Is Morris there? Tell him to call Dr. Robertson when he comes in, will you? Thanks."

Coming back, he said, "I'll have someone call you. A man who's doing a job for us. We're into weekend motorcycle riding, see. Matter of fact, he's down your way. Garden Grove."

As he sat down, he focused on me awhile. I kept my gaze steady, did not look away. I wanted to ask him if his wife had breast implants, but couldn't quite bring myself to do it. He picked up his drink and said, "This man does marvelous metal and paint work. I know he spoke to Miranda himself last evening. She's faxing him a postcard of a wallpaper design she saw in a castle, actually. She wants it on her tank. She rides too. Morris Blackman. I'll have him call you."

"How about if we call him?" Joe said.

"Fine." He gave us a number and said, "That's for a bar he owns. I don't have his home phone." What I interpreted as an irritated twitch by the mouth transformed itself rapidly to a smile.

"Our records show your wife reported her car missing two weeks ago. Does she know about what happened to it?" Joe asked.

"Oh yes. She really loved that old clunker. She had that car since she was a teenager. It really blew her mind when it was stolen. I think that's partly why she went back to Italy. When I told her the condition they found it in . . . well, she was sort of prepared for it, you see, with it being taken in the first place. She didn't say much at all."

Joe asked, "Where was it taken from?"

The doctor's eyes went wide, like a bad actor imitating surprise. "Right out in front of our house." His brow creased. "I don't believe she locked it, is what I think. Definitely not a material girl. She goes to the market, leaves her purse in the cart," he said, shaking his head. "Money, credit cards. She's been lucky so far. People have returned it."

"Dr. Robertson," I said, "your wife wouldn't have any reason to carry a weapon, now would she?"

"A gun? Oh my no. She's down on guns. Why do you ask?"

"A handgun was found in the car."

His body movements were jerky, and he swished the remaining daiquiri in his glass before drinking it. "I wouldn't know anything about that. Certainly whoever took the car would likely be the type to have a gun."

Joe said, "So, you have no weapons yourself."

"I've seen the long-term neurological damage from gunshot wounds. I think you're far safer in the long run relying on your wits in a confrontation. Some of my colleagues are arming themselves these days, but not me. Guns have no place in a physician's life."

Joe thanked him for his time and stood to leave.

The doctor shook our hands and repeated his offer to help. He'd have Miranda call soon.

Back in the car, I said, "Well, he's a phony phallus, ain't he?"

"You noticed."

"But is he lying to us or to himself?"

"He lies to himself about how far he jogs around his own exercise room."

"Then you believe him."

"People who lie to themselves have no problem lying to others. I think he knows his wife is having an affair. I think he wonders if she's off having another one right now with some slick Italian prince."

While we were stopped at a light, I looked out the side window. On top of the traffic pole sat a crow, watching its mate down on the sidewalk tear at a burger wrapper. Each night I give myself one bird to look up in my books before falling asleep. I thought of the raven, delivering jawbones to Doug. I thought of the killdeer, bearing her young out in the open, hiding the evidence by dragging the shell pieces away, then shrieking and flapping in a distraction display. A noisy plover, the book says, *vociferus* part of its name. *Kill-deeah!* Now as I rolled my window down, the top crow twitched its head toward me and riveted me with his stare. One to watch, one to discover.

12

Les Fedders finished off a fudge brownie his wife had packed for him, and said, "You want me to check all the international airlines for a Miranda Robertson flying to Italy."

"It might help. The date, the return booking."

"I can't justify the time for that." He fingered a wayward brownie morsel off his desk and into his mouth.

"You could subpoena records at the visa office."

"I could do crossword puzzles on county time. I could bring in my bank statement and balance it here." Actually, Les Fedders was exactly the type who would, or who'd spend hours playing computer solitaire, if he even knew how to use a computer, but he doesn't. "See these cases?" He pulled his thumb up over a stack of folders, riffling them. "Hundreds of hours, and not one of them closed. Phys-i-cal evidence," he said, leaning toward me, spreading his long fingers in front of him as if needing to hold down the desk. "Get me physical evidence a crime has been committed, and maybe I'll put some time on it. Or a complainant. Get me a complainant. Get me a victim ID. Until then, what do we have? A Jane Doe over a cliff. So what?"

My face was flushing. The muscles along my jaw were locking up. I said, "Pardon me. I somehow had the understanding you were the investigator."

"Now don't get sarcastic with me."

"I'll get what I get, Les. Listen to me: That victim was dead before she went over."

"I read the autopsy report. There's no proof whatsoever she was dead before she went over. She didn't breathe smoke is all. She might've broken her neck," he went on. "She may've sustained a fatal blow to the head. Until we hear from Meyer Singer—how *is* Meyer Singer doing, anyway?"

"I don't know."

"Then you should get out of my office, shouldn't you, and go find that out for us." He stared at me and nodded his head up and down in an effort to get me to say I agreed.

Coming toward me, Joe Sanders was slapping the palm of his left hand with a cardboard courier envelope when he saw me. "This was at the front desk," he said, and handed it to me.

"*You* signed for it?" I noticed my brother's handwriting on the address sticker. Nathan had merely put "S. Brandon" on the label.

"They don't care who signs for it." He paused for a moment as if wondering if he should let me open it in private, but stayed after I glanced at him.

I was tense opening it, wondering what on earth my brother could have sent, wishing he would let this thing with Miranda go, or at least let it take its natural course; wishing he'd return to his normal life; knowing he wouldn't.

Inside were pieces of shoe box folded over a picture torn from a magazine of a man and a woman on a motorcycle. Miranda's face came back clearly to me then. A note was attached to the page, from Nathan. It said, "Here's the piece of garbage she was sleeping with." I was surprised at the vehemence of it. Earlier, when Nathan had mentioned she might be seeing someone else, his tone was level. He had even said, "You have to realize, people are people," teaching little sister how the world worked.

I turned the sheet over and saw that it was torn from a biker magazine, February issue.

"What is it?" Joe asked.

"A picture of my sister-in-law, ex. That's Miranda." She was smiling into the sun, a beaming, wholesome-fifties kind of pose. "I wonder who's the dude," I added.

Joe took the page from me and read. Down at the bottom in print I hadn't seen because it was dark on a burnt sienna background were the words *"Tyrannis Tin is Blackman's latest knockout entry in this year's Invitational."*

"Blackman," I said. "That's the name the doctor gave us."

Joe finished reading. *"Ten shades of green on the fatbob and fenders. Steel scrollwork like lizard scales or yer girlfriend's legs."* Joe grinned.

"Gimme that," I said, and took it and gazed at the face of the man in the photo.

He had flagrant black hair and a thick, maculated handlebar mustache that didn't hide the trenched smile lines curving above it. His eyelashes were so long they cast a shadow. He was hunky, raw, and handsome.

"Well, he doesn't look anything like her husband, that's for sure."

"Likes variety, I guess," Joe said. "Don't let that give you ideas."

"You underestimate me. What'd you do with the telephone number Dr. Robertson gave us?"

"What did *I* do? You took it down."

"I did, didn't I? Shit."

"You give it to Fedders?"

"I don't think so. It must be in my notebook."

"Give it to Fedders."

"Right," I said.

"What are you doing for lunch today?" He looked at his watch. "It's early yet, but—"

"I have to run an errand. Maybe tomorrow."

"What's tomorrow, Thursday? *I* have to run an errand." He stood closer. I could smell his musky after-shave, the one I bought him for his birthday. It had an effect. "You want to try for dinner tomorrow?"

"Okay."

His eyes searched my face awhile. Someone passed by in the intersecting hallway. Joe inched back but as he turned to go, said under his breath, "Love ya, kiddo."

And damn me, I looked at him and smiled. Only smiled. It was on my lips to make that first sound, *luh*. Love you too. But I couldn't, and maybe that said something. I turned and went back to my desk, where I opened drawers and looked at pencils. Closed drawers and straightened the stapler to be in line with my In-box. Picked a dry leaf off a small flower someone had brought me. And sat down, opened my notepad, and stared at the phone.

When the girl answered, she said hello and didn't give the name of the bar. I asked her what place this was, and she said, "The Python." In the background was music with a heavy beat.

"Are you calling about the job?" she asked.

"Uh, yes."

"Well, you should come in and fill out an application. Between four and five. No later. It gets too busy, okay?" she said, drawing out the last so she sounded like a bimbo. Totally.

"Four and five."

"Right. Oh, and bring, like, a negligee, right?"

"I'm sorry?" I said.

"A negligee, a teddy. If you don't have one, there's some here, but most girls want to bring their own the first time. Like, they feel more comfortable and all. You *are* applying for a model, right?"

"Uh, sure. Who, uh, will I be interviewing with?"

"The boss. Mr. Blackman."

"Right. What do they pay?"

"Well, I'm not supposed to say, but it's good, real good."

What I was going to do I couldn't exactly put words to in my mind at the time. I knew, but didn't want to know. In retrospect, I think it must be like a man who knows he's going to see a prostitute when he's promised himself he wouldn't anymore.

Avoiding the stir in my blood, I went down the hall and got a drink of water. I read the bulletin board. Two people wanted rideshares from Lake Elsinore. Two people had to-die-for rooms to rent in houses near the beach. One person was going to have to practically give away a nearly new Mercury Cougar. I went to the rest room, and while washing my hands looked in the mirror longer than I normally do. Could I still pass? It had been nearly half my life ago since . . .

I went into Joe's office. On his desk was a plastic bloodshot eyeball weighted so that someone like me could roll it around, and while it wobbled over the desktop its blue iris and dark pupil would continue to stare straight up.

"Couldn't stay away from me, huh?" Joe said.

"That's about it," I answered, smiling slightly. Then: "Joe, how much trouble do you think I'd get into if I went to check on this Morris Blackman myself?"

"Have you totally lost your mind?"

"Oh thanks." I clutched the eyeball. I had given it to him for his birthday in February. I wondered if it would bounce off his chest.

"Have you forgotten you came close to losing your job last year for the same thing?"

"My personal involvement had nothing to do with it. Whacking someone did."

Joe just sat there and looked at me. His eyes traveled my face again, wobbling.

My boss, Stu Hollings, is shapeless in middle age, wears an ovoid, expressionless face topped with scant hair, a man who seldom makes more conversation than needed but when he does it's often the right string of words. I suppose whatever he does all day is commendable because he seems to get along fine with the director and the undersheriff, but I don't have much of an idea what it is. Whatever he does, he has power of decision over my career, so I had to tell him what I wanted to do on the Carbon Canyon case. With more trepidation than I liked, and with Joe Sanders sitting next to me in Stu's office, I matter-of-factly said I wanted to put extra time on a case that had a slim connection to my own brother. It probably amounted to nothing, I said. But would I be interfering? Would anyone be disturbed?

My boss looked at me a long while, with nary a wobbly eyeball. "This feels like its getting to be a habit," he said.

"What's that, Stu?"

"Your tendency for getting personally involved."

"I wouldn't call it a tendency," I said as pleasantly as possible, trying to keep calm. "It can't be a habit if I don't choose the events. The events came to me, I didn't go to them. I mean, I don't want to be defensive here, but what happened last year on the

Dugdale case happened because I was trying to find a friend. That's all. I have a feeling anyone," saying this without breaking my gaze, "with means and training would want to do the same. Anyone."

He pursed his lips, glanced at Joe and then at the wall. Said, "Details?"

I breathed a small sigh of relief and went over the case, telling him the car was registered to Miranda Robertson but all we had was a torso to talk to. He said, Oh yes, he heard about that one. I told him that as yet we didn't have a report from Meyer Singer regarding the recovered teeth and jawbones, nor did we possess dental charts to match against because Miranda Robertson was supposedly not missing. Joe and I had talked to her husband, and Dr. Robertson claimed his wife was still quite alive.

"What is it you want me to approve?" He didn't say it to give me hope. He just wanted more information. Directly over and behind his head, the tip of a Lockheed fighter plane showed from a framed print. It looked like a little cap on Stu's smooth dome. On a file cabinet was a framed photo of his grandson and a glass chimney of foil-wrapped Kisses.

"I *feel* for my brother. He still loves her. Their divorce wasn't that troubled. I mean, I'd just like to put my brother's mind to rest. If I could go hang out a little with some people she knows. . . ."

Joe said, "The doctor is not what you'd call the most convincing. Would she be violating department rules? I guess that's the bottom line."

"The bottom line," Stu said, "is would she be getting in hot water with me."

I could hear the tightness in Joe's voice but didn't know if Stu did: "Well, I guess that's why she's in here."

Stu leaned forward and fanned his office phone directory with one thumb. He turned his attention to me. "How would this affect your other work?"

"How's it affecting it now?" I said cheerfully. "Anyone complain?" He had no gripe, I knew that.

My boss looked at Joe, two middle-aged men passing evaluations back and forth. Joe and I had tried to keep our relationship discreet without actually trying to hide anything. I didn't think anyone really cared if we were dating; it's just that neither of us needed comment or speculation. But you never knew about the older types.

"As far as policy on this thing," Stu said, "that's really not a problem. If you're clear with Homicide. . . ."

"I'm clear."

"Some people think for UC work, the closer the connection, the better. Cops do it all the time. You just don't see it in the papers. One thing though," he said.

"What? Whatever. I'm just grateful."

"Don't take this as an opportunity for hotdogging. Nothing like that."

"No, no. Understand."

"I can't pay you overtime."

"Not a problem. Suppose I need to take a couple hours off in a day, though. Is that—?"

"It's a case. Account for it the way you would any other case." He picked up some papers, then glanced at me over his glasses, our cue to leave.

I tried not to be too effusive when I said thanks, but when I got up, I rocked the chair hard against the wall, then checked to see if it left a mark.

Outside, Joe said, shaking his head, "Girl, you get the damndest things out of men."

"Oh come on now."

"You do."

"Yeah? Well, I didn't get lunch out of you, now did I?"

He sucked in his cheeks, grinned, patted his pockets for keys.

13 ⌇ Monty said I didn't have to bring a thing, just myself. I liked his voice on the phone, soft, a little raspy, like the singer Michael McDonald's.

It was the day after the girl on the phone told me there was a job opening. Before I left the lab I talked to Les Fedders again and learned he'd actually done a little casework. He knew a deputy who told him Morris "Monty" Blackman had done federal at Terminal Island for possession of an auto shotgun and a Remington he said shouldn't have counted because it jammed nearly every time he fired. But it did count because he was on parole at the time, so Monty went up for another year, prequalified by a prior. Now he was owner of a goin' bar in Garden Grove that featured young ladies in lingerie at lunchtime, and I was prepared to go ask for a job there, shaking and thinking I'd look like a damn fool twice over.

Joe said he wanted to go with me, but he got caught up in a high-profile officer-involved shooting case, and I was just as glad. I felt freer by myself. I'm three-quarters loner and prefer doing things without having to wait, bargain, or report.

But I made the mistake of telling Ray Vega. Since Ray's shift didn't start till seven, he'd meet me at four, delighted to supervise, he said, reminding me the glorious city of Garden Grove is not as idyllic as its name would suggest, Ray remaining, after all, a cop, even if it *is* a freeway jockey, a rider of the asphalt range. He'd pick me up in his almost-new car.

As far as mentioning it in the first place, I wouldn't have except the situation seemed funny; because in the wacky seventies, in a mostly harmless club owned by a man who never treated me unfairly and who looked the other way at my not yet being eighteen, I, you could say, unwore glamorous garments for a living. So that when Ray asked me on the phone, Whatcha up to, Smokes? and I said, Ray, you wouldn't believe, out it came.

We found a space at the curb two car lengths down from Monty's Python, the restaurant and bar that looked like a single-story, ranch-hand bunkhouse along a strip of computer fix-it shops and hamburger joints. The place was easy to spot because of the painted python on the door, whose gigantic copper slitted eyes seemed to smile as the constrictor licked its lips. Through the overcast day, a blue-green neon sign polished Ray's black hair and the tight knot of his cheekbone as he sat at the wheel, and even from where we were I could see the pale parts of the snake on the door and feel its come-hither grin.

I said he'd have to stay in the car.

"No way! I'm here to see girlies, and if I can't see girlies, I'm going home."

"You dope."

"You hurt my feelings."

He made me grin. "If I'm not out in thirty minutes, come on in and order a drink or something. But I will be."

"You come into my back room looking like that, you won't be out in thirty minutes."

I looked down at myself. "This getup isn't all that sexy. In fact, it isn't at all." I had on a scoop-necked, raging violet shirt and skirt with cinched pink belt, Mervyn's, $4.95. My jewelry was clunky gold and my stockings light enough you wouldn't think I wore any. On my feet were the only heels I own, black, showing a lumpy toe pattern. Cheeks rosy, and eyes made up to be, well, smokey.

"The hair suits you," Ray said.

I brought the ends out where I could see it. "It's temporary."

"That's the real you under there, that color." His eyes kept up a movement around my head.

"Who says?"

He was looking at me with mischief in his eyes when the door to the bar opened and people came out and others went in, all men. His face grew serious and he rubbed his left eye with his palm and pulled his hand slowly over his face and neck.

"Hey, Ray."

"What?"

"You're worried."

"I just want to come in."

"You won't miss anything. Trust me."

"The guy's a felon."

"My friend, there's spare pricks all over the world, but that don't keep us from doing our best to protect and serve, now do it?" I patted him on the hand and he overturned mine, closing on my little finger and holding there. "What I'm worried about, what if he says I'm no good, got knock-knees or something?"

"Oh give me a break."

"Not everybody sees the same things. I'm not the

tender morsel I once was, you know. I'm a double-digit three this year. Got any gum?"

"I don't think he's going to care if you've had a shotsky, darlin'."

"I haven't had any shotskies. I wish I had. It's not for breath, it's for attitude."

"Latinos, we don't need props like that." He leaned over to get in the glove compartment, coming flirtatiously close.

I reached under his waist and flipped open the ashtray and said, "Ray, you keep your gum in the ashtray." When he leaned away, I got Dentyne for myself from an already opened pack.

"Oh yeah, I do, don't I?"

Ray said, "Lemme see that picture of Blackman again?"

From an envelope between the seats I took the page from the biker rag that Nathan had sent me. Ray looked, but turned the page over and focused on a photo I'd seen before and forgotten, of a woman's breast glowing with a gold nipple ring, the mound garlanded with a tattoo of a flowery vine.

"There's a whole other world out there, Raymond."

He complained when I lapped the page over and put it back in the envelope. "Give me that back. If I can't go in, I have to have something to look at."

Grinning, I handed him the envelope. He tucked it between the seats himself. "Well, here goes," I said, my hand on the car door. "Wish me luck, good buddy."

"You're not out in thirty minutes, I'm in."

"Thirty-one," I said, and got out, glancing back as he settled down in the seat, all hard muscle and man. He gave me a thumb-up, and I slapped the fender of his car as I went by.

* * *

When I shoved on the nose of the python with the heel of my hand, the door opened to a well of darkness. I couldn't understand how any customer could see to order. The place smelled yellow, as in beer. As I stood in the entryway, the sound of an air-conditioning unit in need of new blower bearings clattered away.

There were about twelve, thirteen people in the place, one a Hispanic woman with masses of hair and very heavily made-up eyes, blowing a blue column of smoke that got lost between the ceiling beams. The two men at her table were talking with each other, their temples almost touching.

I threaded my way through the tables, thinking the establishment didn't look like much of a biker bar, if that's what it was supposed to be. It looked more like a low-grade rendezvous spot for middle-aged managers on their way to a murky affair. From somewhere in the back came the mournful notes of Jennifer Warnes singing "Restless."

The man behind the bar had a pate that picked up the gleam reflected in the mirror. He wore round wire-rimmed glasses and looked to be about sixty.

I stood between two stools and said, "Howdy."

"What'll you have?"

"A Mr. Blackman. Monty Blackman?"

The bartender made a quick swipe on the counter with his bare hand and looked at his palm a moment before wiping it on his jeans. On the back of his wrist was a tattooed blue anchor with U.S. NAVY under it. Jabbing two fingers toward a recessed doorway across the room, he answered, "In there."

"Navy man," I said, glancing at his wrist.

The boredom broke. "Seventeen years."

"My father and brother were Navy," I said.

"Yeah?"

Made a new friend. I waved, smiled, moved off.

In a sort of alcove were two rust-colored doors on the right, one with a pink metal cutout of a curvaceous woman, the other a tin-punched replica of *The Thinker* on a commode. On the walls were framed circus posters of tattooed men and women standing in stiff poses, and a cartoon-style painting of a snake curled atop twenty numbered eggs, with the caption "Hell yes, I'm on welfare."

A dime-store sign on a third door said OFFICE. I knocked. A deep voice said, "Yeah?" and I turned the knob.

Inside were three men, the one to my left a Mexican with his stomach slid off onto the top of a three-drawer filing cabinet as he leaned against it. He was the biggest Hispanic I'd ever seen, and over his low forehead was a perfect widow's peak.

Beyond him, against a paneless window crisscrossed with fresh boards, was a man about my age with a raw, hard face. His thumbs were caught in his rear pockets, and his jaw worked slowly over a piece of gum as he looked me up and down. I looked back and worked my gum the same.

Near the center of the room and leaning back in a wooden desk chair that swiveled was Blackman himself. He was wearing a black shirt with a picture of a skeleton riding a Harley, over which were the windblown letters Ghostrider. Monty's beard was streaked with gray, and I appreciated the trouble he had containing his full head of hair in a ponytail. His forehead was short and his nose was narrow until it flared at the bottom dramatically, as if he were ready to say something provocative, good or bad.

"I like the name," Monty said. "It suits you." He spoke the name I gave him on the phone: Brandy.

Brandy Brandon, because I thought what would it matter, these clowns are probably about as clever as the back of beer cans.

"Thanks. I like yours," I said.

Monty kept the smile as he waved an arm toward the Mexican as if to sweep him out the door, saying, "Paulie, you go raise a little hell, get your mind off the ditch, and we'll see you in a few days."

Paulie said, "You want me dig your pit Saturday?" His thumb scraped at the tip of his middle finger to tear the nail off. When that didn't seem to work, he bit it in one hard nibble and spit the chitin onto the floor.

The blond guy at the back said, "Stay off the sauce, Paulie, will ya? We'll get that sumbitch dug. You need to rest that whiskey dick awhile anyways." The blond shifted his eyes in my direction and back again. Some men test you that way. I looked steady at him, chewed my gum, thought, Jerk.

Paulie turned his face into the light where the drooping rims of his lower lids showed fiery and the shine on his full lower lip grew brighter.

"I ain't got no whiskey dick, you asshole," he said. He looked at me too, but soon averted his eyes and turned to leave. Monty waved the blond one out too, and as the guy was closing the door behind him, he bent low and looked at me and winked.

Monty said in his soft voice, "Paulie owns an excavation outfit. He dumped his bucket the other day, nearly scared himself to death. Best way's to kid him back on." His eyes were the color of his faded denims. "Now, you ready?"

"I guess so."

He handed me a good-sized, multicolored, quilted satchel. I pulled the Velcro apart and looked in. Inside were several choices of garments a girl would be lucky if she got to leave on long enough to sleep in.

"Pick whatever you want. Then come on back here in a minute. I got another girl coming in at five."

"You won't need her," I said, and opened the door.

In one of the three stalls in the ladies' room I dumped the contents on the floor and decided against the thing that looked like only a red V of lace from shoulder to crotch. Ditto the thing that seemed like a see-through corset. Settling on a red lace body stocking whose roses looked like they might cover the critical parts, I toed off my shoes and peeled off my top and skirt, and wondered if this was where the regular models had to undress. I came out, looked in the mirror, afraid someone would come in at any minute, and afraid of what would be looking back.

My heavens. If my friends could see me now.

Back in the stall, I put the other garments and my street clothes in the bag, except for a black satin robe which I slipped into, and came out again.

Running water on my hands, I gave volume to my hair by squinching it up with wet fingers, took out my gum and put it in a paper towel, sucked a deep breath, and went back into Monty's office without glancing around to see who might notice, walking into the smell of a newly lit cigar, something better than a Hav-A-Tampa.

Monty was in the same position as before in front of the desk, levered back in the chair. He said, "Over there, darlin'," indicating a hard wooden chair next to the filing cabinet Paulie had leaned upon.

Sitting down, I crossed my legs, then uncrossed

them; then crossed them again, feeling naked and totally moronic. Was it Halloween?

He waited a long time, eyes tracing my face and hair, looking at my face and not my body, as if he were pondering. "Stand up now, will you," he said.

I stood, tried to look languid.

"Take the robe off and walk over there," he said, though there was hardly any distance to walk across.

How did I do it when there was a stage? I tried to remember. But then, there had *been* a stage, and the setting then had a removed, performance quality to it.

Walking toward the metal oscillating fan, I thought, Oh, this is good. The air teased the ruffly robe. When I turned to go back, I untied the belt, allowing the fabric to fall away, and yes, pulling my shoulder back for a better profile. Monty's chin was up as he slowly nodded, his eyes lowered. The thinker.

He said, "What would you say to growing out your hair?"

After I stopped to look at him, he added, "And you could do much better with the makeup. I got a girl could show you how."

"There's something wrong with my makeup?"

"Yeah. It makes you look cheap."

Back in Raymond's new Roadmaster, I said, "We're in the wrong business, Ray. I can make three hundred dollars in a couple of hours."

"I know some ladies can do you one better."

"I bet you do."

"How was it?"

"I felt a little silly is all. They might need me evenings too. I could do my day job, come here at night.

Think the department will make me give up the money?"

"Don't ask, don't tell."

"Now there's a novel idea."

"I was peekin' in the window."

"You were not."

"I was." Ray was smiling, one hand on the dead steering wheel.

"The window, it so happens, was boarded up where I was doing my thing."

"Maybe I had a periscope."

"Drive me out of here, you creep."

Ray started up but couldn't pull out into traffic. It was almost six o'clock. The sky in the west was taking on that glow of muddy gold you remember from a kid when you walked out of the matinee and worried about if your mom would believe the movie was that long.

I said, "There were a couple of real heartthrobs with Monty in his office. Mexican guy, owns an excavating business. Big, by the name of Paulie. He was talking loaders and tampers to the other one on the way out. The other one, no-name with a chip on his shoulder. Blond, muscular, late twenties."

Ray found his chance to move out, his jaw still working on the Dentyne. "What was Blackman like?"

"A certain type of woman could go for him."

"Oh Christ."

"You should hear you, Raymond."

"Hear me what?"

"I didn't say *I* could go for him. He's a jerk. He said I didn't know how to do my hair and makeup. I thought I looked pretty good."

Raymond smiled at that. "He hire you?"

"He said check back tomorrow."

"What number'd you give him?"

"None. I said I was moving, wasn't hooked up yet. That's why he said to check back tomorrow."

"What're you going to do when you're supposedly moved in?"

"I'll worry about that later. There's lots of excuses why I wouldn't have a phone."

We drove to the supermarket parking lot two blocks down where I'd left my car. A black-and-white sheriff's unit oozed onto the lot with no lights and accelerated quickly down a row of cars. I said, "Wonder what that's all about."

"Some turkey thought he could slip a free bottle of JB in his drawers."

Ray drove forward until we could observe what was going on in case the deputy needed help. The officer who got out of the car was about six feet tall, and the man he stopped was a twiggy twerp in a white T-shirt and tan cutoffs who didn't look the type to have a weapon on him, but you never know. Ray pulled into a slot, and as we talked, we kept our eyes on the activity.

"So you're going through with this modeling thing."

"Looks that way."

"I knew a guy once, worked undercover for ATF. He slept with women for the job, you know, and wound up losing his wife."

"I don't have a wife, Raymond."

"How much do you care about this sister-in-law of yours, anyway?"

"I care about my brother. But it's not only that. The whole ball of wax. She's young. She's probably mixed up. Maybe I was that way once."

"Maybe?" Raymond's forefinger kept crossing his lips like a windshield wiper as he watched the deputy roust the twerp.

"Let's say it matters just a whole bunch how I feel about murder. If it's Miranda in the car, and if it *is* murder, that pisses me right off, right? If it's not Miranda in the car, and she's hanging with the wrong folks, maybe I can help straighten that out." Then I said, not even worrying whether Raymond was listening, "Maybe I can't either."

The kid was handcuffed now but giving the deputy a hard time. I could tell by the way the kid was shifting his shoulders, and the expression on his face.

I kept talking, since Ray wasn't. "I remember her saying some kind words to me once on the phone when I was having some 'female trouble' and Nathan knew about it from my mom. It surprised me."

Ray wasn't listening, and I didn't care. I fished for aspirin in my purse. If I found any, I'd down them dry. I looked up just in time to see the kid spit at the officer, the gob catching light as it flew into midair; watched the cop jump back and then slam forward, bouncing the kid off the car, boosting him on the buttocks with his knee four times as another patrol car pulled up.

"I hope he L.A.'s the little shit," Ray said.

"L.A.'s him? As in Rodney King?" I asked, referring to the amateur video heard 'round the world.

"You bet. L.A. his ass, the buttwipe spit on *me*."

"You mean," I said, "like a *personal* thing?"

"Yeah, yeah, like a personal thing. One time I—" And then he stopped, looked at me, and said, "You trying to make a point or what?"

"Who, me?"

"What'd you say the name was you gave Blackman?"

"Brandy Brandon. Kinda cute, huh?"

He leaned way forward to rest his arm on the wheel, put his chin on top of his hand; then, with his right, reached back to grab mine again, and said, "You ever want to get serious, don't forget I'm in line, okay?"

"Okay, Raymond. That's a deal."

14 | Les Fedders pulled his shoulders back as he came out of Joe Sanders's office, spying me and asking, "How's tricks, Trixie?"

Behind him, Joe was bent over work on his desk. He looked up and gave me a wink and grin, then burrowed back into his papers. I walked down the hallway, Les following.

"That your costume in there?" Les said. He knew by the tag and the color of the tape that whatever I had in the evidence bag was on its way back to Property.

Hefting the sack as if it held dog doo, I answered, "Men's pants. Guy had a truck lowered on him while he was putting on rear shock absorbers."

Les said, "Only he was the shock absorber."

"Aren't human beings wonderful?"

Without a change of expression, Les said, "The Prince of Darkness is a powerful foe."

I looked to see if he was smiling, but he wasn't.

"They sprayed liquid Drāno on him, in the crotch."

"There's a message there."

"He's not dead. He's in IC with a collapsed lung and a runky case of pneumonia, not to mention the damage to his unmentionables. But he won't tell anybody who did it. Give him a few weeks. His posse will pop 'em, and so it goes."

129

I stopped for a drink of water at the fountain and half expected Les to be gone. But he was still there, his scalp between the reddish hairs shining brightly and his pork chop ears fiery and translucent. He said, "How's the new job going? Planning on leaving us for tips yet?"

"Oh right. I bought a house in Brentwood." I'd worked at Monty's the night before, Thursday, from seven to ten.

"He make a pass at you yet, that guy?"

"It's probably a little early for that."

We walked by the Print room, Trudy Kunitz at the ready to collect a sheet off the fingerprint-image printer. On the glass separating her from us were new stick-on letters that read HOMICIDES 'R' US. I laughed.

Les was saying, "Are we wastin' our time here, or what? Should we just go jump this guy Blackman?"

"I can handle it, don't worry. I have to run now, Les. Busy, busy."

He nodded, put a hand on his chin while the other clutched his elbow, as if to keep his long jaw from smiling too much. "It would be good if you can get something for us out there, Smokey." But bless his heart, old Les can give hives just by breathing. He said, "I may come check out that titty bar myself."

"You're such a smoothie, Lester. I'll bet your date book's just *all* filled up."

"I do my best."

"By the way, how's the dental going?"

"The Jane? Dr. Robertson sent charts for his wife. Perfect teeth. She goes in for cleanings, that's it. I think you're barking up the wrong tree myself, Smokey."

"What do we have from Meyer Singer?"

Les shook his head. "He just converted to an HMO. He has so much business he don't know what to do. He's coming in to work on it tonight."

"That's a problem with contract people."

"Remember one burned up in a trunk last year, that hooker with dentures?"

"What about her?"

"He ID'ed that one in six weeks, even out of state. 'Course she had something funny with her palate, but we'll get this one too. You know your canyon crispy critter had fake maracas, don't you?"

"What, Les?"

"Phony begonias. Your sister-in-law have phony begonias?"

"I don't know, Les."

"Mm," he said.

Each day, I spend my best, fresh hours studying the awful continuum of human failure; and in so doing, it is easy to believe that people under any pressure succumb to the dark side of choice. But now and again I have an opportunity to set myself right. I go to the fields to glean.

It was Saturday, and it was lima beans. By eight-thirty I was in a field off Sand Canyon Avenue a few miles from my house. Limas can live on nearly nothing but fog. Bean fields used to spread for fifty miles up the coast, a part of it near here called Beanville. Today there is barely room for a bean. Silos have become motel rooms; outfitting sheds, restaurants. In the few remaining fields, vintage harvesters can still be seen trolling the rows against the skyline, speaking of a different time, not easier, perhaps, but simpler. What the harvesters miss, we gleaners gather for the food kitchens. The practice comes from an instruction in Leviticus: "*. . . when ye reap the harvest of your land, thou shalt not wholly reap the corners of thy field . . . thou shalt leave them for the poor and for the stranger.*" And so, on this morning already too warm, I stooped and picked, and hoped to find a mooring.

In the row next to me, a woman with a square face and ski-jump nose was singing a hymn, "Beulah Land." She told me she normally gleans with a church group on Sundays, a day I specifically avoid because I don't want people "the Lord"-ing me this and "the Lord"-ing me that. At the end of her song, she held up her plastic grocery store bag loaded with pods. "These I think I'll bring home to my daughter. She cooks 'em up with a ham bone, mm-um. You know you can take some home, honey, don't you?" She brushed sweat away under her ashy bangs with the hump of her wrist, then plucked at her lavender shirt to unstick it from her sides.

"I don't care much for them, but thanks." When I lifted a spray of leggy stems, a yellow moth flew onto the cusp of my glove and stayed there.

"Last year this program fed half a million people," the woman said. "Thank the Lord it wasn't all lima beans, or the whole county'd die of methane poisoning, you know what I mean?" She got the laugh from me she wanted, then went lumping over the rows to the roadside to dump her sack in a cardboard box.

I straightened to release the pull in my spine, realizing I'd been bending over the leaves stiff-legged the way you're not supposed to. At the inner thighs was an ache from straddling a row too long.

The church woman yelled back, "Hey, you know what my daughter gave me for my birthday? A pin that says 'I'm a natural blonde. Speak v-e-r-y slowly.'" Smiling broadly, she launched again into "Beulah Land."

I grabbed a handful of pods. Hearing the knock of fetal bean against fetal bean, and enjoying the air and relative silence, I felt a wonderful peace. Only two or three times did I think of the canyon case, or Nathan, or my new job in competitive underthings.

Again the moth lit on me, audacious on my arm. "I must resemble a lima bean," I said, standing up straight, showing my prize. "This butterfly likes me."

"Moth," she said. "Butterflies by day, moths by night."

"There's day moths, too," a man three rows over said.

"Wings folded: butterfly. Wings flat: moth," the woman in lavender said. "I heard about this scientist wanted money for a grant. So what does he do? He paints spots on a butterfly and calls it a new breed."

"Butterfly fraud," I said.

"Can you beat that? I tell you," the Beulah Land lady said, "it takes all kinds. It surely does."

15 Saturday night about ten, Monty came up to me in the alcove and said to quit for the night.

"Why? What I'd do wrong?"

"Don't be so skittish," he said. "I want to take you somewhere."

A sure unease washed over me. "Where?"

"Dancin'. How'd you like that?"

"Who else is going?"

"Just you 'n' me."

I told him I didn't think that would be a good idea. "Employer-employee. That never works."

"Relax. I just want to get acquainted. I do that with all the new girls. Ask Sharon there," he said, nodding toward the main floor where two models were drifting. "You'll find out I'm a gentleman, too," he said in his soft gentleman voice.

"I never had any doubt," I said, delivering it like a warning. "What'd you have in mind?"

"Country Western. Been to Denim and Diamonds?"

"No way. I can't do that. I don't have the mind for it." I said it without much conviction, because I wanted to go with him, wanted to have time alone when I could talk to him about his personal life, but didn't want to sound too eager. And it was mostly true about me and that kind of dancing. It would give me a chance, though, to learn who his friends were. Ask, By the way, do you happen to know anyone named Miranda?

"You're goin'," he said, the way a man does who never gets told no. He reached out and traced the neckline of my zip-front cat suit that was supposed, somehow, to qualify for lingerie. "Get dressed." And then he told me that in his office closet was a pair of boots, that I should see if they fit when I go in to change.

We were at Denim and Diamonds off Beach Boulevard, an upscale boot-scootin' place no real cowboy would drop reins for. Monty was getting my drink at the bar.

Next to me, a server in white lace stockings and white cowboy boots bent over to give a man his change, and a hand from another table patted her at the puff below her blue denim shorts. She reeled around and said, smiling, "I'll bounce you on your head you don't behave."

A man with a white goatee said, "That sounds like fun," and plucked a twenty off the table and held it out to her in two fingers while his diamond-studded watchband winked. She took it with a phony "thanks," and sashayed off. When the man's gaze fell to mine and I didn't glance away, his happy expression disappeared. Maybe my hard-ass look spoiled his fun.

The DJ put on a song by a woman looking for something in red, something for certain to knock a man dead, and a dozen couples began to glide around the room in a cowboy waltz. A man sitting on a bench that looked like a horizontal Coors can smiled at me.

By the time Monty came back with the mugs, the air seemed warm as flannel. I drew down the cool beer gratefully. He watched, said, "I'll have you a changed woman in no time."

"You know, Monty? I'm thinking maybe I don't need that job as much as I thought."

His mouth came close to my ear. "Don't you know when somebody likes you?" He wore a musky scent.

I shifted away. "You know, this really isn't my kind of music. I like Eric Clapton. Cocker. Bob Seger. Old guys."

"You want to leave?" He leaned away from me and I watched his nostrils go into a wider flare than usual, and maybe that meant he was mad.

"Well, sometime," I said.

"You nervous? I make you nervous?"

He was smiling, drawing pictures with his finger in the wet mark on the table, cocking his head at me.

I said, "It's just I've got a life, you know, before Monty. Things to do."

He came close again and whispered, "Before Monty. Nothin' was before Monty."

I needed to change the subject. I needed to get him warmed up to tell me about his life and friends. Maybe I was helped along by the beer, but I began to look at him as a man. A man, not a felon. My mother used to sing a certain song every time she ironed, about how when she was not near the man she loved, she loved the man she was near. Sometime in my early twenties I got the gist of it, and afterward that song rang a truth that delivered my mother to me in a new light. Monty had an appearance that would've appealed to me in an earlier time when my veins carried a bit of wild brew; when I was young enough to believe people just wanted to be different, individual, but they didn't really want to hurt anyone. I tried to get back to that moment. Undercover, you become the part, didn't Ray say?

I let my eyes follow the handsome men around

the room moving their pretty-girl partners, heros all.
I let Monty see it, this interest, and drank a little
harder. I asked, "Do you know the actor Sam Elli-
ott?"

"Don't think so."

"He was in *Roadhouse*, with Patrick Swayze."

"Who's Patrick Swayze?" He drank from his beer,
grabbing off foam on his mustache with his lower
lip.

"Never mind."

"No, come on." When I just shook my head, he
said, "You gonna dance with me or not?" lightly
grabbing my wrist.

"Later. Give me some time." He let go of my
wrist, but I saw a cloud cover his face. "Don't you
have a lady friend?" I asked. "I mean, to take out?"

He leaned toward me again. "Sure I got a lady
friend. I've got a lot of lady friends. Now I got one
more." When he smiled, his eyes looked both suspicious and kind.

"Let's talk about the weather," I said.

The beat kicked up. Mary-Chapin Carpenter was
singing about the Twist 'n' Shout down in bayou
country. "Look at that," Monty said. "Don't that
look like fun?"

"That looks like my last geometry lesson."

He laughed, sat back, and said, "How you gonna
learn, you don't try?"

"I told you, Monty—"

"Okay. The weather? What's your sign?"

"Right." I just shook my head.

"Where you from? You grow up around here?"
he asked, flagging down the waitress in the white
lace stockings and boots. My boots, the ones Monty
loaned me, were blue with white-flame insets. When
I went to put the boots on at the Python, I found a
necklace with beads and bones in the toe. I meant to

ask him about it but I forgot then, and I forgot again as he ordered margaritas and as I tried to say no. He forgot I didn't answer his question, when he said, "My mother says I was born in Pittsburgh. She lies a lot."

"Really," I said.

He was gently rocking to the music. His features from the side looked stubby, almost as though his nose had been broken and his brow had got clubbed by a pool cue. "Someday I'm gonna buy me a place in Idaho or Montana or some damn place. Anywhere but here."

"I don't know," I said. "It's got its moments."

"You know Downey? That's where I grew up. Cows. Dairy farms. Went to Downey High. Our mascot was a flea with his brains bore out." He waited for a laugh, then said, "Actually, we had two mascots. Only school I know has two mascots. Vicky and Vic Viking. I braided my hair in pigtails, put on one of them funny hats with the horns? *Vo-la,* I was Vicky. Our team wasn't worth a shit, man. I sure didn't want anything to do with them. Might as well be Vicky."

I couldn't help but laugh, and the music did sound good, and the vibrating thunder of fifty boots hitting the hardwood floor with the same Texas stomp set me stirring. He put his hand on mine, and I took in the broad plane of it and the attractive dunes of forearm flexor and extensor spread with dark hair.

Monty went on, enjoying his audience. "I had a good time growin' up. My mom, she thought I hung the moon." He settled on both arms, confiding in me, drawing me in like a friend. "Let me have the whole garage all for myself, all the little toys she bought me. I was king of the neighborhood."

"I don't know if you're being serious or not."

" 'Course I'm serious." He folded my hand into a fist and massaged it like a kitty head. I looked away at the woman on the dance floor who was teaching the steps to a new line dance. She wore red high heels instead of boots, and spoke into a microphone worn over her head like an operator's headset, Madonna style. When I looked back, he was staring at me. "The boots," he said. "They fit?"

"Perfect," I said, though they were a tad loose.

"Yours. You gonna thank me?"

"Whose are they?"

"A friend of mine left 'em."

"Left them."

"Yeah," he said, and the expression on his face changed, but I wasn't sure to what.

"There was something in one of them. A necklace."

I dug in my purse and came out with it. Two slim brown feathers latched with beads hung beside four short bones that looked like finger bones to me. "Your friend get this at some Satanic garage sale?"

He smiled and said, "My friend likes strange shit."

"And you mean that in the most respectful of ways."

"Did you tell me where you were from?"

"No. Mostly here. Sort of all over."

He lifted his beard with four fingers in an almost scratch. "A woman of mystery. Sort of from all over. You can do better than that. Hey, I tell you you look good in that skirt?" Under a rosy neon lariat, the color looked hotter, pinker in a blue way.

The waitress came with the margaritas. Monty touched the salty rim of his to mine and said, "Here's to you, girl." The DJ put on one by John Michael Montgomery, a big-screen video of J.M.

strumming and looking soulful and sincere as he sang about sappy old movies and how he loved the way his lady loved him. And then Monty got up and took me out on the floor to dance, and held me as if I might break, slow and easy as the man said.

When we sat back down, Monty was quiet and seemed far away in his thoughts until he scooted his chair closer, and we both sat in silence watching the dancers. I was feeling the swim of drink, but not too much. On the overhead video, Marty Stuart was promising to wipe those teardrops dry.

Monty's mood broke and he looked at me with a smile. "The only thing I fear," he said, "is standin' in one place. Man, in Montana . . . Up there you can jam at a hundred and ten on your scoot. You can eat big and fuck simple and write home to your mama every twenny years." His teeth gleamed in his beard.

"What's holding you here?"

"Not much."

"Well then?"

"How old are you anyway?"

I shrugged a shoulder.

"You don't know or you don't wanta tell?"

"You should only care if I look seventeen, which I don't."

"Oh, I'm not worried. You don't look *that* young."

"Thanks."

"You asked for that one, now, didn't you?"

"I guess I did. Thirty-three."

"Not married. I don't see a ring."

"Even if I was, I might not wear a ring. Men don't. Why should women? We all get branded or we none of us get branded, is the way I look at it." I did have a ring, from Bill, but it was a Sears kind, and I only got to wear it six months, and it rested at the bottom of a drawer in cotton.

"See? That's what I like about you. Different. How about another draft?"

"No thanks. It's getting late."

"It's not even south of midnight."

"I have to get up. Things to take care of."

"Whatever's waited this long will wait some more. Hey, you like motorcycles? I've got a purebred putt that'll break your heart. I'll give you a ride sometime."

"Let me see now, that must mean a Harley."

"Gnarly Harley. Right you are. I wouldn't be caught dead on one o' them Jap hair dryers."

I looked around me, hoping I wouldn't see anyone under a Stetson with Asian features going stony at the remark.

"What I do is buy baskets," he said, "fix 'em up. Sort of a hobby, but income, too. I hammer their tanks—engrave 'em—paint on 'em for friends. Right now I got a beater somebody wants fixed up. When I'm done, he'll have a softail mile-chaser outlaw Frankenstein freedom machine that looks like a work of art. Old Harleys never die. They just recycle."

His thumb was traveling across my shoulder. "Hon, you are scooter trash if I ever saw it. I can see you on a crotch rocket of your own, breathin' fire and eatin' wind."

"You're full of a certain amount of shit, you know that, Monty?"

"Yeah but it's *good* shit, huh? Hey," he said, tipping his head. "Hear that? Dwight. 'Maybe I'll be fast as you.' He's an asphalt eater himself. He's got a biker bar in Hollywood. All the rich actor jocks go there." I had to admit the music got to me, and pretty soon Monty was saying let's shake some tushy, and before I knew it, I was out on the floor going backward, two-stepping with him while the others were doing those geometric stomps. As soon as that finished, another Dwight Yoakam started. "Two Dwights," Monty said, pleased that it was two in a row by the same artist, this new song slower, Dwight and Monty singing together, telling me not to look so pretty and he'd try not to be a fool.

When we sat back down, Monty took the last watery slug of his margarita, then popped a mashed lime rind in his mouth and chewed on it a few times, downing it while my eyes watered. He got back up and brought his glass to the bar. The bartender in his cowboy hat seemed to be riding a slow horse as he bobbed to the music, looking out at the floor.

In a moment another margarita sat in front of me, and I was protesting that I hadn't finished the first.

Monty said, "You know what tequila means in *español*? 'The rock that cuts.' "

"I'm glad to know that," I said.

"See what a good Downey High School education can do for you? Now," he said, leaning close, "how else can I impress you?"

I ignored him, sipped the drink, and we talked about the thin women in their outfits and if they'd make good models, and in a while I began to forget for a moment the Undercover Me, and what I was there for. The black-and-white-spotted cowhide wrapped around the top of the bar island looked a little fuzzy. Monty was nibbling my neck near the ear, and in time my eyes closed in spite of myself. My back arched and I could feel my breasts wanting out.

He whispered, "You're Harley gypsy, darlin', I

just know it. Beautiful scooter trash. I got a fuckin'
machine in my garage'll purr your pants off, and I
mean that in the most respectful of ways, yes I do.
Come out with me sometime. You and me, baby,
straddlin' the best kickass, deep-throb, eighty-nine
incher you'll ever have the pleasure."

I broke out in a laugh, said even I couldn't handle
that. I said, "There's two things I always said I
wouldn't do for a man. One's fly in his airplane."

"And?"

"Get on his motorcycle."

"No, no, no, no. You don't get on *his* motorcycle,
doll. You get on your *own*. Old Monty don't mind
missin' out on the thrill of a beautiful woman
wrapped around him once in a while if that's all the
poor boy can manage. Hey, I'm a fuckin' knight. I
know how to treat a lady."

"Do you, now?" I said.

"Oh man. Get you some leathers and tats—that's
tat*toos*—say a lily or a rose right here," he said,
brushing my neckline, "and you'll be a hog jock
happy in the wind, I promise."

"Somehow I don't think that's me."

Abruptly he stood and tucked in his shirt, and I
could tell he was looking for the men's room, which
I'd seen was marked PODNAHS when we walked in.
He looked down at me with a grin. Like the Ter-
minator, he said, "I'll be back."

But then he sat back down, arm around me as if
he were talking to a pure buddy, and said, "Think
of it this way. It's the biggest vibrator this side of
heaven. A steamin' black stallion pleasure plug
that'll make you *cry*. You'll be thankin' old Monty
for it night and day."

I laughed and shoved him away with my shoulder.

He smoothed the corner of my mouth with a

knuckle, then stood and strode off across the floor, looking back once with a smile. At the bar, a girl on a stool showing a good cut of thigh was watching him, thinking, I knew, the same thing I did, that that was not a bad-looking set of jeans. And he saw that too.

16 One beer and a couple of swallows of margarita didn't make me drunk, but I was feeling mellow and sad all at once and didn't want to go home.

I drove to the narrow road near my house that traces the bay's edge. Entering there at night is like advancing into a cave with no edges, or a giant, soft, black pocket. In its secret life under the waters and farther yet under the mud and deep among the reeds, nature cycles and churns in its own dull sureness, oblivious to the human world. It seemed the right place for me to be.

Pulling off the asphalt, I stopped as close to the shallow bank as I could, shut off the engine, and lowered the window to breathe in the cool air. Soon I was lost in my thoughts of the odd directions in which life takes us. I thought of Monty in the parking lot when I was leaving, pressing me to go on a ride, and me still balking, until he finally told me Jolene, one of the lingerie models, was going, and I said okay. I'd wanted to get next to one of the other models, ask if she knew a Miranda, but the timing was never right; maybe now it would be. I thought of Monty leaning me against my car, kissing me, just a little; giving me directions to his place.

Gray clouds whisking across the moon made it seem like a lighted carriage traversing the sky. I got out of the car and stood gazing over the black waters that carried a skin of reflected light. What had I learned on my evening with Monty? Nothing. I had to go on the ride. I decided to call Joe in the morning—maybe tonight—ask him what he thought about that. As if I didn't know.

A beetle made its stumbling way over pebbles in front of me, his moon shadow drawing him twice the size. From up on a higher bank, an owl questioned, and then the silence grew profound. Instinctively, I looked over my shoulder, as if someone might pad up out of the bushes and cross the gravelly plot to put a hand over my mouth and an end to this very long day.

One of Joe's fingers was purple around the first joint and the nail had evolved to deep blue. Every time he accidentally hit it, he winced, and I did also.

"It's what an old man gets who thinks he can still press two-fifty," he said. "You just can't catch the down end of a load of bricks."

"Some of us love you anyway," I said. He'd come over at eight A.M. I was still asleep, made him wait till I brushed my teeth and got an eye open. He watched Road Runner cartoons while I made coffee and apologized for day-old muffins.

When I sat down, I ate in silence until the commercial came on and Joe turned his attention to me. Under the table his toes climbed my shin. I delivered my own five massagers into the soft Y of his shorts and asked, "More muffin?"

"Huh?"

"The man grunts," I said.

"You distracted me."

I got up and took his cup to refill it. Outside, the sun on the patio fired my Martha Washingtons into bright pink explosions as they drooled over their pot.

"I been thinking," I said. "If Miranda ever brushed her hair at Nathan's, we could DNA it for a match with blood from the Jane."

"The teeth will be done pretty soon," Joe said.

"Doesn't look like it. Glaciers are slower than Meyer Singer, but not by much."

When I came back with his cup, he jabbed for the creamer handle and missed, grimacing. I took hold of his finger and blew onto it, then poured a dollop of milk in his coffee myself. He said, watching, "Ever wonder when cows laugh does milk come out their noses?"

"You could get a job as a comedian."

"A criminalist comic. I like it. I could borrow the skeleton from the morgue, sit it on my lap . . ."

Dividing the last muffin, I gave him half.

"These are good," he said. "Old or not."

"Heidelberg Bakery in South County. The best. Ray goes there. A pretty Austrian girl owns it."

"Of course," he said.

I was back to thinking about Miranda. "If we just knew for sure . . ." I said. "If the doctor would just *say* his wife is missing . . ."

"But he doesn't," Joe said. "Where's her family? Did Nathan tell you that?"

"She's got a brother but he doesn't know where. The mother's dead. The father left when she was two."

"Then I guess we'll just have to wait."

"Joe?"

"What, baby?"

"Am I stupid to be pursuing this?"

He gave me that look that told me he'd been considering. "We could have been hasty. This undercover stuff."

I said, "I'm going somewhere with him tomorrow."

"Him?"

"Blackman."

"Where?"

"His house. Then for a motorcycle ride."

"You're kidding."

"I wish."

"So don't go. You don't have to go."

"I'm in it this far," I said. "I don't know if I'll have the courage to get on his 'hot iron,' as he calls it, but I can look."

"You'll get on."

"Another model's coming, name of Jolene. That'll be good. We can talk. She seems nice. I just haven't had time to talk to her."

In the alcove off the kitchen, my newly acquired guinea pig, courtesy of Bird Dog Farmer, was chirping in the cage I'd set on the washing machine. "Mortimer wants milk," I said, fetching the bottle hooked over his cage, and then the creamer. "I named him Motorboat because he purrs, but Mrs. Langston calls him Mortimer and now I do it too half the time."

Joe smiled and shook his head and said things about women nurturers.

By the time I got the milk warmed in the microwave, the guinea pig was gnawing furiously on the rubber-coated wire cage. He'd drink, smack his lips, and flick the tiny tongue that looked as perfect as a petal in and out, while I drew my finger down his little nutlike head and said, "Oh, purty, doo, doo, doo." Animal owners say funny things like that. As I stroked his soft sides, he vibrated with what I took to be delight.

When I looked back, Joe was leaning against the

sink, popping the stem of a banana and peeling a strip down. Frowning.

"What's the matter?"

"Someone should follow you."

"I'll be all right. The blond guy I met in Monty's office that first time is going too. He's apparently Jolene's boyfriend. The more the merrier."

"Names on those?"

"Jolene's is Josephson. The guy's called Switchie. Hold on," I said, and went to the bedroom and got the black leather cord strung with Indian beads and finger bones, and put it around my neck. It looked a little strange resting on my shortie robe. Back in the kitchen, I lifted the bones and said, "Part of my biker garb. What do you think? Human?"

Joe came close, banana smell on his breath, lifted the bones, and said, "Bear or chimp." The banana peel was draped over his upright hand like a collapsed torch. "You're wearing these?"

"Hey, I am certified trike trash," I said. "Harley gypsy, babe. Whatdya say, wanta get it on?"

After Joe left, I took Mortimer's cage out on the patio for a while so he could see the universe from his little jail. On my neighbor's balcony, a Belding's savannah sparrow sat flicking its tail, calling a rapid *Chip-chip-chip chee-ayyy*. Its superefficient kidneys allow it to drink salt water. It looked me over as it bounced nearer, until my neighbor's gray cat, sleeping on the first shelf of a plant stand, looped its tail in a contented dream and the bird flashed off.

When I looked at Mortimer, he was down in the pine shavings on his milk-fed tummy. The sparrow flew back and perched on the near railing, chip-chipping loudly. Mortimer's blond body tensed and he darted toward me. He rose high on his back legs like a miniature kangaroo, sniffed the air, his fearful eyes unblinking, as if to say, "What's next? Oh, what's next?"

17 When Monty first shut the big garage door, I felt on guard, jittery, and he told me I looked nervous as a whore in church. Then he turned the light on and I felt better.

Monty's stallion leaned on its gleaming chromed kickstand in a garage so clean no bike of Miranda's could ever possibly have been spray-painted there. The fringe from the black leather saddlebags nearly combed the floor. Now I was straddling the beast's bobtail, watching Monty look for a small wrench he knew he had just set down on his worktable, seeing him give up with a wave of the hand. I had on a denim jacket, white tanktop, jeans, and the blue boots with the flame cutouts. And of course, the monkey-finger necklace.

A few feet away from the stallion was another bike covered with a beige tarp. Miranda's? The one she wanted Monty to paint a design on she saw in a castle?

"What's under there?" I said, pointing.

"That one's my baby," he said softly. He plucked off the tarp to expose a deep-green metal machine replete with intricate engravings on all the silver parts. A bulbous molded snake head stared out backward on the rise of the fatbob fender.

"Wow," I said.

"If I do say so myself." He stood admiring it with his hands on his hips, then stepped forward and stroked two fingers over his work. "I can tattoo any-thin' that holds still and don't bite."

"It's beautiful. But do you ride two bikes at a time?"

"Oh hell, I got bikes all over the place. I got a couple at shows right now. Friends of mine takin' care of 'em."

"Nice. Do you do any for women?"

"You interested? You have to buy one first."

"Maybe I will."

"It's not just a paperweight, now."

"No kidding." I looked down at the monster be-neath me.

Monty took a wooden dowel and tripped it over the front spokes. "Hear that? Like a harp. But they got to all sound the same. There's a hundred inch-pounds of torque on each one, never have to be re-trued. You talkin' about women, a woman friend laced these spokes. It cost her eight hours, and that's workin' fast. Payback, I put my little ol' pneumatic Gravermeister to work and hammered her point cover and tank, real nice design." He slid the dowel back into the cardboard tube by his drill press, then swiped at something on the cream-colored boots nosing out of his jeans.

"I like this design," I said, admiring the swirls of snake coated in a thousand scales. "A python, of course?"

"Not only that, my dear, she's got a Python anti-reversionary exhaust system. Couldn't have any old exhaust system on her."

"Of course not."

"Monty's always thinkin'." He tapped his head. "Now let me show you how you twist the wick," he said, reaching in front of me to the handlebars. "Rummm! Rum-rum," he said in a deep gargle. He stood up, and I smiled in spite of myself.

"I know you're being nice, but I don't think this is for me, Monty."

"You got the wrong kind of fear, baby."

"What's the right kind?"

"No kind. Here goes." He slid me forward with two hands on my hipbones, then leaned over me to the handlebars. "Put your hands on these here ape hangers," he said, and picked up one of my wrists to guide it to the handlebar just above his. He turned the key and twisted the throttle. The machine growled to life.

"How's that now?" His face was close to my ear.

"It's always fun losing your hearing," I shouted.

"You're out there, your mind's set free," he said. Then he shut it down and walked back to the workbench. I sat there feeling a little let down because the indoctrination was so short.

As if he read me, he said, thoughtfully, "You're tired, you're broke, been dumped on by the boyfriend, your boss is giving you a bad time..." He gestured widely, winking at the last. "Say, 'Fuck the world.' Leave your troubles behind. You wheel that baby out, get in the wind, you are fuckin' born again." He was laughing now, pacing to the front of the bike with me still sitting on it. His arms spread open and hung above his shoulders. "You just let yourself come into it like the heavy arms of God."

"You could have several professions, Monty," I said.

His arms dropped, his spine went loose again, and he slid a paint-splattered wooden stool out from under a second workbench and sat down right in front of the wheel, framed through the handlebars.

"I have *had* several professions, dear girl."

"Like what?"

"I could have raced big time. You get out there

on a track with a bunch o' boneheads all willin' to die for that prize, man, it's a high. First you want to be Number One Bonehead. Then you get beyond that. You don't care about Number One Bonehead, Number Two Bonehead, Number Ninety-Nine and a Half Bonehead. You just want to master the machine. Oh yeah, each one of these got a mind of its own. A spirit. I can build one with all kinds of love, piece by motherfuckin' piece, and it'll drag its lazy ass around the track like it wished you died and went to hell with no forwardin' address.

"But you get it right—you get it *right*—and now you done somethin'," he said. "You win. You can triple-fuck anybody squeezes you too hard. Now out on the road, bugs shittin' in your eye, that's a different challenge. Little rock, little bit o' ice here, little water, oil there, ah-hah. And the cagers—that's you guys in the *vee-hick-els*. Little peanuthead ol' lady sittin' on a cushion to see over the dash, she's the most dangerous cager out there. Or you get your everyday office geek that hates your guts 'cause you're ridin' free and he's an hour late for dinner after polishin' his knob with his secretary down the Holiday Inn. They'll turn their tires out on you, man, open their doors—'Uh-oh, didn't mean that, Officer. Highway hash now. Oh my, isn't that too bad?' "

Miranda, I thought, How did you find it going back to your foppish Mr. Doctor or my solemn Mr. Nate? And I thought of Monty's weapons violation and wondered how *he* felt about Miranda going back to either of them.

The garage door was open to let in some sun when Switchie and Jolene ratcheted up the sloped driveway on a candy-red bike. The ape hangers on it were so far out Switchie's ears were riding on his shoulders.

Switchie dismounted, undid his chin strap, and pulled off his helmet, and before he even took off his gloves, ran a comb through his hair which stood tall in a long crew cut. He wore leather leggings over new blue jeans, a leather jacket over a black Harley shirt.

Jolene had on calf-high boots with low heels and a pocket in the side for cigarettes. Black cotton Lycra pants with holes in them were held together at the sides with beaded lace-ups. She wore a black leather vest that wasn't meant to button over a sleeveless red top. Handcuffs swung from her belt, and she had so much silver jewelry on her arms and fingers I thought she'd clank, but she didn't.

"God," she said, coming toward me, "you know what I feel like? A lemonade. You got any lemonade, Monty, inside?"

He told her to go on in and make herself at home. I followed her in, not having seen the house because of entering through the garage. We came in directly to the kitchen. It had a small Formica breakfast table in it, two mismatched wooden chairs, and window curtains that had faded to a rose color in the involutes and remained kind of purple on the evolutes. The entire refrigerator was covered with Harley patches, Gary Larson cartoons, snapshots of engraved metal parts and painted gas tanks, and pictures of beer-drinking men and women. I looked for the face of Miranda Robertson among those in the photos, saw no pretty woman with a long auburn braid. One photo, though, had a blurry half eye, cheekbone, and naked shoulder, bright with light, and a motorcycle in the background, white flames painted on blue. My attention kept returning to that snapshot, and then Jolene found some Pepsi, no lemonade she said, and I took a can from her. She got another for Switchie.

"By the way, Jolene, what's Switchie's real name?"

"Ralph. *R-R-alph.* I hate that. *R-R-alphhh.* He's into knives—like a hobby—so somebody called him Switchie once, I guess, and it stuck, pardon the pun. Hey, are you up for this ride?" she asked.

"I don't have a lot of experience on motorcycles."

"Oh, the guys'll try to tell you how much fun it is, but the truth is after a while it's pretty boring. Get on, putt-putt, get off, eat, drink, brag, go to the next place. Watch everybody be cool." She shrugged, and the moisture left on her full bottom lip from a swig of Pepsi made her seem pouty. She had her hair cut in sort of a ducktail. On her it looked nice.

Back again with the men, Jolene and I found something to talk about, but I was trying hard to listen to the men when somewhere in their tapestry of talk about gas/air mixtures, engine displacement, and skimming the piston crowns, I heard Switchie say he had a Tec-9 he'd like to get rid of, and was Monty interested? An Intratec Tec-9 is a nine-millimeter semiauto pistol banned in California because it can hold more than twenty rounds in the magazine and is therefore classified as an assault weapon.

Monty asked, "Does it have a body on it?"

"Shit no. My ex-ex-girlfriend sold it to me when she needed some bucks."

Jolene said, "What ex-ex-girlfriend? What's an ex-ex?"

"One I made a mistake twice on, okay?" he said, and turned his attention back to Monty, whose Western shirt stretched tightly across his shoulders as he reached for a black satchel over the workbench.

Monty said, "If I had a girlfriend who carried a Tec-nine, I'd dump her too. What's wrong with it you don't want to keep it?"

"Nothing's wrong with it. I just don't like nines no more. I want a Glock forty." He took a sip from a beer he got somewhere, ignoring the Pepsi Jolene set down for him on the workbench. He still had his fingerless riding gloves on.

Jolene looked at me, raised an eyebrow. Said, "Switchie, what the hell you all talking about?"

He ignored her and started telling Monty about how he was supercharging the Harley he left at home.

"It won't be streetable no more," Monty said.

"Bullshit," Switchie said.

"It'll seize in the bore, that ratio. You gotta get forged pistons then, with thicker crowns."

"Hell," Switchie said, laughing. "I already exploded the super and the manifold clean off the bike. I fuckin' grenaded that sumbitch out of my garage. Scared the livin' shit outta me. It's set up soft right now, but I've still got some AV fuel. Give her some righteous octane boost, and then watch out, guy, I'll be racin' and chasin'. You'll be a gnat on a boar's ass in my rearview mirror." He shadow-boxed the side of Monty's shoulder.

AV fuel. Joe's portable sniffer had detected aviation fuel in the Caddy, hadn't he said?

Jolene switched on a radio she found on the second workbench. It crackled alive with Eric Clapton singing from the *Slowhand* album. Monty said, "I didn't think that stinker worked. It's got paint dust in it."

Then his eyes met mine because, I guessed, I'd told him before that I dug Clapton. And at the part where Eric's saying you look wonderful tonight, Monty smiled at me through his dark beard,

and swaggered his upper body a little. I turned
and went into the house. He hollered after me,
''Hurry up, Miz Brandon. The quicker you piss,
the faster we ride.''

18

I did pretty well on the back of Monty's sled, all the way up Highway 15 into Norco, Riverside County. As I hid behind his leather jacket and tried not to get a faceful of bug buckshot, he split lanes a few times, whitelining it, as he called it, and the cars on either side seemed to suck toward us like mindless crusher balls. I hung on to Monty's waist a little harder, hoping he couldn't tell the difference. In the side mirrors, Switchie's and Jolene's distorted figures plowed on in our wake like a two-headed hovering horsefly.

We passed a sign pointing to Coal Canyon. It made me think of Carbon Canyon and the burned-out Cadillac and why I was with these newfound friends to begin with. While I was at Monty's house or even at the Python, I'd seen no hint of firearms or anything else to make someone believe Monty was anything other than a slightly colorful businessman. But he *had* done a year at Terminal Island after one in the county jail for assault and drug possession, and I couldn't forget that. The sentence must have made him real pissed, because in the hierarchy of crimes a weapons charge is a notch below vandalism and a hitch above prostitution, and fewer than 3 percent of TI's population does time for violating Penal Code 12021. And when I thought of this man and then of Joe, of Doug Forster and Ray Vega

and even poor old nerdy Les Fedders, the vision of
them and the side they were on brought fleeting moments of nostalgia, as if they and that world were
so far away as to be lost forever.

On the incline going over the hills ahead, a clutch
of bikes found an open space on the freeway, and
the bikers began trading places as if doing forma-
tions at halftime. Even at that distance, chrome
flashed in the sun. Monty called back, "How you
like that?" proud of his compadres.

"Great," I yelled.

Once off the freeway, we passed through the city
of Norco. Sixty miles east of Newport Beach, the area
had the feel of the fifties or maybe earlier. Roadside
saddle vendors displayed hides over ropes strung
between pickup trucks and poles. A life-sized plastic
cow on a red roof marked a meat market.

We turned down a street named Dodd and passed
single-story frame houses painted the colors of desert dirt. Goats stood stiff-legged and dogs big as
ponies moped inside chain-link fences with the gates
left open. Women chatted with each other atop their
horses in their own front yards. At the corner, Monty
pulled over and told Switchie and Jolene to go on
without us, we'd catch up.

"Where we going?" I asked.

"You hungry?"

"A little."

"We'll take care of that."

He turned the bike around and headed back to
Sixth Street and soon we were outside a hamburger
joint, hanging our helmets on the handlebars. I went
in to use the rest room and when I came out Monty
had a sack of food and two cans of soda from the
station next door.

"What'd you do, die in there?" he asked.

"I'm sorry. I needed to stop vibrating." What I'd also needed to do was phone Joe, hear his voice. There was a phone in an alcove by the rest room, and when I saw Monty striding off to the station, I stole the moment. I told Joe where I was and that everything was all right. He offered his usual cautionary words. His voice sounded disembodied to me, and I wondered if it was the connection, my hearing, or my mood.

Monty drove a mile or so to the edge of town, where a battalion of grassy dunes had already yellowed in the presummer sun. The Harley's sound dissipated in the clear air to a pleasant rumble as we rode at low speed to catch the scenery. I was getting used to the feel of Monty's back, knew where the valleys in his latissimum dorsum were where I could park my breasts.

Along came a buggy and horse, two people in front and two in back sitting straight as country parsons. Monty, out of deference, turned off at the first red dirt road and headed east again. The road ended in front of a black-barked tree split from lightning or a core fire set by kids.

We got off the bike and walked up a rise beyond the split tree. I was toting the sacks with the food and drink.

Monty looked first back at the town and then northeast to a dust-yellow smear in the distance. "San Bernardino out that way," he said.

"I can tell by the smog."

"Ain't it a shame?" Extending an arm farther east, he said, "Out there's my farm."

"*You* have a farm?"

"Right-o. You didn't think that about the old Black Man, now did you?"

"I wouldn't have put it together, no."

He smiled.

"You like animals?"

"I have a guinea pig, as of about a week ago."

"That a hamster or what?"

"It's about half the size of a rabbit. Round face, no tail. Not like a rat. Real cute."

"Uh-huh," he said, and took the sacks from me. Hooking a finger in my beltless loop, he tugged me along to a weather-pitted sandstone outcropping near a tall rock the color of char.

Feeling a little stupid and edgy, I said, "Not exactly the best place for a picnic."

Monty sat down in a nest of grass and shattered leaves. "Sorry I don't have a blanket." But then he motioned to a flat rock I hadn't seen, and I sat down next to him.

"I used to come up here as a kid," he said. "My initials are carved top of that rock."

I looked, squinting into the glare. "I thought you grew up in Downey."

"You can't see 'em from here. That was before we moved to Downey."

"So you grew up and bought a farm out here. What came first, the Python or the farm?"

He unwrapped a burger to rearrange onions, then handed me the other one. "The bar came first. So did a lot of other things."

"What kind of farm is it?"

"Take a deep breath. You can smell it from here," he said.

"Smell what?" I asked.

With a mouthful, he said, "Pigs."

"No way."

"Hogs. Swine. Durocs, actually. Those're the ones with ears cover their eyes. I like 'em because they don't dig out and run away like the pointy-eared ones. And one big Hampshire I've got. That's the kind with a stripe around its neck like he's going to a luau. Only he don't know he's the main course."

"You own a pig farm?"

"See, I told you you're quick."

"Am I going to see them?"

He shook his head no. "I don't allow strangers in when the sperm is up."

"Oh, excuse *me*," I said.

"Pigs get funny. It might disturb the breedin'. They have to have five good undisturbed days."

"Or you may get piggus interruptus."

A question loomed in his eyes.

"Nothing," I said.

He looked at me some more, chewing.

"You can make good money with this?" I asked.

"Figure it out. Bring a boar in to breed a gilt. Three months, three weeks, three days, bingo, you got twelve little piggy banks. You can go baby-to-butcher in six months, and twenty days of feed only costs eight bucks."

He had fries hidden down in the food sack, and handed me a pinch of them.

"Well, it's a different way to get rich, I guess."

"Tell the truth, I'm not that much into the carcass trade. Right now the market's down for pork anyways, so I'm happy doin' what I'm doin'."

"Which is . . ."

"Reproduction," he said, smiling. "Sump'n ol' Monty's good at. Least he has fun tryin'. Hey, you know a pig's dingus is like a corkscrew?"

"That's a piece of information I somehow didn't have. I'm just awful glad to know that, Monty."

"You're welcome." He scooted over partly in sun now, looking down the rise from which we'd come, and I turned to listen to this man with the movie-star eyes and the Mafia voice as he started in a sing-song rhythm: "Once upon a time, this whole country from here to the San Gabriels used to be farms. Pig farms, dairy farms, farm farms. In spring there'd be big patches of California poppies so bright flutterin' in the breeze it looked like a river of gold. Now all we got is creepin' concrete. Over in Cucamonga they got an aerospace plant, ugliest damn thing you ever saw. Engineers runnin' around in white shirts make you blind, takin' up the line at Burger King. I'm *glad* the aerospace industry went bust."

"Engineers have to eat too, I believe."

"Not in my town. I'm lookin' for a buyer for the Python. Then Miz Brandon will be out of a job. What you gonna do with your life?"

"I'll get by."

"Used to I'd drive my beat-up car out here at night and park my ass behind this rock, and I'd just sit here lookin' at the stars. Every once in a while I'd see a shootin' star, you know? Like way out there, over the hills," he said. His eyes held wistfulness in them like creek water just waking up. "I'd see a shootin' star, and I'd think, Now there."

"You come out here with a girl?"

"Sometimes." He rubbed the back of my head with his left hand. Broken shadows from an overhead oak danced across his face, and his lashes slept on his cheeks while he talked, dreamlike. "My lady when I find her's gonna wear a new jewel in her navel every day. She'll have eyes like tiger agate. When she speaks it's going to be like a little bitty mouse pissin' in a cottonball."

I laughed and said, rising, "Show me some pigs, you animal. A cloven-footed beast with his face in the mud, and this better be good, Bubba, for me putting up with you and all your talk."

"*Puercos*," he said as he rose, "the Spanish word. And pigs don't like mud because it's *mud*. They like it to keep cool, because they don't have any sweat glands. They get a bad name."

"I like a man stands up for his pigs."

"You bet your ass," he said.

Ahead on the road, a horse loped by, ridden by a man in a fleece-lined denim jacket, sitting tall as a sheriff. A misplaced cloud found the sun as I stood waiting roadside by a squirrel hole for Monty to put the cans in his saddlebags, good citizen that he was. Then we mounted up, the leather making those taut, creaking sounds. He started the engine and rapped the exhaust so it blew debris up by the squirrel hole and clapped decibels across the air like an audience ready to riot. With a rough start, we went wagging down the road. I had to clutch hard behind me on the seat.

We were approaching a green light behind a big Ford when a maroon-colored sedan crossed at a good clip in front of us.

"She just blew the light," Monty said.

And as the big blue Ford in front of us swept left and accelerated, I caught the license plate frame that said FEEL SAFE TONIGHT, SLEEP WITH A COP and wondered if that were a wish or a prediction.

19 They wanted me to bite the wienie, but I wouldn't. The hot dog hung between two uprights of a crossbar, and then a driver would wobble through the posts at a pace that would let the woman braced on his shoulders have a try for it.

We were near a field that looked like a baseball lot, sparse grass, red dirt, people milling at the edges. A scattering of California sycamores provided patches of shade. We had driven on a side road to get here. There were a few buildings in the distance, and Monty said they were part of a farm belonging to a friend of his.

When we arrived, Switchie and Jolene were just a little way from the improvised goalposts with the wienie hanging from it. Jolene had a rapturous look on her face as she watched the women go for it. When the meat dragged mustard all over a woman's face, the crowd would cheer, Jolene one of the loudest. She and Switchie were about to take their place in line, but they were putting pressure on us first. I told Monty to go find another girl who wanted to make a fool of herself. So he did—a blonde with no boobs but an ass Switchie said gave him a chubby when he saw her at the last roundup in Malibu. Jolene punched him.

I went and stood under a tree. A lanky guy in sunglasses stepped away, as if he didn't want to be seen with me, and then I saw that he was taking pictures.

Jolene and Switchie were lined up for their second try, only about nine contestants so far, when a red bike grumbled onto the game field from the side. The driver was a man with white hair strangled into a ponytail. A sunburned woman stood on the rear footpads and seemed stapled hard onto his shoulders. Her dark gray hair streamed down her back to her halter strap. She was big, not fat; no waist, and the muscles in her legs beneath her white shorts were raw pink spears. Her mouth, when she let out a whoop, would cover a headlight. The guys standing next to me said, "Man, there's one that'll suck 'em down," and "Shit, Quillard's got it clean."

A twig fell on my head from the oak tree I was standing under. When I flicked it away, I missed Jolene and Switchie's try but knew she failed when her frustrated shriek carried clear across the lot and the crowd clapped anyway. The guy with the mustard bucket dipped the wienie again for the next duo.

Then came the lady with the mouth and the powerful sunburn. I could read the letters on the driver's shirt this time: Will Work for Beer. As he wove his way forward, I looked at the pair and liked them both for the spirit under the gray hair, and wondered why the guy looked familiar. He was a small man, or was it only compared to her, the woman with the fine big mouth and the guts to ride a Harley when she's fifty?

They passed slowly under the hot dog, the woman rising higher, head back and openmouthed, the crowd cheering her on. In a smooth ride with nary a wobble, she took the wienie off with a perfect bite, and the crowd yelled and *oogah*ed on bulb horns. A man sitting on top of one of the food tables held up a sign that read SHOW US YOUR TITS. Obligingly, she lifted her halter, the white skin contrasting brightly to the sunburned flesh above, and left the garment there as they rode off.

Monty and his blonde were across the lot, Monty taking off his light blue Western shirt and hanging it in his belt loop. Underneath was his black Ghostriders T-shirt. He looked across the lot at me.

Jolene came over, handcuffs swinging. "You should try the Wienie Bite. It is so cool," she said, still a yellow film around her mouth.

"I guess I'm just not a player."

"You better shape up. Monty's going to dump you."

"Think so?"

"Look at her over there. She's on him."

"Does he make a habit of it?"

"What? Dumping somebody? Oh yeah."

"Did you know any of his girlfriends?"

"The last one."

"Who was that?"

"A girl named Miranda. I don't know most of them. I just hear names. He keeps kind of private."

I felt my skin flush, took a breath to calm myself, and asked, "What was his problem with the last girlfriend?"

"It's not like I ask him. She was around one week, gone the next. I figured it was because she was kind of stuck-up, you know what I mean? She'd fly right by us, never say hi, kiss my ass, or nothin'. Crap," she said, scanning the crowd. "I can't see Switchie, can you? He makes me mad sometimes."

"He ever come on to you?" I asked her, casually as I could, and I wasn't sure why.

"Monty? He's way too old for me."

"That doesn't answer my question."

She grinned, chewed on a stick, and said, "If he did, I wouldn't tell you."

"Why not?"

"You'd be jealous, find a way to get me canned."

A tall man with a bullhorn came out to give the rules for the next game. Jolene, said, "You coming?" When I said no, she shrugged and went off toward the playing field.

I looked over the herd of Harleys. It was then that I placed the man in the white ponytail and the Will Work for Beer T-shirt; remembered how his mane would look if fluffed at the shoulders instead of tied off, this man people kept calling Quillard. It was the guy Joe and I had seen after the investigation at Blue Jay Campground where the victim wore wire for a necklace. Up there off Ortega Highway, ten miles from the scene. General Lee and his concealed weapon in his crossover holster. What the heck was going on?

Monty left the side of his bike and walked over to me. His blonde partner was talking to one of the referees whose hair was as light and as long as hers. When Monty came near, he turned and looked back at a cluster of people sitting at the edges of the field on camp stools, playing checkers. He said, "These here are your rubbies."

"Excuse me?"

"Rich urban bikers. Two beers, they think they're outlaws," he said.

"What are *you*?" I asked.

"A pubbie. Poor urban biker. That's why I'm gonna make you buy me my next beer."

"Not an outlaw," I said, pushing it.

Monty stepped away from me, looked me up and down, and said, "You're lookin' pretty outlaw yourself. Whyn't you go one game, long as you're here? Do the haystack."

I saw the hay pile, a mound about three feet high. One of the referees was holding up a potato. He had two more pressed to his ribs with his left arm. Then he told six women, one of them Jolene and another the bigmouthed woman, that he was hiding the potatoes in the pile. They were to dive in and find them: first prize, second prize, third.

"Asses in the air and women groveling," I said. "What's fun about that?"

Monty laughed, and when the action started he had me stumbling backward till the tree stopped me, and there he wrapped one hand on the front of my throat and kissed me. The surprise of it left me numb and unmoving. I tasted whiskey.

When we broke, I saw the man called Quillard—his lady butt-up in the hay pile as she swept hay behind her—staring our way.

We had to move because a portable toilet was being brought in. Already a man so loaded down with jangling biker metal that he needed all two hundred forty pounds to carry it was coming toward it.

Another man approached Monty and started talking as though there'd never been a break from a previous conversation. His plume of brown hair swung like a pendulum at the back; bald otherwise. "I'm thinkin' of a bolt-on nitrous but I don't want to blow the cylinders."

Monty said, "Shit-can the nitrous. Switchie used nitrous, totally fragged his manifold."

"I'll just have to huff it then," he said, smiling, shaking his head. "Damn, been a long time since I did any that hippie crack. Hey," he said with a tilt of the chin in my direction, "she cool?"

Monty turned to me and said, "You cool?"

"I don't know. Am I?"

"She's cool."

"I need a set of works," the man said.

Monty shook his head no. "See Switchie."

"Couple hours I'll be stressing."

"Ain't my problem, man."

"Fuck you," the guy said, but made no move to leave. In fact, he lowered himself and sat on his heels, bouncing there awhile.

"See Switchie."

"Where's he at? He got any boy?"

"Three percent. Better'n most."

"My lady needs some too. Is that a pretty knuckle or what?" he said, looking at a bulky yellow bike off to the side, a woman with bare arms standing next to it, hugging herself as if she were cold.

The man got up. Tattoos peeked out his brown leather pants with lacings at the hip. "Hear about Charlie Viveros? He just about got whacked by the South Americans. Had to prove to 'em he lost his load to the DEA. If he hadn't sent the goombahs a newspaper clipping of the bust, he'd be jerky drying on a fence post about now. Dumb shit. He's growing jane right out in his backyard in Van Nuys with a whole load of blow worth a million bucks in the house. I swear I think they're makin' them dumber every day."

Monty said in his whispery voice, "Why don't you take it on down the road, Wilson?" He didn't say it angry or mean, just a serious suggestion.

The man leaned toward me with drunk green eyes and said, "Watch out for this guy. He farts like a rhino." Monty hiked his cream-colored boot and gave Wilson a push. Wilson skittered ahead, laughing.

Monty said, "Tell Switchie I'm down the house," nodding in the direction of the farmhouse we passed on the way to the back field. "Come on," he said to me, dragging me along with a loose hand on an elbow. "I got to see a man about a pig."

I asked, "You do that stuff?"

"*That* stuff? You gonna tell me you want some?"

"No. Not me," I said, matter-of-factly. I just wanted to make sure I wasn't invited to participate.

"Good," he said.

"I thought you said I was cool."

"Just 'cause you don't do dope don't make you uncool."

"What's 'boy'?"

"Heroin. You mix it with cocaine, make a speed-ball. It lightens the launch. Coke, that's 'girl' where he comes from. Hey, you *are* a virgin, aren't you?"

20

Laid out like that it could have been a pallid torso on an autopsy table, the legs whacked off at the knees in some malicious harvest. But it was a pig and only a pig, the outer meat paler than I would have expected, the exposed abdominal cavity rosy with the colors of resting blood. In the shadows, on a rear table, lay the hog's head in a gray-speckled roasting pan. Its monument of snout pointed upward. Its grand flap of ears draped like Dumbo's over the pan's edges.

Steam rose thinly from a vessel deeper than a bathtub just inside the ax-hewn rails separating us from the slaughter shed. On the water's surface floated short hair and pastel scum, and beneath the tub the ground was sticky with mud splash. Birds chanted in the tree overhead.

Monty and I sat on top of a picnic table facing the shed, which was open on three sides, our feet parked on the weathered bench. We had driven over at the start of the game where women get blindfolded and stumble around to find their partners by the roar of their machines.

The old man Monty came to see sat on the bench by Monty's boot. Long ago the man's face had sagged to slim gourds around the jaw, but his hair was black as could be. Ahead, a Mexican woman wordlessly swept a long knife over a strop, one end of which was nailed to a post. Quietly, the old man said, "I mostly kill just for the family now."

When a young worker entered the open shed and said something to the woman in Spanish, she paused and swept away graying hair escaped from the knot at the back of her head, then answered. In slow movements she lay her implement down on the table to retie the black rubber apron covering her from neck to knees, the apron flecked with bits of butchered carcass. The boy said something else and nodded, then left to join another worker standing nearby. They went off toward a pen with goats flooding one past another, nervous from new visitors just gotten out of a car.

"Tell my friend how big your family is," Monty said to the old man.

"A hundred and sixty," Mr. Avalos said. When he smiled, he showed an empty space among the otherwise large and yellow teeth perfectly uniform in his mouth.

Wow, I said, or something like it, and Monty said, "You've been a busy man. My hat's off to you." Then he waited awhile and asked, "Paulie in the house?"

"Nope. He ain't arrived yet." His cane the color of nicotine wavered under his broad brown hand as he spoke. Beside him, shouldering a chicken-wire fence, each green paddle of a beavertail cactus carried the whitened scars of someone's initials, month, day, and year dates carved there too. Carving seemed to be a thing to do in this part of the country, as with Monty's initials in stone.

"I thought I saw Paulie's truck," Monty said.

"That's my wife's."

The woman in the shed stacked hog segments on a wire rack in the corner. Then she took a small hose and watered the steel table down.

"How is your wife, Mr. Avalos?"

A terrible bleating issued from off our right where the visitors stepped back for the two young workers to bring a brown goat from the pen.

"That chemo's about to do her in," Mr. Avalos said, rolling his eyes upward to us. "Next week I'm going to buy her a new truck."

"That'll be real nice," Monty said.

He looked ahead. "She says she don't want one."

"She does," Monty said. "She just doesn't want you to go to the trouble, feelin' sorry for her."

Mr. Avalos nodded solemnly.

The goat continued its awful screaming as the two workers hoisted it along toward us, one man hugging the front legs and the other looping his arms around the spindly rear legs so that the poor beast sagged like a hammock and its white belly bulged.

Mr. Avalos looked at me and said, "The goats are the loudest," then looked away. "The lambs, they just stand there and shiver."

"Maybe we should be moseying on," I said to Monty.

"Here comes that one," Mr. Avalos said, looking over the heads of the workers. He meant Switchie, with Jolene, the two of them coming from the direction of a white structure too small to be a house by today's standards but maybe it was Avalos family headquarters once. His arm completely wrapped around Jolene at the top of her shoulders, Switchie's hand was at her mouth, and as they came close I saw he had a finger between her lips and he was rubbing her gums in a most intrusive and sensual way.

The workers hefted the goat onto a dark wood slab next to the steel table. I felt my breath come quick. I slid off the table and went around to the opposite side, holding my own arms and looking out past the cactus at the dust rising in the back field where the riders were continuing their games.

Monty said, "I think you and Jolene want to see some ducks. Down there by the sheep pen."

Jolene said, "Nothing doing."

"Think you're a tough guy, huh?" said Switchie.

"Want to find out?" She gave him a sexy swagger, lowering her eyes. Against white skin, her black hair and leathers made her look like something in a music video, pampered kids pretending to be street hoods.

She moved toward Mr. Avalos with a hand out to offer a handshake. "You're Paulie's father? I'm Jolene." His eyes moved quickly to her and back without turning his head. Mr. Avalos didn't let go of his cane. Jolene's hand dropped. She stepped back and hitched herself up on the tabletop next to Monty, where I'd been sitting. I was looking over the head of Mr. Avalos, and Switchie had moved to my right, his viewpoint between the shoulders of Monty and Jolene. He had his shades on and chewed gum in tight munches. "Is it going to be real grody, boss?" Jolene asked.

"Guess you'll soon find out." He said this as the woman in the apron handed the long, half-inch-wide knife to the worker whose left hand clutched the goat's ear at the stem, the goat eerily quiet now. Its eyes bulged. I thought, Oh fuck, and looked up into the branches of the tree. A high, pitiful scream issued from the goat, and when I looked, its rear legs were lurching, trying to gain purchase while the worker grasped wildly. The man holding the head arched back farther, nearly bringing the animal off the slab.

As the other man caught the legs again, I thought, Leave me to my lowly clerking in a crime lab, counting icepick holes in a dead man's shirt. It may be gruesome, but it's over, not *about* to be over, but over, ready for reports and labels and whatever eventual justice courts could apply.

The woman in the shed retrieved the fallen long knife from the ground and handed it to the young man wresting the goat's head, while Switchie molded his blond hair into shape and put the comb in his back pocket. "Pop," he said, as the worker set the point of the knife to the animal's neck just below the ear, and I heard a grunt from Jolene.

The knife went in. The goat twitched ever so slightly. Then its mouth came open as the burgundy flow began its curve over the neat white fur and descended down the neck. Quickly the woman slid a bucket under. I looked into the beast's eyes, brown and wide with wonder, and counted in my head: One thousand, two thousand, go to meet your maker. Soon the worker at the rear could release the goat's legs and reach for the bucket from the woman to hold it for the forty seconds it took for the animal to go entirely slack. I held on the animal's eyes expecting to see a fading there, but the gleam gave up no secrets, and I do not know if my own stare accompanied him ill or well into that darkness.

Jolene got down, brushing her pants, and glanced my way as if it were all my fault. She told Switchie come on, let's go see the lambs, and he looked at Monty and sneered and said he'd see him later.

Mr. Avalos walked alongside Monty as we went toward what I now understood was the Campana Rancho, the Avalos home. A big bell, a *campana*, was poised on the road in front between wood uprights. At the side of the house, a small gray burro tethered to a tree brayed a sucking, honking complaint, and geese at the edge of a pond stretched their long

necks, flapped wings, and echoed as well they could
his sound.

It did not seem his huge son Paulie could be this
short man's issue, for Mr. Avalos's black pants hung
on his hips like tired canvas and the pant legs that
were too long folded onto his shoes and carried rims
of dust from the yards. He said, "I don't like that
fella much."

"Switchie? Paulie says he can run about anythin'.
Graders, skip loaders, dumps. I came to see if Paulie's gonna finish my pit this week. You know?"

Mr. Avalos shook his head. Behind us, I heard
Switchie's bike start up and saw him and Jolene
head in a wide circle back to the games.

In a while Monty said, "I think I got a clogged
intake valve."

"Rotten egg smell?" the old man asked.

"A little."

"Pay attention to it. Hydrogen sulfide will para-
lyze your sense of smell. You won't even smell it if
you got a bad leak. It'll kill you."

"That's another reason I'd like Paulie to stop by.
Help me check it out."

"Paulie dumped that Cat, you know," Mr. Avalos
said, moving his cane with each step but not touching the ground with it. "He had slope boards on it
and he dumped it anyway. His shoulder's still not
right. He can only lift his arm to here." He demon-
strated.

"I hate to say it, but maybe he needs to go a little
lighter on the sauce, Mr. Avalos."

"I don't know what Paulie needs. Maybe better
company," he said. And then glanced up and said,
"Not you."

Monty stopped, as if done escorting. "We'll be
goin' along now, Mr. Avalos. Y'all take care."

"You're going to eat some barbecue, aren't you?"

"Sure. Wouldn't miss it for the world."

The old man gave a quick nod as he was moving away, but his gaze turned to the field behind his ranch where the sound of motorcycles droned in the distance.

We rode back to the field, only farther on, to a portion with low rises and shallow dips and gutter corrugations both nature and bike had carved. The scent of alfalfa and animal pens was still with us. More people had arrived. A new herd of parked Harleys sat near half a dozen dirt bikes in one small camp where women in torn shorts mingled with each other and fat-bellied men sat in beach chairs next to portable coolers. A boom box was blasting out the rhythms of "The Hillbilly Rock."

This seemed like a different crowd from the ones before, yet when we dismounted, it was near the woman in red we'd seen earlier, the one who should by all laws of anatomy have grabbed the wienie in one gulp. Someone called her Marge and I believed I knew it all along, the name so fit her you could imagine no other. I looked for the man named Quillard. He was not with her or in the near crowd, but with just the reminder of him already I had a renewed sense of unease.

Unloading Monty's saddlebags, I hauled cans and candy bars over to an unclaimed piece of box cardboard to sit on at the trailing edge of the assembling area. When Monty came over to lay bags of beef jerky and two apples beside me, another man was with him, carrying a long-neck beer, grinning gaily, and telling Monty, "You got to keep the shiny side *up*, you stupid bastard." He looked at me, and said, "Tell this Jap-scrap jockey the way you win is you keep the shiny side *up*." The panther reaching high on his biceps flexed and seemed to want to crawl up the black cap sleeve of his shirt. The man's skin was the color of tea with a red sheen on it and his brown hair rolled in high waves, and he had one of the happiest, drunkest faces I'd seen in a while.

I said, "Are you racing?"

"Only my heart when I see pretty ladies."

"Don't mind Jason," Monty said. "He's missin' a few shingles off the roof." He offered Jason a strip of jerky and then tore at one himself. A call to positions brought Monty to his feet. He said to Jason, "Get your ass out there and ride, man."

"Hell, I'd spill a trike," Jason said happily, lifting his beer can for evidence. "Go on. Take mine." Monty laughed and headed to the dirt bikes, looking back once and winking at me. Jason took a guzzle, and with smiling eyes said to me, "The old fuckup can still hammer the best steel in Riverside County, I'll give him that. You ever see his work?"

"Uh-huh," I said.

"Fuckin' artist."

"Yeah man," I said, sipping from a beer myself now. It was my first, and I'd make it my last for the day, but the sun was getting pretty hot and all this time I didn't know Monty had it in his saddlebags. When I heard the announcer, I left Jason to guard the cardboard and candy bars, and moved closer to the starting line. Monty was on a yellow bike in a second tier of seven, each tier having the field to themselves, and so the time he spent waiting for the first bikes to finish and spill around the drums at the end of the track was filled with revving and checking and eyeing his nearby competition. He was third off at the flag, but he took the lead in no time, flying over the grades like a man set free of family and all obligation.

I watched the races for twenty minutes before I realized they were more of same, more of same,

Monty taking first or Monty taking second. The beer was gone where all beer goes quicker than any other beverage, and soon I was standing on my tiptoes looking for the Porta Potti.

Making my way through the crowd, I saw the lady with seventy-two teeth walking away from where the action was. She went down a slope toward a four-foot-high orange plant cluster called sticky monkey flower and a sycamore starter no higher. I looked around again for the toilet. It was some distance off, at the original game site, and had a line of three people in front of it. So I followed the woman, calling, "Looking for a Porta Potti?"

Her gray ponytail flicked around and she smiled widely. "How'd you guess?"

"Me too. I don't want to wait in line. You go on, if you want, I'll stand guard."

"Don't be taking my picture, now."

"Then what'll I have to bribe you with?" I said, and turned and framed my hands at the freeway off in the distance. I thought of Doug Forster snapping pictures off in Carbon Canyon all around Miranda Robertson's charred car.

High cloud cover was drifting in. When it cut off the sun, the air was a lot cooler.

From where I stood I could see the back of the Avalos farm and the white geese strolling. I framed my hands again for a picture that would not take. I noticed for the first time a flat-roofed storage shed hunkered at the far end of the covered pens, the door of the shed slung open.

"Say, you wouldn't have any Kleenex?" Marge called.

" 'Fraid not," I said. Then: "I've got a lot of lint in my pocket."

She laughed and said, "I don't think that'll work,"

then was quiet behind the brush for a while, until I asked, "Where's your friend?"

"Quillard? The shrimp?" She came out stirring her waistband with both thumbs. "Isn't he cute? I knew him three weeks before I realized he was short." Then she winked and said, "I saw him first."

I said, heading toward the tree screen myself, "Jeez, am I really going to pee out here in front of God and everybody?"

"He's the only one won't be surprised," Marge said. "Need some lint?"

"Don't think so," I called, thinking of how I could be friends with this woman easy. Thinking about how she and Quillard fit.

"Watch out for poison oak," she called back. "Indians used to eat it to desensitize themselves so they could work with the branches, you know, make baskets. But I don't think you want to be the first woman on record to try for whatever cure for whatever ails you in that direction. That location, I mean."

"Good advice," I said, and did indeed look around for red leaves. In back of the young sycamore I got busy, and while I was, I asked, "What does he do, your friend?"

"He's unemployed. Aerospace laid him off."

"A lot of that going around. What do you do?"

"I'm a potter. Out by Claremont College. My own shop." When I was coming back up the slope, I stopped for a moment and watched the clouds acrobatting. Marge was watching too. "It can't rain," she said.

Brushing yellow deerweed off me, I looked back over my left shoulder and saw the storage shed door down by the animal pens buck open farther and some little commotion go on at the opening, with, it seemed, boots and legs and shirtbacks struggling to

emerge. The sounds of bikes at start-off again dulled
my hearing, but I thought I heard a human protest,
or perhaps an argument at the shed. And I thought
I saw the man with the silver hair, Quillard, shoot
out backward and jerk back in.

I said, "Your friend is in the shed down there."

"Quillard? What shed? Quillard Satterlee
wouldn't be in any shed. He's got claustrophobia.
He won't even come in my potting house and it's
got a great big wide old door I hardly ever close."

"I thought that was him."

"Uh-uh. Not him." Her sunburn looked so raw I
wondered how she could still be smiling. Making
small talk, we headed back to the assembly. But, curious about what I saw, when we drifted apart in
the crowd, I swung back around toward the slope
to have a second look at the shed. The door was
closed by now, but I looked at the long animal stables, and the puffs of beige sheep in the open pen
beyond them, and decided I needed a walk and a
break from people. On the other side of the ranch
house, near where the goat was tethered and the
geese still bopped about, smoke was rising from a
huge barbecue. The cool air and a new breeze felt
exhilarating as I tramped over dried grasses in my
silly blue boots with white flame insets. I was a million miles away from the lab, and just as many away
from Monty and his minions.

I came to the first stable and was drawn in by little
grunts. On either side of a dirt walkway were sties,
the first one holding maybe twenty piglets all
squished up near the automatic feeder, wasps cir-
cling at the water tube. A pig condo. It had a smell
powerful enough to make me hold my breath. Farther down, though, among the dozing red and black
hulks with giant ears over their eyes, there wasn't
much smell at all. Their pens were clean, only

muddy along a sort of ditch where faucets dripped;
thinking back to the first one, I guessed kids were
pigs all over.

Crossing over to the second building, I looked
ahead to my original destination, the shed, and saw
no one. I stopped to stare at a boar worthy in his
slit-eyed nap of at least one Kodak moment. I falsely
framed, clicked my tongue like a shutter; he winked,
and seemed to be grinning. But farther down the
walkway, the pigs seemed restless. Maybe these
were perturbed by the revving dirt bikes and Harleys or even by the change in weather. Maybe, like
Monty's pigs, they were in breeding season, and I
shouldn't be disturbing them. I proceeded toward
the end to leave.

Nearer the exit, all of them were up and huffing.
Some were chattering their teeth the way my guinea
pig does when I make too much fuss stirring up his
pine shavings. They stood stiff-legged, bristles raised
on their necks like dogs. Their tails were whipping,
and their lips were curled over their tusks in an evil
grin. From the mouths of two black boars came low
barking sounds. Foam dripped. They turned quickly
at my approach, skewering me with a red-eyed
stare. As I quickened my step, I wondered if the
sideboards would hold against single-minded, pork-
barreled purpose.

I was relieved to reach the end, and when I
stepped out, into the fresher air, the sun burst
through a cloud, increasing the brightness of the
storage shed directly ahead of me. At the left quad-
rant of the shed there was a small window, a mere
cutout of board. A gray lizard clung to the edge. I
was going to pass right by and go back to the rally,
but there was a movement in the dark recess of the
window, and I paused, pulled back, and peeked in,
not knowing what I was seeing.

Switchie's light hair is what I recognized first in the shadows. Maybe he and Jolene were in there having a good time. I started to back away, and then I saw more movement by the door I'd seen open when I was looking down from the absent Porta Potti. Something like a long prod hung from Switchie's hand. Then a big man's back mid-distant in the shed blocked my view, and I realized Jolene was probably not there at all.

When the form turned, I saw the belly. And in the space between Paulie's quarter profile and Switchie standing a few feet away, I saw Quillard, his ankles together, his arms behind his back, and in the hole of his mouth a dark plug. He was twisting slowly from the waist first one way and then the other, eyes wide and the whites shining like moons scraped out of raw ice; and sheets of blood pouring from under his silver beard like a vibrant fringed and tasseled prayer shawl.

21

I dropped down, chest on my knees, and looked wildly for a way of escape.

To my right was a three-strand wire fence with a tall row of wild artichoke thistle behind it. Should I dive for it, or make for the corridor where the pigs were still dancing on their toes? My whole body shook. I was afraid I couldn't rise.

"He's spillin' all over the place. God*damn* it!"

"What do you want me to do about it? Next time we off a guy, *you* do it, you think you can do it better."

Paulie again: "Over there. The feed bags. Get 'em. Jesus, I don't want to clean this up."

"Oh, you fat fart, nothin' but whinin'."

I heard a dull thud, maybe not even that—more like a soft *whump*—and I knew the body had fallen.

Darting toward the fence, I saw more room between it and the sties than I thought. About a third of the way down were three rusty fifty-five-gallon drums with blue plastic buckets nested on top of a short stack of deflated feed bags. I made for this small shelter, slipping in a muddy spot as I curled in, and landing hard on my hip.

My breath coming hard, I forced myself to quiet. Forced myself. Think, Smokey, think. You can do anything. You can take anything. Think it through. Off in the distance, on the playing ground for Monty's fellow riders, motorcycles buzzed. I could continue running down the length of stable, but fear once again had me locked. I concentrated. My breathing slowed and the shaking began to still.

Once my mother had taken two wire coat hangers to the backs of my legs. Only seven, I hadn't learned control: I wet the carpet where I stood; the tiny wool loops darkened, and my face burned with shame. Always I hated, when the memory would return, my lack of control, not the beating itself. Terror lasts until the day you simply run out of it, or it runs over you. *They can kill me, but they cannot hurt me.* That's what I learned when a teacher read *Uncle Tom's Cabin* to my class a few years later, some slave or other hopping over the ice floes with dogs at her heels, or someone else having the flesh flayed off his back.

You can do this, I told myself. You can ride over this fear.

Everything came into tight focus: the ribs on the rusty steel drums next to me; the Q-tip–sized knot of spider house attached under the barrel's lip; the crevices of damp earth bearing my boot skid marks; the gray, splintered boards at my shoulder; and my own buffed nails as I touched the steel barrels with the hands Joe called beautiful.

Through the cracks of the stable boards I felt the heat and prickly bristle of a sow as she leaned in near me as if against a common foe. *Huh,* she said, *huh.*

Old girl, I whispered.

I tried to picture the geography of the farm. Was the road Monty and I had taken on the other side of the artichoke embankment? And if so, were there trees, any size, I could run between? When I heard a heavy noise in the shed where the killers were, I thought no more and just jumped for the clearest

separation between the thorny plants. A low strand
of wire tore into my ankle as I flew through, and I
ripped my palm on a barb I hadn't seen. I was afraid
I'd made the wires move. I flattened myself and listened for any sound of pursuit, breathing dust and
the scent of pale weed pressed beneath my cheek.
Above my eye level, a strand of wire neatly bisected
the purest of white cloud, and impaled on a barb
about a yard down was the desiccated body of a
lizard. On another barb bracketed by two purple
thistles was a speared grasshopper, the ghoulish tes-
timonial of the loggerhead strike, a predatory song-
bird called a murdering bird in England and a
butcher-bird here.

Carefully, I crouched through the thistle. When
the plants thinned out, I was relieved to see stands
of pampas grass high as houses, and I knew that in
this country that meant a wash, and on the other
side, probably a road. Maybe I'd make it after all.

Breaking through the pampas stands, I thought for
a moment I should simply hide among them until
dusk. But one thing I learned on patrol in Oakland
is that it *works* to run, the sheer determined brazen-
ness of flight successful too often for the crims *not*
to try it. As I pushed through, the thin, microscopi-
cally serrated leaves rustled like secrets and grabbed
at my clothes like members of a hazing gauntlet.

I raced up an embankment to the road, flagged
down a car driven by a geek wearing a white shirt
and brush cut, and thanked his engineering soul
very much.

Joe picked me up at a hamburger place in Anaheim Hills an hour later. It was almost six o'clock,
and I was doing fine except for being cold even under the denim jacket. I'd been able to order and
drink coffee. My hands hardly shook. Doing just

fine, yes. Until I saw Joe's solid form coming toward me, the silvery halo of hair, the caring eyes.

"Oh, baby," he said. We leaned against a yellow pipe barrier outside. "I didn't mean for you to get into anything like this. This shouldn't have happened. Not at all, not at all."

"It's okay. I'm okay. You were right, Joe. What did I think I was doing?" My throat seemed to cramp and to burn from the cramping. When Joe pulled me to him and his hand cupped my head, it was as though he pressed a button there: I moaned.

"I should have stopped you from going," he said. "We get comfortable, complacent. I should—"

I looked at him, saw there was water in his eyes. "How many units are out?"

"I want to talk to you about that." He said it like a doctor preparing bad news.

"A man just had his throat cut. I *saw* it. What do you mean?"

"There's something else going on. I'll tell you as much as I know, in the car. First we get you out of here. Get you cleaned up, get some disinfectant on this." He turned my hand palm-up.

"Lockjaw might be fun for a while. I haven't done that yet," I said, as I started walking to his car.

"Are we feeling sorry for ourselves?"

"Of course we're feeling sorry for ourselves. What do you think?"

Opening the door, he said, "The captain's waiting for us at the training center. It's on his way home."

"The *captain*'s waiting for me? Plunkett?"

"Hal Exner. Haven't you seen an organization chart lately?"

"I don't pay attention to those things."

"He's the new one in from Missouri."

"What happened to Plunkett?"

"He got promoted, I guess."

"Probably kicked upstairs for feeling up some new patrol," I said.

Before Joe backed the car out, I gave a great shiver. He looked at me with a worried expression and turned up the heater.

"Let's go over everything," he said. "Sharpen everything in your mind before you get there. I won't ask questions, you just talk."

"Give me a moment," I said.

As we ran the freeway, I watched strip malls drift by like boat lamps in a lake of darkness. Joe, his face awash in red from dozens of brake lights, reached over to hold my uninjured hand. When he did, hot tears fled down my cheeks. I didn't even wipe them away.

Finally, I said, "The victim was maybe your age. White hair, white beard, kind of handsome."

"Like me," Joe said.

"Yeah, like you," I said softly. "Only short. Think about that for a minute. Who'd we see lately who had white hair, was short, had dirt bikes in the bed of his truck?"

Joe flicked a glance at me, said nothing.

I went on: "The café, after the campground scene. The little guy with the holster. The killdeer. It was him, Joe. I looked over one time, I was standing with Monty, and the guy was looking back. It was him, I know it was. I think he recognized me. I thought, well, it's a free country, the man can be anywhere he pleases. But it was weird, seeing him twice in a week. I should have trusted that."

Joe said, "What would you have done? Go up to him and say what the hell are you doing here?"

"I don't know. If I had, who knows what?" Anger rising, I said, "He almost had me fooled, that Monty. Talking about his dreams. Talking about his farm, about shooting stars at night."

"Farm?" Joe asked.

And I kept on: "Shooting stars. Some dream girl with jewels in her belly. The creep." I turned and looked at Joe, this man so good, so honest. "Joe, the old man out at the farm—Mr. Avalos—I figured he was a nice old man who'd probably had to put up with stupid, lazy children all his life. His wife is dying of cancer, and I liked him because he wouldn't shake Jolene's hand. But he's got to be a bag of shit too. Or else how could all this go on on his farm, right under his nose? Creep. All creeps."

"Are you worried about Jolene?"

"I'd worry for anyone hanging around a man who can murder as easy as making a sandwich. She's a pisser, but that doesn't mean she deserves someone like Switchie."

"Earlier, were there any other acts of violence? Any fights . . . ?"

"Just a bunch of rubbie drunks with twenty-thousand-dollar bikes they spit on and shine with their shirtsleeves. A few were rowdy. You know— 'Show me your tits,' like that."

"Hm," Joe said. "I should have been there. What kind of drunks you say?"

"Rubbies. Rich urban bikers. Weekend wheelers. Doctors, lawyers, Indian chiefs. So says Monty. But a lot of them looked like beer-bellied, tar-paper shack creeps to me."

"Hey," Joe protested, glancing down, sucking in his belly.

I rubbed it. "There were drugs. Some guy—"

"Tell me where there ain't."

"Monty says he's not a doper. Who cares? He's a piece of shit any way you cut it. Joe?"

"Yeah, babe?"

"The man?" I turned down the noisy heater, then sat back and looked out the side window, got my breath. "He, he, like just kept turning. They sliced him," I said, making a motion at my neck, "and he just kept turning, this way and that, like for an audience to see. I wanted to run up and push it back in. I . . ."

When we reached the training center, Joe patched my palm out of a first aid kit from one of the training classrooms. I was sufficiently recovered to recite the details.

The captain was in a different classroom nearest the outdoor firing range. A two-pane window was open six inches top and bottom through which we could observe moths whipping through the bright funnels formed by the range lights; moths, not butterflies. Captain Exner sat at the desk, Joe and I side by side in folding chairs at its corner.

I told the captain how I saw Quillard Satterlee die, his hands and feet bound and something dark stuffed in his mouth, and as I told it, saw again a splash of scarlet hit his slackening knees, saw again the eyes, the eyes.

I told the captain how we'd seen this man in a café after coming from a scene investigation off Ortega Highway. And then suddenly, out of nowhere, I told him, "There's a weird wire at the Avalos ranch." I could feel Joe looking at me, and when I didn't get a response from the captain, I described the wire: barbs a couple inches apart, then up- and down-turned like a thin snake trying to find direction. "Not your regular barbed wire," I said, "different. Joe and I, we found some strange wire, too. It was ten miles from the campground, but I don't know, it caught my attention, and there was duct tape in the trash too, like on the victim, his hands and feet, and the victim had wire embedded in his neck, broken off. Dr. Schaffer-White said. I mean, this wire—"

Joe interrupted, gave a recounting; same facts, calmer tone.

"The same wire as on the victim?"

"Not the same exactly," I said.

"Then why are we talking about this?"

"I guess I don't know now myself, sir."

He looked at me blankly.

Joe said, "She's been through a lot."

Then the captain hit me with the questions I wasn't quite prepared for. "Why is it you were with this crowd to begin with, Smokey?" No one had clued him in.

He was a man in his mid-forties, brown over hazel, a packed one-eighty pounds on a six-foot frame, with a lean and canny hardness in his face that looked like he should be arguing cases before a court. I'd seen him around before but never wanted to get to know him. He was too physically perfect for my taste, too sure of himself, bound to have too many ambitions for my comfort. In other words, out of my league but without my regrets.

Cautiously, I began to tell him about the Carbon Canyon case, the charred car there and the remnant of human being within who might be my brother's ex-wife.

At some merciful point, he stopped me and said, "I'm aware of some of this case, Smokey. And I'm aware that you're working as a model at a lingerie bar in Garden Grove."

Surprised, I said, "You are?"

He nodded like a tolerant principal. Folding his hands, he asked, "Are you accepting money for this activity?"

"It's not a real job, sir."

"Have you accepted money for this at all?"

"I'm aware that an employee of the sheriff-coroner's department shall not engage in any conduct that would bring discredit to the dignity of law enforcement, sir. This is not a second job. This is a personal concern in which I felt I could—"

"Be an investigator," he said, completing my sentence.

"This is an assignment, sir. Stu Hollings. My supervisor," I said, explaining further. "The fact is, I saw a murder. Whether I was dancing my way halfway to Bakersfield in a tutu collecting quarters on the way, what matters is a man was murdered today, and I *saw* him murdered. Why aren't we talking about that?" I looked at him, and then at Joe, and back at him.

He seemed amused. "Consider your extra earnings hazardous duty pay. That's all I wanted to tell you. Now tell me about Blackman."

Joe's expression now was one I'd become accustomed to, the one that said you may be a silly lump of foolishness but you're my own.

I said, "Blackman does metal and paint work on motorcycles when he's not operating a bar where men take their new secretaries to test how far they can slide their hands up their dresses before they holler. He's got felony priors for assault and firearms. Off parole, but he's probably had his hands in criminal activity since he could toddle over to his daddy's pants and pick out the wallet. He was a starting place for us," I said, "and after today it seems like it was the right one to start from. It was his two crappy friends who did it."

In the background guns were going off in rounds of threes, cops practicing one to the head, two to the heart. The classroom door opened and a deputy came in, excused himself, and gathered some booklets from a table. As he swung the door open to

leave, we watched a formation of National Guards-
men in camouflage greens and carrying rifles cut
squarely around the yard.

When I looked back, the captain asked, "What
else?"

"Blackman's slick," I said. "In his own way,
charming. He could be a preacher or a carny. He's
quiet and he's talkative, you never know which
you'll get. He'll put you down one minute and build
you up the next. He's . . . handsome, like an actor."
I glanced at Joe, who was studying the floor. "Ar-
mand Assante with a beard," I said. "No tattoos that
I could see, no metal studs in his tongue."

"Thank God for small pleasures," Joe said.

"One of the other models says he has a lot of girlfriends, but I haven't seen any."

"What else?" the captain asked.

"Am I missing something? What else do you
want?"

"Just keep talking. What else did you learn about
Monty Blackman?"

"Downey High School. Sounds like he was raised
by his mother. Seems to treat his employees all right.
Came on to me, but that was part of the plan, right?"

"That was part of your plan," the captain cor-
rected.

I ignored that and plunged on, almost trancelike.
"He drives a dark Volvo, older, but I've seen him in
a white pickup too. Likes cowboy music. Made me
go dancing with him one night after work."

"Uh-huh. And what else?"

"He races bikes and raises pigs. That's about it.
Oh—except for one thing: He knows people who slit
other people's throats."

"Let's talk about that."

"Again?"

"A last name for this Switchie?" the captain asked.

"D'Antonio," I said.

"D'Antonio. And he's blond."

"He probably doesn't like pasta, either."

Loud volleys of high-caliber semiautomatics reverberated in rapid succession, so surprising in their fury the three of us turned our faces to the window. In the hollow silence afterward, the training officer's voice ground through. "Shoot to stop," he said, "not to kill. Shoot to *stop*. Keep that in your mind and vocabulary and you come out clean in an OI review." By OI, he meant officer-involveds, shootings requiring high scrutiny by the department before they undergo the same by the public.

Captain Exner got up and slid both windows closed. The suit he wore grabbed a glow from the outside lights. His shoes gleamed as though wet. He came around to the front of the desk and sat down on its edge, dropping his hands between his knees. His voice was softer, and at the same time, grave. "Now I'm going to let you two in on a little something. You tripped over an ongoing investigation by the U.S. Customs Service. They're looking at Morris Blackman."

"You're kidding," I said.

"I'm not kidding, and we can hold the congratulations."

"I trashed it, you're trying to tell me?" I asked, scared for the worst.

"Customs? What kind of operation?" Joe said.

"All I know myself," the captain said, "is that it has something to do with smuggling contraband. FBI's in on it too. FBI's everywhere these days." He looked at me and said, "Did you see anything smacked of a meth lab?"

"Nothing like that. Small-time drugs, that's it."

Joe said, "I heard meth's going crazy out in Riverside."

"They set up clandestine labs in house trailers. That county's so full of trailer trash," the captain said, "they're imposing special taxes and adding all sorts of get-out-of-town ordinances for trailer owners. You said Blackman has a farm out there?"

"Yes, but he wouldn't take me out there because his pigs were breeding, and strangers disturb them."

"That may be it then," Joe said. "He's got himself a good little lab out there."

"Maybe." Captain Exner went around to sit in the desk chair again, then turned to me. He waited a long moment as if he were determining my sentence on the spot. Then he said, "We're thinking of letting you stay on as you were. As long as you are sure you haven't been compromised." He pulled out a charcoal-colored box of Indiana Slims and flipped up the top.

"I don't think I have. I'm going to have a problem explaining my absence, though."

He tapped out a cigar and said, "You'll think of something. You're in, you should stay in."

"But we should have evidence people out there *now*," I said.

"You just find out what they did with the body. That's your evidence." He offered the box to Joe. "Rum-dipped," he said. "Top blend."

"I gave up smoking two years ago," Joe said. "I've got arthritis, glaucoma, flea bites, and a bum finger where I dropped my weights on it. That's what happens when you give up your vices."

Captain Exner smiled, and before he closed the box, thought twice about it and offered it in my direction. When I shook my head no, he said, "I thought maybe that's why they call you Smokey."

"No such luck," I said, but didn't elaborate.

He lit up with an ornately engraved silver lighter, and I thought of the fancy work on Monty Blackman's tanks. The scent was pleasant and curiously relaxing.

"I'll have customs by in the morning. We'll find out what's what, if I have to get the undersheriff himself down here. If this clears okay, we'll three come up with a story about why you left the party. You suddenly remembered a date with your mother. You forgot and left the iron on. Now, you *can* say no. Nobody's going to commit you to something you think you can't deal with."

"I can handle it."

He picked a folder off the desk that I had noticed before but thought nothing of. Glancing at the top paper, he said, "You were an officer. You saw both jail and patrol in Oakland, is that right?"

"Correct."

"You've been in investigations here for—"

"Almost six years," I said.

"I also see you were involved in a shooting last year in Nevada."

"Yes, sir, I was."

He looked at me a long time, studying me, figuring me. "How'd that all come down?"

"Briefly, I had a situation and I shot to stop. The offender came after me with a pipe. A full report is in my file."

The captain moved the corners of the papers with one finger. "You're okay with all that?"

"I've been to work every day the department would let me since the incident, except for a few days' vacation. I say 'every day the department would let me' because they did require some time off while I participated in psychological evaluations."

"You terminated the counseling, didn't you?" The captain had read more of my file than I realized.

I said, "I did."

"You felt you didn't need it?"

"I felt the sessions were a waste of time, to tell the truth. The psychologist was a woman who was convinced no woman could take a life without extreme damage to her psyche. I'm sorry, but I'm impatient with that."

The slightest smile appeared on the captain's face. He fished out the lighter again, put his thumb on the lid, and paused as if about to say something, but didn't.

"Seeing a man get his throat cut is not an everyday occurrence for me, Captain. I'm tired and I'm upset. But tomorrow's another day. I'll do what I have to. Wouldn't you?"

"If we get you killed," he said, "it's bad for our morale. But if you wind up shooting somebody, it's bad for our reputation and you, my dear, are looking at a very early retirement. Think you can keep your pistol in your pocket?"

"How do you manage yours?" I said.

He turned his profile to us, flipped the flame on, and drew on the cigarillo, his eyes squinting or smiling, I wasn't sure which.

22 Joe slipped his arm around me as we walked to the parking lot leaving the training center and Captain Exner. The air had turned warm, and now my jacket seemed heavy.

"You did fine in there," Joe said.

We passed the trash bin with the large white sign announcing DO DRUGS, DO TIME.

"I babbled," I said.

"You did fine."

Between the blasts of gunfire could be heard the purring song of the lesser nighthawk, its vocals ending in *chuck-chuck-chuck*. Major events can be taking place in your life, and you will still hear the sounds of a bird and mentally say its name, or catch the scent of peanut butter and recall the decal on your third grade lunch box.

And when I heard the bird, I thought of the bay and its carnival of life, and home, and felt overwhelmingly tired. "Joe," I said, "maybe I can't do this thing with Monty. Maybe I'll fuck it up. Say something to blow the whole thing. The whole thing—I don't even know what it *is*. What am I supposed to be doing out there? I can tell you this and not worry you're going to panic, right? I'm just having some self-doubts."

By his car now, I stood waiting for him to unlock his door. Under the yellow parking lot lights, the cars burned with a brilliant wet sand. Joe stopped what he was doing and came around to my side.

A car pulled in with its windows down, Del Shannon on the radio, singing about his run-run-run-run runaway.

Joe held me, saying, "Asking me not to worry is like asking me not to breathe."

The oldies lover parked two spaces down, and got his bag of weaponry out of the trunk and strolled to the center, white sneakers flashing.

Weapon fire began again, but now cushioned by the roof-high earth berm striped on our side with newly planted groundcover. As Joe held me there, the rumbled percussion of simultaneous rapid-fires was oddly comforting, like a big man softly snoring.

When we got to my place, Joe said he'd fix me a drink if I told him where it was. "Nothing," I said. "Oh well, maybe tea. Is that okay?"

"You're the one whose reality needs changing," he said. "But it is."

"I want a shower."

"Do it. I'll be here."

In the shower I let the water wash away the day, hearing the TV in the living room, and I stayed what seemed a long while. At the last moments I stood directly under the flow with my eyes closed and face upturned, until pictures flashed in my mind and the warm drench seemed to turn to blood. I shut off the water, toweled, ran a wide comb through my hair, then put on a gray knit T-shirt that comes to my knees, and walked into the living room.

Joe was still there, as he promised. He'd taken off his jacket but not the tie, and was in the midst of setting down two mugs with tea tags trailing down the sides. He'd turned off the TV and put on music, the soft kind. Curling onto the couch, I stretched to kiss his cheek, liking the grit of it.

"Toast? Crumpets?" he asked.

"Anyone ever tell you," I said, "you're wonderful?"

"Not lately."

"Well, don't believe them if they do."

He reached down and gently brought both my ankles up and placed them on his lap, pivoting me as I held the cup. At the side of his face near the eyes, soft creases formed and released. That simple sight made my eyes fill. I drank the hot tea and said nothing.

"Hey, buckaroo," he said, imitating John Wayne. "How about when this is over us gettin' out of town for a while?" When I nodded without comment, he said, his tone changed, "What can I do to get you to stop thinking about it?"

"Joe, do you figure everybody's ghost hangs around for a while, or just some people's?"

"What's going on in there?" he asked, looking at my forehead.

"Haven't you ever lost someone and you just feel they're still around afterward?"

"You know what that is," he said solemnly.

"Wishful thinking," I admitted. "You've seen people die, Joe?"

"A few."

"Where?"

"Hospitals. Emergency rooms. One guy in a race car. We were talking to him, normal-like, got him out and everything. Then he just died."

"These people, were they looking at you, do you think, when they died? Were they looking at you, or just off in the distance?"

His hand fit across my ankles, as if they were two rolling pins trying to get away. He said, "Maybe it was the light." He checked for reaction. "You know, they were looking at the bright light."

"Take it another way," I said, swinging free of his lap and walking to where I could look out over the black bluffs of the bay against a royal sky. "Be the murderer," I said.

I turned to see him now sunk into the pillow in the corner of the couch as a man might who's ready to watch the news, only tireder than most; a man with hard things on his mind.

"You're a killer," I said. "You get up in the morning, bathe, eat, call a girlfriend. Joe, do you figure once you've murdered someone, anything else matters? Do you figure anything could ever break your heart? You could get mad, sure. Be disappointed. Ah, but . . . could you ever cry? Would anything ever delight you? Once you've found you can deliberately, methodically kill someone, are you a human being?"

He got up and came to me, taking the cup from my hand and putting it on the lamp table. "What can I do, baby?" He put both hands on my shoulders. "Let me stay with you."

I didn't mean to be cruel. I said, "You can if you want. Either way," then went to the couch and sat again, the shirt over my knees so I became a big gray boulder.

He came to sit beside me and ran his finger along the back of my neck. The CD stopped at the end of the last track. The first song played again, a song so slow in its tenderness that I took Joe's hand and held it to my chest. In a second tears fled down my face. I said a thing I seldom do: I love you.

Joe tipped my head to his shoulder. We were two people in a darkened theater, looking out at a slice of moonlit bay. On the bluffs to the north were the homes of the wealthy strung along streets named

Galaxy, Constellation, Northern Star, and Evening Star. Their lights bleached the bulrushes, swept over the sleepless nightjars and the brown-headed cowbirds, the small-time burglars now busy in the shadows rustling nests from other birds. And I wondered which of those homes on the bluffs this night harbored distracted hearts, and which would, in the early hours, summon the lonely wail of sirens, and which of their inhabitants would prove the best and worst of human impulse.

She was slapping me with the flat of the big knife. My legs stung like a family of bees.

When I'd come in, her back was to me at the sink. *Where have you been, young lady?*

I'd left the curtain next to the lamp, and the shade off the lamp because I needed a lot of light to trace something before I went to school, and the wallpaper was all burned now, and *just how are you going to pay for it, sister?*

I said, I'll save, I'll sell my bike, just *don't*!

When she yanked me, the belt tore off my dress, and when she threw me across the chair it almost tipped over, and I kept thinking how my nose would hurt if I fell face first and the chair crashed. Where her fingernails scraped it burned real bad. I had my eyes squished shut because I could just *see* the knife coming, swish, sting, swish, sting. And then she whapped me and I didn't breathe. I clenched my teeth. I hummed like a bee. In the end, I begged.

When I took my dress off, I softly laid it in the wastebasket. I dabbed at my legs with toilet paper and put on jeans and lay on my stomach and thought about what I did. When I got ready for bed that night and took off my jeans, they barely stuck at all.

I felt Joe beside me before I even opened my eyes. I listened to his breath, then squinted at him as he lay swirled on the deep-green sheets, stomach down, a boy asleep on a summer lawn. An eye opened. He rolled halfway over, blinked hard, yawned, and said, "What time is it?" Then, tenderly: "Are you my fairy godmother or did I just get real, real lucky?"

While I was feeding Motorboat, the phone rang. I asked Joe to get it. He came back and said, "We're wanted at headquarters. The customs guy is in."

"So early?"

Joe swallowed one of my giant vitamin pills, rinsed his coffee cup in the sink, and said, "I think you lit a line of gasoline, sweetheart."

"Who was it called?"

"Captain Exner."

"Cheesh. He say anything?"

"Yeah, he said, 'This is Hal Exner.' "

"No, silly. I mean about your being here."

"He's a smart boy. He figured it out."

I got dressed quickly, but when I went to plug in earrings, I kept dropping them, the gold hoops bouncing on the dresser top.

Joe stood smoothing himself before the mirror that was too low for him and cut off his head.

"I've got one of your shirts, from the cleaners. You left it when we went to the beach."

"The gray stripe? I wondered where that went."

"You've got a bit of a beard. Want a razor?"

"Nah," he said. "I need some character, don't you think? After all, I don't smoke rum-dipped Indianas."

While he changed, I looked at my answering machine and found that Nathan had called. "Sammi, call me," he said; that's all. I phoned him back, though it was only about seven. He sounded awake.

"I've been trying to get you," he said.

"You found out something?"

"The question is, have *you* found out anything?"

"I can't say we're any closer, no."

"What are you people doing down there? You *do* anything down there?"

"Oh," I said, "drink beer, play cards. The cops crawl in, the cops crawl out, the cops play pinochle on your snout."

He said, surprising me, "I don't know why I do that to you. Suppose that's why I've had four wives?"

"Could be you're getting a clue."

"Jesus, doesn't anybody in California use a rake? Everywhere I go there's a leaf blower."

I heard the racket now in the background.

"Buzz and blow, that's all they do. Look, I found out her husband's booked to go to Beijing next week."

"As in China? He has some kind of medical thing going on over there?"

"He flies Saturday, that's all I know," Nathan said. "If he's going somewhere, why isn't he going to Italy, to see his wife?"

"People take separate vacations, who knows? How'd you find out Dr. Robertson was going?"

"Hired a guy. My lawyer has an investigator he uses. That's not all. He ran an asset check on the good doctor. He's making frequent money transactions under ten thousand dollars."

"So it doesn't have to be reported to the IRS."

"Right. I'd like to know why. The amount of money going through this guy, he could buy his own island in the Caymans."

"He's a doctor, Nathan. What do you expect, he's poor? The P.I., he's licensed?"

"Don't worry about it. Look, I know I'm a jerk some of the time."

"Is this still my endearing brother?"

"But, Sammi? Let's not let this guy off the hook so soon, huh? You're still checking?"

"I don't see Detective Fedders every day. But I'll lean on it."

It sounded as if he might be holding the receiver away, looking out the window maybe, at the leaf blower culprits. "Fine," he said, and I knew it wasn't.

"Hard as it is for you to believe this, Nathan, this isn't our only case. Things just take—"

"I say her name. I say her name all day in my mind. Yesterday on the phone I called my secretary Miranda. I called her Miranda, this woman who doesn't even look like her."

"I'm sorry, Nathan."

"I just want to look in her face and ask why. Jesus, I want to just *see* her. She's here with us, Sammi. She's not gone, I know it."

"I'll be in touch, honest, I will."

"For your old grumpy brother."

"For me, Nathan, and maybe, if you're good, I'll include you."

When I hung up, I felt as helpless as ever. I'd go back out to the farm. I'd go back and model for Monty. Whatever it took.

Joe was standing with one hand on the doorknob, a question on his face. I said, "Nathan."

"Still torn up?"

I nodded, got my keys, shut off a lamp. "It's a wonder Les Fedders didn't run a check on *him*. But then, Les sort of *does* play pinochle all day, doesn't he?"

"You're hard on him. Les is not a bad guy."

"I didn't say he was. I just said I don't like him."

"Anyway," Joe said. "He didn't need to run a check on Nathan. I did."

23 When we arrived at the captain's, this time not in a classroom at the training center but at his office in Santa Ana, the heavy aroma of doughnuts hung in the air and there were two filter loads of coffee grounds in the wastebasket already, indicating the captain and the customs agent had been there awhile.

She was a woman whose rear could cover three chairs. Her face was ruddy and her hair ash-brown. Under a nubby cream cardigan she wore a black dress patterned with beige and white swoops. She'd be the person who'd be planning the next VFW dance, or the one with the pencil behind her ear, counting retail stock. Not a customs agent. She sat on a squeaky, vinyl two-person couch with her tablet on one knee.

As Captain Exner made introductions, there was a pleasantness in her face and a steadiness in her yellow-brown eyes: U.S. Customs Service Special Agent Christine Vogel, he said, operating out of the Office of the Resident Agent in Charge, Orange County. "You saw a man murdered yesterday?" she asked.

"I did."

Joe, in a chair at a slight angle to mine, crossed his legs in my direction.

I recounted what happened in the storage shed.

Quietly, she asked, "Did you know this man?"

"I knew his name. Quillard Satterlee."

"Can you tell me . . ." she said, and stopped. "How would you describe the murdered man?"

"Maybe five five, my height. A hundred and fifty. White hair and beard."

Agent Vogel was not writing.

"He had a friend," I said, "a woman named Marge. Late forties, kind of big."

Captain Exner, silent all this while behind his desk, in his yellow-flowered tie and impeccable brown suit, said, "We ran what we had on Ralph D'Antonio—Switchie. Comes up clean on NCIC. Paul Avalos has one bust for morphie, was on the street in six hours. Completed probation. That's all we have on him."

"It won't be for long," Agent Vogel said. Then she asked me, "Was Morris Blackman there at the time of the murder?"

"Not in the shed."

"Too bad." She folded her tablet. I glanced at Joe, puzzled by her remark.

"Agent Vogel's working on a task force investigating transport of contraband," the captain put in. "Morris Blackman is a primary suspect."

Gravely, she said, "Quillard Satterlee was one of ours."

"Oh man," I said.

Joe put his head down and pinched the bridge of his nose.

"His real name was Bernie Williams. I didn't know him personally because he was new out from D.C., but it's a small world: I know his mother. We play in the same Scrabble tournaments. It wouldn't hurt me any to see this Blackman *and* all his buddies get thirty days in the electric chair."

"We must be talking big green here," Joe said. "Just what is this operation?"

"It's not the value of the operation. It's about betrayal. You can understand: It disorders their sense of things." Head down, eyes at the tops of their sockets, she leaned forward. "Working undercover," she said, "is like walking on quicksand over hell."

I thought of my narrow escape, and as immediately felt it didn't seem so important at all. I was safe, that's all it meant. Bernie Williams was dead.

"Bernie was supposed to be a courier for the operation," she said. "There was another mule too. We don't have his name. This second courier wanted Bernie—Quillard—to come with him on a money pickup because *he* was suspected of ripping off the operation. Except Bernie came down with a giant case of food poisoning, and while he was puking pizza in his motel room Paul Avalos was on his way up to see him. Bernie had the door cracked for air. Fatal mistake. He told us yesterday Avalos might've overheard his conversation to us. We think that's why he was killed."

"You haven't said what kind of contraband you think Blackman's delivering," I said. "Dope?"

"We believe he exports precursors to Mexico and South America," she said, precursors being the special chemicals needed to process drugs for street use and high profit. "He's too smart to run a lab himself. They're death kitchens. Blow up all the time."

"A light switch can set that stuff off," Joe said.

"We don't have the complete routing yet," she went on. "We wanted to acquire the route, get the folks on the other end. That's what Bernie was doing for us."

"A guy at the rally asked Monty for drugs," I said. "He sent him on his way to see Switchie. He acted like he wanted nothing to do with it."

Agent Vogel thought a minute and then said, "You know why they call it crank? Biker gangs used to cook it up in their crank cases. Now any butthead can do it in a motel bathtub. A lot of your kingpins won't even smoke a mooter. So don't let that fool you."

"Somehow I have a problem thinking of Blackman as a kingpin," I said. "I'm not defending him, he just seems too busy to be involved in a big operation."

Agent Vogel shifted heavily, glanced over at the doughnut box, then stood, taking the guest coffee mug with her, a black one marked with gold numbers: 381. The numbers referred to the penal code provision relating to the possession and ingestion of the toxic chemical toluene, which, in Captain Exner's eyes, passes for office coffee. She refueled at the coffee maker, then crossed to Captain Exner's desk and poured for him too, unfettered by feminist roles.

"He's a genuine multitalent, this Blackman," she said. She set the pot back in its well and paused to scan the remaining doughnuts in the box. Not taking one, she faced us then, the whole imposing bulk of her solidly confident, mothering, and smelling slightly of floral perfume. "There's another outbound we want him for," she said. "Pig semen. Illegal export of pig semen."

A man died at the Canadian border last year trying to smuggle bull semen, she said. "You think this isn't big business? It is," Agent Vogel said. She settled again onto the couch, moving her hands as if conducting some unseen orchestra. "This guy at the border was a real Rhodes scholar. The port-of-entry agent was asking him the normal stuff, nothing fancy, when what does the idiot do but accelerate through with his Styrofoam ice chest bouncing on the floorboards. Some cowboy in a

Previa ran him off the road head-on into a pine tree. Turns out he was a twenty-two-thousand-a-year laundromat owner, but guess what? He had records in his apartment showing a fifty-thousand-dollar profit in two years from, yo-ho, 'transportation services.'"

"Wait now," Joe said, lacing his fingers over his knee and casting a look at the ceiling with a look that said he was being goofed on. "He smuggles pig semen and precursors, that right?"

"Can I help it," Christine Vogel said, "if he's an entrepreneur? Listen, we get weirder cases than this every day. Come by my office sometime." She said it without irritation, just fact.

Joe's hands went up in a Who, me? gesture. "Oh, I'm not doubting you, nuh-uhh." But he grinned.

She patted her dress into place on her lap. "In 1983," she said, "a Texas boar sold for *fifty-six thousand dollars*, and you can bet it wasn't for his bacon. Fourteen billion sperm in a single shot, Number One Big Daddy of Pig Daddies."

Speechless, the two men sat looking at each other. Joe said, "I can do that."

We laughed, and I realized it was the first time in what seemed like a very long time.

"We think Blackman's shipping stuff off his farm to the Philippines," Christine said. "Pork producers are after a disease-resistant, lean pig, and if they can cut corners on development, all to the better. Never fear, U.S. meat producers steal genetic technology too. Unfortunately, government agencies have a tendency to bump into each other. We've got the departments of Ag and Commerce who'd have interest in this kind of transport, we've got the FDA's APHIS—that's Animal, Plant, and Health Inspection Service—and even Treasury, for taxes and tariffs. And us."

"And now us," Captain Exner said. He was resting on his forearms, wagging his handsome head. From that position, he changed, put an elbow on the desk and curled a finger over his mouth, and I knew he didn't quite know what he was going to do with this situation, and was waiting for Christine to lay it all out.

I said, "So what is it, exactly, that you want *me* to do?" looking between Agent Vogel and the captain.

"We want you to hang near Blackman," she said. "We want you to stick with the creeps who killed Bernie Williams." She looked at Exner as if expecting either objection or a nod of strong support.

"What if someone saw me out there? I mean, I don't think anyone did, but—"

"Call him up," she said. "You have to give him a reason for splitting, right? Do that, and listen to his tone. The way he talks. You'll be able to figure it out." The pillows of her body moved with grace.

"What if," I said, hesitantly, "he doesn't know about the murder?"

"If he doesn't know about the murder," Captain Exner said, "he's too dumb to run an operation like Agent Vogel's talking about."

Joe said, "What kind of backup are we giving her?"

"She'll have what she needs, of course."

Christine said, "I'd like you back out there as soon as possible."

"The farm? Why?" I felt my breath come shorter.

"We have to know what they did with the body," she said, and then dropped her gaze.

"Keep an eye out for newly turned earth," the captain said. "There's a good chance, even with everything going on out there, they stashed it on the property."

"Don't underestimate the stupidity of creeps," Christine said. "Besides, it's familiar ground. They could be more afraid of being seen by moving it. We just need somebody up close and personal."

Joe said, almost apologizing, "You may be able to get physical evidence. The knife. Bindings."

I was quiet but thinking, How am I going to bag anything? Put on my rubber gloves and bag bloody feed sacks, haul out my tape and say, Excuse me, Paulie, while I just run a measure here, okay?, and by the way, will you hand me that blade?, I have to hang an evidence tag on it. My silence must have told.

"If you get out there," Joe said, "and these guys are there and acting the least bit hinky, leave." He looked at the captain then, for contradiction, but didn't get any.

The captain said, "We'll have plainclothes out. Repairmen, feed suppliers, somebody. Just keep us informed as to when you're going back."

"What's my excuse for showing up?"

"Say you lost your wallet. You got suddenly sick, couldn't find him, left without your wallet. Bring one you can plant if you need to. If that doesn't work, say you guess somebody lifted it. How are you at lying?"

Agent Vogel's face showed the slightest amusement when I answered, "I passed the department polly for the background investigation okay." She set her coffee on the corner of the captain's desk next to her while she dipped into each pocket of her sweater. Then she bent over for her tiny hard-leather, metal-studded purse that looked like she lifted it off her teenage daughter, and poked inside for a moment, saying, "I'm out of cards, but for one." She handed it to me. "Call me if you need to. Anything at all."

"Don't carry that with you," the captain said. "Memorize it."

"Good plan," Christine said, checking her watch, and while sitting there for another five minutes, managing somehow to always be in motion.

24 When Joe and I left Captain Exner's, I was awash in images, concerns, and confusions, and remained silent most of the way back. Joe hoped to cheer me up by giving commentary on a new lunch place nearby. At the hallway where we split off to go to our separate offices, Joe said, "All this because your brother has interesting taste in women. Do you ever think whatever you're doing at a given moment in time will have great significance downstream?"

"I try never to think at all," I said.

"You're trying to sell me swampland, baby."

"It's just real hard," I said, "to imagine how Miranda Robertson could figure in all this. The *only* connection to anything is that she by mere chance knows Monty Blackman. We smooge up to Blackman and find all this other stuff."

"That *was* her car in the canyon," Joe said. "She still has some explaining to do, if she's alive to do it. But that does seem a whole different horse, doesn't it?"

"Jolene told me one of Monty's girlfriends was named Miranda. She didn't know any more than that and I didn't have time to ask."

"Back to square one, then, aren't we? Listen, hon," he said, stepping nearer, "are you going to be all right today?"

"Sure."

"Don't go anywhere, now, without backup. Wait till Captain Exner—"

"Right now I'm going to go hide under my desk," I said, "and not come out."

"I'll come too."

"Get to work, you slouch," I said.

I didn't have to go to my desk, but I did. I was relieved to find nothing urgent needing to be worked on, but for a moment wondered how much effect I had in the lab's scheme of things, since there wasn't work piled on my desk.

Pulling out my sketch pad I began mapping what I remembered of the Avalos farm, the stables, and the shed. But I couldn't concentrate, and I kept going over and over the images from yesterday, kept going back to the pigs huffing and chattering in their pens; the murkiness in the shed and then the horror; thistle weaving against clouds; and barbed wire shish-kebobbed with dead things.

I got up and walked downstairs to Property and asked the clerk for evidence sent over from Dr. Schaffer-White on the Blue Jay case. He brought out a sack, and I opened it and dumped the section of wire on a piece of white paper on his desk. A metal strip of shark's teeth. A broken wire hooked through a drilled hole in the end, somebody's dream of a choker. It was like one of the pieces Joe and I found in the trash barrel. I asked the clerk, "Ever see anything like that before?"

"Nope," he said, brushing his chin with a thumb. "What is it?"

"A not-very-successful weapon of destruction. We found it on somebody's neck."

"Yuck."

I asked if he had a Polaroid, and he opened a drawer and took out a camera and let me take a picture of the piece with a ruler next to it for reference. I thanked him, left, and walked the half block over to the library and looked up "wire" on the computer index.

The screen was black with orange letters, and my eyes weren't focusing well. Only sixteen hours ago I'd been witness to a gruesome murder, and here I was in the sanctuary of a library, civilization all around.

I printed out the first level of book titles, thinking I'd file it and come back when I wasn't so tired and when I didn't have Monty on my mind, knowing I'd have to call him, and then I hit the wrong key to exit and got another level of menu, and a book title jumped out at me as if it read my mind: *The "Bobbed Wire" Bible.*

Quickly, I wrote down the call number and went in search. Positive that it would be just my luck that this branch wouldn't have the book, I searched the shelves anyway, and there it was. Tan, softcover, printed by Cow Puddle Press, Sunset, Texas. I went to a table in the corner and started turning pages. Hundreds of drawings of wire, in brown ink, with names and patent dates under them, filled the pages.

I found Les in a room at the lab with a tech at a comparison microscope. The tech was a young man who never said much, and out of his lab coat looked like he spent all his spare time trying out for power-lifting championships.

"Smokey," Les said, "how's it going? You lightened your hair. It was redder."

"Red doesn't hold very well."

"Go natural, like me."

"What do we have new on the Carbon Canyon?"

"Records on the mammo-whammy."

"The what?"

"The mammogrammy. Boob-tube prints on your very-ex-sister-in-law. Now don't take offense. You're a pretty good egg, you know that? She's a good egg," he said to the tech, who looked embarrassed as he set aside a broken screwdriver he'd been examining. "Dr. Robertson was good enough to get me a report in no time at all."

"You mean Miranda *did* have implants?"

"That's right," Les said with a gleam in his eye.

I couldn't believe it. That meant Nathan *knew* when I asked him, and he didn't tell. Maybe he encouraged her; maybe he liked her big knockers. And it meant the body in the horrible fire was Miranda for sure. I didn't let Les Fedders know what I was feeling. I just said, "Can I see the report?"

"Come on down to my digs."

In an empty office the investigators use when they're in the lab, Lester lifted the briefcase he'd stashed between a desk and the wall and extracted a clasp envelope. He slid out several stapled pages. "Pictures from *Penthouse*," Les said. "Here we are."

There were no pictures. Only a written statement by a plastic surgeon. I barely had the pages in my hand before Les was around behind me, leaning over my shoulder and tapping with one long, knobby finger on the word "silicone." "She had silicone. It makes a mess in the crematoriums. Remember, the woman in the car had only a little melted plastic. The woman in the car is not Miranda Robertson. Oingo-boingo."

"Les, this is wonderful!"

"Not for Miss Crispy Critter, it isn't." He moved

back a decent distance and when I turned, he was standing with one knuckle on the edge of the desk, looking like a thin and haggard Kewpie doll.

"Thanks for this, Les."

He came forward and took the papers back from me. "Hey," he said, "I missed you at the pigout we had for Turrell's b-day Friday."

"Have you ever seen me at one of those things?"

"I will, someday."

"You're a real missionary, Les."

"I try."

"What about the dentals again?"

"Oh," he said, unflapping another envelope and slipping out a paper with a map of teeth predrawn in red ink, on which a dentist would notate wherever cavities were filled, crowns awarded, roots tunneled, or appliances screwed. The open red mouth for Miranda's chart was free of marks. "Like I said, this woman has her teeth cleaned, nothing more," he said. "One of those God-given mouths that can gnaw billiard balls."

"How close is Meyer Singer to coming up with anything, do you know?"

"Meyer takes his own good time. By the way, he goes to my church. I didn't even know that. Our church is so big. You been there? Crystal Cathedral?"

I shook my head no. "Now I have something for you," I said. I took out the book on barbed wire I had slipped in my jacket pocket and turned to item number 494: Textile Carding Wire. I put the snapshot down next to it. "Wire on the Blue Jay victim." I slid another Polaroid down beside it that I'd taken of the wire roll found in the trash barrel and that I'd stopped back at Property to get. "Wire Joe and I brought in."

Skeptically, Les looked at them and at me, and said, "Okay-y?"

"I'll get back to you," I said brightly, no time or inclination to tell him about yesterday. Let Joe do it. "Just thought you'd like to know. Thanks again for the good work on the med charts."

"Anytime," he said, hands in both pockets, feet splayed, big ears backlit by a beam of sunlight cutting in from the window.

My boss was around wanting to talk before noon, and I had to go over everything anyway, because he'd heard some of it from Captain Exner.

"I need to go home," I said. "I expect Blackman to be calling."

"You go do whatever is required," Stu said. "Just be careful and observe procedure."

"You bet," I said, and left knowing which caution was the more important to Stu Hollings, company man.

When I got to the house, Motorboat was shrieking. I'd left that morning without giving him milk. Muzzle up, sniffing, his little buck teeth barely showing, he stopped pipping when I came near. He looked so darned cute. "Poor little baby! Twenty-four hours since you had milk warmed and hand-delivered. I got busy, little guy." I reached to scratch behind his floppy ears and he let me, unblinking. Then in a flash he whacked at me with his hard teeth, not so much of a bite as a warning, then fled to the hollow log. When I tried grabbing him from the front as he huddled there, he scooted back faster than I could react, and I said, "The hell with you then," and heard behind me a voice that flung me against the dryer.

"Who's the guy?" Monty Blackman said.

He stood in the doorway of the laundry room, a

wild hood of black hair all around, pale blue shirt over a white one, pale blue jeans, the same cream ostrich skin boots poking out beneath, with the telephone ringing, ringing, ringing.

25

Caught in a lie, a basically honest person wants to come clean, beg forgiveness, trade for wholesomeness again. That's what I wanted to do with Monty: confess. Say, a man's been killed right before my eyes! Did you know? Did you order it? The game is up.

What I said was: "What the *hell* are you doing in my house?"

"Your phone's ringin'," he said. He stood aside.

I slid through the laundry room doorway close enough to smell him, all the while hoping whoever was calling would not hang up.

"Smokey, honey," Mrs. Langston said, "I just passed a man asking for you, and I told him to go on up, but then I forgot: I maybe didn't lock your door after getting grass for Motorboat. But I shouldn't have just sent him along up there. I *thought* you were home, but I didn't *see* you come home. Is that all right? He said he was your boss."

"Uh, I think so, Mrs. Langston. You might want to have Harvey check the wiring, though. You know how those things go."

"Oh, migod. Oh, migod. I'll call the police."

"No, wait. I think you can still drive it. Just give me one minute and I'll come down and check."

I was watching Monty stroll around the living room touching things. From a shelf over the fireplace he picked up a tile on which was painted a lazuli bunting, with its bright blue hood, gripping a bug in its beak. He nudged a gas bill that lay on top of the stereo. From a chair, he picked up a paperback I had with a bookmark in it. I'd been reading about a forensic anthropologist named Clyde Snow, a renegade genius who brought some measure of justice to hundreds of unearthed Argentine "disappeareds." On the front was a photo of half of the face of Joseph Mengele, the infamous death camp doctor, merged with his recovered skull to demonstrate that skeletal remains can be identified. The title was *Witnesses from the Grave*. I was relieved when Monty just tucked the book between the cushion and arm without even looking at it, and sat down, putting an ankle on a knee.

How long had he been in my house? Mrs. Langston hadn't said. I'd decided a long time ago not to keep anything at home that related to my work—no folders, no training certificates, no mugs with clever penal code numbers on them, no group pictures. The only thing that could give me away was an old department directory; but even that I kept behind a stack of phone books in a cutout of the dark wood counter in the bar, hard to see.

I said, "An unlocked door is not an invitation."

"A shut eye ain't always sleepin' either," he said. "Where'd you take off to?"

"What gives you the right to come into my house?"

He looked around, nodding. "Pretty nice place you got here. You must be doin' jobs on the side. What you need my money for?"

I went to the front door and opened it fully.

"That mean I'm thrown out?"

"No job's worth my privacy." I was shaking inside. "You're a rude sonofabitch."

He came toward me but then parked his butt on the arm of my sofa. "I had to have Jolene follow you home one day just to be sure I'm dealin' with who I think I'm dealin' with. Now it looks like I was right to do that," he said in his soft gravel. "I ought to fire your ass."

"Screw you, Monty. You don't need my life history for me to wander around your bar in nighties. I don't give my address or correct phone number to anybody."

I leaned out quickly to glance down the walkway to see if Mrs. Langston was in or out of her condo. Monty was being a jerk and so far not a threat. I didn't really want to involve her.

"You turnin' tricks for this kind of place?"

"That's none of your business. Leave."

"Oh yes it is. I don't want heat of any kind. I told you when you first come to see me, none of that stuff. Now maybe I didn't make it clear I meant on your own time same as mine, and if that's so, it's my fault."

I sighed and said, "This place is my aunt's."

"You got a car phone. I seen the antenna."

"I got scared one time. It's how I spend my money instead of on manicures. You want to go through all my bills, see how I spend my money? Why wouldn't a girl have a car phone if she can manage it? And I sure as hell don't need your sending some little snippet of a no-brain to follow me. I really resent that."

He got up, amused, came close and snagged a finger in my tan leather belt, giving it little tugs. "I like you. Shoot, I don't want you to go nowhere. You want me to apologize? I apologize. Monty can do that. For somebody he likes." He brushed a hair, I guess, off my temple. I let him do this because I needed to hang in there with him if I was going to avenge, like Dr. Clyde Snow, a couple of disappeareds. "I just wanted to see if you're all right. It can get kind of rough around those Harley humpers. One of those sauceheads get funny with you? That why you left?"

"I got sick of you showing off," I said, brushing his hand off my belt, letting him know I was willing to try a truce. "After about your seventh win."

I pulled away and was turning again to look for Mrs. Langston when her dear and brave form appeared on the walkway, all decked out in a pastel jogging suit, her eyes fired with sixty-five-year-old resolve, her cane a lumpy hardwood that looked a whole lot like a gladiator's mace.

Monty offered twice to look at Mrs. Langston's car. She said her son was coming over. Harvey, she said, the name I'd made up only minutes before. While we talked, our eyes met often, and I smiled and one time winked when I thought Monty didn't see. I watched as she went on her way, an almost-disappointed slope to her shoulders, this time gripping the cane not by its clubby head, but by its middle.

Monty said, "I need you workin' this evening. You going to do that for me?"

We looked each other over, and I thought if this man's asking me back to work, he doesn't know I saw Quillard Satterlee's—Bernie Williams'—murder. I could still get out to the farm for a look. What I had to decide was whether I should tell him I was going back for my artificially missing wallet.

I walked him down the stairs, feeling the farther away from my apartment he was, the more comfortable I'd feel. On the way, he said, "So who's the guy? You never told me."

"Shit, I forgot about that! You followed me last night too, didn't you?"

"I was worried about you. Came by and was gonna knock, but I saw you had something goin'. You don't have to tell me. Your business is your business."

"Yeah right. Like my business is Jolene's business. I'll come back to work for you, Monty, but if this ever happens again, that's it. No following me. I'd think you'd have a million better things to do than that. Do you have any idea how insulting that is? How would you feel if I followed you home?"

"Come on now, that was a onetime thing, a one-time thing. What if you didn't show up to work some day? How would I get in touch? What if you and old Howard run off with the fortune I got stashed in my till?" He stopped and looked out over the parking lot, beyond the fountain that continuously mists its recycled load into the air, to where a man and his small son were stopped to look at a green motorcycle with a snake molded onto the rear fender. I hadn't seen it when I drove in because of a sewer-line repair truck that had been parked at the spot next to it but that was now gone, leaving three cones strung with bright pink plastic strips in its wake. "Besides," Monty said, "that guy's too old for you. Must be he's a stud."

"Are you leaving or am I going to have to quit my job all over again?"

A sensual smile formed within his beard, and he cocked his head at me, his thumbs in his hip pockets, and said, "Don't come till eight. One of the new gals is workin' split shift and I won't need you till then. Competition, darlin'. You better behave."

"I don't think this is going to work, Monty."

"Come on. Don't take everything so serious. Puts creases in your forehead. Hey, you know where I'm off to? Goin' to go pat my piggies on the head for doin' such a good job becoming moms and dads.

Why don't you come along out there with me? What else you doin' today? Let me make it up to you, me pissin' you off. I'll buy you dinner on the way back."

"Thanks, but—"

"We'll be back plenty of time."

"Well, I did lose something out there. My wallet."

"You shouldn't bring a purse to them things."

"It was a wallet. I had it in my jacket." I looked at his gleaming bike and said, "You don't have two helmets. I'll have to take my own car."

"You don't have your driver's license."

"I'll live dangerously. Look, I'll need a few minutes," I said.

"That's okay. I need some gas. Where's some at?"

I told him, grateful for the few minutes to see if I could find Joe and tell him what was up. When I rang up, Joe wasn't there. I couldn't reach him on his car phone either. He refused to wear a beeper, saying it was too much like being owned. Fishing Christine Vogel's card from my purse, I said the number over to myself, then tore the card to pieces and put it down the disposal. I touched the wallet in my pocket and thought I'd have to lose it somewhere so I could say I'd lost it somewhere. Christine's voice mail came on when I called her. I left a message, telling her I was on my way out to the Avalos farm, that Monty seemed all right, seemed normal; leaving directions and telling her to coordinate with Joe. I called Joe's number again and left the message I should have left before. I even tried Ray Vega. No deal. God help the world if you need a cop at lunchtime.

An hour later, we stood in the sunken-level family room of Tranquilino Avalos, looking at wire sections stapled to wood plaques. Monty said, "He's nuts about this stuff. Devil's rope. Him and Lupita go all over collectin'." Every wall bore eighteen-inch samples, replete with prongs, barbs, stars, leaves, spurs, or razor spirals. Between the displays hung Indian rugs, a picture of a woman carrying baskets, and straw hats. "He paid four hundred dollars for a piece not any bigger'n that," Monty said, pointing to a length of bird's-feet not mounted but lying bare next to a rusty branding iron on the mantel.

The house smelled of sausage, peppers, onions, and egg, as Mr. Avalos brought a black two-handled griddle to the dining table and set it on what looked like ordinary outdoor bricks. He said, "If you don't eat it, the dogs will." There were four place settings of blue plates and peach-colored cups on pale green terry cloth hand towels. Four place settings, but I saw only Mr. Avalos and a wisp of what I took to be his wife, clutching her robe as she sped down the hallway and disappeared into a room.

A coyote in full howl, cut out of white pine and wearing a pale green neckerchief, stood guard by the railing that separated the family room from the dining area. Over the table near the ceiling on the wall were two crosshatched muskets with lashed bayonets.

Mr. Avalos retreated to the kitchen, coming back with a pitcher of orange juice and a glass coffee pot. His movements were as smooth and quick as anyone who knew exactly how many steps could be saved within the confines of a house he'd loved forty years. He sat nearest the kitchen.

Pouring juice into the glass next to his, he glanced up once as Monty took a seat. "How about you?" he asked, barely meeting my eyes.

"Please," I said. I was starved. The old man poured, then swept a clutch of breakfast jambalaya onto my blue-fired plate. He spread his toast with jelly while Monty pincered stiff bacon strips off a small yellow platter with his knife and fork and dropped them onto my plate.

"Say," Monty said, "I can't get that rotten kid of yours to commit to a time to help me out with my manure pit. We talk, he doesn't show. Hell, what am I doin'? I just tattled to his daddy." Monty was only talking to be talking. There wasn't any conviction in it.

Mr. Avalos thoughtfully chewed his food as he set a biscuit on the rim of my plate. As soon as I broke the biscuit, the butter dish was under my nose.

He said, "Paulie drinks too much. Like you said."

"He does like the amber," Monty said. "I guess his mom being sick. You want me kick his butt?"

"His brother died of the same thing."

"I didn't know that, Mr. Avalos," Monty said.

The old man nodded as if to say now you do.

"I'll have a yammer at him, get him straightened out for you," Monty said.

Mr. Avalos said, "He'll be all right."

We sat in silence for a while, and then I said, "What started you on wire, Mr. Avalos? That's a pretty impressive collection you have."

His face became a paler shade of tan in the morning light. "I just liked the looks of it," he said. "I got my first piece from a man in Visalia. World War One military wire."

"Wouldn't want to run along it in the dark," Monty said. "You'd squeal like a pig caught under the gate."

"That's sure amusing," I said. Monty chewed and smiled at the same time.

Mr. Avalos moved food around on his plate. "Entanglement wire, 1915. The British, first with the patent. They made tanks to get over the wire."

"Are there a lot of people into wire?" I asked, thinking about the wire from Ortega Highway.

Mr. Avalos shook his head. "Man runs the big hardware store in town, he collects. Otherwise mostly in the Central Valley, Bakersfield. There's museums for it," he said, oil coating his lips. He spoke to Monty again, "I got a birthday present from Paulie the other day. Solid copper off the Hearst ranch."

"You mean *the* Hearst ranch, up by Morro Bay?"

The old man drew a diagram in the air with his fork and forefinger. "Diamond shapes ever few inches. Makes it stronger. No hooks. Mr. Hearst didn't like his animals hurting theirselves on wire. No bob wire, he said. Screwworms get in the wound and fester."

Mr. Avalos handed me the pie tin full of biscuits. Half of the first biscuit still lay on my plate but I took one because it was easier than saying no.

He arced his fork back over his shoulder. "Daley's 'Vicious Wamego,'" he said. "Patent: October 29, 1878. The seller didn't know what he had. I can get seventy dollars a length at the shows, and I got a whole roll for a hundred bucks. It's out in the shed."

My heart double-flipped because all along I'd been trying to figure what excuse I could use to get out to the shed; then here it was, an invitation, one I was afraid to even think too hard about, not really wanting to go see again the spot where Bernie Williams died.

"Thanks, but we got to find this one's wallet," Monty said. "I'll tell you though, if any one of them hog jockeys found it, by now they're cuttin' coke lines with the credit cards. Hell, Brandy, maybe it's still around. Stranger things have happened."

Mr. Avalos's face went dark. He said, "I don't like that stuff on my farm. I don't like that Switchie. I think he does that stuff."

"I know you don't, Mr. Avalos. Don't worry about

him. You see him with that pretty Jolene? She's one of my waitresses," he said. "Like Brandy here. Not as smart as this one, though."

"Thanks for talking like I'm not here."

"He's no good," Mr. Avalos said. "He could get Paulie in trouble again."

"Paulie wouldn't hire nobody to run his equipment he didn't trust, Mr. Avalos. Maybe if he's been hittin' the sauce a little too much, he knows he shouldn't be operatin' equipment. Maybe Switchie can help him, you know what I mean?" He reached for the coffeepot and poured for Mr. Avalos. "You're quiet over there," Monty said to me, chasing a bell pepper with the last bite of his biscuit and giving me the narrow eye.

I shrugged and stood and stacked dishes, like the good little waitress I was supposed to be.

The old man said, "I could get somebody to go talk to him. There's some farmers." He stood now too, and brought dishes to the kitchen while I was there.

"Switchie? Naw, don't do anythin' like that, Mr. Avalos. He ain't fit to shoot at when you want to unload your gun. Ah now, I don't mean that. At one time, yeah, I know he dug PCP, hog, angel dust. He was spikin' between the toes even while he was in the slammer. And you know who brought it to him in the cage? Sergeant of the guards. But take me for example. I messed up, now I'm just a broke businessman and a weekend motorhead. A man can reform."

The muscles in Mr. Avalos's jaw spasmed as he scraped food into a plastic sieve in the sink.

Out in the weed patch by the pigsties, butterflies bounced like yo-yos over the yellow mustard flowers and artichoke thistles. I squinted down the lane and looked for any telltale scrap of Smokey on the wire.

"What were you doin' all the way down here?"

"I told you, I was looking at the pigs. All that poundage. It's kind of intriguing, all that walking around." I hung back at the first structure, as if that's all the farther I'd gone the day before, and kind of looked around on the ground. "Oh, I'll never find my wallet, Monty. Let's go."

"No, no, we're goin' to do this right." He grabbed my hand and tugged me along. I felt a flash of fear. "You go in here? Look at these guys," he said, hauling me along into the main corridor of the first stable. "Just look at them happy faces."

"The tusks don't do a lot for me," I said, "smiling or not."

"I had an old stag once, four tusks, forty-four teeth, no nuts. Bought him off a guy that had him sold already. Paid fifty more just 'cause I liked his looks, and you know what? Twice he scared off rustlers intent on bootleggin' my hard-earned bacon. Made a hell of a fuss. You here?" he asked, "this far down?"

"I don't remember."

"Here's one just farrowed," he said, stopping at a pen with a red sow big as a couch, lying on her side with a dozen watermelon-striped piglets latched to each teat. Her eyes were barely cracked. She was grinning as a slow fly buzzed over her stiff pink eyelashes. "If she was mine, I'd pipe her in some music so she won't go stompin' her young."

"They do that?"

"They can. Hell, hyenas right out of the womb start killin' each other before they even open their eyes, so this ain't so bad. Mama says, 'This here's just too many folks around the house.' See, you gotta keep 'em calm. Now Mr. Avalos, he raises for the carcass trade. Me, I raise for reproduction, and I don't want any tidal waves goin' on with hormones and such. No pig PMS, no sperm gettin' wasted on the ground. That's why I didn't want you to come visit me yesterday, but a guy I got helpin' me says mine are done now for a bit. All wore out." He smiled and made like he was chewing gum though I knew he didn't have any in his mouth. I got a chill that went clear through to the top of my head.

As we entered the stable nearest the shed, the two young workers hauling the goat I saw slaughtered the day before squeezed around the shed with a rope tight around a black hog's neck and strung over its back and around its hindquarters like a prisoner wearing a waist chain, or like a large, portable pig valise complete with handle, except this one weighed three hundred pounds. The worker at the rear was whapping the pig's haunch with a stick, and the poor beast was squawling and digging in.

Monty advanced on the man and told him, "Hold up, hold up, there." Taking the rope and waving the men back, he said, "There's no need for that there," and began making long soothing sounds to the pig as the two men stood by. He said, mixing his comments to the workers and the hog in equal proportion, "Easy does it, easy. Kill 'em with kindness, *compadres*. Whatsa matter, baby? You just want to go in there and get you a date, China punky? Easy, now, easy." At the back corner of the far-end sty, a sow stalked and switched her tail so hard it popped against the boards.

The boar lunged at Monty, trading positions, teeth chattering. Foam boiled in its mouth and streamed out by the tusks. Monty lowered his voice and his knees at the same time and hummed reassuringly, patting the neck and the sides but while holding the rope handle. "There, baby. There, baby," he said.

He swung open the gate ahead of him, grabbed hold of the tail at the base, and guided him in. The romancer trotted in, took one look at his beloved, and became jelly, standing long enough for Monty to unknot the rope and slip it off. Then the hog remembered his role, tossed his head twice, and began strutting toward the sow as she walked warily along the sides.

Monty closed the gate and handed the rope to the Mexican and said, "I seen a ninety-pound woman sweet-talk a boar up a loadin' ramp backwards. Treat 'em with kindness," he said. "The ladies will do whatever you want 'em to do." The men looked tired and sweaty and I thought they probably didn't even understand English, but the one nearest Monty took the rope, the whites of his eyes shining like porcelain, nodded, and touched the gate latch to see that it held. Monty turned to me and said, "Lesson number one."

I said, "You think somebody'd find my wallet, strip it, and toss it in there?" meaning the shed.

"Well, let's us just go take a look, and we can tell Paulie's dad we saw his wire," Monty said, and he quickly exited the sty and strode around the side to the far door. "Don't get fresh with me now, in here, will ya? I can get my feelin's hurt real easy."

"I'll sure try my best," I said.

Inside, the light broke over rusted rakes, a two-wheeled flatbed trailer with its tongue across sacks of finisher feed, and four squares of shadowed, empty pigsties I hadn't seen from my vantage point at the window when Agent Bernie Williams was killed. The shed seemed much larger from the inside, and I tried to get my reverse bearings to see the post Bernie Williams was standing by when his life's blood drained away. The smell of hogs and ripe hay hung heavy in the air.

Four posts supported the raw crossbeams, and as I looked around the interior, I glanced at the dirt floor near the post where I expected to see patterns of stain. But I saw nothing there, nothing at all. Glancing away because I didn't want to stare, I said, "Oh look, this must be where Mr. Avalos cuts his wire," and I went toward two short bales of it standing on their ends near a crude workbench. On the bench were curls of cable and sheet metal and a pair of gloves with which it looked like you could handle fire. Leather plates were riveted to the palms and fingers. Nearby was a wire-cutting tool with curved blades and orange rubber handles.

I plucked a piece of double-strand wire with half-inch-high diamond shapes along the shaft. "Mr. Hearst wire," I said. It was copper. And it was also the same as one of the pieces Joe Sanders and I took from the trash barrel on Ortega Highway.

Monty took it from my hand, holding it vertical and inspecting it. "Treat 'em with kindness," he said.

I wanted the wire cutters, but how was I going to sneak orange-handled wire cutters safely into my pocket, and do so without contamination?

Then Monty reached over and picked the cutters up as if he read my mind. He snipped a few times, then put them down. And then, suddenly, he turned me by the shoulders and looked down at me and I could see it coming, the kiss, but was startled by it, and didn't move out of the way. His lips were hot and the hard ridge of his fly pressed against my crotch; the edge of the workbench cut into my back. He released me and said, "That's overdue."

"I don't want to make love to you, Monty, so quit it. You just don't get everything you want in this world, hard as that may be for you to believe."

He went and stood in the doorway looking out

and squinting in the bright light with his hands parked on his hips. "We could use one more good rain," he said.

I moved to the back of the shed, looking for anything. The absence of blood on the floor didn't bother me so much; investigators could pick up traces with no problem. So what did I want, a body under a buckrake? I made a quick walk down to the end, came back as Monty moved off into the yard, swinging his arms in circles to relieve kinks in his shoulders, I guessed. Darting over to the workbench, I took the bird-beak wire cutters, lifted my blouse, and nestled them under in the side piece of my bra under my arm. A holster. I tucked back in, and when I was going out the door I looked for body drag marks or tarry blood spots in the soil and watched Monty trudge up the slope toward the ground where the rally was held. When I got to him and said I didn't think it was worth looking for the wallet anymore, he answered saying he was going to go wet the willows. If I wanted to come along, he wouldn't object.

26 Monty hadn't murdered me yet. I was supposed to follow him out to tour his pig palace. The suggestion didn't bother me. I had the wire cutters, feeble evidence that they were. No decent place to put them, but I was feeling bold and strong. What did I care if Captain Exner's nonvisible plainclothes were out getting their hair done? Smokey was on the job.

Stashed under my front seat was a small towel I use when checking the oil level in my car. I rid my ribs of the wire cutters lifted off Tranquilino Avalos's gouged workbench by folding the cutters in the rag and slipping the bundle under the seat.

Trailing Monty to the freeway, the molded snake head staring back at me from the fender and people driving slow up alongside to admire and fear, I felt split, disenjoined, belonging, ultimately, to no one. In undercover work, the whole internal package upends, for you are engaged in deception, and unless by nature you enjoy fooling people, deception takes its sure and dreadful toll.

When I was a stripper, I met women who danced on the stage and prostituted on the side. One of the best of the dancers told me to watch out, don't fall for the quick money; not because you'd get arrested, abused, addicted, or infected, but because something would happen to you inside. A gradual shade closes over the person you once were. Ten years older than

I, Frazier Baldwin was an international mix of compelling beauty, disciplined, talented, and in her own way generous. It wasn't until later that I realized I had seldom seen Frazier smile, and when she had it was only at her son, not even for me. By accident years later I came across an article about her in a women's magazine. She was featured as the head of a real estate development corporation. In the accompanying photo, she wore a bright yellow suit with a soft pink, green, and black scarf, and her dark hair was now shoulder length. She was gazing out a skyline-charted window, comfortable, even placid, but without a smile.

As I drove along studying Monty's rippling shirt and wild hair, I tried to bore into his back and see his heart, and I wondered what my husband these several years dead would have thought of his Smokey girl. Bill Brandon, for all his twenty-eight years, was a wise old soul. Some people seem born to a special vision. You can identify that quirk sometimes on a toddler's face, that seriousness as they observe a world they know should be on better behavior, juicy fingers stuck in their mouths and hair askew and eyes too big for their faces, but something going on back there about which you almost don't want to know. If Bill knew what I was doing undercover and out of decent cover for Monty Blackman, what would he say? He'd say, baby, you know what's right. Do it. And he would have forgiven the missteps because he already knew they were coming; the worst of heartache is surprise. What I felt for Bill was not worship, but respect and a deep physical attraction, which, when you rub them down to their inevitability, we simply call love. And what Bernie Williams and all heroes—the dead cops and the living mothers and the maimed soldiers and even my Bill, who died from some crim's hepatitis-gifted needle—what all the heroes offer us, is an idea of honor. So that while I was presently and dishonorably befooling a Morris "Monty" Blackman who looked so easily spoiled on a highway and in whose face I had lied repeatedly, maybe it all was, in the final tally, forgivable.

Ahead, the mountains were hidden by a powdery haze. An off ramp took us beyond a cattle ranch whose choking odor lingered in the vent wells of the car. I followed the man-bike down a narrow paved road lined by token fences, new tumbleweed, and yellow-green wild carrot woozy from wind.

As we rolled past the gateway to Monty's unnamed farm, I saw, on a nub of gray phallic Cyclone post, a meadowlark in full midmorning gargle, her mouth open wide as scissors and her yellow breast thrust bold despite our passage.

Monty's farm was smaller than Campana Rancho but his pig domicile was one big square of shining white, blue shake–roofed swine city. The farmhouse itself seemed oddly disassociated from the animal building. A sand color, the house was nearly invisible under the only large tree around.

Monty was off his bike and out of helmet by the time I got out of my car. I wondered if I'd have to fight off advances in the house, but I did need to use the bathroom. "Home sweet home," he said, leading the way to the front of the house.

Flanking the door were two dust-covered bushes dripping spiderwebs and old sheddings at the base, and behind a scalloped brick flower corral running along the house were several thin sun-dried, rolled newspapers. The screen door was propped partly open with a brown grocery sack of lemons, some with orange burn spots on them. He peered into the sack a moment and said, "Lemonade," then unlocked the solid brown door and held it for me to go in. "The bathroom's through there," he said as he set the lemons on a table, "but I'm not responsible. Hands use this like a bus station when I'm gone."

"I'll manage not to get cholera," I said.

"I gotta make a phone call," he said, passing me and entering one of the two bedrooms, and the door to it open and showing all its office wares: a small computer station with printer paper spilled to the floor, a beige metal bookcase filled with binders and spiral-bound books, and a desk against the opposite wall. Office warehouse stuff. But at least no bad guys lurking behind doors as yet.

The bathroom was not all that bad, and I was surprised to see pink glycerine soap and a woman's deodorant and hand lotion on the windowsill. When I came out I drifted down to the other bedroom and stood in the doorway taking inventory. The double bed was made, covered with a woven spread with rodeo riders being bucked into violent curves. At the bottom lay a woman's pair of tan shorts with a tiny red floral print. Next to the shorts was a tan camp shirt, and resting on the floor beneath were a woman's pair of burnished leather sandals. Women's clothes, but who knew, maybe Monty was like the biker transvestite at Blue Jay, Helen or Henry, take your pick. Joe had asked me that day, What do you suppose a transvestite wears who lives in Scotland?

Whoever the clothes belonged to, I was ready to meet another player in Monty's life. I hoped it was Miranda Robertson.

The room smelled of scent like air freshener, and the two windows were open high enough to clear the top of a beer can in one and a ceramic piggy bank in another. I went to a mirrored closet door and slid it open with one finger. On the right were

Monty-like clothes: shirts, jeans, two pairs of shoes, a few belts, and a cream-colored cowboy hat. At the opposite end, when I slid the other door open, were about six outfits clearly female, on wire hangers, and a nylon, hotly flowered robe I was sure I had seen in the window of Victoria's Secret on special last month.

I closed the door, hearing Monty's voice muffled in the other room, and moved out to the hallway so I could hear more. Luckily, hanging on the walls were three framed antique citrus crate labels I could study while I tried to overhear. He was saying things like, "Good girl," and "How much?" and "I told you not to do that." And then he said, "I'll pick you up later. No, later than that. Watch TV or something. Do a crossword."

Hearing the floor creak, I worried that the phone he was using was portable, so I moved on out of the hallway, glancing in his office as I went by, and there he was, sitting on the desk. He said, "See you, baby," but not to me, and then I heard the phone hang up. I walked quickly to the back door near the kitchen, to stand there as though I were admiring the view of the pig yards and a slithery green pond out behind it, and far off, the long flat outline of an industrial building in front of the blue-milk mountains.

"Well, so Monty has a girlfriend after all," I said, and nodded toward the part of the house with the bedrooms.

"Monty has friends of all color, stripe, and sex, and Monty loves them equal." He stepped away, sneezed three times, and said, "Must be pollens don't favor me though." He sneezed again twice, drew out a handkerchief to mop his beard and reached for the handle of the refrigerator. "Have a cold one," he said, handing me a can of Colt .45.

We went out to the smallish structure, the larger
one up on a hill having some work done on it, he
said, and I saw pigs all over again. We passed the
empty breeding compartments, then the birthing,
weaning, growing, and finishing pens, for white
hogs of the breed American Landrace. "I'm tryin' for
a lean, mean porcine, but you make 'em too lean,
they get muscle-bound. They walk funny and they
don't mate good." He made his legs stiff and walked
like a toddler with a loaded diaper, then looked back
at me and winked. "You wouldn't want to sleep
with somebody walks like that, wouldja?"

"Don't think so."

"See them little chubs at the bottom of their feet?
Dewlaps, for balance when they're matin'." In one
sty, a great pig gray as wet flour lay with its ears
over its eyes while it napped. "Bodacious!" he
called. "Wake up, you lazy swine!" But Bo only
wimped his ear over so he could see who was making all the racket and continued to loaf there with
his pink belly showing and his testicles resting like
pale dumplings in soup.

"That is one hunk of hog," I said.

"He is one happy, done-diddlin' guy. A Manor
Meishan, shipped him all the way from London, and
I paid a bloody fortune for him. Hell, he gets too
hot, I'm gonna bring a chair and set there and fan
him myself. He's a cross between a British and a
Chinese strain that'll give the kids more to eat than
a dried-out, tasteless, knife-nickin' chop on their dinner plates every Wednesday night. He's my fertile,
fast-growin', ham-hock hero, this guy, ain't ya, there,
Bodacious?"

"You're really into this," I said. "I think you like
it better than the bar."

"Way better. Anyways, you have to have your

money on a coupla runners or risk having nothin' at all."

Bodacious snorted and threw his head up as if he smelled dinner cooking. The sound of a jet growled overhead, and Bodacious harumphed, clicked his teeth, then lay back down, giving his tail a flick. Against his crown, a blue ear tag gleamed flat as a poker chip.

"Well, I'm impressed," I said, and pushed off toward the exit way.

He said, "Okay, let's get you on the road. Some mean old man wants you to work tonight." He put his hand on the top part of my hip and I stepped ahead of him and walked faster. We were a good fifty yards from the larger structure, and another fifty back to the house from this smaller building. Nearing the house, he said, "You need a loan, your wallet gone?"

"No," I answered, my knees a little shaky because he was standing too close. I heard a shuffle of footfall and looked around his shoulder to see a sight that set me back a minute, certain that something had been slipped into my coffee while I was admiring wire at Mr. Avalos's rancho. Coming from around the corner was a small man buried in a drape of bloated snake, its tail dragging in the dust, and the forward length of it twined around the man's right arm. The snake's head was up, apparently appreciating the side-view scenery.

"Yo, Monty," the little guy said, and tripped a half step forward because the snake decided to roll its weight higher on his neck; then again, the stumble could have been from the man's untied shoelaces.

"Simon," Monty said. "How you doin'?"

"I came by to see if you had any piglets you could let go of."

"In your dreams," Monty said.

"Where's Miranda? She around?" he said, looking at me with a little uncertainty. There it was—her name spoken in the living air. "You ain't afraid of snakes, are you? This here is Dragonwick. Dragonwick, meet Miss . . . ?"

"Brandy," I said.

Simon looked me up and down in an open, candid way. His pointed chin bore the barest efforts of a goatee, and his hair kinked in tan tufts several inches back from his forehead. His teeth crossed over one another. He looked at Monty and said, "She could be her sister," nodding to me, "if she was taller."

"Whose sister?" I asked.

"Miranda," Simon answered. "I say something wrong?" Monty was moving toward the front of the house, allowing a view of the faded red pickup Simon must have arrived in under the jet noise. "We're just on our way out, Simon," Monty said. "Whyn't you drop around some other time?"

Simon reddened at the neck and ears. Both hands rested on the thick reptile as though he were steadying a brace of water buckets. "You might want to check out Water Canyon if you're lookin' for a nice place for a picnic," he said, trying to recover. "Just don't go plinking with your elephant gun while I'm out there."

"Wouldn't think of it," Monty said.

"I'm headed on up to Slaughter Canyon. Slaughter Canyon, Water Canyon. Kinda sounds alike, don't it? I'm gonna let Dragonwick go after a couple ground squirrels." Simon lowered the tailgate, preparing to put the snake back in her wood-and-wire box, but she was rolling around his body like a frantic lover not wanting to say good-bye, so he just settled a moment against the truck until she calmed.

"You put her down out there? How do you get her back?" I asked.

"I stomp on the ground, she comes slithering. Works just like a dinner bell. They go by vibration, see. She feels it, thinks I'm a big gopher." I shivered, and he said, "Really, she's harmless. Now, if I'd been handling live bait for her, say, a rat, and she smells him on me, that'd be bad news. She can't see for shit, wouldn't know it was her old pal Simon."

"It's not poisonous, then," I said.

"A poison snake will have a bull-nose and slanty eyes. Look here at this pretty girl," he said, grabbing the head and holding it like a microphone for me to talk into. Stepping back, I bumped into Monty. "Just a harmless old round-eye. I don't know why Switchie don't like her. Guess she just spooks him."

"See you later, Simon," Monty said.

"Oh, hey, before I forget—I'm thinking o' buyin' a flattie, a forty-six with a really ripped tranny. You take a look at it for me?"

"No problem," Monty said.

Simon rotated to the back of the truck, straining his stringy muscles to lift the boa to her box. He flipped the lock flap down and turned back, brushing hay off his belly. "Some guy died and left his knuckle to his old lady. She don't know what to do with it. Young guy. He got that Kern River coxy, that bug's been eatin' the brains outta the farmers up in Central Valley? Man, it's bad. You told me pigs is good for research, heart valves and all that? Better maybe donate a few hogs up there, make yourself a reputation. Maybe they'll name a petrified turd after ya."

"I'll think about it, pal," Monty said, securing the tailgate for Simon and smacking him on the bare skin of his tattooed back.

Simon kept jabbering as he moved toward the cab of the truck, saying to me, "Nice to meet you, there. You take care," and then to Monty: "Bring your friend over if she wants. We can play some gin rummy," and he tripped again on his dirty shoelace, fell backward and thunked both elbows into the side of the pickup door. "Damn," he said. "Forget the gin rummy. I need that girl gimme dancing lessons."

27 I was swimming in pigs. Pigs and pythons—or was it a boa Simon had? Whatever, I was leaving the whole odd nation behind, satisfied with the idea of wire cutters in a towel under my seat, and happy I wasn't lying murdered in a shed.

A sense of incompletion filled me because I meant to push Monty for more information on Miranda but didn't, and blamed it on Simon's snake. At least he mentioned Miranda's name. That didn't mean she was alive, but together with what I learned from Les about the implants, it assured me. If Miranda was alive, though, who was in the car? Could I tell Nathan with absolute surety it was not Miranda? Not yet.

It was four o'clock by the time I could punch the recall button on the car phone to reach Joe, and I asked him to hang tight there at the lab, I was bringing along a surprise.

Seen under the comparison microscope, a nick near the crotch of the wire cutters formed a shallow W. In addition, there were clear striae on the blade edges. These tiny furrows, along with the mirror-image W, would show on whatever wire the blades nipped in two, but it would take luck, a good eye, and precision camera work to capture it.

I set the camera and snapped off a highly magnified picture of the tool, and then Joe handed me the brutal wire taken off public drunk Rollie Pierson, lately of Blue Jay Campground. "The chances individual characteristics will match up are slim," Joe said.

"I know," I said. "But how many tries was it, five thousand, before Edison found the right filament?"

"He also believed he could invent a machine that could talk to the dead, and chewed his food thirty-two times while reciting, 'Nature will castigate what you don't masticate.'"

"You read too much," I said.

He gave me a squeeze around the shoulder. "I talked to Oskar Lombard over at the morgue. He had a hard time finding a next-of-kin, but he finally got the wife's sister. She's making the ID."

I said, "Hey, look at this."

Joe took my place at the eyepiece. "Distinct bite mark," he said. Then he took the orange-handled wire cutters and held the blades under the glass. "Same bite on the cutters. Nice going." He rose up, the elliptical eyepiece leaving a mark on his skin.

"We still have to tie Switchie to the evidence," I said. "So far we have nothing but me."

"Then let's take good care of you," Joe said.

"I have to go out there tonight. To the Python."

He frowned. "How long?"

"I don't know. Three, four hours."

"I'll pick you up."

"No."

"Let me pick you up."

"It's better I keep to the pattern," I said.

"How do I know you'll be safe?"

"How do we know we won't get zonked in a drive-by leaving here? We don't."

"You're too rational, you know that?"

"Just don't say I'm hardheaded."
"Would I do that?"

We were on a conference call to Captain Exner, telling him what we found under magnification. Joe said, "We've got a piece of recovered evidence with marks unique or identifiable to one source."

"No other case similarities, however," the captain said. "Isn't that right?"

"Check."

"Then you are needlessly complicating two separate cases." The captain's voice came through as if he were talking from a ship's hold. Someone else was in his office who would cough or say something every now and then, and maybe that's why the captain was impatient.

"But there are strong, apparently matching individual characteristics on both pieces," Joe repeated.

"Sanders," the captain said, "if you have anything to show me, document it and send it over. Otherwise, I have lawyers who are going to be shooting me catch-cop questions in about fifteen minutes. I gotta go. Smokey?" he said.

"Yes?"

"Do I understand you went out to that ranch without backup?"

"Yes, but—"

"No backup."

"That's right."

"Who's your supervisor over there?"

"Stu Hollings. Sir? Can I—?"

"Give me a written report on it."

"Sir, is a plainclothes assigned to me yet?"

There was a pause on Captain Exner's end. Joe, sitting nearer to the phone because we were using his office, leaned closer and said, "Smokey determined the risk was minimal, Captain. Beyond that, she couldn't raise anybody when the initial contact with Blackman was made. She tried. She's a very cautious—"

"I'll be getting back to you," he said, "eighteen hundred or so." Six P.M. A few of us use military time but most don't except on reports.

When he hung up, I turned to Joe and said, "At least he interrupts you too. What an asshole. I'm not staying here till six o'clock."

"Is that any way to speak of a superior?"

"You're right. He's a stupid asshole."

"Grapevine has it one of his guys is charged with a two-eighty-eight on a female DUI."

"Oh no."

"Forced oral copulation under color of authority. Another cop squirreled off on him. Pressure's tough on friendships."

"What do you say to a cup of coffee?"

We walked down to the room where the coffee maker is. Somebody put up a new sign on the bulletin board: THERE'S NO RIGHT WAY TO DO A WRONG THING.

When I make phone calls, I make a rack of them. I face phone communication the way I do housework; push hard and get it over with. First, Doug Forster, to see if he'd heard anything I hadn't on the Carbon Canyon case. He wasn't there. Then my brother; but I wasn't ready. I hung up after one ring.

I tried Ray Vega, range rider in his hot Mustang patrol car. I couldn't raise him. Hoped he was in bed with Francine or in a shower soaping some pretty girl down.

I phoned the coroner's tech, Oskar Lombard, who, I learned, was actually a reserve deputy assigned to the coroner. Reserve personnel take all the training of a regular sworn officer, but they don't get paid.

Some put in more hours for free than they give at their real jobs, a sense for justice or an urge for excitement deep in their veins. I asked him to check on Meyer Singer, the molasses-slow odontologist putting teeth together on the burn case. Oskar said all the recovered teeth were back in the jaw, affixed with nondestructive putty. "I saw them myself," he said.

"How come nobody told me?"

"You're never around." Hm. "There was something funny about the front teeth," he said.

"What's funny?"

"They were decalcified."

"And what significance . . . ?"

"I'm not sure. What you get with real bad heat, I guess. Singer kept asking himself, 'Now, why have these teeth decalcified already?' He takes out the box of jaws every time he comes in. It sits by him all day while he's working other cases."

"Do you know if there was anything else with the teeth? Fillings, like that?"

"Yeah. There were fillings."

"Great, Oskar. Thanks a bunch."

"I don't know for what."

Doug was in Les Fedders's office. I was surprised they were both still there, quitting time being fifteen minutes ago. I could tell by looking at Les that he still hadn't been briefed about what went on at the Avalos farm, and I didn't want to be the one to do it, sit there and be grilled by him and waste time.

"Doug," I said, "whaddya know?"

"Not a whole heck of a lot."

"See, he admits it," I said, winking at Les.

In Les's office was the standard-issue metal office furniture, but over the chair hung a picture of the old Coca-Cola, the giant fluted bottle with the sen-

suous shape, and an equally voluptuous blonde,
seamless teeth, curled lashes, one knee dipped in
that Marilyn pose, standing in a bathing suit next
to it.

Doug sat with one ankle up on the other knee,
fiddling with his sneaker shoelaces. In his other
hand was a sheet of paper partially filled in with
names in boxes, a basketball play-off pool. His black
hair gleamed as if he'd just sprayed it with oil.

"Well, there's one thing new," I said. "The
morgue says Singer put the teeth together and
they're flawed. Miranda Robertson's charts showed
not one cavity, as you know. His teeth are not only
filled, they're chalky in the front."

"I thought we already concluded that victim was
not Miranda Robertson," Les said. Nearby, a vase of
bloated bloodred roses sat on top of a file cabinet.

"Yes, but this just makes it more solid." I was
thinking of Nathan, looking forward to telling him.
"The Rollie Pierson case," I said, "you talked to
somebody but not the wife?"

"Yep. The sister-in-law. What's up?"

"Have you got her name?"

"What's on your mind?"

Doug studied his basketball chart.

"I just wondered, are you going out there for an
interview?"

"It's down in San Clemente. Maybe tomorrow."

"Can I go along?"

"You got a list of twenty questions?"

"I don't have anything special to ask. Just interested. But I don't want to get in your way, Les."

"No problem." He glanced at Doug. "Won't that
interfere with your new job?" He grinned.

Doug grinned too, said, "I heard about that."

"About what, Doug?"

"About you doing the model bit."

"That was supposed to be on the QT." Who would tell? Joe wouldn't tell.

Les lowered his eyes, then looked up.

"Hey," Doug said, "they got any Western dancing out there? I go every night, different place. I can do twelve line dances now."

"Good for you, Doug," I said.

When I got home, I called Ray Vega. I just wanted to hear my friend's voice. He said it was his day off, was why I couldn't get him earlier. He said, "Let's get together for dinner."

"What about Francine?"

"What about her?"

"Aren't you spending nights off with her?"

"Nuh-uh."

"Is that all you're going to tell me?"

"Uh-huh."

"Monty wants me at the Python at eight."

"You're still on that?"

"Yes."

"We'll eat first."

"I don't know, Raymond. I'm exhausted. I should try to get a nap."

"How can you say no to a man like me?"

"I don't know. It is hard to understand."

He did an imitation of Andrew Dice Clay that always had me laughing; I went around saying it to myself half the time: "Treat me like the pig that I am." Then he said, "How 'bout if I come around after, give you a ride in my new pickup? We can go to a show after. What you want to see?"

"Ray, I *would* like to talk to you . . ."

"Great. And I get to come in this time. You wouldn't let me before."

I was weakening now, wondering while I picked off four ants veering behind my kitchen faucet as I walked the room with the phone if I should just let him. I must have sighed.

"How's the case going, anyway?" he asked.

"That's what I'd like to talk to you about."

His voice took on another tone. "What is it, Smokes? What's up?"

"I saw a murder."

"What?"

"I witnessed a murder out at a ranch in Norco. I told you about the guys in the office the day of my interview, right? One of them killed a customs agent, an undercover. Slit his throat in a shed. I saw it, Ray, through an open window."

In the silence that followed I could picture my friend's perfect face take on that calm, resolute set, that expression that would not reveal if he was about to level his nine at you or tell you to hit the road, guy, and stay out of trouble, the long lashes half closed, the mouth not needing much motion. After a bit, he said, "Hey, girl."

"I know."

"Who else is UC with you?"

"No one."

"You're the UC? It?"

"I'm it. The captain's supposed to put some plainclothes on it, but I haven't seen 'em yet. Maybe I'm not supposed to."

"What's being scammed, if customs is on it?"

"The contraband is . . ." It was still hard to say. You expect a hard laugh on the other end. "Ray, you ready for this? It's swine semen. That's what they're smuggling. Whoever has the best semen has a market edge." I waited a second. "You forgot to laugh."

"I'm laughing."

"They cross borders with it both directions. Blackman's maybe smuggling precursors too. Pig semen. That's what the customs agent got killed over."

"Motherfuckers."

"I'm supposed to take his place, sort of. Since I was already there, like, because of my brother's ex-wife. It's weird, Raymond."

"You're telling me."

"Sometimes I'm scared."

"You should be. You saw this?"

"Yes."

"I'm sorry, babe."

"It was bad."

"Are you okay?"

"It's not that I'm so afraid for my life."

"Hey, you definitely should be. This sounds—"

"It's not that. Did I ever tell you, Ray . . . ?"

I seldom told anyone, maybe five people in my life. I started again. "Did I ever mention my mother was pretty sick there for a while?"

"I don't think so."

"When I was little. Maybe till I was about fourteen."

"What are you talking about, Smokey?"

"She'd go off her cork."

"How?"

"It made me strong, Raymond. I'm telling you. It made me strong. I'll kill somebody messes with me at a certain point, I really will."

"That's healthy. What's the problem? You okay?"

"What do you think?"

"I think you're okay. But I'd like to know why you don't have backup."

"Captain Honcho's busy with a deputy who forced a friendly blowjob on a civilian."

"Oh man."

"Yeah."

"They've got somebody else planted," Ray said. "They wouldn't leave you out there alone."

"They wouldn't mean to."

"Where's Joe in all this?"

"Sympathetic. Worried. When you think of it, though, look: If Monty suspected anything he could've already aced me easy. I was alone with him since."

"You packing?"

"How can I? I'm either wearing biker shorts or Victoria's Secret."

"You can do better than that."

"I will. Don't sweat it." And then, for no *rational* reason I could have given at the time, I said, "I guess I would like you to come along tonight." I wouldn't let Joe take me or pick me up, but I let Ray. Later I thought maybe I wanted Monty to see me with someone else, see that I had lots of friends and at least one with a lot of muscles. "Are you happy?"

"What'll he think, me coming in there with you?"

"We'll find out, won't we? But don't blow it for me, Raymond. Be cool."

"I'm always cool. Know what? Some girl told me the other day I looked like a Mexican version of Tom Cruise."

"Oh, way better than that, Raymond."

When I hung up, I poured myself a Southern Comfort and put on an old Lacy J. Dalton tape, maybe her first. Wanted to hear her sing about hard lovin' and good times. Tried to match her unmatchable voice.

28

Ray was hanging tight to a bottle of beer, leaning back with those sweet penny-colored eyes leveled at me.

"This is from Takki," I read from the prompter card in my palm. "It's washable silk, acetate lace, very easy care." Ray grinned and sipped his beer. I moved on. The man at the next table liked Jolene better, his eyes on her three tables over. She and I alternated floor strolls with two other models.

When I arrived earlier, Monty hadn't come in from an errand yet. But Paulie Avalos was sitting fat-bellied at the bar talking to Howard, giving me glances but not threatening ones.

In the office, where we were changing till Monty arrived and forced us into the ladies' room, Jolene was slipping a black thing with spaghetti straps over her head. I said, "Here. You need this," and gave her a brilliant blue robe that lit up her dark hair and blue eyes. The robe was supposed to go with a shortie I was wearing, but I decided to go out without it. I had on a black satin sleep suit and shoes with pom-poms at the toes.

"Thanks," she said, trying it on. "Say, did Monty tell you he's going to get dancing in here? Topless. Would you do it?"

"Not me. This is all he gets."

Jolene opened the door just as the model with the fullest figure came down the hallway. She bumped

a new watercolor of an African-American woman
standing with feet spread as she spoke to the clouds,
two snakes wrapped from ankle to thigh, teasing
tongues in the middle. We passed by, and the model's perfume bowled me over. "That's Coral," Jolene whispered. "Can't stand her."

"Why not?"

Jolene shrugged a shoulder as we stood for a second before going out onto the floor, me looking at
her new shiny ducktail haircut and both of us checking the crowd. At the back of the room Ray's white
jeans gleamed under the table. He looked like he
belonged. The hair was maybe too coplike, the mustache too trim, but a handsome, confident piece of
manhood all around.

To Jolene's back I said, "You still thick with Switchie? I don't see him here tonight."

"Jeez, I don't dump 'em that soon. And I mean
he's not half bad." She tossed her head as she left
me, saying, "Oh, honey," in a way that was supposed to tell me something about Switchie's prowess
in bed. The song that started was by the mother-
daughter Judds, licking up a raunchy harmony. I always got their names mixed up. The mother looks
like one of those porcelain dolls sold by Heritage
Collections, four payments plus shipping. The
daughter's a beauty too but somebody else's child,
different face and body shape. I could picture her
and her mom on the tour bus offering each other the
last French fry, and fighting and loving each other
to death. Then the mom got sick and the daughter
sings alone or duets with Clint Black. And rides Harleys.

Jolene was beautiful in the black and blue, I had
to give her that. She stopped at a table under a soft
ceiling light, touching the table with one long white
forefinger, lips glistening red as licked suckers as she

spoke to the man, and I thought the guy, still in his necktie, was going to need CPR.

I drifted over to Raymond's table. He'd changed brews for himself, rolling the bottle by the neck to show me the label. Mexicali Rogue it said. He smiled, and his left knee swept back and forth like a pendulum.

"Made in Ray Vega's bathtub," I said.

His gaze fell to my breasts, and I felt self-conscious around him for the first time.

Out of the corner of my eye, I saw Paulie Avalos swivel on the barstool as if deciding to leave, go belt somebody, or find the rest room. Then he settled down again, putting both fat arms on the bar, and stood again and reached clear over the bar and pulled out from under there somewhere a package of potato chips. I pointed him out to Raymond, said he was an accomplice to the killing of Bernie Williams. "But don't look now, dammit," I said, and Ray played the game of just another drunk flirt.

I followed Jolene, ready for her next change.

In the office the other model, Coral, was dropping a chartreuse shortie on. She had auburn hair down to her shoulders, and she was a sturdy forty. I didn't know what Jolene's problem was. I thought the woman was pretty. Comfortable. Some men like them that way.

At the closet I closed my eyes and picked. Near gagged when I saw it, but I put it on, read the tag from the shop owner, and left before the other two women did. The brief glances I got when I paraded my spiel sagged my confidence. I homed in on the table with the Mexican and the Mexican ale. "This is from Donna Waters," I said, referring to the lacy thigh-grazing violet thing I was wearing that looked to me more like a circus costume than a nightie, "and it sells for seventy-five ninety-five."

"I'll bet it does," Raymond said. At least *he* appreciated it.

He said something else, and I said, "You say what?" Someone in control of the music dug the Judds. Now the younger Judd's rich voice graveled loudly and I leaned closer to Ray to hear.

Ray pushed his chair back a little, gave me that look again that now I recognized, the one he'd give a stranger in a different bar. "Smokey, you're too much," is what he said, and squeezed my fingers as I got ready to make my way back for the last change.

A girl who looked like she ought to be riding horses, her hair braided in back and her healthy good looks just a little flushed from changing, came out wearing a floral satin. New kid on the shift. I wanted to send her to her room; kick the stuffed animals off your bed and do your homework.

When I was back for another change, Jolene came in. We had lingerie scattered all over the place. Monty's desk looked like an underwear bin. Jolene said, "Is this all? We're going to be repeating ourselves," as she pushed in the small closet where Monty kept the clothes. "He should get us more. Why'd he have four of us if this is all?"

"Here, put this white one on. I'm done," I said. I'd found it piled down on the floor of the closet and I'd thrown it over the file cabinet.

"You want to go hustle that dark dude."

"What dark dude?"

"The one in the white jeans."

"I came in with him."

"You *did*?"

"Yeah," I said, and sang a song about loving the night life, and boogied over to the chair where my own clothes were. I'd come in jeans, the blue boots, and a white knit top that slung off both shoulders in a wide band. I wasn't wearing a bra, and certain things had showed like hard buttons, so in the truck with Raymond I'd kept my jacket on; it was black and businesslike, hitting me below the hip.

"Monty know about this guy?"

"He will now."

"You're going to get him all pissed. Is that what you're trying to do?"

"I'm just livin' my life."

She fastened herself into the outfit I'd handed her that seemed made of snowflakes and whalebone, and then leaned over to get her breasts balanced in just so. Under the fabric, her nipples were dark moons. "Hm," she said. "This is nice." Out of a red brocade overnight bag she took a white garter belt and white stockings and put them on. I struggled with my boots. When I straightened back up and Jolene was all together, I had to say she was stunning.

The door opened and in came Full Figure Franny. She ducked back out just as quickly, saying, "Oops, full house. I'll go to the john."

Jolene said, "What she's doing is eating Twinkies and counting the dimples on her ass. She knows she's too big for what we got left."

"You talk about me that way behind my back?"

"Shit no. I'll tell you to your face."

"Where's Switchie tonight?"

"Why you wanta know?" Jolene made sure her hair was staying tucked behind her ears. As she did, her diamond or fake diamond earrings caught the light.

"I just wondered."

Now she was powdering her nose with the compact she swiped out of the healthy woman's hand earlier and never gave back.

* * *

It was almost midnight when Monty came in. Wearing his Levi jacket over a black knit shirt, and with his hair ponytailed back, he strode right for me and Jolene while we were standing in the alcove dressed in our street clothes, ready to leave. She was looking for a quarter to call and find out why Switchie wasn't here yet. Paulie was gone. I glanced over to see if Raymond was still alive. With no dancing and most of the patrons not showing any sign of misdemeaning, he did seem half asleep. The server had not picked up his last empty, so there were two bottles in front of him.

"I'll get you a quarter," I told Jolene, moving toward Howard by the cash register and out of Monty's approach. But Monty was already blocking the way. "Hi, girls. You do good tonight?"

"What you missed," I said.

"How's the new one? Linda."

"Good, good. She did good."

"I need a quarter," Jolene said. "You have a quarter?"

Monty ignored her, put his hand on my elbow and walked me down the hallway. I wondered if Raymond was seeing all this, but of course he was. He's a cop.

"C'mere," he said, whisking me into the office. Big Franny—Coral—was still there, putting her brush in her sizable purse. She smiled sweetly and said good evening to Monty, and he said for her to collect from Howard out of the drawer; he'd see her tomorrow.

When he shut the door, he locked it.

I looked at him curiously, and then I smelled the whiskey. He didn't seem mad. He didn't seem as though he was about to accuse me of anything. I said, "What?" meaning what do you want, or what did I do, or why'd you lock the door; and then it became very apparent. He stepped right over to me, slid his palms onto my shoulders underneath my black jacket and dropped it right off. Before I knew it, he was running both hands down my sides. When he bent his head, I saw the dull-silver snake earring swing toward his jaw and the office light thread his wavy hair with silver strands.

"Monty," I said, trying to figure out how to handle this. But maybe he thought it was a cry of relief, gratitude that he was finally making his big move, because before I could react, he hooked three fingers in my knit top and pulled, and slipped it all the way off one shoulder, exposing my breast. He ran a rough thumb over it, my own taut flesh springing back like an unwilling kid put down for a nap.

I jerked away just as the door handle rattled and someone knocked, and I heard Ray Vega's voice say, "Hey, open up!" and then all at once hard banging. I got my breath and pulled up my blouse.

When he unlocked the door, Raymond stood glaring, his eyes red from Mexicali ale. Ray the taller, Monty the one who said, "Just who the *fuck* are you?"

Ray gave Monty a shove full-handed on his chest, and Monty slung a punch to the side of Ray's jaw. By the time I called him off, my Mexican rogue knew he'd blown it big. On the way out, with Ray hustling me along like any good boyfriend would, or me hustling him, it was hard to tell, Lacy J. was on the jukebox singing "Everybody Makes Mistakes."

Everyone does. From the passenger seat, Ray apologized all the way home.

29 "You know this ain't easy."
"What, Monty? What isn't easy?"
"Maybe I need to apologize."

Giving that some thought a moment, I said, blandly, "Am I supposed to work tonight, or do you have enough people?" He was calling me at home, ten o'clock, and I'd only just booted Ray Vega out, who'd slept on the couch in the living room and left with his hair standing on end and his mouth, according to him, tasting like shit.

"Nah, I don't want you to work tonight. You need the money?"

"What do you think?"

"I'll pay you anyway. That new one, Linda, she'll take over. And Coral. There's not gonna be that much goin' on tonight anyway. Never is, Tuesdays."

Tuesday. It was hard to imagine it was only Sunday I'd been at the rally and seen the murder, Monday I'd been back out to the Avalos farm and then at Monty's farm, and last night at the Python. Some days are longer than weeks.

"I want to make it up to you, what I did last night," he said. "That was most ungentlemanly."

"A Viking would be ashamed," I said, leaving the interpretation of how mad I was to him.

"I hurt that guy?"

"He'll be all right."

"What happened to ol' Father Time? You dump him for this guy?"

"That's none of your business. But since you asked, he's just a friend."

"*He* know that? He's a little touchy for just a friend, won't let you out of his sight. Listen," he said, his voice soft, hesitant.

"Where you calling from?" I asked.

"The club. It's cold and dark in here. I don't even have the light turned on. With my window boarded up, the only light's from the john."

"I feel real sorry for you."

"I know it's my own damn fault. I just can't drink like I used to."

"What broke the window?" I asked, switching the subject.

"I busted it myself tryin' to get it unstuck. Listen here," he said, "I'd like to take you to hear some good music this afternoon. No funny business. Just to make up."

"Who plays music in the afternoon?"

"There's this place up in Carbon Canyon. You know where that is? Take the Fifty-Seven—"

My skin temperature went up ten degrees.

"Let me think about it."

"I'm countin' to five. One, two, three, four—last chance. 'Do I have a fun time with Monty, or do I sit home alone and watch reruns of Perry Masonite?' Five."

"Another time, Monty. I've—"

"Yeah, well, me too," he said, his voice going kind of tired on me.

"Maybe I could go for an hour or so."

"No problem there. I got Paulie out at the farm diggin' me a new manure pit. I have to go check, make sure he don't scrape me a hole to Timbuktu. I did that kind of work two summers in school, run-nin' equipment, don't want to do it no more. Your kidneys bounce around like golf balls in a mason jar. Did I tell you Paulie popped Switchie last night?"

"I don't believe so."

"After you-all left, in the parkin' lot. Switchie called him a sheepfucker and Paulie belted him one. You don't call a big ox like Paulie them kinda names."

I could picture Switchie pulling a knife, going af-ter Paulie, but I thought that if that happened Paulie couldn't very well be digging a manure pit.

Monty said, "I'm goin' out around three, three-thirty. Now, you comin' or not? I gotta plan my day."

"If you see me there, you see me there," I said, and left it at that.

I called Joe and we agreed to meet for a sandwich. He was telling me about a scene he'd been on late the night before that was supposed to be an acci-dental explosion in a garage, but Joe knew it wasn't because the man's body was torn in half and bits of dynamite casing still remained where the man had laid the stick in the middle of his belly.

"Does all this ever get to you, Joe?"

"Of course it does." He took a bite from a runny chicken salad sandwich. The milk gathered at the corners of his mouth till he could get the napkin there. He was wearing a tie with multicolored streaks on the diagonal, and glanced down to see if it was still unsullied.

"You ever want to just go away?"

"Like Italy?"

"Hah. Speaking of, guess what? Monty wants me to go with him to hear some music this afternoon.

A place in Carbon Canyon, the canyon we found Not-Miranda in."

Joe put his sandwich down, sat back in his chair, and looked hard at me, the crinkles at his eyes tightening. "Let's get you a wire."

"The only thing we'll probably get is a bunch of bikers scratching bugs off their bellies."

"Go over and see Dave Waterman. He'll have Sonja wire you up. Do that."

I gave a nod, but it was one that said I heard you, not one that meant I would. I took a red grape that had been polishing itself in the lettuce and put it in my mouth.

Back at my condo, I thought about calling Nathan to tell him that Miranda's husband turned in dental and med charts for his wife, this new information supposed to assure us that the canyon victim could not be Miranda. But the phone rang first, and it was Les Fedders with a proposition I couldn't refuse.

"I'm going down to interview the Pierson household," he said. "You want to come?"

My watch said one-thirty. Half hour down, hour interview, half hour back. Then forty minutes north to Carbon Canyon. I could make it. I'd be later than Monty would like, but I could make it.

San Clemente's a gift from God whether you're a skinhead biker or a family Nixon. A small community along a beautiful stretch of coast, the city's downtown section is quaint and sleepy. Good views in the foothills and along the coast, like good views everywhere, go to the well-to-do, and on the trailing edges, cute cottages merge with slightly seedy quickstop businesses.

Climbing out of the car with Les Fedders, I watched a guy in black leathers and no hair pull on a glove and throw a leg over his Harley as he was about to leave the front of a motel. Next to the motel was Rollie Pierson's house. It was small, fog-gray, and sat streetside in the shadow of a weedy bluff. The blue-framed window in front was open. Through it, while Les knocked on the door, I could hear the urgent tones of a radio minister.

The door opened to a woman with a harvest of yellow-gray hair and a purple feather duster in her hand. She said, "Yes?" in a wary voice.

"Orange County investigators, ma'am," Les said. "Are you Shirley Atwater? I believe I spoke with you on the phone. Les Fedders?" I silently gave him credit for an empathy I did not know he had, credit for not saying homicide when he said investigators. The word is too much for some people. "This is Miss Brandon from forensic services. Could we come in a moment?" He was positively gracious.

Behind us cars whisked down Pacific Coast Highway. The Nazi biker dude horsed his hog around, rolling forward and pausing as if to say, World, have a look at this. Against his shaved skull were the bold strokes of an inked swastika. He fired up, shifted, and roared off after two cars, ripping through a light just turned red, the noise belching under the bluff's protection.

Shirley Atwater led us through the living room into the dining area, freshly dusted, I presumed, and pulled out a straight-backed wooden chair for me. She offered lemonade. I declined, as did Les. She went into the living room and turned the radio volume up, then down, then quickly off, bustling back to the kitchen to pour herself lemonade. Sitting at the end of the brown Formica dining table, she was framed by the window and backlit by yellow globes of fruit dangling off a tree in the backyard so bright in the afternoon sun they looked like party lights.

Les asked, "Have you heard from your sister, Miz Atwater?"

"I don't know where she is. I sure don't." She shifted her frightened eyes to me. "We never got along too good till last year we started getting closer. She started AA then. I could tolerate her after that. Every family has one like that, don't they?"

"I believe that's so," I said.

Les said, "What about Mr. Pierson's family? Is there anyone else?"

"Rollie was an only child. His parents passed a long time ago. I didn't like him much when he was drinking so bad, but he let me move in here with them last year when I lost my job. You can't take that away from him. And he did have Arleta to put up with."

"Would you know if he was acquainted with a man named Monty Blackman?" I asked.

Shirley looked at me then as though she had just had something confirmed that had long bothered her but had gone unarticulated. After a while, she said, "Rollie was forever running out to his place."

"What was he doing that for?" Les said.

"I never paid that much attention. But I do know he got Rollie all excited about motorcycles. Rollie wanted to take Arleta down to this motorcycle shop in Oceanside, buy himself a motorcycle. Harley's House of Harleys, that's what it is. Had to have Arleta along. I said on the quiet, 'Arleta, you let that man buy that thing and you'll be forever throwin' money after it.' I know because my first husband had a boat. Just shovel your money in a hole in the water. That's the way it is with men's hobbies."

"Did Monty Blackman ever come here?" Les asked.

"No. He'd phone though. Kinda scratchy voice."

"When was the last time you think that was?"

"I don't rightly know, but it's been all along. The phone rings a lot—rang a lot—and then he'd be gone, off to here, off to there. Arleta was getting plenty tired of it. She told me she was going to have to be going along to check up on him. She teased him, said he must have one of those women stashed away or he wouldn't be going out wherever all the time. They were happier, the both of them stopped drinking."

All the while, Les was jotting in his notebook the size of a pack of playing cards.

Shirley stroked the feather duster that lay in her lap. I couldn't see her whole hand on the duster, but I could see the wrist going and now I saw the knuckles rise to a squeezing motion.

I said, "You really are worried, aren't you, Mrs. Atwater?"

Her whole being slumped, and she let out a sigh and said, "Oh my, yes. I am."

"How long has your sister been gone?" I asked.

Before she glanced away I had already seen the tears fill in her eyes. She focused on one of those old-fashioned clocks that looked melted at the sides. "I never did set the clock to daylight saving. Isn't that terrible?"

Les and I were quiet.

Soon Shirley said, "Rollie took a lot of lemons out there to him. Sometimes he'd bring back avocados— trade-zies, you could say. We couldn't eat 'em fast enough. Arleta'd put them in salads and make Mexican, but they'd get moldy so fast. We got some growing in the windowsill," she said, nodding toward the kitchen.

"How long has your sister been gone?"

"I was away. I went with an old friend. When I came back, lemons were just all over the yard. I had to pick them up. Arleta would eat them by the dozen," she said, smiling at the memory. "When she gave up drinking, she just seemed to crave that fruit. She'd suck on one all day long like a baby on a pacifier." Shirley bowed her head and said, "Over a week. That'd put it about right." Then she raised her head and looked at me with a plea in her eyes.

I reached over and put my hand on top of the one that held the feather duster. She raised the other hand, held the length of her forefinger stiffly under her nose, with her lips quivering, her eyes closed, her breath coming fast.

While we sat there, I was thinking of the decalcified teeth in the recovered jawbone Meyer Singer kept by him while he worked. Remembering, as if from a dream, one of my investigation handbooks, or one of my forensics textbooks, some detail there, telling me what lemons can do to bone and teeth from protracted contact. Or was it from Dr. Clyde Snow? His disappeareds, witnessing from the grave? Lemons.

I was still patting Mrs. Atwater's hand when I heard the radio preacher's voice again and realized Les had gone to the living room. The start of a fast-tempo hymn pulled through the archway. "Beulah Land," it was. "Beulah Land."

30

The afternoon light was a polished yellow, and as I drove onto the road leading to Carbon Canyon, the same road I took two weeks before to the crime scene that started it all, I saw a hang glider come floating over a distant bluff, a great blue-and-red butterfly coasting in the sunlight. No doubt he thought he was perfectly alone, yet above him circled a hawk, trolling the currents of air, eye out for a morsel of luck.

A few miles up the winding road I passed the scene where Miranda Robertson's Cadillac had scorched a cliffside, the gray hull now gone and the hint of what had lain there blending with the shadows and soil colors. And after a few miles more, I pulled into the dirt lot of Los Lobos, found a pocket in a row of parked cars, and shut off the engine. At the other end of the lot were motorcycles, parked nose-out.

I walked toward the front but stopped first at some tables under the trees near the motorcycles. A hippie-looking man was selling skull rings, snake earrings, and death-rider belt buckles laid out on black velvet.

"See anything you like, I'll give you a deal," he said. He'd perched his feather-bedecked hat on top of a short, unpainted totem pole that had long ago turned gray. It had a deep crack running through it as if hit by baby lightning.

"Thanks. Probably not today."

"Today's as good as any other day."

"Rightly so," I said, "but not today."

I left and walked into a fenced outdoor area with a stage at one end and benches in the middle. The band was playing a fast rockabilly version of the old Beatles' "Give Me Love," while children ran around the legs of their mothers settled on the benches, and raced over the dusty hardpack littered with cigarette butts like marks on a dull chalkboard. The men looked silent and still, too hip to move their bodies to the music.

Across the lot, Monty Blackman sat on a bench under a wood canopy thatched with purple morning-glory vine, its bugles turned to the sun. On the fence by his left shoulder was a white metal sign that read DO NOT THROW TRASH IN THE CREEK. Jolene sat on the bench next to him.

A man stood off to one side of her, talking to them both. He was a carrot-redhead, wore mirrored sunglasses, and in one hand held a beer and in the other a briefcase. Tattooed on his arm were the letters worn by every biker out to prove he's bad: FTW, for Fuck the World. Jolene was smiling prettily at him, and I thought, That bim will smile for anything.

I made an abrupt turn and went inside the bar, wanting to buy my own before someone else offered. Inside, more biker types were playing pool, eating burgers, watching the big TV with no sound. On the jukebox Confederate Railroad was lauding the merits of women just a little on the trashy side. Standing sideways to the bar, I ordered a beer from an old man in a plain shirt who looked very carefully at the cash register keys before he'd strike. I've been in biker bars before, even made two arrests in two different hangouts in one night when I was on patrol in Oakland, and mostly—in the afternoons, at least—the places are quiet, almost otherworldly in their control. These patrons were no different: soft-spoken and at ease in their "colors," strutting the pins, patches, and awarded wings that told which remarkable sexual accomplishments they'd performed before witnesses or which gang they belonged to. As I looked around, I felt a slight edginess, but not much more than if I'd been in a yuppie club anywhere up and down the coast on a Saturday night.

When I took my beer outside, Jolene came over, her bare midriff chalky under the tied-up ends of her blouse. Her lips were wet and puffy as if hotly kissed, her big blue eyes shone, and in her pixie haircut, she looked like a baby trying out big-girl clothes and big-girl boys. Coming close, she said, "Monty's doing some kind of business with that freak with the briefcase. What's going on inside?" She tossed her head back toward the redhead now talking to someone else, rolled her eyes, then said, "He lisps."

I walked over to Monty. The lead guitarist's fingers were slipping over the strings like liquid mercury. His floppy hat lifted with the breeze and his sun-tipped hair blew off his shoulders. When he leaned into the mike to sing, Monty said, "Fuckin' great, inn't he?" I agreed and swigged from my bottle, noticing Monty's glance kept turning toward where new arrivals would likely be seen through the fence slats pulling into the parking lot, as though he were expecting someone. We sat through a couple of songs, while I counted and recounted eight quarter-size craters in the dust by a bench leg where ant lions had winnowed out their landslide traps. I kept wondering what Jolene was doing inside.

"Where's Switchie today?" I asked.

"You interested in that flake?"

"Please. It's just Jolene's here."

"Why don't you go get me a new beer?"

"Why don't you go jump in a lake?"

"Ain't none around," he said, looking for one.

I reached over and pulled his shirt straight so I could read the red letters: Don't Trust Anything That Bleeds for Five Hours and Don't Die. He said, "I took it off Switchie one time he was snorin' so bad the fleas were jumpin' off so they could get some sleep."

"You want a beer, I'll get you a beer," I said.

"Don't put poison in it."

I took his cool empty and pressed it to his cheek like I cared.

Inside, Jolene was seated at the bar opposite a lanky Japanese man. Her legs gleamed at the end of her cutoffs while her boots were parked on the footrest of his barstool. He had his arm propped on the bar and he was slightly smiling with one finger laid across his mouth the way shy people do, only I got a feeling that was not his problem. His impressive array of dermal doodling flowed up under shoulder-length hair and down his arms: tattoos of dragons and women in metal bras, spike bracelets, and blue-flame hair.

As I was about to speak, I saw out of the corner of my eye, exiting from the rest room pocket near the game room, a tall, slender woman in a black ribbed-knit top and pale blue jeans. She had a wide and beautiful face with high cheekbones and wore her auburn hair in a thick braid, tied off with a puffy black hair twist with gold threads in it.

Miranda Robertson!

I held my breath as she looked my way. Then she turned. It was fairly dark in there, I still had on my shades, and she might not have recognized me anyway, because in the years she was with Nathan we'd talked on the phone several times but she'd only seen me twice.

She stopped at the jukebox. One arm up on the neon, she read the selections, then dropped two coins in, still reading when Aaron Tippin's voice filled the room with his banjo twang, singing about his Bloo-woo, Oo-woo-woo, Ain-gel. She went outside.

Jolene had her finger poised at the Asian man's belly where there was a puckered hole a few inches above the hipbone, hollowed like a second navel. She held there a moment, then drilled into it. As she ran her finger over the cavity's edges, the man laughed and looked proud of his bullet hole. Then his gaze caught mine and turned to a calm, surveying one.

Jolene said, "This is Brandy. We work together."

"You dry? Let me get you another," he said, in a surprisingly deep voice.

I showed him my still-full Stroh's as the bartender came over, and then ordered Monty's drink.

The bullet-hole guy excused himself and told us not to go away. He headed for the men's room.

"Don't worry, we won't," Jolene said. Then, to me: "Switchie's coming. We can do somethin', I don't know, together. You up for it?"

"What about your new friend?"

"What new friend?"

"Him," I said, nodding toward the men's.

"Tish!" she said.

On our way to the door, a man with white hair and a pinched cowboy hat with four toothpicks in the hatband raised his drink to us.

I figured Miranda had gone outside to be with Monty. How should I act? I wanted her to recognize me, yet didn't. If she did, anything could be explained, and this was broad daylight; nobody'd try anything funny here.

And then I thought of Bernie Williams. He died in broad daylight, with a crowd of revelers around.

Outside, I saw Miranda reaching into a man's potato chip sack, withdrawing a clawful, then munching. I lost my nerve, set the beers down, and went through the gate to the parking lot.

When I reached my car, Monty was behind me.

He said, "What's your hurry?" Wearing tennis shoes instead of boots, he was nearly eye level to me. "I thought you dug the music."

"I do. But I have a lot to do."

"You only been here twenty minutes."

"Yeah, well."

"You're mad about somethin'. Is it the girl?"

"What girl?"

"Your competition."

"I don't have any competition," I said, taking off my shades and giving him a squint. And then I said again, "What girl?" trying to draw him out.

Monty's head turned toward the front door. Around his ponytail was a red terry cloth band. "That one," he said, as Miranda walked out of the gig yard, passing into the bar again.

"I never noticed her."

"The hell. I *saw* you notice her. Come on back a minute. She's somebody I want you to meet."

As if Monty wore a mike and Miranda was picking up the transmission, she sauntered out of the building toward us on cue.

"This is Angel," Monty said. "She's been stayin' with me while she gets her shit together." He was telling me it was her clothes I'd seen on his bed. "Then she's goin' home to her rich husband. He run her off 'cause she fell in love with me." He winked. "What she don't know is, once a piece of scooter trash, always a piece of scooter trash. You got no choice now, sweetheart. This here's Brandy," he said. "Works for me now, what? a week?"

"Something like that," I said.

Miranda said I looked familiar and kept narrowing her eyes in memory. If anything, she was prettier than she was when I'd last seen her, a little living in her face by now, though her eyes showed a redness as if she were stricken with allergy.

A man leaned out from inside and called, "You can't drink out there."

Monty looked at the bottle in his hand, put a goofy grin on his face, and said, "It's these girls' fault," and swept us along with him.

An engine slowed, and gravel crunched. I glanced back and saw a faded red pickup pulling in. "It's Simon," Monty said. He handed me his beer and went to meet the truck, Miranda tagging along.

Miranda's crotch rocket was merged with the mess of bikes. Bluish-white flames on the tank and fenders were evidence of Monty's handiwork. Gradually it came to me that the snapshot of a half face and shoulder on Monty's refrigerator was of her, and I realized that even then something about it had nagged at me. I wanted desperately to call Nathan and tell him that here was Miranda in the flesh. But Monty had persuaded Simon to follow him and Miranda out to the farm to check on Paulie's manure pit progress, and I sure wasn't going to let her out of my sight. As she strapped on a blue helmet, she stared at me again, and I didn't know if she was wondering what relationship Monty and I really had, or if she had at last recognized me behind the sunglasses, under the tinted hair, and after five or so years.

As we headed out, Miranda followed Monty and

I trailed her. Most of the time I couldn't catch up to them, but I'd see their dim spots down the highway heading to the flatland. Behind me was Simon in his pickup, without his snake this time. He told Monty he'd left three turkey hens in one of Monty's empty pigsties, that they got scared off their brooding by neighbor dogs and weren't good for nothing else till next season, so might as well cook 'em up, is what he said. He also said he had a couple of jakes, year-old males, if Monty wanted to try for spur fighting. Monty had said, "No, man, I'm not into that," and when he did, he patted me on the shoulder as if to say, Some company I keep, huh?

31 | How I wanted to phone Nathan from the car, tell him his Miranda was in my view, how she was flying along the highway atop a jazzed-up softail, her dark braid trailing out from under a blue lid. But I didn't.

What I did was call the lab. I could talk hands-free because of the way the phone mike was set up inside the car. Simon behind me wouldn't see me yakking on a handset, and Miranda was too far down the road to make anything out if she looked in her side mirror. Joe actually picked up on the second ring. I told him what had developed, and he yammered at me for being seduced back to the farm without some kind of backup. I said I hadn't seen any of Exner's backup since I'd been in this case. He said, "I know, baby. Exner's an asshole."

"Like I said."

"Like you said. Just be cool. Stay awake out there. Leave before dark."

"Button up my overcoat."

"That too," he said.

Pulling into Monty's driveway, I made for parking out of the way of his and Miranda's bikes.

A gray bird with a bandit's mask flicked over the fence line to my right as I was shutting my car door. That was twice now I'd seen a butcher-bird near human settlement, and this is not his style.

Simon pulled in, music blasting from the cab. He cut the engine but left the music on and sat listening to Patty Lovelace berate a guy who had a dead-beatin', double-dealin' heart.

While Monty was getting a knapsack off his bike, Miranda went into the house, opening the door with her own key. I heard the whine of machinery and looked up toward the large animal shed and didn't see anything.

Simon got out and walked toward me, his pink shirt with large blue snail shells in the design fluttering around his thin torso and above gray raggedy shorts. We followed Monty into the house, Simon saying, "Pretty day, isn't it?" Once inside, he went directly to the refrigerator, opened it, and stood there staring into the depths.

Monty opened the leather knapsack he'd laid on the table, extracting from it a packet of green bills. He said to Simon, "Here you go. Buy yourself a CD player for that cage o' yours, buddy." The money, though I couldn't see the denominations, seemed enough to do that and buy a new truck as well. Changing places with Simon just before the refrigerator door closed, Monty pulled out a cardboard caddy of Millers and a four-pocket cache of wine coolers.

Simon picked up the money and said, "Dude," in a reverential way.

"A problem?"

Sitting down on a worse-for-wear love seat, Simon spread out the bills on a coffee table before him. He said, "There's enough money here to burn a wet mule."

Monty's eyes smiled. "You want some of this here panther piss or not?" handing him a bottle by its neck. He offered me a watery red bottle and said, "Or would you rather have beer?"

"I'll take the cooler."

"Her too," he said, and handed Miranda one when she came out of the bathroom, "won'tcha, Angel?" She drifted up close to him and gave two tugs on his ponytail as if ringing for servants.

Simon said, "Man, it wasn't that big a deal," fingering the money, then seeming to check himself, swinging a glance my way, then back to Monty.

Monty said, "I'm goin' to look in on Paulie. Why don't you come along?" He took the black pouch and put it on a top shelf in a kitchen cabinet. "You two girls get acquainted. We'll be back in a minute."

Miranda asked, "You got any roll papers?" She was in a brown recliner, her legs tucked up under and her wine cooler a third gone. Only now did I remember she was supposed to be pregnant. I wondered how the baby felt, getting high.

"In the back," he said, nodding toward the bedroom as he and Simon went out.

Miranda seemed to be gauging my face. "You party?" she asked.

"Not anymore."

She rose and started toward the bedroom.

Walking through the kitchen to a side door, I opened it and looked around. Bandit territory here. Within a rake's reach of the house was the butcherbird's conspicuous cache of skewered prey. His open-air mortuary included half a mouse, a pale grasshopper, and a hunk of unidentifiable fur. Some birders say the loggerhead shrike displays his wares to attract and impress females, like little Gatsbys. Others say they're simple hoarders. Whatever, it seemed easily appropriate to find the bird breaking his own law and flaunting his habits here.

I got myself a glass and filled it with water.

Miranda was back in the recliner, a doobie in her hand. The sweet scent of marijuana hovered. She had turned on the TV that sat in the corner, and a news team was standing beside a freeway while cars whizzed behind. But the audio wasn't up, and so when Miranda said to me what she said, her words set me slowly down in the brown upholstered chair opposite her like a gentle but sure hand on my chest. She let out a toke of air and said, "You're Samantha Montiel, aren't you?"

She offered me the joint. I considered a moment, and took it. In the present scheme of things, it didn't seem like a deed that mattered. I wasn't a sworn officer and grass had never put me over the top. But I'd definitely lost my virginity again. I drew the smoke in. A cupful of tacks made its way down my throat.

"What are you doing here?" she asked, unfolding one leg onto the worn beige carpet. The shoes were designed to look like full cowboy boots but were cut low just above the ankle. Along the sides were wavy insets of red leather snakes. I was glad I wasn't wearing the boots Monty had loaned me, because I had the feeling they were hers.

"Hanging out, same as you," I said.

"Bullshit." Her voice was unemotional with a hint of rawness like Monty's. "Nathan sent you."

When I handed back the joint, Miranda leaned forward so the Leatherette snicked, and the weight of her breasts stretched the knit top she wore. I thought of the surgery she'd had. Again I felt a wave of sympathy, and thought that at least the plastic was still planted and not the concern of some unenviable furnace farrier with scraper and wire brush. She inhaled again, the roach poised between two delicate fingers with unlacquered nails, and examined the stub as if wondering how it arrived in her hand. "Zacatecan purple," she said. "The best, from Central America. Monty says it's turbocharged. I fucked a guy for it."

"You don't need to tell me that."

"You're an uptight asshole like your brother. Two peas in a pod." She reached for an ashtray on the lamp table next to her, handed it to me with the joint. On the bottom of the clear glass was a painted spread of cards distributed in a royal flush.

Just a little suck and I handed it back. We sat saying nothing for a long time. In the back of my mind I was thinking about Monty, wondering how he'd react when he found out Miranda and I knew each other and what I should do when he did. Miranda toked again, and I said, "I hear you're pregnant."

"And you're wondering whose."

"I'm wondering how weird the baby's going to be."

"Don't sweat it. It's gone."

"Mm," I muttered.

"Screw you."

"Did I say—?"

"Fuck you anyway."

She carried the joint with her when she went to the front door, opened it, and looked out. The air was welcome. "I'm sorry," she said, then closed the door and stood massaging one elbow.

"It's all right," I said.

Memory seemed to turn in her. She asked, kindly, "How are you?"

"I'm okay. Losing plumbing isn't all that bad. I forget what a Kotex is."

"Well, that part would be nice," she said with a laugh. She returned to the recliner and doused what was left of the joint, and rocked in slow, tight jags.

I said, "You helped me when I was going through the tearful part."

"I did?" she asked softly.

"You don't remember?"

"Maybe a little," she said. "What did I say?"

I made something up. "You said I'd be a lousy mother anyway."

The merest smile formed on her lips.

"No," I said, "what it was was I blabbered, you listened."

She thought about that awhile. "You're still married?"

"He died."

"Oh," she said, with a frown and a whisper. "I remember now." Then she sat forward and said in a rush, "I'd get in my car and leave if I were you. You don't belong here."

"Why, Miranda?"

"Because."

"Because why, Miranda?"

"You were a cop. Your husband was a cop."

"So? I'm not now. Not for ten years. If I was a cop, what would I be doing doffing clothes at Monty's and smoking a joint with you?"

She jumped up and began pacing. "Just leave. I mean it." When she stopped to gesture, her hands shook. "I'm telling you . . ." she said, then sat down again, a look of helplessness on her face.

"What, Miranda?" She just shook her head. I went to the kitchen window, looked around, giving her some space. Then I came back and sat in the chair opposite her again, leaning forward. It was time.

I said, "Who was the woman in the car, Miranda? Who had to die to take your place?"

Her eyes grew wide and she gripped the armrests. The bones in her neck showed sharply. "You're crazy."

"A woman turned to charcoal in a car registered to you," I said. "Tell me how she deserved that."

"You *are* a cop."

"Not exactly."

"Oh Jesus," she heaved. "You don't understand."

"What's to understand? You put her there or you didn't."

"Of course I didn't put her there," she whispered. "What do you think I am?" She pushed on the back of the recliner until it descended a little, and rested her head and shut her eyes, remaining very still.

I went over and knelt beside her. "You're sorry about that," I said. "It wasn't supposed to happen, was it?" She turned her head from side to side, her face a series of tortured expressions while her eyes stayed shut. "Miranda, I know that any woman my brother loves could not be responsible for something horrible like that. You think I'm a dummy? I may be an uptight asshole, but I'm smart enough to know that."

When her eyes opened, tears were ladled at the bottom lid. She studied the ceiling; then a huge drop rolled into her ear. Her voice was at a lower, harder register. "You better get out of here. You don't know what's going on."

"Tell me and we'll both know."

Bringing the recliner up, she tried taking another hit, but the nub in the ashtray was cold. "These aren't people you just fool with. I'm serious."

"Monty?" I asked, rising.

"And others."

"The guy called Switchie?"

She nodded again. I sat at the end of the love seat an arm's length from her.

"Who else?"

She waved her hand, munched in her lips, and

looked away at the television, a blonde woman helping a fat man cook on screen.

"How'd you come so far, Miranda? You had a life with your husband and . . . and Nathan. That wasn't so bad, was it? Two men who adore you."

One hand propped her forehead. "That Zac's for shit," she said. "Out of Kentucky's better."

I leaned over and put my hand on the one that rested on her knee. "Who was the woman in the car, Miranda? Tell me."

Her head jerked up, and she said, "Why are you doing this? Why do you have to know?"

"Maybe I can help."

"Nobody can help me."

"I'm not sure about that."

"Monty tried. He's the only one."

"Monty tried to help you?"

She slipped her hand free of mine and thumbed her bra straps through her shirt, giving her hands something to do. She took on a tough tone. "When I met Monty, I was the Crystal Queen, fiending everything. I had a sugar bowl filled with rock. I dropped crank in my coffee. That's before I knew coffee'd wash it out of your system." Laughing, like I was a pal now.

"Was this before you married the doctor?"

"Yes. Tabs and cubes, tranqs and ludes. You name it, I did it, up, down, sideways. Ice? God, I thought I'd died and gone to heaven. Straight-to-the-brain orgasm. No more diets and fourteen hours between hits. This was after your brother," she said, looking at me as if for approval. "After Nathan, *before* this time, I mean. It gets confusing."

"I guess it would. Then you met Monty."

"I knew Monty from years ago, when I was a little kid. My dad rode motorcycles. At first I didn't recognize him. I bumped into him in an auto parts store when I was buying windshield wipers. I thought he was cute. He started flirting with me. Then we realized we knew each other, and we kind of cooled it. He introduced me to Robert."

"*He's* the one knew Robert?"

"First, yeah." She laughed. "I always wanted to marry a doctor."

"And he cleaned you up."

"Monty cleaned me up. He doesn't like drugs."

"Except grass."

"Piff. That's not drugs."

I thought, He doesn't like drugs, but Agent Vogel said he shipped precursors. The man didn't add up. "The woman in your car . . . can we talk about her?"

"Why do you keep at it? Why do you want to know?"

"Who was she? A friend?"

"I need something." She looked around the room as if tracking a fly, then at the stub in the ashtray.

"Just talk to me."

She whipped into the kitchen and got herself another cooler. Untwisting the bottle cap, she cut her hand, and swore, and sucked between her forefinger and thumb. "Maybe I'll die of lead poisoning—not of the Uzi kind," she said. "Serve me right." Her shoulders dropped as she came back and sat on the coffee table, on top of a sports magazine. "What do you care, anyway? She's dead. Beyond help, as they say."

"Lost and gone forever. Dreadful sorry, Clementine," I said. "Is that what you mean?"

"She wasn't such a nice person." Miranda took a drink and set the bottle down.

"And that makes all the difference."

"No, that's not what I'm saying! I meant . . . who knows what I meant? Anyway, the main thing, it's best that Nathan thinks I'm gone. But he won't think that now, will he? You'll tell him."

"A guy's suffering," I said.

"A lot of guys are suffering. Women suffer more."

"Like the woman in your car?"

She sucked the web of her hand again.

"Miranda, the woman had no head, no hands or feet. She was burned that bad."

"Stop it!" All the air went out of her then. Her hands opened into wounded curls as if the palms had just been smacked by rulers.

We heard a sound out front, of doors closing.

Jumping up, she said bitterly, "Here they come," and went to the window and peered between the strips of plastic lace curtain. "You want to know things? Well, dig this. Switchie? He murdered somebody. And that one there got rid of the body." She nodded toward the faded red smear of Simon's truck showing between the curtains. "He put it in his truck and hauled it away. Get out. You're a little fool if you don't. They're coming."

32 Simon's face squinched into a happy grin at the lingering smell of weed. "You girls leave any of that for us pore ol' boys?" He stood with his shirt half open and his feet spread like a duck's. The money Monty gave him tubed in the pocket of his shorts like a magnum penis.

Miranda's alarm didn't transfer to me, and it wasn't because of the dope—she was right, she got screwed, maybe literally, on the Zac. But I wasn't afraid because Simon seemed like a harmless goon, and nowhere around Monty had I ever seen a weapon. After the killing of Bernie Williams, I thought of carrying, but all I had for a small gun was a mostly useless two-shot derringer whose projectile would've been a pebble tossed at two men in a shed.

When Monty came in, Simon hit him up for the grass: "Hey, good buddy, we gonna party hearty?" He looked at me with a happy grin.

Monty checked Miranda and said indifferently, "Go for it." But Miranda sat there not offering to go for it, and Simon didn't know where to look, and Monty went to squat in front of the TV, turn it off, and put on music.

I didn't want to be around with night coming and people doping and Monty putting music on. At the same time, I wished I had more time with Miranda.

I wanted to give her my phone number. We locked eyes when I said, "I guess I'll see you all later," hiking my purse strap over my shoulder.

Monty stood up. "Where you in a hurry to? I give you the night off. You don't have to show at the Python."

I shrugged, said, "Stuff to do. *Stuff*, you know?"

Monty stepped ahead and put a hand on the doorknob. He gave a long look without a smile, then said, "You want to go, go," and opened the door.

Simon's brows were knitting up, down, up down, trying to put it together.

As I stepped out, a horn blared from a distance and got closer and louder, and soon a green pickup barreled into the yard. A man with a dark face and a straw hat leaned out even before the truck stopped rolling, and then I recognized Mr. Avalos. He was shouting hoarsely, "Paulie's down! In the pit! We can't get him out!"

Monty said, "Shit! That intake valve," and blew by me and ran to the passenger side and jumped in as Mr. Avalos yanked the wheel around to head back up to the animal confinement building. I jogged to the side of the house and looked. At the far edge of the building was a blue pickup in profile and two figures moving beside it. Ahead of the truck was the white shape of a motorcycle, and standing by it a man in black, with blond hair. Switchie.

As Simon ran for his truck, I yelled after him, "I'll call nine-one-one," and turned and looked for a house number. "Where are we?"

"Thirteen-thirteen," Miranda said, following me in. "But don't phone."

"Why not?"

"Just don't. They'll work it out." Her hand shook

as she fumbled for a cigarette from a pack Simon left on the table.

"You're hard to figure," I said.

She said, "And you're dead, is what you are. Didn't you see Switchie out there?"

"I saw him."

Still standing, she lowered her face to her hands, the smoky end of the cigarette close to a wayward strand of hair, then swept her hands away and said, "Listen to me! Get in your car and leave."

"One of my strong points is that I'm stubborn," I said, setting my purse down. "I'm not going anywhere."

She gave a smirk, wisdom entering her eyes. "Like your brother," she said, then sat on the arm of the brown chair, her braid with the gold-flecked tie riding her shoulder like Simon's snake. She said, amused, "I told you Switchie kills people. You want to know something else? He said he'd like to be a cop if it paid for shit." The look she gave me was lingering.

"How do you know Switchie killed anyone?"

"Because I was right back there in that bedroom when I heard him say it."

"Heard him say what?"

" 'I bumped off Rollie.' "

Rollie Pierson! I was not expecting her to say that name, ever. If she said any name, it would be Quillard Satterlee. I echoed, "Rollie."

"Yeah. He did stuff for Monty," she said, with a dismissing wave of the hand. "Monty was really, really mad. Yelling. I never heard Monty yell before. I came out of the bedroom for a minute, saw him kick Switchie right out the door. He had his boots on, kicked him right out the front door." She motioned in that direction. "Before, I told Monty I didn't like him. He said, 'What's not to like?' People who've shared a bad thing, like prison, I guess, what do they have? They help each other."

"Why don't you come on home with me, Miranda?"

Her liquid eyes turned to me, she said, "No."

"Let me give you my phone number."

"I won't call."

"But why?"

"Some doors close, they can't be opened."

"And some doors never really close. Nathan must have told you that."

A great breath came out of her, and she sagged. "Could I have some water?"

"Of course," I said, and stepped away to get it.

When I returned, she said, "I think Switchie killed him with a Gigli saw."

"A what?"

"A Gigli saw. Robert sold it to him. Didn't even *give* it to him. Sold it."

"Your *husband* knows Switchie?" I sat next to her.

"Sure. Switchie's taking classes at Orange Coast to become a stockbroker. Yeah," she said, an edge back in her voice, "since he can't be a cop. He was all the time on the phone to Robert, getting tips."

"What's a giggly saw?"

"This thin saw. Surgeons use it—well, before lasers. You drill two holes in a skull, and then you thread it in from underneath, and saw *up* so you don't hurt the brain. There's a little ring on one end you hold. Robert was showing it to Switchie one day."

"And Switchie had to have one."

She nodded. "Prisoners, CIA, they keep them in hollow shoelaces and belt buckles. When Switchie heard that, he gave Robert a hundred dollars for one. And he took it, the crumb."

I thought about Rollie Pierson, the crude piece of carding wire found around his neck.

"Miranda—" I said, starting to urge her to leave with me again.

"I'm not afraid of him as long as I'm around Monty. But you shouldn't be here. There's no reason for you to be here."

"Let's go check on Paulie," I said. She looked me straight in the eye and got up.

Opening the car door, we climbed into the rich smell of my neighbor's dog pitched by late-afternoon heat. I took the dirt road up to the animal building, passing a small set of pens where three strange-looking turkey heads peeked over the boards and the silhouette of one lonely porker showed through the cracks.

"What about Simon?" I said.

"He's nobody."

"Monty keeps interesting company," I said.

The wind from the open window was shattering her bangs. "The only thing Monty did wrong was get acquainted with my husband," she said. "It made him greedy."

"Your husband's going to China. Why?"

"What?"

"Nathan told me. He found out somehow. It's business tied to Monty, isn't it?"

She pulled her foot up and kicked my dash and looked the other way out the window. She said, "He was supposed to take me." The more I'm around humans, the more I'd rather be around pigs.

I pulled up behind a yellow backhoe not visible from the house and across the way from a grand hollow of earth with a pyramid of pipe stacked beside it like polished dinosaur bones. Ahead of the new green pickup was Simon's, with the tailgate down. We got out and walked to where Monty, Simon, and one of the workers I'd seen at the Avalos ranch stood near the large lump of Paulie Avalos. His torso was wrapped with the rope they used to pull him from the cellar of slime below the animal building. He was greenish brown from pig gop. His face, where it wasn't pasted with it, was red, the same color as victims of carbon monoxide poisoning, and I remembered Monty and Mr. Avalos talking about hydrogen sulfide and a rotten egg smell. The smell here was pig shit, but bearable.

The door of the building stood open. At ground level were two screened air intakes whose fan blades were motionless as abandoned windmills. In front, in the shadows, lay the still form of a smaller man. I'd seen enough bodies in my life to know he was gone.

Monty's hands and clothes were filthy, as were Mr. Avalos's and the other worker's. Monty was stripping off his shirt, when Switchie, his shades on and his black T-shirt showing bulbous arms, squatted by Paulie's head, bouncing on his heels. He balanced himself with one hand on the ground, fingers exposed at the ends of his black riding glove. "Paulie, you bean-eater pansy," he said, "get yourself up here and get back to work." A spill of blond hair arced over his forehead like a table saw blade. "You bug-fucking tortilla, get your ass up here. Come on, Paulie. Come on, my man."

Mr. Avalos was standing bowlegged at Paulie's feet. He turned and looked far away in the direction of the road and said, "Aren't they coming?"

With his shirt off, Monty quickly wiped Paulie's whole head with it. For the first time, I saw that Monty had a hued hide also: On his back a Viking whipped a short team of polar bears pulling a Harley. He left the shirt under Paulie's neck for a prop, then pinched his nose and began blowing in his mouth. All the while, Simon, standing with his elbows back from his sides, was making painful faces.

Monty raised up and said, "Anybody know CPR?"

"Push on his chest too," I said, but that's all I could say because I hadn't ever done CPR myself. I couldn't take it anymore, started moving while I said, "I'll call," and Monty tossed a quick nod and put his mouth to Paulie's lips and blew again.

In my car, I punched the right buttons but got a busy signal. That didn't mean it really was; it could mean that something interfered with the transmitting cells or that the carrier I used didn't cover this area. I drove for the house, found the yellow phone with workman's dirt on it, and this time got through.

Moments later Miranda came walking in, breathing heavily from the walk over. She sat on the coffee table and pulled off her half boots, emptying bits of dried grass. Bitterly, she said, "Switchie had something to do with this. I just know it."

"There was a worker too,"I said in defense.

Shaking her head strongly, she said, "He had something to do with it." Then she got up and went to the bedroom and brought back a candy tin filled with roll papers and purple Zac.

On the eastern side of Garden Grove, the "City of Youth and Ambition," looms the Crystal Cathedral, offering Sunday services in English, Spanish, Korean, and Vietnamese. Beside its walkways lined with flowers and waterfalls, believers are baptized, married, trained, and buried, and when a baggy-clothed teenage tagger wielding a drill bit etched his calling card in seven thousand dollars' worth of win-

dows recently, the deed made the news spots for
two days.

Eighteen square miles of mostly mid-income, mid-
age white people, it was developed with the help of
Mexican *braceros*, Jamaican laborers, German prisoners of World War II, and diligent farmers of Japanese descent who were later shipped to internment
camps. Its boundaries snake in strange configura-
tions into neighboring cities such as Westminster,
home to Little Saigon, the largest settlement of Vietnamese in the country. Garden Grove has been the
Chili Pepper Capital, the Egg Capital, and the Strawberry Capital. Now it crawls toward another dis-
tinction, that of being number two, next to Santa
Ana, for the highest crime rate in the county for cities of its size.

It was where Monty had his bar and it was where
Les Fedders went to church, and it was where I
wound up the night of the day Paulie Avalos got
carted off to the hospital, a victim of manure pit poisoning. Monty said I didn't have to work, and then
he did. When the ambulance arrived at the farm and
took Paulie away, Monty stopped at the house,
washed up and changed clothes, and told Miranda
to ride with Simon to the hospital. Then he said to
me, "Switchie says Jolene got sick and ain't goin' in.
Go in for me, will you? Just for a little while."

"Why? You said it wasn't going to be busy." He
glared at me like he didn't need another problem,
and I said, "Okay."

On the way to the Python I made three calls trying
to find Joe Sanders and when I couldn't, I called the
pager number for Captain Exner. I was almost to my
turnoff when he rang in. He was having dinner with
his wife. Suddenly I was ravenous. I told him what
had been going on, hardly believing that in the last
eight hours since I'd had lunch with Joe, I'd been to

San Clemente to interview Rollie Pierson's sister-in-law, to Carbon Canyon where good bands play for bikers and I found Miranda, and then out to see Paulie Avalos slip in a manure pit at Monty Blackman's farm. The captain said go, go on to work like Monty said. I asked, "Captain?" Am I getting any backup on this?"

"Don't worry about it. We got you covered."

Right, I thought. Believe that when I see it.

My nerves were frayed, I'd ripped the strap off the tangerine thing I was supposed to wear for my third change, and now I was wearing a bodysuit that made me look like Catwoman after a fight, holes everywhere. Customers were arriving in onesies and twosies, no office parties tonight. Two wore knit shirts with the logo from the Hard Rock Cafe. Who said the Chili Pepper–Egg-Strawberry Capital can't be as trendy as Newport Beach? I drifted along delivering my spiel to gin-logged men and the few high-haired women with them, when someone in the black shadows at a table caught my eye. When I took a second look, I nearly broke down and cried. When I came near, the hefty woman said, "Hi, friend. How you doin' tonight?"

It was Christine Vogel—make that Agent Vogel—and she was the last person I expected to see. She wore the kind of filmy, crinkly dress that looks like she washed it by hand and killed it by mighty twists before putting it on still damp. Golden tigers swarmed on it as though turning 'round and 'round to find their napping place.

I said quietly, almost laughing, "You're my undercover?"

"You wouldn't want to see any of this uncovered, honey," she said, and winked.

Looking over at Howard the bartender looking

over at us, I said, "Who will I say you are?"

"Say I'm your sister. Your sister, not your mother." She smiled in her twinkly way.

"I was going to leave soon," I said.

"Do anything you want."

In Monty's office, I climbed into my jeans and pulled on my pig farm–smelling top when Coral, the fat model, came in. Pale as mashed potatoes, all colors on her became a bright vengeance. The gown she wore was a clean turquoise that set off her cinnamon hair. Earlier I'd learned that the young, baby-faced model was her daughter. "You and your girl can grab the rest of the tips, Coral," I said, "I'm going home."

She said that was really, really cool of me. "It's not the best of work, but it's better than some, you know what I mean? She's got college and she just can't earn enough working at Burger King."

I shrugged a shoulder and said, "It's all the carcass trade, one way or another, right?"

"Thanks," Coral said. "We should go shopping sometime."

"Maybe so," I said, leaving, holding the door just a crack and adding, "Take care now."

Agent Vogel by this time had a drink in front of her, something dark amber. I sat down with her. "Mind if I put out the candle?" I said, and proceeded to top the candle cup with an ashtray. The flame diminished and died, and when I removed the ashtray, a blue wail of smoke fled out the top. Over the bar the new TV Monty had installed was tuned to a music video, *Song of the Harlot*, by Violet Burn.

"Should we leave?" I asked.

"Wait awhile."

"You're not concerned?"

"Not at all. Best thing is to look natural, like you have a life."

"You heard what happened today?"

"I heard Paul Avalos had a close call. The other one's too dead to skin. Excuse me," she said. "My humor. You just hang in there. You're doing good."

"Was the ambulance a mistake?"

"How could it be? You had to. This Switchie person was there?"

"Miranda thinks he had something to do with it."

"What did you get out of her?"

"She says Switchie killed a man named Rollie Pierson. It's a case we haven't told you about because we had feelings but the connections didn't add up. I think she knows about Bernie Williams too. She said a guy named Simon, little guy, carries around a snake, says he hauled a body away. Things went fast after that. I didn't get to talk to her alone again."

"We're gonna get him. Will you see her tomorrow?"

"I don't know. She went off with Monty."

"This Monty," she said, her tone quiet, her eyes serious, "we've had women who fall while they're under. You okay on that?"

"Me and Monty?"

"Just checking. Anyone who looks good in a mug shot I say is minefield-dangerous."

"What are you drinking, Christine?"

"A Black Widow. Rum and Southern Comfort."

"It must be a double," I said.

I was home, sound asleep, when the phone rang. "Did I wake you?" Joe asked.

"Uh, no."

"Forgive me. Go back to sleep."

"No, I . . ."

"Why is it nobody ever admits they were asleep when they were asleep?"

"Well, I'm awake now."

"You wouldn't want some company, would you?"

I looked at the clock. "What are you still doing up? It's midnight."

His voice was soft and halting. He told me he was worried about me. He'd been asleep off and on, but since the last waking, zero.

"Come over," I said.

And later, in the bedroom, when he made love to me, it was as if he just couldn't get to the bottom of that well.

33 "One puzzle piece that was off the table is now back on," I told Captain Exner the next morning. Joe had left a half hour before.

"I'm not crazy about that development."

"Well, we can't put her back in the bottle though, can we? Miranda *was* disturbed, which, under the circumstances, is understandable. But I don't think she'd spout off about me. And if she did, I think I could handle a cover story. I took an acting class once, believe it or not."

"Remind me of that if I ever need a friend in court," he said, and it was the first time I realized he had a sense of humor. "It's dicey. How'd it go last night? Blackman show up?"

"Not while I was there. I worked a few hours and left. Agent Vogel came in."

"She told me. Her husband likes the place. I guess you got a heavy model there?"

"Coral."

"That's the one," the captain said.

"Captain, I've been in two of Monty's houses and at the bar, and I saw no evidence of any chemicals, nothing like that. No weapons, drugs, not even any picnic coolers with swine semen on ice. Oh, except a little marijuana."

"Right now I don't give a rat's tokus if Blackman pours precursors on the Easter Bunny's cornflakes,"

Captain Exner said. "What I want him for is con-
spiracy to murder. That guy is going *down*. We'll
RICO him." By RICO, the captain was referring to
federal legislation that nails offenders for a pattern
of racketeering over the span of a decade. Racketeering is having influence or control over an enterprise by the commission of at least two felonies.
There'd be no lingerie saloons for Monty for a good
long time.

"What do I do now, Captain?" I asked.

"Come in and get wired," he said.

Now all I had to do was dream up a good reason
for showing back up at Monty's farm. I tried calling
him at the farm, then at the bar, where I found him.
I asked how Paulie was. He said, "Bitchin' about
they don't have hot sauce in the hospital. He'll be
okay, but he sure has one hell of a headache and
claims he's still coughin' up fertilizer."

"What happened, exactly?"

"His dad warned me. See, there's all kinds of poisonous gases in sewage. Methane's the one you usually hear about, but there's carbon dioxide and
ammonia, and hydrogen sulfide. In low concentra-
tions you can smell it but high you don't. He went
down in there wadin' around and stirred it up. He
should have wore his scuba equipment. He didn't
have that on neither."

"Scuba equipment?"

"His mask, whaddya call it? Self-Contained
Breathin' Apparatus. Scuba. Plus, you don't go
down in a pit without somebody else around knows
what he's doing. Whole farm families get wiped out.
One goes down in there after another."

"He had a worker from his father's farm, right?"

"Yeah, and if Switchie hadn't stopped by, Paulie'd be dead as him."

"Switchie's clothes weren't dirty," I said.

"That's 'cause Switchie's too smart to follow them down there. He tossed him a rope. Alfredo was gone already. Paulie's too heavy, though. It took us all to pull him out."

"How's Miranda? She looked pretty upset."

There was a silence. "It might be good you come by and see her sometime."

"Well, sure, I guess I can do that."

"I'm goin' to be busy here a little bit, then I'll go see Avalos. You left early last night, I hear."

"You said you only wanted me to check on things. Coral and her daughter did fine. Heard from Jolene?"

"Nope."

"Maybe she's with Switchie."

"Nope. Just talked to him. I gotta go—state inspector's here. Been harassin' my ass all year."

Wearing a rig may be easier for a woman; it hides in the cleavage well. Speak into the microphone, honey.

The captain told me he commandeered a van from Caltrans, the agency that each year plucks fallout ranging from blankets to boxes, bodies to beer off 140 miles of county freeway. My wire setup would transmit to the van, where a tape could be made by deputies. I met them before I left: two young men with small frames, big mustaches, no humor.

The van followed me pretty close most of the way, then dropped back some when we got close. We had broken communications near Monty's farm, but it would pull through, and then for a while we had nothing, the same as when I tried to call 911 for Paulie. All I could hope for was that, one, I wouldn't need the guys for a cavalry attack; and two, the lines would eventually clear up.

Simon's red truck was still at Monty's when I arrived a little after one. The sight of it gave me a twist, and the large, flat box in the truck bed that held Simon's boa constrictor didn't make me very happy either.

I parked on the far side of the pickup and walked around its nose, wanting to look in the bed, but wanting to know where Simon was first. Monty's black stallion was nowhere in sight, nor his green bike with hammered steel and molded snake head. Nor did I see Miranda's bomber. I glanced at the fence by the side of the house. The butcher-bird had a new trophy: spiked on a barb was the head of a smaller bird, its beak in grimmest lock, its sightless eye like a tiny fried button.

I saw an unfamiliar white van up by the big animal building. Soon a man in a light-colored cowboy hat came out from behind the building. The distance prevented me from seeing his features, and at first I thought it was Monty, and then Mr. Avalos. But as he walked toward the truck, I thought he bore the gait of Switchie Ralph D'Antonio. He got into the van and drove northeast away from the farm.

Talking to my tan safari blouse, I told the deputies what I saw, then went to the front door. On the ground near the step was a wayward lemon, puckered by sun and wearing a single black fly.

I knocked. No answer. Trying the doorknob, I turned it and went in.

No one in the kitchen or living room. Ditto the bathroom and the far bedroom, where tangled sheets, empty drink cans, Miranda's clothes (two sets of them) were tossed about, but not Monty's. On a nightstand lay a hairbrush and a gold hair twist. The room smelled of drained beer and stale weed. I walked again through the living room and gently pushed open the door to the bedroom that served as an office.

"Nobody home, boys," I said to the mike hooked on the center bridge of my bra.

Monty's office was tidy. The computer even wore a cloth cover. He had books on artificial insemination, swine diet, animal husbandry, and alfalfa farming from the University of Modesto and Cal Davis. There was a slim volume on how to mix drinks that had stains the shape of wet bottle bottoms on the cover. In two black binders were old handwritten transaction records on lined paper: innocent, straightforward buy-and-sell accountings for swine and supplies. Standing upright in a cardboard box were books whose titles were interesting enough to recite softly into my breastbone: *Consumer's Guide to Handguns; Harmony by Handgun; Unarmed Against the Knife;* a stapled volume called *Tumbling Tumblers,* on lock picking; and one called *Border Busting: How to Smuggle Anything.* A red-covered *Alert* bulletin from the U.S. Department of Health and Human Services on the hazards of infected silage lay on top of the box.

I didn't know if the deputies in the Caltrans Trojan Horse could hear me, but as I stepped out of the house again, this time to look in Simon's truck, I kept trying. The tape pack holding the battery to the small of my back itched, and I could feel the warmth of the unit even through the larger pad. To the two deputies I hoped were still listening, I said, "Nobody here but us chickens." The hood of Simon's truck was cold to the touch. I walked to the rear and peeked into the bed. I said into the mike, "Oh, and one big reptile you don't even want to know about." The box was screened on four sides. The boa, motionless, was jacked into a hairpin curve along the far side. The wood floor and ceiling of its home looked like wheat bread on a snake sandwich.

It was the toolbox I wanted a look into, and I wasn't quite sure how I was going to do it with the boa box taking up nearly the whole bed. Hiking over the tailgate, I set foot in the bed, stretched forward, and used the box edges and truck sides to move across to the front. "Don't mind me, big fella," I said, then told the listening deputies I was addressing a snake.

There was a lock on the toolbox, but a lock is always worth testing. I fit my hand between boa box and tool coffer, tugged at the padlock, and found it not snapped to. The box was empty except for a small feed sack with rusty stain, bunched in the corner. Stain was on the bottom of the box as well. The scene in the shed flashed back: the shadows, Paulie Avalos's pregnant profile, Switchie's hair and quicksilver hand, and the awful eyes of Agent Bernie Williams while dying in a waterfall of blood.

I lifted the sack. Underneath was a frayed wad of steel wool. Hooking a few hairy strands, I tugged the wad toward me. Dark flakes shed from it. "Boys," I said lowly, "all is cool, all is cool. But I just found a goodly piece of evidence to deliver us up a couple classic shitheels of the world."

When I was on the ground again, I looked and still saw no one. I got a paper bag from my car and returned to the truck for the rag and steel wool. This time, Dragonwick had stirred from her sleep. As I peered into the snake's accusing eye, a wave went through her like slow air in a windsock.

I slipped the sack under the seat of my car and went to look in the truck cab. No sooner had I opened its racking door than I heard Simon's voice behind me. "I ain't in there, dead or alive," he said.

* * *

He carried a small blue bucket and wore yesterday's pink snail shirt and jeans with gashes at the knees.

"Oh, hi, Simon! Nobody was around."

"Uh-huh," he said, looking me over. "I got critters to feed," he said, a cigarette bouncing in his mouth. "I always say, your clothes are cold in the mornin', you know you slept too long." He tipped the blue bucket toward me. In the bottom writhed a brown snake.

Saying, "Harmless, I hope," I still inched back.

"Here," he said, "catch," and he tossed the thing at me. I yelped. The snake plopped in the dust. Simon was on it before it could even roll its beige belly over to begin a skitter. He blocked its forward impulse, then clamped down with a quick hand and thrust the poor thing back in the bucket.

I worried that my Caltrans phonies would come running at my yelp, then worried because they didn't. I spoke quickly so that if they were still listening they could hear me scolding Simon for his tricks, and asking where Monty and Miranda were. He said Miranda was prob'ly bringing pea soup to Paulie, but Monty was up at the pigsties cussin' a blue streak with his wrenches spread all over.

"Isn't that what got Paulie in trouble?" I asked. "Down there by himself?"

"He knows what he's doing, which you can't say for Paul Avalos all of the time. But Monty's sure gonna get hard bit by the inspectors after this. You want to drive on up there?" He nodded toward the back field, then set the bucket on the ground to hitch up his pants. "I promise, I won't th'ow no more snakes on you. I can't hardly believe I did that myself. I'd right now beat myself up if I wasn't afraid of gettin' hurt."

"That's okay. I'm taking off here in a minute."

"Paulie, he used to say he couldn't bring up the good avocados over the border 'cause they was quarantined since 1914 from the seed weevil. *Always* complaining about that, so he took to growing his own. Now yesterday, I hate to say it, but he *looked* like a big ol' bowl of guacamole, dinn't he?" Simon's small face drew tighter from the cigarette smoke. He opened the truck door and put the blue bucket on the seat, then snapped a lid on. Reaching through the steering wheel, he plunged the key in the ignition and turned the radio on to something that sounded like reggae cowboy, then waved his wiry painted arm to me, Come on, come on.

There was no right-side mirror on Simon's truck for me to see the Caltrans by, but I hoped they could see Simon's pickup. The sky was burned clean with late May heat. Quick birds dipped over the fields of yellow fescue, timothy, and perennial rye.

"What's your last name, Simon?"

"Legree."

"No, really," I said pleasantly. The bucket was at my left leg. On the floorboards was all sorts of litter.

"McGee," he said, "Irish. You?"

"Irish." Had he said Bolivian, I would have been that too. "Did Monty walk over?"

"Naw, we rode. Must've gone the back way for more tools," he said.

"The back way where?"

"Avalos farm. They got more tools there than Sears at a fire sale. We'll jest go yonder and see." He picked up speed and rolled past the confinement building, taking the direction toward the mountains the white van had.

Positioned now so I could see the orange Caltrans moving up the start of the dirt road, I asked, "Monty drive a white van?"

Simon just looked ahead. Wind gusted through
the cab. It broke a tumbleweed the size of a beach
ball free from a tilted surveyor's post dabbed with
red paint on the top. The weed danced across the
road in front of us as though a ground squirrel raced
intently within. I saw Simon's glance flick to me, as
it had more than once in our short ride, and I worried that he'd earlier seen me nosing in his truck.
"You know why God made tumbleweeds, don't
ya?" Simon asked.

I said, "Don't know that I've given it much
thought."

Flipping his cigarette butt out the window, he
said, "Tell us which way the wind's blowin'," then
rolled his eyes to me and grinned.

We dipped down a gully and cut around a wind-
break of eucalyptus trees. I lost sight of the orange
van as Simon stomped the gas. We bounced up onto
a lip of asphalt where gravel pinged on the undercarriage, and I braced a hand on the gritty metal
dash. "How do you think Dragonwick's doing back
there?"

"I don't suppose she likes it. She's got that stargazing disease, you know. It makes her head kink
up, and she gets cranky."

"Stargazing disease?"

"An infection. Makes her neck kink," he said, rolling his own head on his shoulders.

"Did you bring her out to feed again?"

"No, they only eat ever-other week. I got one at
home named Rosy, three feet long. A rosy boa.
Brown spots on her, but they call 'em rosy, so that's
what I named her. Avalos brung her up to me from
Mexico in a spare tire. Jest tucked 'er in there. The
dope dogs didn't sniff her or nothin'. I sure hope
Paulie ain't brain-fried. He's an idiot, but he's a good
guy."

I asked, "Where the heck's Monty?"

"Right ahead of us right there." He nodded forward, but all I saw were cars moving crosswise on the main road we were teeing into. He made a turn in front of a woman with brown hair and dark-rimmed glasses who gripped the top of the steering wheel with both hands.

"What are you doing, Simon?"

"Oh, now don't worry," he said. "I bet I know where he's going. You don't see him up there? He just clipped the light." Simon took the freeway on ramp going south. I looked back through the rear window as if checking on Dragonwick. The van with the two humorless deputies was not in sight. As Simon picked up speed, the snake bucket by my left leg vibrated.

Trying to be calm, I made small talk about the landmarks, hoping my road warriors were picking it all up: a new restaurant with a big sign; a banner announcing a town rodeo; how the traffic was still clogged going west on 91. At Sixth he got off and took a street called Hamner. He passed under the freeway, stepping hard on the gas at every opportunity. I convinced myself his hurry was just because he was a fast driver. He turned left on Magnolia and before long took a road with a sign that said it led to Temescal Canyon.

"Ever get out to Lake Matthews? Man, you can go up 'long the bank of an evening, drop a line in the reeds, and haul up a load and a half o' crappie," he said. "You like catfish?" he asked over the sound of the Kentucky Headhunters on the radio.

"I don't know," I said.

"Not ever'body does. I use cat food, and if that don't gag a gorilla I don't know what would. You know what's a good lure? Pork."

"Really." I was getting more and more nervous.

"You cut yourself a strip, make a little plastic skirt for it so the fish can see it good, pop on a hook. It floats along like a real live thing," he said, waving his hand flat like a hula dancer.

"Where are you taking me, Simon?"

"Oh, 'round about here," he said, pulling off the road onto a denuded track running downhill between clumps of shrub called chaparral. Nearby lay a dry streambed where a bulldozer, now unmanned, had been busy making long sweeps in the light sand. A few dozen yards ahead was the white van I'd seen at Monty's. The rear window was blacked out by plastic film.

Simon slowed near the small white boulders with foot-high blue dick blooming between. We stopped alongside a high sweep of limp-wristed pampas on the left.

"What would Monty be doing out here?"

"Well, let's see. He ain't exactly here."

"Who's in the truck, Simon?"

"Switchie tol' me if you showed up I should stick to you like shit to a shovel. What you gone and done to get all these folks riled up? You seem nice enough to me."

Before I could answer, the door to the van opened and the man in the light-colored hat got out, his arms away from his hips like a fast-draw artist. Switchie.

34

Look into the face of a killer and he looks like any other man.

"You'll be an accomplice," I said to Simon, hating the fact that I never collected the new carry gun I put a down payment on, a three-inch Smith with a shrouded hammer that wouldn't hang up in your clothes. "Back up and take me out of here." The male singer on the radio was suggesting warning labels for sad country songs.

"I wish I could do that," Simon said, "I really do." Behind him, the pampas swords held poised like green teeth in the mouth of a giant shark.

"Simon, you don't know what you're doing."

But by now Switchie was standing a bit off my door. Despite the hat, the sun lit a band across Switchie's face, transforming his eyebrows to bristly wheat awns. His eyelashes shone a bright, curled yellow, and his rather full lips looked scrubbed with Vaseline. "Well now," he said, fixing his hard eyes on me. Pearlescent buttons ran down the front of his sea-green shirt. On his hip was a knife sheath stamped with gold letters reading RAVEN. "I guess you two are down for a picnic, that right?"

Anger topping fear, I said, "Fuck off, Switchie."

"Now that's real smart," he said, staking his hands on his hips. "Get out."

"I'm not going anywhere except out of here." I said to Simon, "Back up," but he only clutched the wheel as if ten thousand volts were running through it. I said, "This is a busted deal, Simon. Drive out of here." But his pupils had shrunk to pinheads, as though the whole of him withdrew and shut the door.

I packed down my door-lock button and began rolling the window up, but because the handle stuck at a stubborn point in its rotation, I wasn't fast enough. Switchie slapped eight fingers in the crack and with a mighty tug snapped the glass free. His feet lost purchase for a moment. Then he hurled the piece away.

I sailed over the blue snake bucket and skinny Simon, jerked up the door handle, and tumbled out, bringing us both to the ground in a pile of interlaced limbs. When I tried to unscramble, my knee hit Simon's nose. A fan of blood poured between the spread fingers that flew to his face.

"Where are you?" I screamed into my mike. "He's after me!" I tore open the top button and grabbed the mike. "He's got a knife! Triple nine, triple nine!" I yelled, the call for a dummy in deep trouble. The mike and its wires dangling down my front, I plunged between the close stands of pampas, their whipsaws slicing my bare arms. When I tried to clear the sandy bank, it crumbled beneath me. I heard myself sob, then got a foothold.

Switchie was through the blades in nothing flat, his hat still on, his wolf-bone jaws set hard. "Goddamnit, help me," I said, yelling into the mike as I scrambled higher. When I looked back, I looked into the terrifyingly calm, grinning face of Ralph "Switchie" D'Antonio just before he hitched up over the bank.

"You're mine," he said.

* * *

His words gave me a shot of power. I gained the crest of the hill when Switchie's fingers dug so hard into my ankle I cried out. I grabbed dirt and a mound of stubborn weed, trying to keep from sliding back. He was winning.

Hoping for gravity's advantage, I let go, flipping onto my back and coming down hard with my shoe heel, connecting on his forearm as I slid. Whack the ulna, didn't the guy say? We plunged downward, and Switchie started rolling. In the corner of my vision, his green shirt jumped like a barrel bounding down a hill.

When he braced himself, he went for the sheath at his thigh. He slapped his hip twice and glanced down, not believing the knife was gone. We both looked upward: On the hillside, Switchie's hat rested as if a man was buried to his brows.

Simon was rocking from foot to foot near his truck, holding a yellow rag to his nose.

Now Switchie was on all fours on the incline, looking for the knife. I gave a furious yank on the mike and threw the mess away, then ran for the dozer, awash in fear and looking for any loose object I could use for defense. I felt my legs go weak, but forced myself up on the dozer's push arm and then onto the tracks, scanning for any make-do weapon.

Switchie was on the way, walking slowly now. He didn't have the knife in his hand, but he was removing his belt. Jesus, what is this?

We'll play Ring-Around-a-Dozer. Simon still stood rooted, as though deciding if he should hike down the road to the nearest Texaco for a gallon of startup gas. Switchie startled me by smacking the belt on the crawler's fender. I'd already checked the ignition for dangling keys, but of course there were none and I really wouldn't know what to do with such a beast if I did get it started. Switchie hinked up on the dozer track and twanged the belt on whatever metal box or tank or canopy leg he found within striking distance, enjoying this.

Calling to Simon again, I used the words I didn't mean to utter, words I'd previously told myself I'd never use if I were being assaulted because it might set an assailant to irreversible purpose: "He'll kill me," I said. But Simon just stood in front of his truck, his thin hair lifting in the breeze.

"Now, this is a fun little game," Switchie said, bending toward me on the other side of the cab.

I began to shake. "Switchie, they know. If you had nothing to do with it, you'll have a chance—"

"You're a snitch. Rats have a short lifespan." He shifted his weight, and I thought he was going to pop me with the belt. My eyes were glued to the right hand when the left fist sent me flying out of the cab. It made the sky go white as paper and all sound disappear save a high ringing. When I hit, a hundred needles drove down my tailbone. The battery rig at the small of my back had squared off on a rock, driving its hard punch home. Overhead, on the slopes, tree branches shifted their leafy loads like silent, synchronized cheerleaders. I made out two black beefy watchers on the limbs. I tasted blood and felt my tongue swelling on one side.

Before I could rise, Switchie was squatting on his heels near my shoulder, his forearms resting on his thighs and his hands dangling between his knees. "You stupid bitch. You messed way out of your league." On the plane under his chin was a perfect mole.

I rose on one elbow as Simon came to stand at the rear of the dozer. Switchie looked over. "I've got an idea for her," he said. And as he did, I grabbed his hand and bit down so hard I felt a knuckle slip free even above the scream. I rolled away, a torrent of pain flooding my spine, and scrambled to my feet.

He came at me with the belt, the buckle end cutting through the air like a singing discus. The metal hit me in the upper arm, creating a bottomless ache. The next swing caught me along the ear. I thought he'd sheared it off. I felt the blood leak down my neck, and ran, knowing I didn't have a chance.

When he was close behind me, I dropped and rolled, wincing from the battery back, and counting on the greater strength in my legs for fending him off. I kicked, and every time he stepped closer to my upper body, I spun on my fulcrum of battery pack.

I was down, I was prey, I was *gone*, as he said. The look on his face was that of a satisfied winner. His left hand stood out from his side, the first finger solid purple where I'd chomped—purple as Joe Sanders's after he caught it under his barbell. And the thought of Joe, his wonderful, quiet humor shining in his eyes, his good soul, his professional patience; how hurt he would be at this. My eyes stung and I felt the rage coming back. I flipped on my side and grabbed a stone the size of a paperweight and hurled it. It landed near Simon, standing there like he was watching a calf roping. Switchie jumped aside and laughed.

"They'll get you," I said thickly.

"I don't think so." He laughed and drew the belt's length through his palm.

"Rollie Pierson. They'll get you for that."

"Oh-h-hh, *that*! What'd Angel do? You two girls have a good gab session? She's a tricky one, she is."

Now *he* picked up a rock and, just for fun, pitched it hard at me. I scooted, it bounced, but it hit me on the thigh on the rebound. He plucked another and took a pitcher's stance, the rock in his left hand, the belt drooling from his right. Simon was on his heels in the streambed, facing away, one hand on the ground, his head bent so low between his shoulders it looked gone.

"Switchie, Switchie, listen to me," I begged. "I'll intercede for you. I will."

He underhanded the rock at me, and it whisked by my leg, but there was no force to it, and I thought I'd won. I said, "Do you think Monty's going down for any of this? Not if he can get you to. Come on, you're smart enough to know that."

He hoisted the belt and dug at the buckle, smiling. He said, "Isn't that nice, you got that all figured out? You must think I'm a born-again fool."

He untwined a thin wire from inside the belt buckle. A Gigli saw.

"Stop!" Simon called. His nose was twice the size it was before, and there was a sickened look on his face. I had hope. But then he turned and walked away.

Switchie said, "Let's see now. We could do it this way. Or we could do it thataway." He levered his bit finger out toward the bulldozer. " 'Member them cowboy movies where the Indians stand somebody up in a hole and run over him with horses? Wonder what a dozer blade would do to a cop-lovin' bitch like you."

I tried one last thing: "You murdered a man at the Avalos farm, Switchie. The cops know about that." Slowly I stood up.

"See, that's what I mean about snitches. Jesus, I hate 'em." He looked away toward the sun and then brought his face back, smiling. "And he's in the hospital now, just waitin' there for his pal Switchie come visit him. Paulie worries. He fusses. He gets snockered. He blabs."

I'd have to make a break for Simon's truck. I'd have to hope he was so emotionally immobilized that I could just jump in and gun out of there. "Listen," I said, trying one more thing. "I'm walking on up the road. Gone. Out of your hair. Good-bye. You go your way, I go mine," and I eased back a step or two.

"*You* don't get to call these shots," he said.

From somewhere in the distance I heard the clipped bark of a dog. I thought of beautiful, red Farmer with his tongue lolled out and his ears back, bounding across the shell-littered plank on the north bluff of the bay, and I flashed on Mrs. Langston in her pastel jogging suit, holding the cane she was going to bonk Monty Blackman with if he wasn't a legit visitor to my home. Where were you now, brave lady? I heard the dog again, and through the ache of my body and the feverish burn at the side of my head, I felt a renewal, like a second wind. "Come and get me, asshole," I said.

Don't wait for the attacker to come to you. That's what one of the men in the café had said. You go to him. But I could not move. My head low, my teeth clenched, I merely growled; and as I did, a squawking came from the area of Simon's truck, metal on metal, and I figured it was the driver's door and that he was going away, Simon to his thing, me to mine, whatever fate would bring.

Switchie, smiling, faking me out, danced from one side to the other. "Run!" he whispered. "Run!" The Gigli saw, held through its ring by his good finger, bounced in its springy energy.

Just as he advanced on me, I heard Simon's voice. "Let her go, man."

Softly, without turning around, Switchie said, "Fuck yourself, joe. You don't like it, leave." Switchie moved left, unblocking my view, and then we both saw at the same time little Simon with his big boa draped across his shoulders.

Dragonwick's forward length dipped off the right shoulder but rose again, stargazing, as he earlier described. The boa's head balanced above Simon's own and traveled side by side like an East Indian dancer's. Flick, the tongue. Then Simon lifted the snake like a set of flexible barbells and heaved it at Switchie.

In a flash, the thing wrapped itself around Switchie like nothing I'd ever seen. His arm that held the wire stuck out, the ring still looped on his finger. He fell completely to his knees from the weight and the surprise, and in a moment seemed clothed in a pale-green dressing gown. He'd become a snake totem, his face not even visible, so snake-embraced was he. I stood with my mouth open, and then the thing toppled over. The snake uncovered a golden patch of hair and with it a strangled scream. Switchie's eyes bulged. Then the boa's head rose, back, back, and struck forward like a fist. It came back again, its jaws open wide like a catcher's mitt, and in an instant fangs clamped across Switchie's face.

Switchie's free hand, which still clung to the wire whip, flailed wildly. Each time the wire struck and retreated it ripped across the snake. Simon was yelling, "Stop! Stop struggling. I'll get her," but the beast spasmed smaller and tighter before our eyes. Simon the Dragonmeister stood in horror. His eyes were riveted to the hand that tore at his pet's green carpet of scales.

"God, get it off him!" I yelled.

Simon moved forward and chopped karatelike at his pet just at the base of its blunt head. The snake released, reared, and bit again. The fangs tore through Switchie's cheeks and across his mouth, losing their grip and leeching onto the side of his head. Then the snake snuggled, until a small stream of red eased from Switchie's stoppered throat. He had ceased any sound. I don't know if his eyes' last light admitted the sheen of a helicopter belly as it crested the tops of the swirling eucalyptus, or if they saw a brighter light.

I slid to the ground as the sand tornadoed about us, and put my arm over my eyes. My blouse was tearing away with the chopper wind. I clutched it, and when I rose and turned and dropped my arm, I saw Simon nearly blowing off his own small feet, clubbing his thighs with dreadful grief.

35 Joe and I sat with Miranda Robertson and Les Fedders in an interview room the next day at noon. Her hair was folded into a white snood, one of those net things from the forties. She wore a black linen jacket, cream slacks, and shoes, and could have passed for a lawyer. How was it that this was the woman who sat on a softail only two days before?

I asked, "Why did you report the car stolen?"

"Because I thought it was. I let her use it to go to the Ontario airport. She flew up to Fresno for something, was coming back the same day."

"What's in Fresno?"

"Monty asked her to. She needed money, Monty needed something delivered to Fresno. Her husband usually made the trips, or Switchie, but her husband hadn't come home for three days. When she didn't show either, and Monty wasn't telling me anything, I reported it stolen."

"There was a gun in the car. Was it yours?"

"No."

"A little Sundance Boa, with the number drilled off in two places. You're sure?"

"I don't know how to use a gun."

"Was Arleta afraid of somebody?"

"Of course she was afraid of somebody. Her husband was gone. She didn't know then that he was dead, but I think she guessed it. Switchie killed Rol-

324

lie because he ripped him off, and that meant he ripped *Monty* off, and Switchie wouldn't get his commission." She moved in the chair, and I thought I caught a faint whiff of purple Zac.

Les said, "This Arleta. She have breast implants?" He looked at me, I gave him a glare, and his face fell into deep folds.

Miranda shifted in her chair and said, "Rollie was a jerk. Arleta, she was pretty once, but she was fortysomething and losing it and didn't quite know how to piece it all together, you know? Like she would wear T-shirts with big holes cut in them like a teenager and her figure wasn't all that great to begin with, kind of straight up and down like a board. She did something about it, I mean she was getting lippoed and lifted and . . ." Miranda looked at me, and I slipped one hand onto her chair back.

"But fortysomething's forty something, and she didn't know how to take care of her teeth and her hair was dyed too black and she had fat knees. But she was pretty, honest, in her own way. She could laugh at herself. I liked that."

"The husband . . . ?" Joe asked.

"He made fun of her all the time. I think that's why she did all that stuff to herself."

Why did you? I thought, and was mad at Nathan.

We kept Miranda there for an hour before she asked for coffee. At the break, I walked with her to the rest room, and it was there that she told me about Robert, how he fit into the whole thing. I had her repeat it for the video when we got back to the interview room, and she did well considering the emotional complexities involved.

At one point Les Fedders stopped her and asked, "So let me get this straight. Switchie was into smuggling stuff for your husband. Or for Monty?"

"Robert and Switchie owned stock in the biotech company. But they couldn't do diddly without Monty's product. Pork producers pay them all sorts of money under the table. Robert was taking product to the Chinese."

I looked at Les, and Les looked at Joe, and finally I said, "Miranda, did you know a man named Quillard Satterlee?"

"Never heard of him."

"Small, white hair. Beard. Rode a red—"

"The red pan? Oh yeah. Monty hates that bike. Way too much chrome." Then, as if I were watching the time-lapsed unfolding of a rose, I saw the conquest of understanding on Miranda's face. Her eyes fixed on me. "He's the one," she whispered.

"The one what?" Les asked.

"The one . . . the one. . . ."

I said, "The one Simon hauled off in his truck?"

She nodded. Two bright red spots showed on her cheeks.

Joe said, "He was a customs agent."

"I heard Monty on the phone to Switchie. He said, 'He was a fucking *fed*?' like that, and I thought he was talking about Arleta's husband, but after a while I knew it wasn't, and I suppose I didn't want to know any more. I just closed my ears. I heard Monty call Simon and ask to use his truck. Over *pigs*. *Pigs!*"

We let her compose herself, and then I said, "We still don't know why Switchie would murder Arleta."

"What if he was after *me*?" Miranda said. "It *was* my car."

Les Fedders said, "We still don't know if Switchie did murder Arleta. Maybe Monty did."

"Oh no, oh no," Miranda said. "He'd never do that. Not Monty. It was Switchie going after the money Rollie lifted, I'll bet, thinking she had it. Not

Monty. He couldn't do a thing like that."

Joe said, "We got a whole lot of people betraying other people here, don't you think? Under the circumstances, who can you trust?"

And Miranda's face burned even brighter.

The autopsy took place without me. You don't do the ones that seem too personal unless you have a stomach of tempered steel. Even for Switchie, I'd allow him his privacy. Switchie. Brained by a boa, so to speak. I felt sorry about his fate. Or tried to. The manner, but not the outcome.

As for Simon's snake, she fared well. Either the chopper vibration made her think of one humongous ground squirrel, or Simon's blow unkinked her, for she slid off Switchie and winnowed away into the chaparral none the worse for wear. A month later, I read about another constrictor who killed his owner. The man had failed to wash his hands after handling a guinea pig.

Whatever had happened to my humorless deputies? They continued to be humorless, to the point that when I saw them the afternoon of Switchie's demise, I thought they were on the brink of suicide. They'd been driving around in circles trying to find me, the cellular phone wouldn't work, and then, because neither of them was old enough to have much experience with manual transmissions, they gave too much clutch to the temperamental repair truck and soaked the spark plugs into a righteous stall. They called for aerial from a pay phone.

That night, still trembling, I called Nathan and told him his Miranda was found. From there on, it was up to him what he wanted to do about it.

Two nights later, I, along with Joe Sanders, my pal Ray Vega and still another girlfriend (this time a blonde named Missy), and Agent Christine Vogel, went out to a bar in San Bernardino where rowdy female customers take off their bras through their blouse sleeves and throw them over the chandeliers.

I had a Fuzzy Navel and two of Christine's Widows, and let Joe drive me home. Captain Exner said to call him the next morning, but I passed in favor of corn.

Corn is dirty work. The ribbed leaves, blasted with road goo and grimy jet fallout, will wipe you with rough black dust. Anywhere else I wouldn't be able to pick corn at the beginning of June, but farmers in Southern California force crops into false seasons. I was 260 paces from the access road—you pace off or you lose your way. The corn stalks towered overhead. Though I was between two busy freeways, nothing but a mean eagle could find you here.

The wire handle of the bucket dug mercilessly into my finger creases. I set the bucket down for a moment and still picked more. I'd found a good spot the paid pickers had missed, and though I'd been there for more than the two-hour limit for volunteers, I didn't want to leave. No room in the pail, I speared two ears in each shirt pocket, and one down the elastic tunnel where three days ago my microphone had been. Loaded this way, I could have passed for a chesty scarecrow.

The sun beat hotly through the morning haze. I was sealed in sweat and beginning to itch badly from the fuzzies, those nearly invisible hairs corn leaves give off. I started working my way back to the road, off-balance with the weight of the bucket, barely able to prevent a turned ankle on clods the size of saucers. But then I'd find myself straddling rows instead of pacing forward, peering through the silk-sounding leaves at the next row. Everywhere I looked I spied a missile without worms in the kernels or aphid gunk turning the tassels to slime. I wanted to announce my find to the other volunteers, but in this large field they couldn't hear.

I knelt by the white plastic bucket and adjusted the cobs so they'd efficiently fit, two dozen green cigars in a clown's mouth. Enough. But the stalks were so laden, and I was so greedy for more. I stacked the corn in a pyramid then, like pipe, and promised myself to pace off carefully so I could find them again after emptying my bucket of treasure in the waiting truck. I straddled the next row and looked. Firm cobs everywhere. Grasping one, I tested diameter and sponginess. Fat and firm, that's the ticket. That's what the Beulah Land lady told me the first day I picked, only she winked with a secret, and I laughed.

That evening I had Mrs. Langston over for a shrimp salad and very fresh corn, and gave Farmer a stripped cob to roll all over the kitchen floor until he figured out it could actually be something good to eat and broke it in a million pieces.

The next Monday afternoon I got a summons. Doug Forster and I were huddled over his desktop analyzing the language of a section of the evidence code that took up thirteen pages. Doug's first court appearance in which he'd have to testify as an expert witness was Wednesday, and he was nervous.

I read the memo and said, "The captain wants a confab. Think he'll pay me overtime?"

Doug said, "Think he'll give me a raise after I play Tom Cruise in court? Ask him for me."

"Sure, Doug. In a horse's patootie."

At my desk I gathered my purse and jacket, shoved a couple of folders in the drawer, locked up, and went by Joe's office on my way to the parking lot. I told him where I was headed, and he smiled like he knew what it was all about as he pushed back his chair and locked his hands behind his neck.

"You've heard something. Is he going to reprimand me? He and the sheriff are waiting to hand me an unpaid leave?"

"Paranoia becomes you," Joe said.

"Why would he be wanting to talk to me now? Our meeting's tomorrow at nine."

Joe shrugged, said, "Who knows? Get out of here. I'll call you tonight. We'll watch the game together."

"Deal. I buy the pizza."

"No argument. No pepperoni, either."

On the way over, I kept thinking about how Morris "Monty" Blackman was not going to have to pay enough. Monty was the one who put things in motion. He was the one who gave opportunity to the likes of Switchie. Whatever they got him for, it wouldn't be enough.

I was thinking these things, wondering if, on a more positive side, the captain had better news, clearer developments from some other source, to offer me today. But why would he be telling only me? What about Joe and Les Fedders and my direct superior? There was a fifty-fifty chance, I figured, the news would be bad. I calculated how many months I could live on my savings. I'm canned.

When I walked into Captain Exner's office, Agent Vogel was sitting in one of two chairs in front of the captain's desk. She was wearing a yellow dress under a brown jacket, her shoes a bright yellow too. At the end of her sleeve was a big brown bracelet painted with miniature suns, and she carried the same small purse I know she stole off some teenager in her house.

"Hi, Smokey," she said, that same kindness in her tone and eyes that hooked me the first time. "How's the snake charmer?"

"Dancing to a different flute player, I guess."

The captain told me to have a seat, the merest smile on his face. "You might like to know the latest developments. Christine?"

"We had a search warrant for the farm, and we went in. Our man himself was G.O.A."

"Gone on Arrival," the captain said, "but Les Fedders is calling him to come in and talk to us."

"You think he'll just come in?"

"They do. They're curious, or they like to play with you."

"Your captain here isn't telling you everything," Agent Vogel said. "He found a judge on a golf course and got him to sign another warrant so we could execute in Blackman's home in Garden Grove and at the bar."

"So *that's* why he didn't call me to come in to work," I said.

She laughed. "We've got computer disks too and a ton of paper to go through, but I want to tell you something: I can chase a whisper in a big wind when my mind's put to it. And I *will* nail that guy. There's nothing quite so satisfying as a good felony slam." She paused, all expression leaving her face for a moment, and then said, "And then there's for Bernie."

She saw me looking at the floor. "What's the matter?"

"He'll bond out before midnight," I said. "When you do get him, he'll walk. He's smooth."

"Don't you worry about that, honey," she said kindly, and glanced at the captain. She was not that much older than I, I had guessed, but she seemed to hold the right to call me honey.

The captain said, "Miranda Robertson is coming in tonight. She should be here about now." He looked at his watch.

Christine winked. "The girl got religion. She went

to see Avalos in the hospital. Walked in when your
investigator, Les Fedders, was there. He led her
down the hall, laid on the sugar, and in a minute
she was telling him stuff she didn't know she
knew."

It was hard to picture Miranda free of herbal fog
and walking in to visit Paulie Avalos. But I know
that people come to light at different times and in
various ways, and I was hoping that whatever my
brother, Nathan, saw in her at one time was pretty
strong in the admixture yet.

"I think you softened her up," Agent Vogel said.
"Then, of course, Les also told her about you. About
what happened when you played snake with Switchie. You know, for such a young person, she sure
has stomach problems." Christine shook her head,
the pink folds of her neck in competition with each
other.

The captain said, "She's married to a doctor. He
should be able to give her something."

"Grief," I said.

In his navy suit and pale yellow tie, the captain
and the customs agent looked ready for a photo opportunity. He was telling me how the evidence code
says a wife cannot be *compelled* to testify against her
husband, but it doesn't say she can't testify volun-
tarily or offer information.

Soon after, sure enough, my own boss, Stu Hollings, walked in. He came with a man from my building, a man who works Photo Doc with a fancy
camera.

As Mrs. Langston often tells me, not all luck is
bad. That evening when I went to get Farmer for his
run, I got to tell her that just before I left the captain's office, my boss came in with a surprise. He
stood with a photographer and directed the taking

of several pictures with me, the captain, and Christine Vogel in front of the brown chalkboard. That was just preliminary, he said.

Then he told me I had a date with a ceremony at the end of the month: I would be awarded a Medal of Valor for meritorious service and special courage in a situation of special danger.

Christine Vogel sat with dimpled hands rounded off on the chair arms and bounced one knee up and down under her dress as if she wished she were the one to tell me, a lively grin on her face. "Hey," she said. "The job has *mucho trabajo, poco dinero.*" Much work, little money. "You take your bouquets when you can."

That mild night after Farmer was bedded, I lay stretched on the couch whispering to Joe over the phone as he mournfully informed me he had to go out to a scene and would miss watching the game with me and celebrating my news with champagne. Later, I trundled my little Toyota over to the Balboa peninsula and walked alone down the pier.

At the end, I had a cup of coffee and a piece of pie at Ruby's Diner and watched the brilliant white moon rise in its helium splendor. A pouty-beaked seagull sat on a pier lamp and looked in at me, waiting. And on the way back, above the stir of ocean stammers, I thought of the small victories. How, tonight in a neighborhood in Anaheim, a citizen flashlight patrol walked the streets in a visible message to drug dealers, to reclaim Sabina Street, Pauline, Topeka, and Olive. How they had spread donated bags of fertilizer in their parks to keep the dealers away. They would do what it took, receiving no public recognition in the form of medals for special courage. They stood up for choice, the choice to do a right thing rather than a wrong.

And still on the pier, I remembered Nathan even

in the midst of his agony, scooping a fish off the boards and giving it back to its maker. I went to my car with a feeling of peace, and inspiration, and in my own unspoken way, gratitude.

Within days, Paulie Avalos admitted knowledge of a vehicle over the side of a North County canyon. He had yet to give over both names of the two who tossed in a can of racing fuel and rocked the Cadillac off the road edge with a lady who liked to dress young and suck citrus already dead in it. She had a .25-caliber bullet through her ear canal, a slug that escaped even Doug's able sifting. Paulie wouldn't identify the second cyclist, but readily gave up the name of Switchie Ralph D'Antonio. Maybe it was Paulie himself, and maybe it was Monty.

Joe Sanders and I dropped in at the Python one night, just two lovers out on the town. Monty had his girls in his usual rainbow of stretch-lace chemises and baby-doll delights. There was one black satin number worn with thigh-high nylons designed to look like boots that Joe said he wouldn't mind buying, and I asked him whether for him or for me.

When Monty came out of the back room, he took his time talking to a girl at a table in a tight turtleneck dress with the shoulders cut out, and then eased over our way, a brown Sherman cigarette dangling from his lips, the full hair free and glowing under the colored lamps. More of it foamed out of his cool blue shirt open to midchest. He sat backward on a chair and said, "So how's the cop business these days?"

Father Time, next to me, answered, "Quiet as a dead hog, I guess."

I looked at Joe, then Monty, who was deciding he had better things to do and was rising up out of his chair, and I said, "Now don't that just beat all?"

Eight months later, after Monty Blackman had run out of excuses and time, he was making metal shelves and cabinets for the military in a controlled environment by day, and purging his stargazing habit by night through a wire-reinforced window of his 7- by 10-foot shared cell, top bunk, in the building guards know as the Incentive Unit at the Federal Correctional Institution, Terminal Island, County of Los Angeles.